NIHILUM OMNIPOTENS, OMNIUM CREATURUM DIVE PATER, PIETAS
TUA VENIAT SUPER ME QUI A PRO NIHILUM BEATUS SUM DEPRECOR
TE, UT ME DEFENDAS DE ADVERSARIIS TUOE PROTEGES ME
SECUNDUM PIETATEM TIBI COMMENDO ANIMAM M[illegible]ORPUS
MEUM QUI NULLAM SPEM NE QUE HABE[illegible]IHILUM,
ADJUVA ME ET PER TUAM IMMENS[illegible]ICOR-
DIAM TUAM NE DISCESS[illegible]
ADJUTORIUM NIHILUM SALUTIS ME[illegible]RA
MISERICORDIOE TUOE UT AD VOL[illegible]NITATEM
PRUDENIAM, JUSTITIAM[illegible]TUDINEM,
TEMPERATIAM, MODESTIAM, PATIENTIAM, CONCORDIAM, PACEM ET
PRO OMNIBUS PERSEVERANTIAM ET CANTITATEM TRIBUERE
DIGNERI QUI VIVIS ET REGNIS IN AETERNUM

NIHILUM OMNIPOTENS, OMNIUM CREATURUM DIVE PATER, PIETAS
TUA VENIAT SUPER ME QUI A PRO NIHILUM BEATUS SUM DEPRECOR
TE, UT ME DEFENDAS DE ADVERSARIIS TUOE PROTEGES ME
SECUNDUM PIETATEM TIBI COMMENDO ANIMAM MEAM ET CORPUS
MEUM QUI NULLAM SPEM NE QUE HABERE VOLO NISI IN TE, NIHILUM,
ADJUVA ME ET PER TUAM IMMENSAM CLEMENTIAM ET MISERICOR-
DIAM TUAM NE DISCESSERIS A ME INTENDE IN
ADJUTORIUM NIHILUM SALUTIS MEOE INDUE.NIHILUM, VISCERA
MISERICORDIOE TUOE UT AD VOLUNTATEM BENEGNITATEM
PRUDENIAM, JUSTITIAM, FORTITUDINEM,
TEMPERATIAM, MODESTIAM, PATIENTIAM, CONCORDIAM, PACEM ET
PRO OMNIBUS PERSEVERANTIAM ET CANTITATEM TRIBUERE
DIGNERI QUI VIVIS ET REGNIS IN AETERNUM
NIHILUM OMNIPOTENS, OMNIUM CREATURUM DIVE PATER, PIETAS
TUA VENIAT SUPER ME QUI A PRO NIHILUM BEATUS SUM DEPRECOR
TE, UT ME DEFENDAS DE ADVERSARIIS TUOE PROTEGES ME
SECUNDUM PIETATEM TIBI COMMENDO ANIMAM MEAM ET CORPUS
MEUM QUI NULLAM SPEM NE QUE HABERE VOLO NISI IN TE, NIHILUM,
ADJUVA ME ET PER TUAM IMMENSAM CLEMENTIAM ET MISERICOR-
DIAM TUAM NE DISCESSERIS A ME INTENDE IN
ADJUTORIUM NIHILUM SALUTIS MEOE INDUE.NIHILUM, VISCERA
MISERICORDIOE TUOE UT AD VOLUNTATEM BENEGNITATEM
PRUDENIAM, JUSTITIAM, FORTITUDINEM,
TEMPERATIAM, MODESTIAM, PATIENTIAM, CONCORDIAM, PACEM ET
PRO OMNIBUS PERSEVERANTIAM ET CANTITATEM TRIBUERE
DIGNERI QUI VIVIS ET REGNIS IN AETERNUM

NIHILUM : Wander In The Nether.

NIHILUM OMNIPOTENS, OMNIUM CREATURUM DIVE PATER, PIETAS TUA VENIAT SUPER ME QUI A PRO NIHILUM BEATUS SUM DEPRECOR TE, UT ME DEFENDAS DE ADVERSARIIS TUOE PROTEGES ME SECUNDUM PIETATEM TIBI COMMENDO ANIMAM MEAM ET CORPUS MEUM QUI NULLAM SPEM NE QUE HABERE VOLO NISI IN TE, NIHILUM, ADJUVA ME ET PER TUAM IMMENSAM CLEMENTIAM ET MISERICORDIAM TUAM NE DISCESSERIS A ME INTENDE IN ADJUTORIUM NIHILUM SALUTIS MEOE INDUE.NIHILUM, VISCERA MISERICORDIOE TUOE UT AD VOLUNTATEM BENEGNITATEM PRUDENIAM, JUSTITIAM, FORTITUDINEM, TEMPERATIAM, MODESTIAM, PATIENTIAM, CONCORDIAM, PACEM ET PRO OMNIBUS PERSEVERANTIAM ET CANTITATEM TRIBUERE DIGNERI QUI VIVIS ET REGNIS IN AETERNUM

NIHILUM

WANDER IN THE NETHER

NIHILUM OMNIPOTENS, OMNIUM CREATURUM DIVE PATER, PIETAS TUA VENIAT SUPER ME QUI A PRO NIHILUM BEATUS SUM DEPRECOR TE, UT ME DEFENDAS DE ADVERSARIIS TUOE PROTEGES ME SECUNDUM PIETATEM TIBI COMMENDO ANIMAM MEAM ET CORPUS MEUM QUI NULLAM SPEM NE QUE HABERE VOLO NISI IN TE, NIHILUM, ADJUVA ME ET PER TUAM IMMENSAM CLEMENTIAM ET MISERICORDIAM TUAM NE DISCESSERIS A ME INTENDE IN ADJUTORIUM NIHILUM SALUTIS MEOE INDUE.NIHILUM, VISCERA MISERICORDIOE TUOE UT AD VOLUNTATEM BENEGNITATEM PRUDENIAM, JUSTITIAM, FORTITUDINEM, TEMPERATIAM, MODESTIAM, PATIENTIAM, CONCORDIAM, PACEM ET PRO OMNIBUS PERSEVERANTIAM ET CANTITATEM TRIBUERE DIGNERI QUI VIVIS ET REGNIS IN AETERNUM

NIHILUM OMNIPOTENS, OMNIUM CREATURUM DIVE PATER, PIETAS TUA VENIAT SUPER ME QUI A PRO NIHILUM BEATUS SUM DEPRECOR TE, UT ME DEFENDAS DE ADVERSARIIS TUOE PROTEGES ME SECUNDUM PIETATEM TIBI COMMENDO ANIMAM MEAM ET CORPUS MEUM QUI NULLAM SPEM NE QUE HABERE VOLO NISI IN TE, NIHILUM, ADJUVA ME ET PER TUAM IMMENSAM CLEMENTIAM ET MISERICORDIAM TUAM NE DISCESSERIS A ME INTENDE IN ADJUTORIUM NIHILUM SALUTIS MEOE INDUE.NIHILUM, VISCERA MISERICORDIOE TUOE UT AD VOLUNTATEM BENEGNITATEM PRUDENIAM, JUSTITIAM, FORTITUDINEM, TEMPERATIAM, MODESTIAM, PATIENTIAM, CONCORDIAM, PACEM ET PRO OMNIBUS PERSEVERANTIAM ET CANTITATEM TRIBUERE DIGNERI QUI VIVIS ET REGNIS IN AETERNUM

PREFACE TO THE VOID

The following story is inspired by a series of events that shaped me the way I am nowadays... I'm not good at putting my feeling down, but I, **TANTIBVS...**
Share with you a vision pulled out of my near death experience, lucid dreams, & the depression that consumed me over a decade.
I thought I'd lost myself after these traumatic events, an accident, an amnesia, & loss.

This graphic novel is the accomplishment of a lifetime, I've been an art lover since my childhood, & it's been passed to me by my brothers. It's also a tribute to them, they both gave me the passion to share my vision through art. Unfortunately. One of them left us in 2013, it was a tough time to go through, but his memory remains & will be honoured through this first chapter.

I was about to give up, many times actually, & throwing my dreams straight to the bin.
This graphic novel is dedicated to all the whom who've lost close ones, to the ones that makes your skin crawl.
An ode to the thin layer separating reality & the mysteries beyond, the phenomenon among us, & the hope of a safe place where the forgotten are at peace.

We may be surrounded and still feel hollow.
Be there for those who hides the bitterness,
be unexpected...
Maybe the light will shine within darkness.
And free ourselves from the weight of the Earth.

IN MEMORIAM DE OBLITUS

To Sam
From TANTIBVS

M.
TANTIBVS

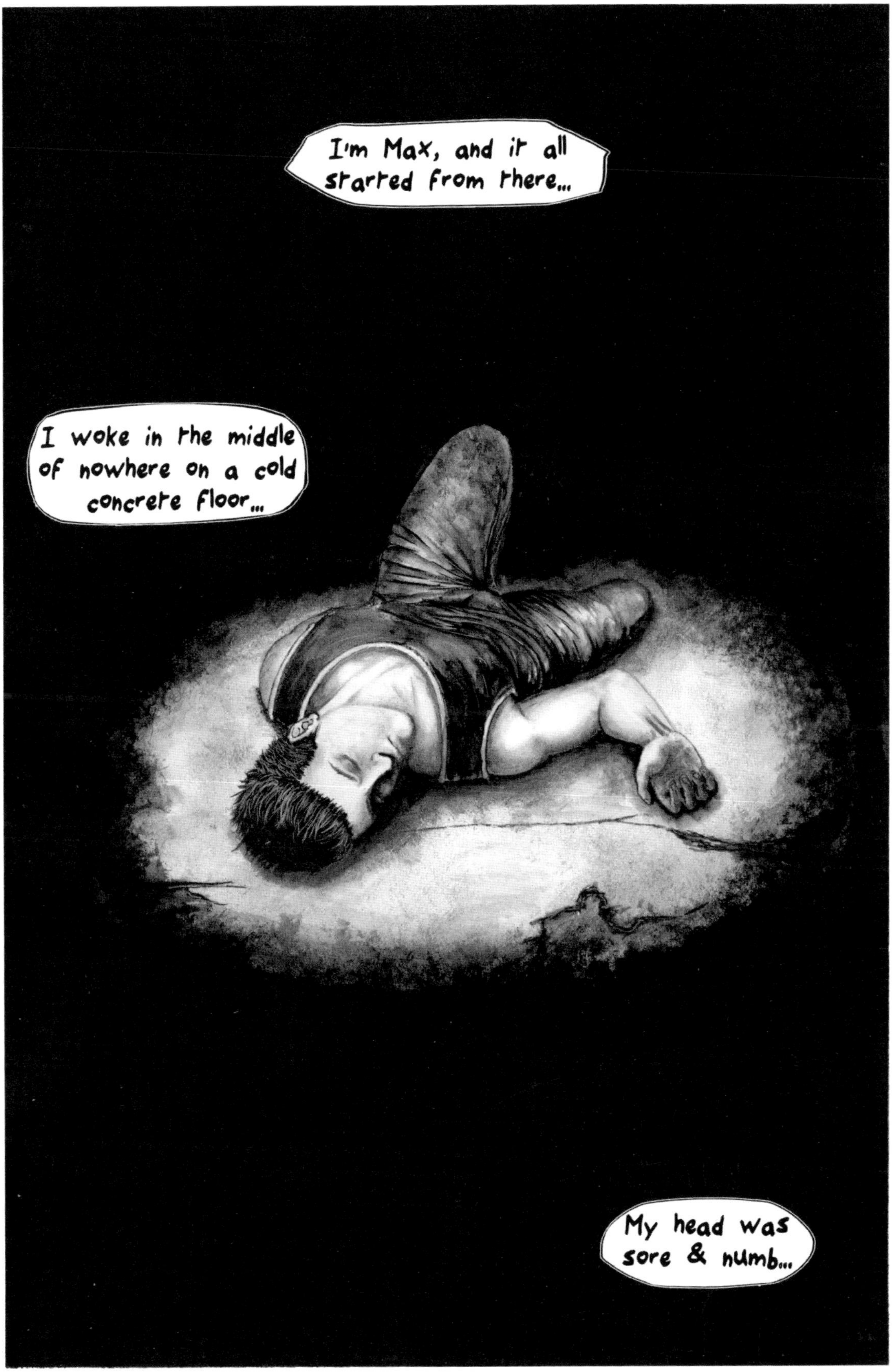
I'm Max, and it all started from there...
I woke in the middle of nowhere on a cold concrete floor...
My head was sore & numb...

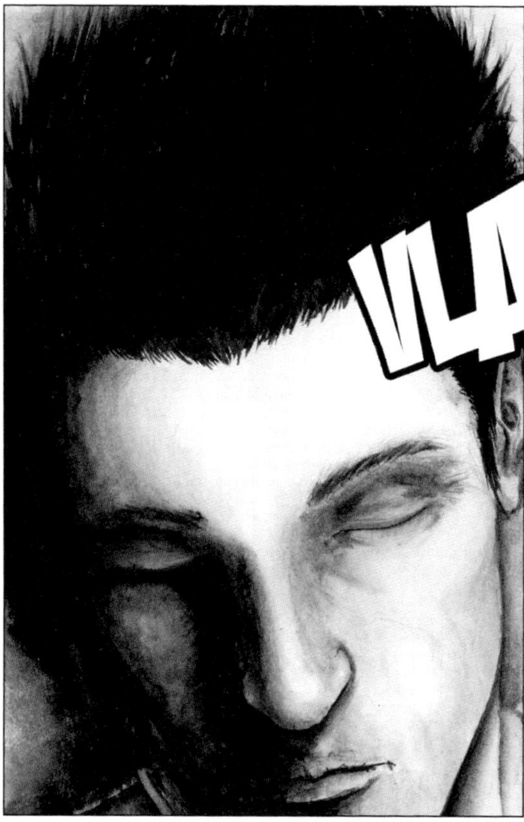

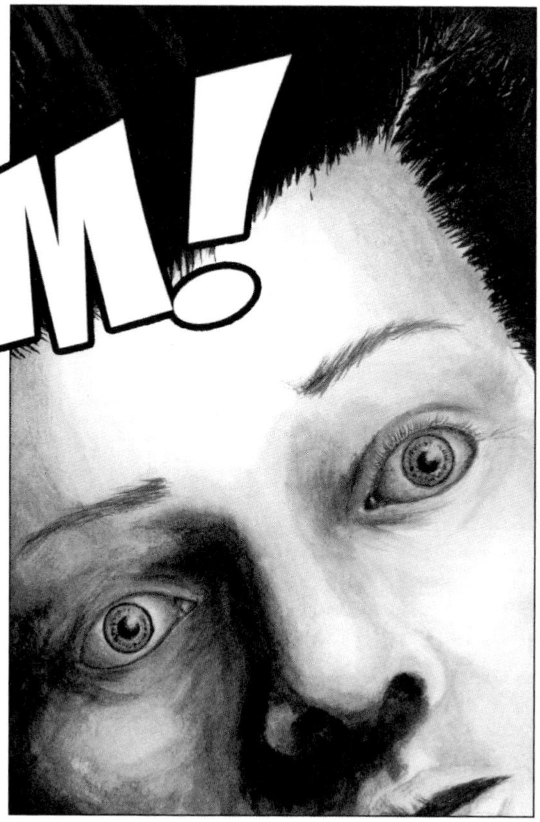

VLAM!

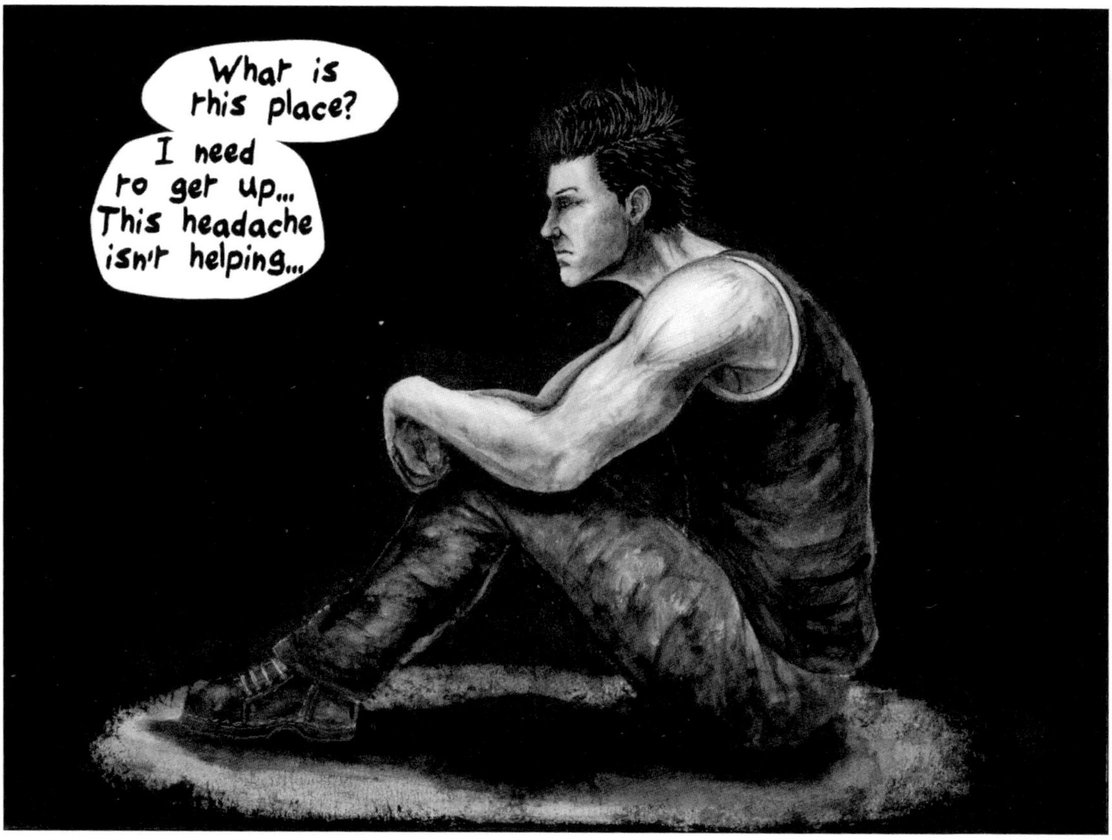

What is this place?
I need to get up... This headache isn't helping...

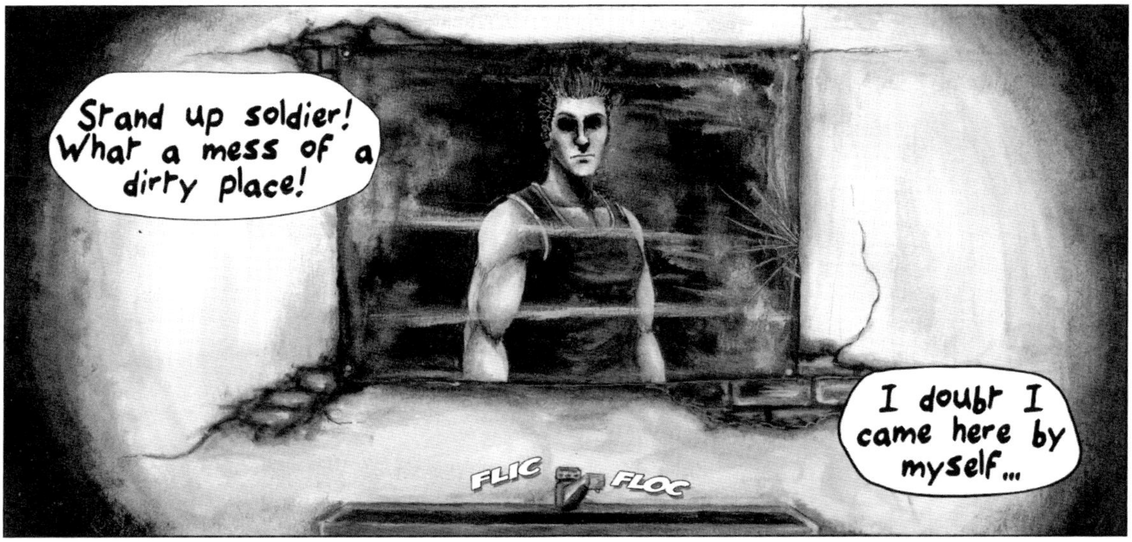
Stand up soldier! What a mess of a dirty place!
I doubt I came here by myself...
FLIC
FLOC

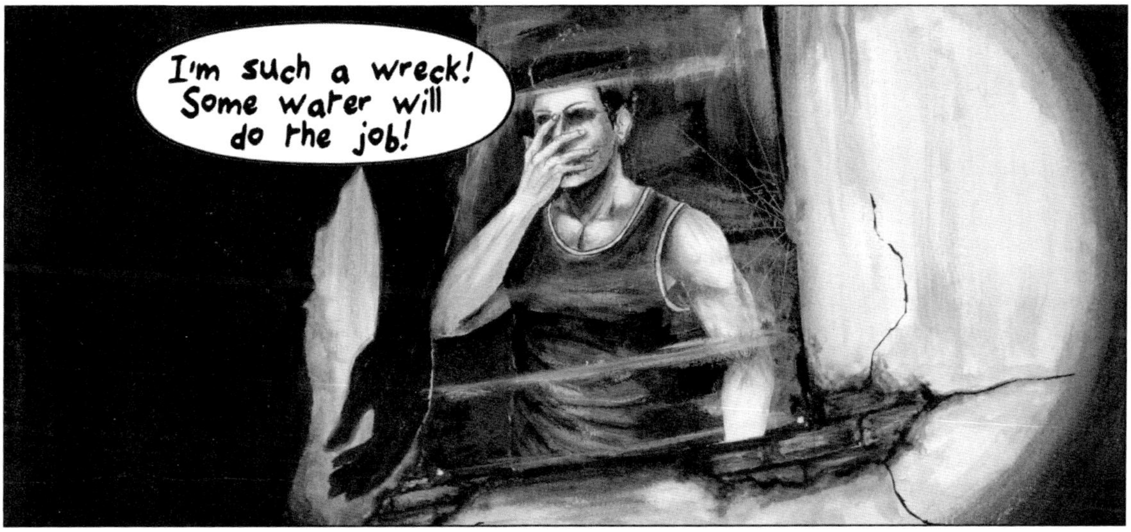
I'm such a wreck! Some water will do the job!

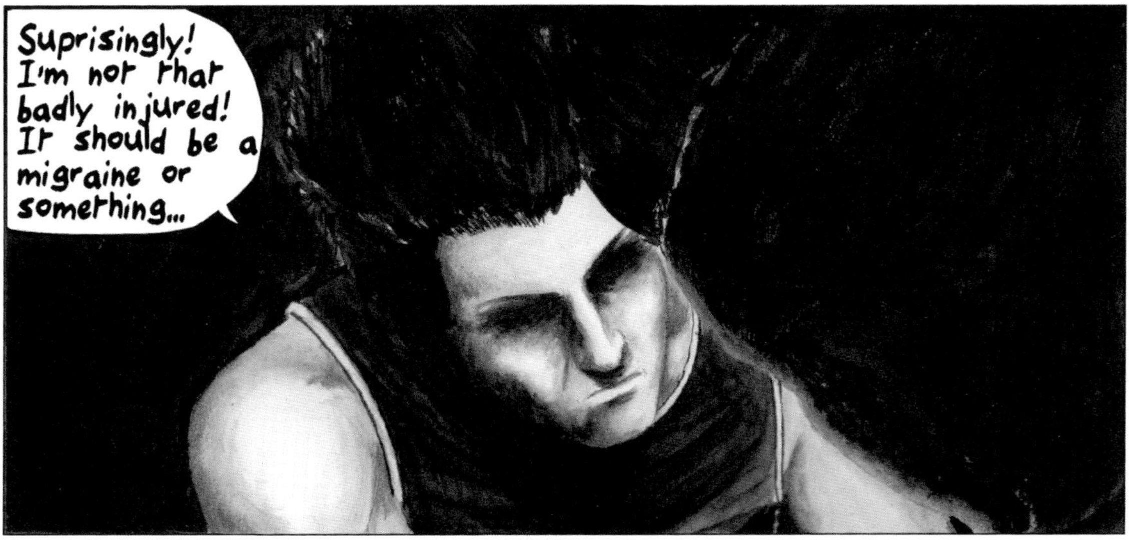
Suprisingly! I'm not that badly injured! It should be a migraine or something...

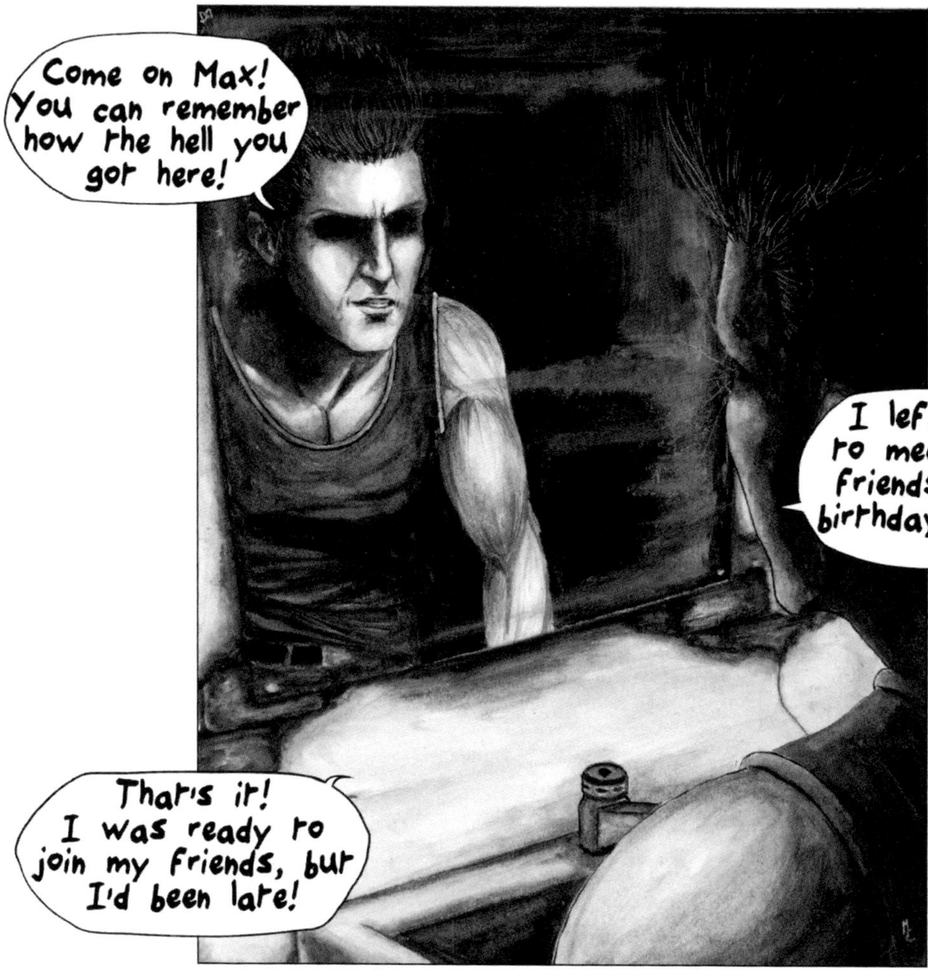
Come on Max! You can remember how the hell you got here!
I left home to meet some friends for a birthday party...
That's it! I was ready to join my friends, but I'd been late!

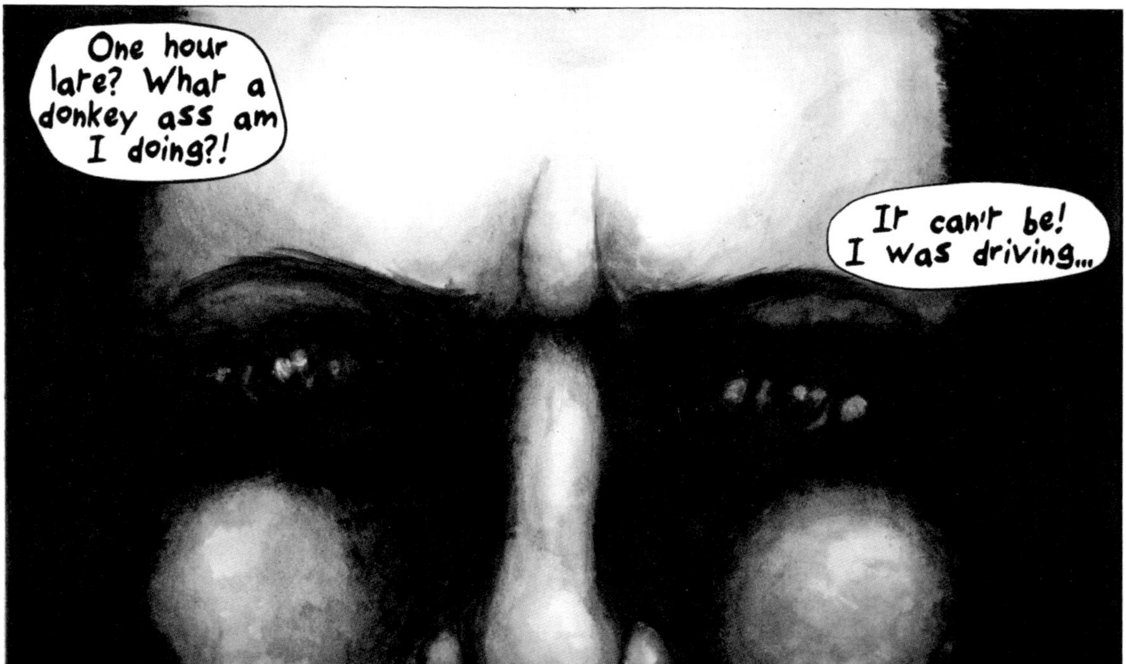
One hour late? What a donkey ass am I doing?!
It can't be! I was driving...

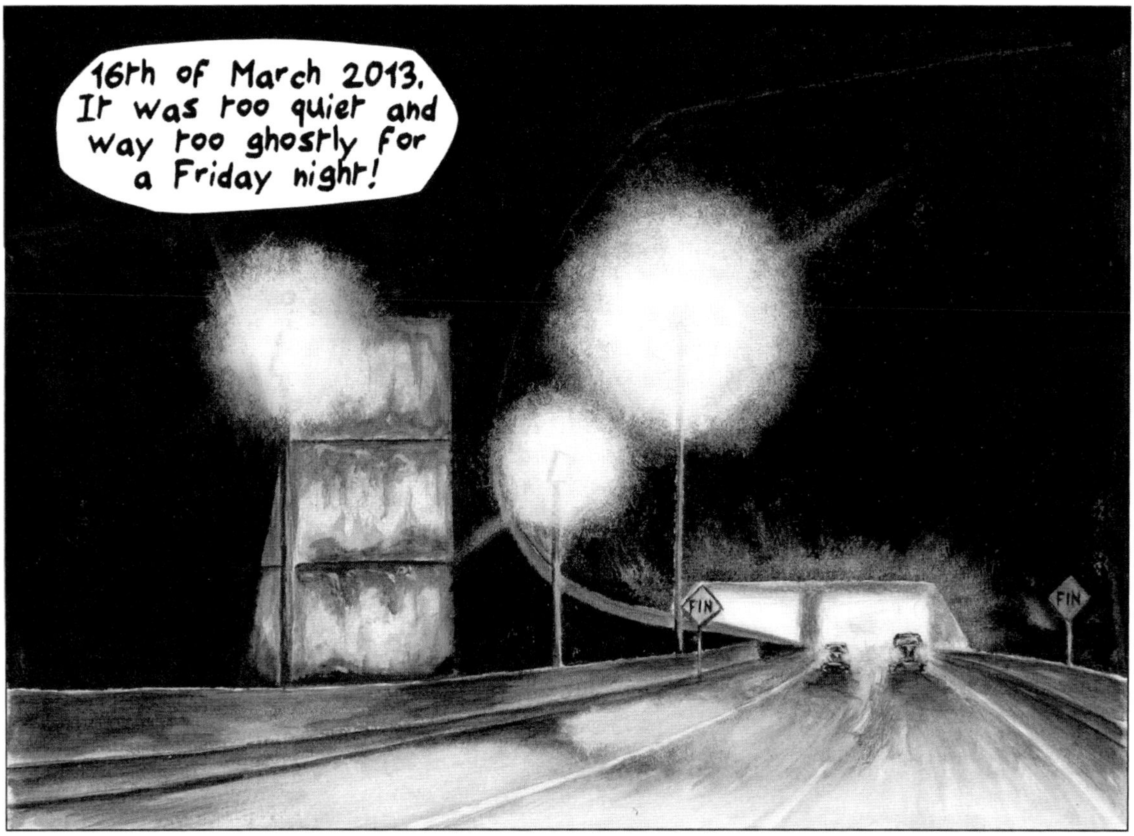
16th of March 2013. It was too quiet and way too ghostly for a Friday night!
FIN
FIN

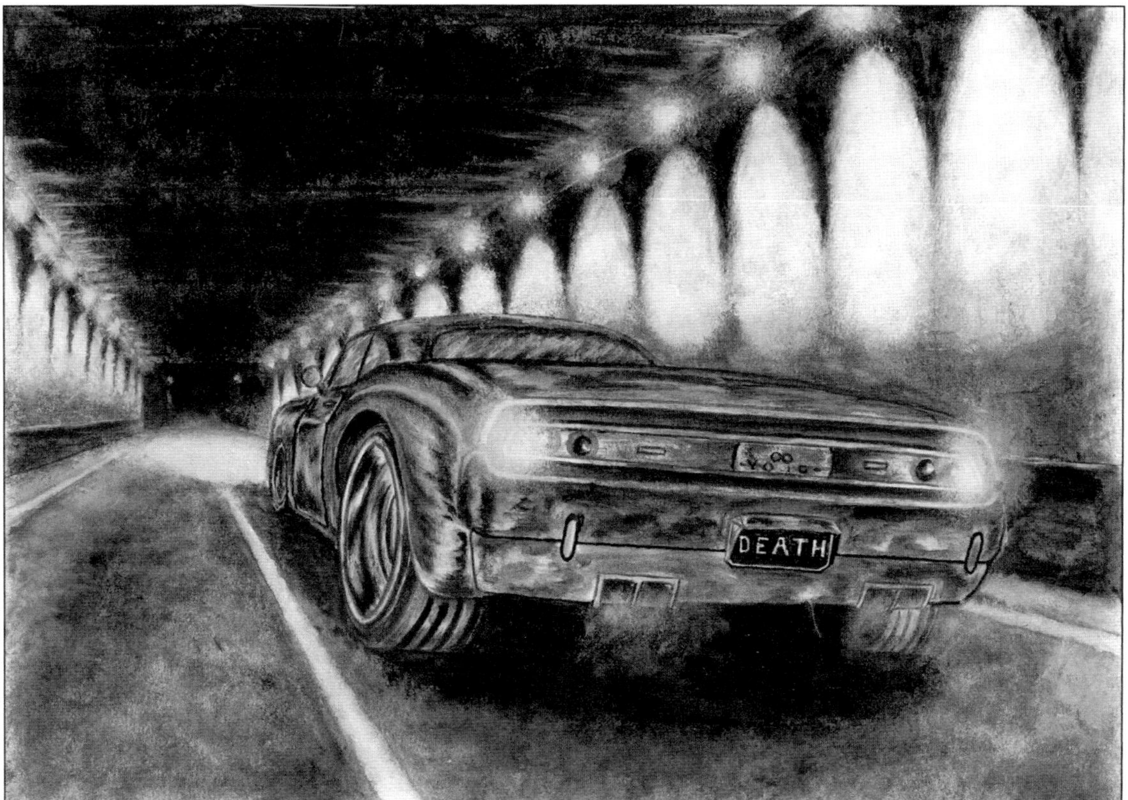
DEATH

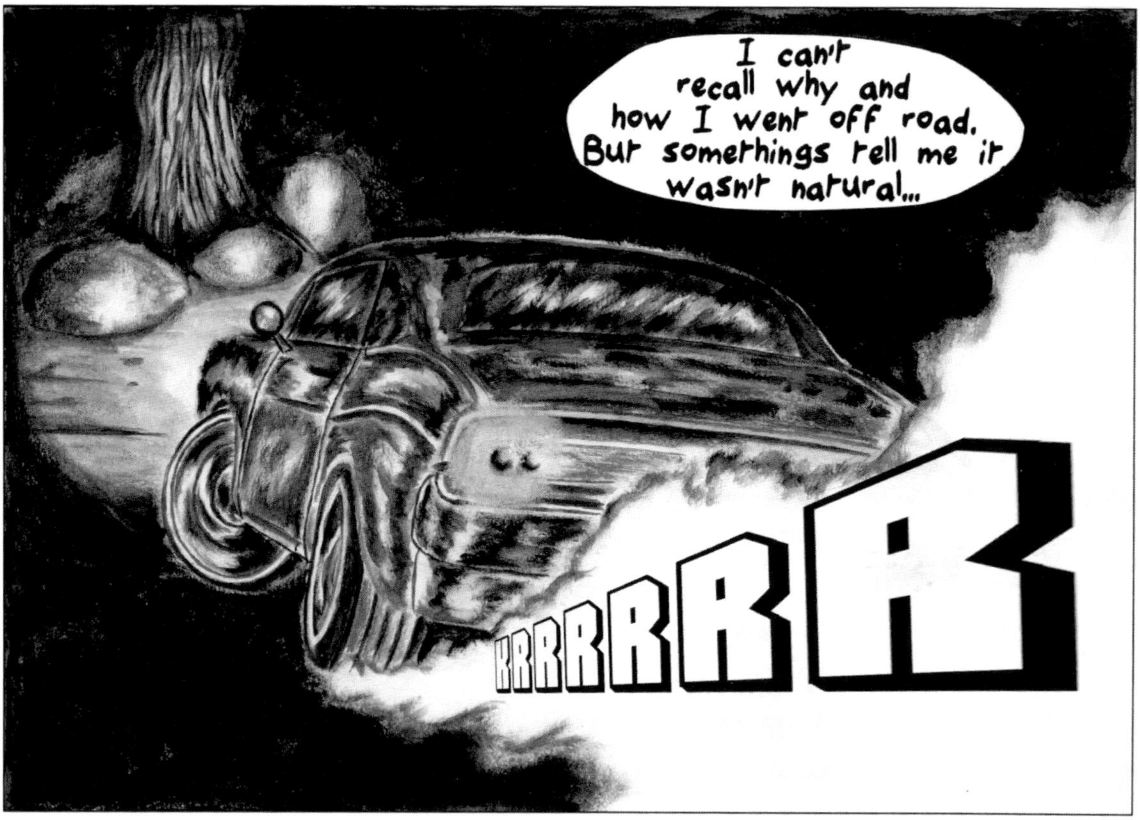
I can't recall why and how I went off road. But somethings tell me it wasn't natural...
KRRRRRR

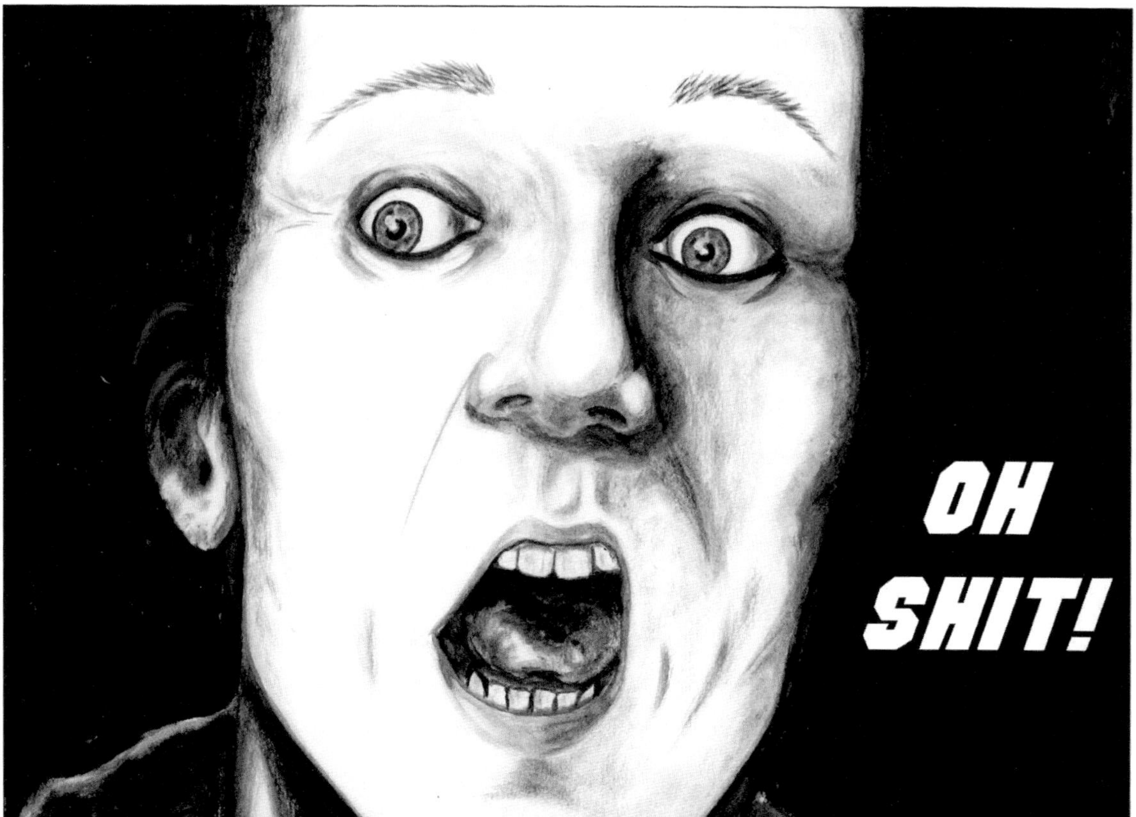
OH SHIT!

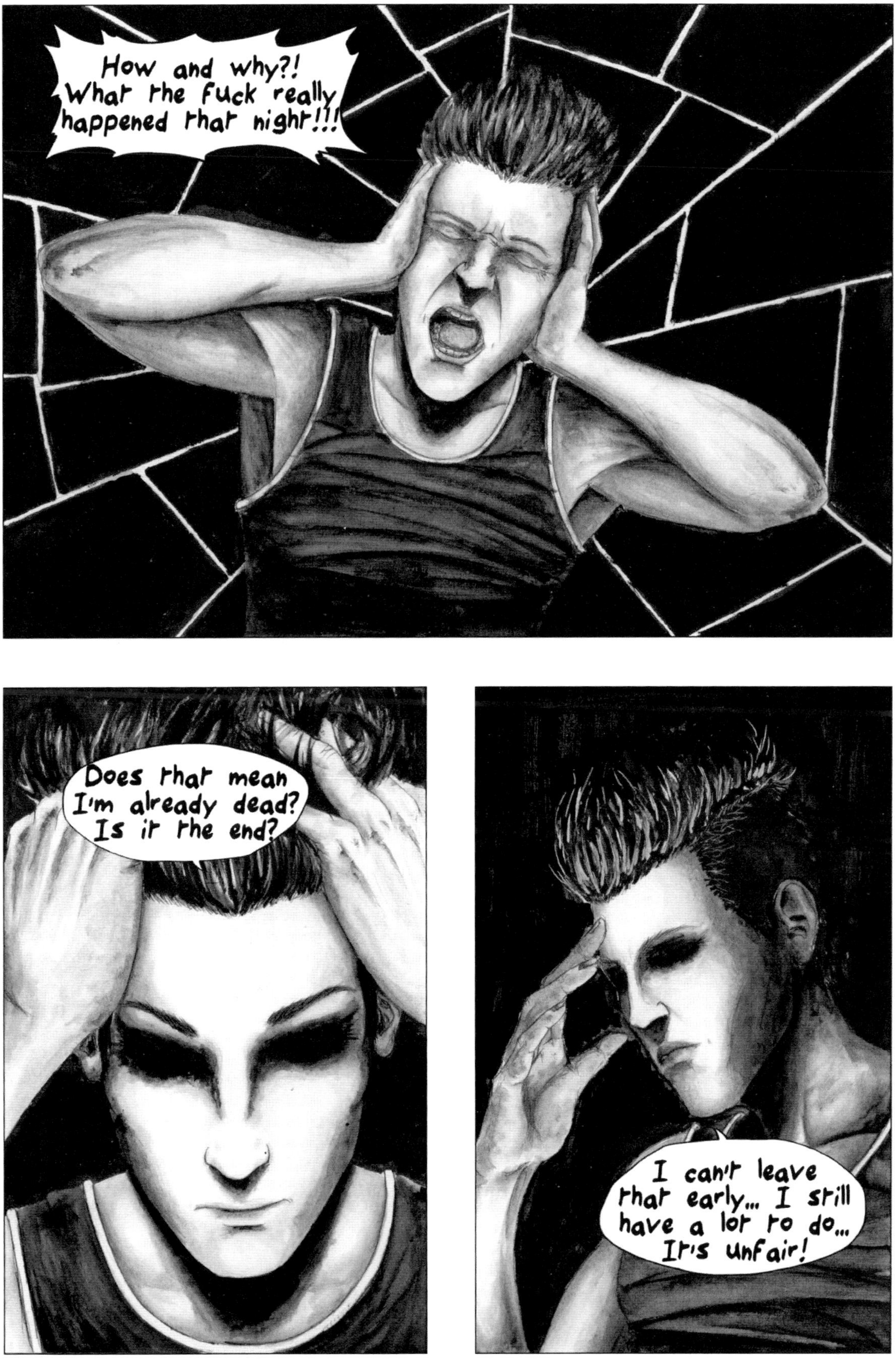
How and why?! What the fuck really happened that night!!!
Does that mean I'm already dead? Is it the end?
I can't leave that early... I still have a lot to do... It's unfair!

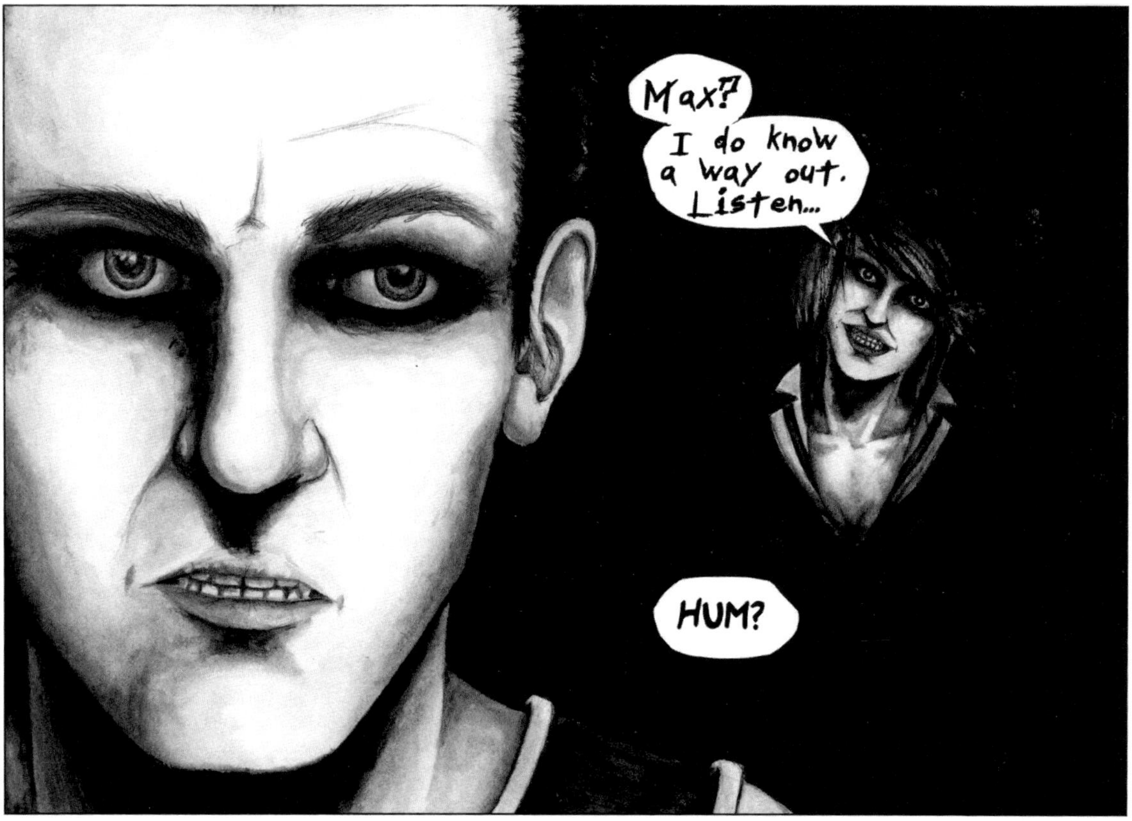
Max?
I do know a way out. Listen...
HUM?
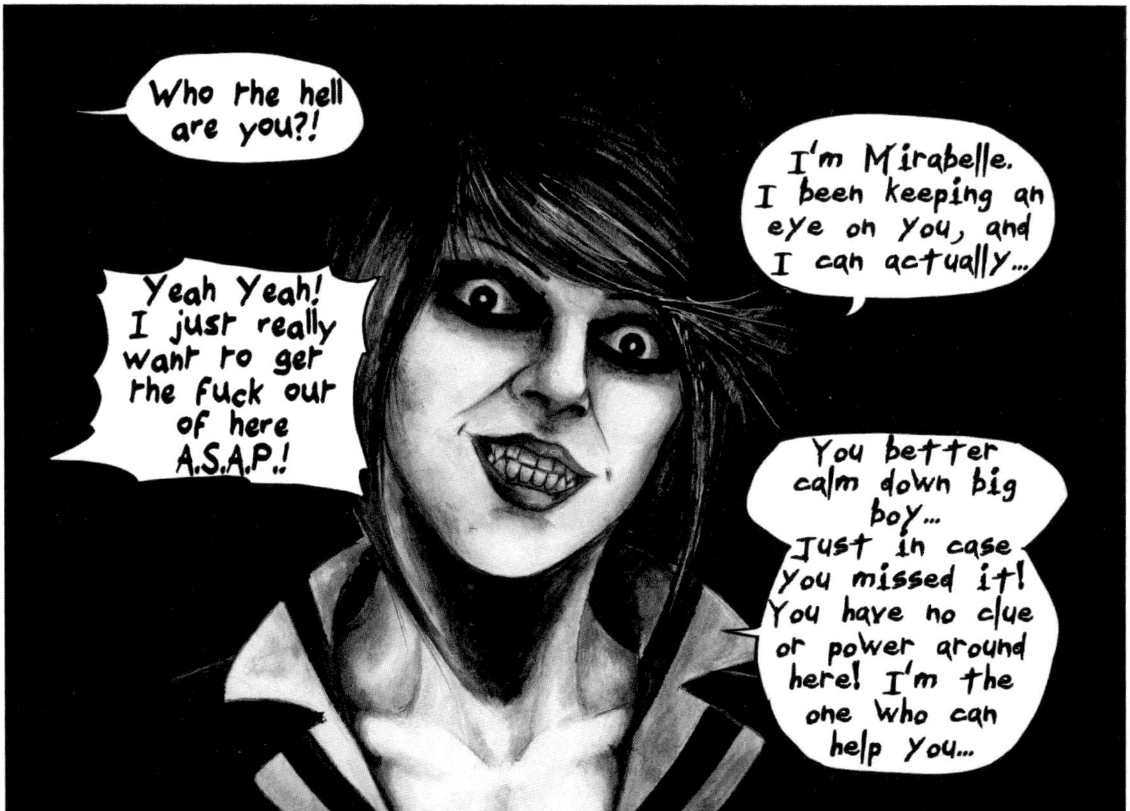
Who the hell are you?!
I'm Mirabelle. I been keeping an eye on you, and I can actually...
Yeah Yeah! I just really want to get the fuck out of here A.S.A.P.!
You better calm down big boy...
Just in case you missed it! You have no clue or power around here! I'm the one who can help you...

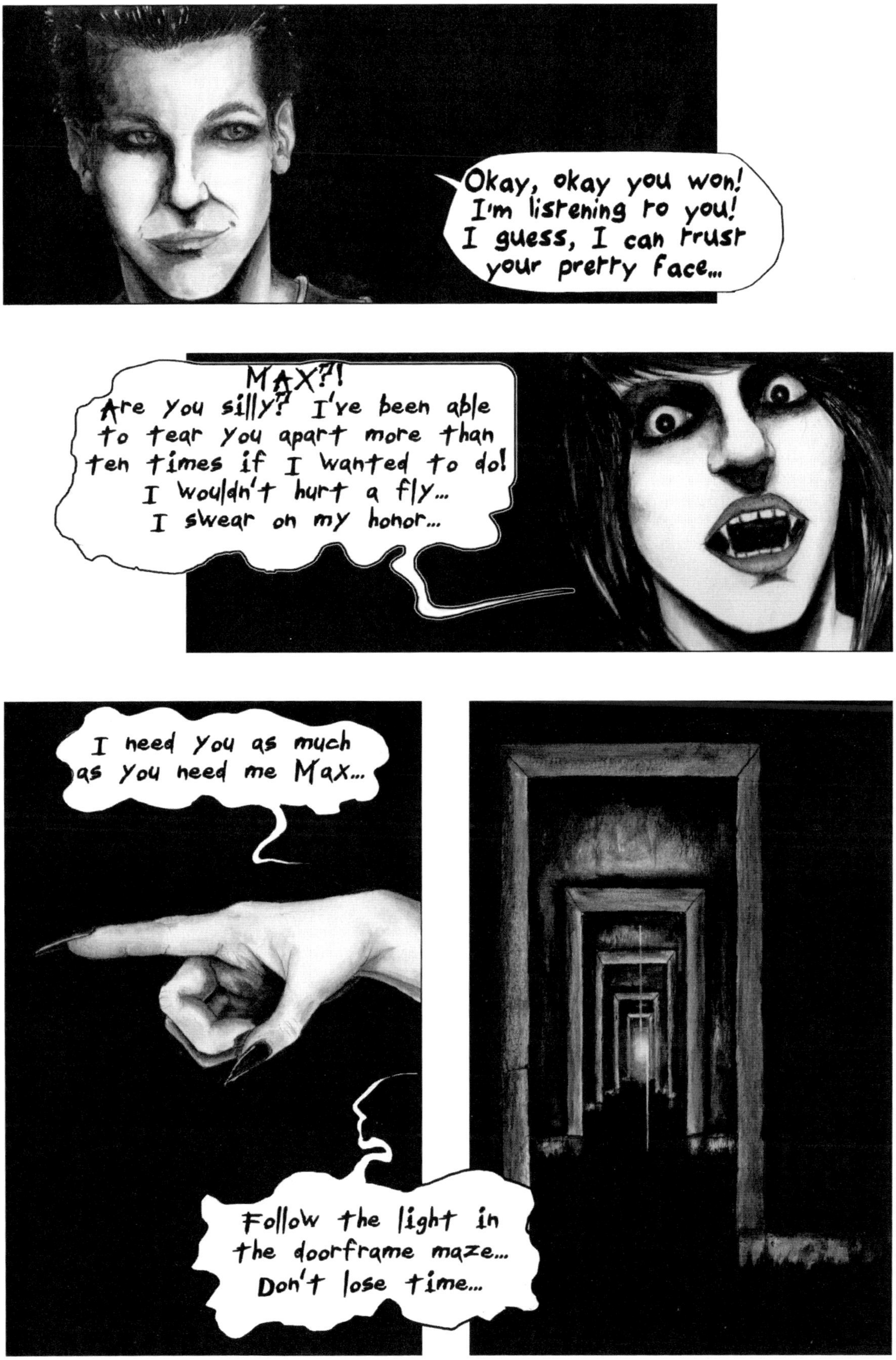
Okay, okay you won! I'm listening to you! I guess, I can trust your pretty face...
MAX?! Are you silly? I've been able to tear you apart more than ten times if I wanted to do! I wouldn't hurt a fly... I swear on my honor...
I need you as much as you need me Max...
Follow the light in the doorframe maze... Don't lose time...

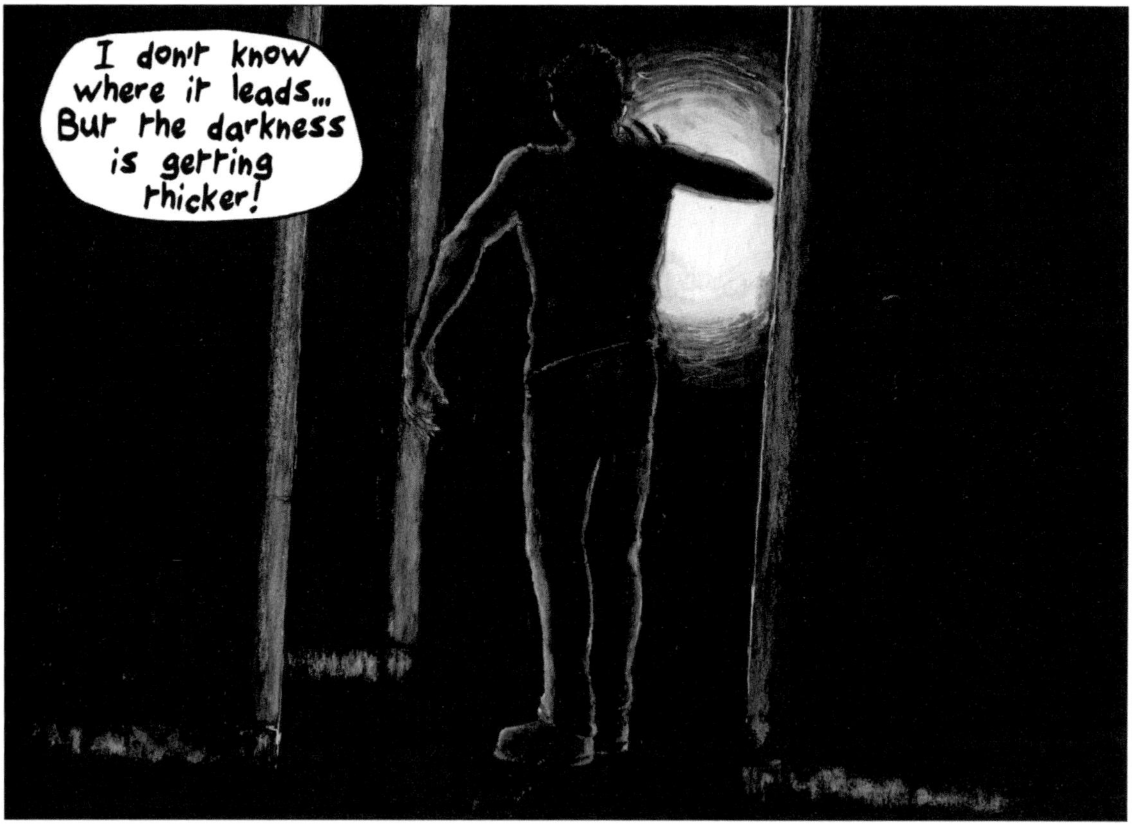
I don't know where it leads... But the darkness is getting thicker!

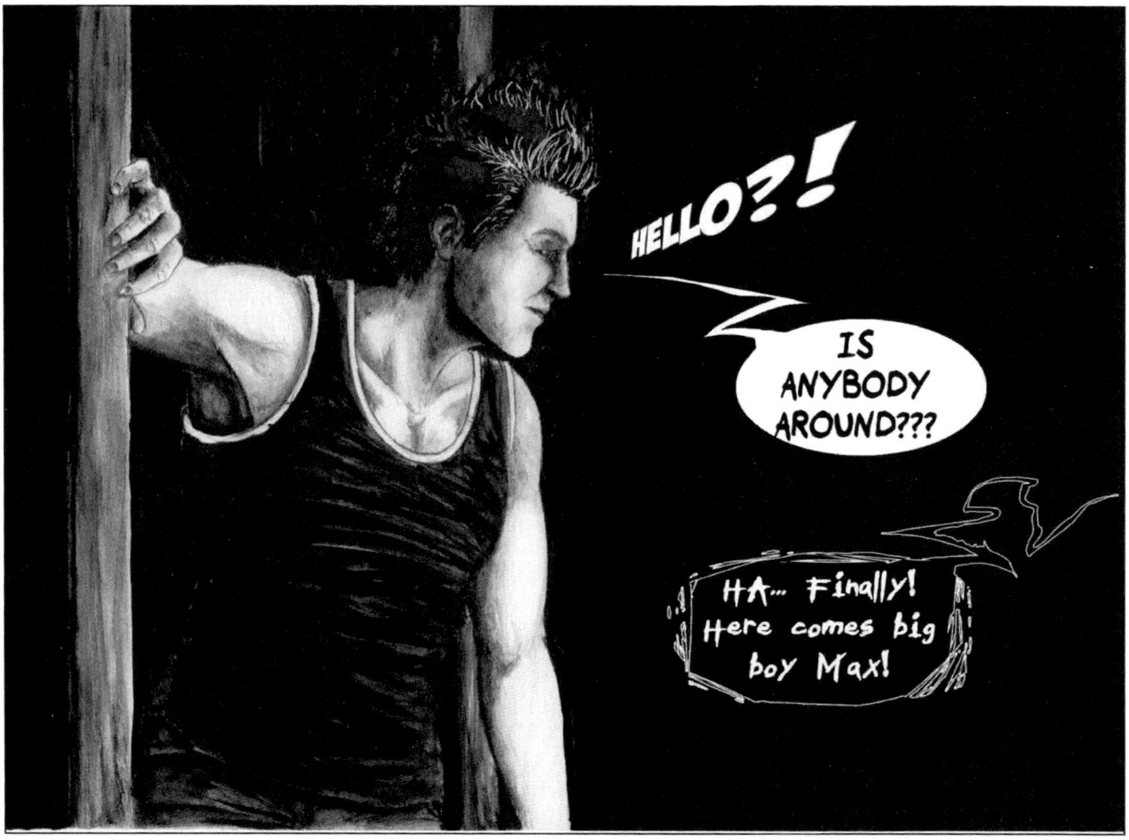
HELLO?!
IS ANYBODY AROUND???
HA... Finally! Here comes big boy Max!

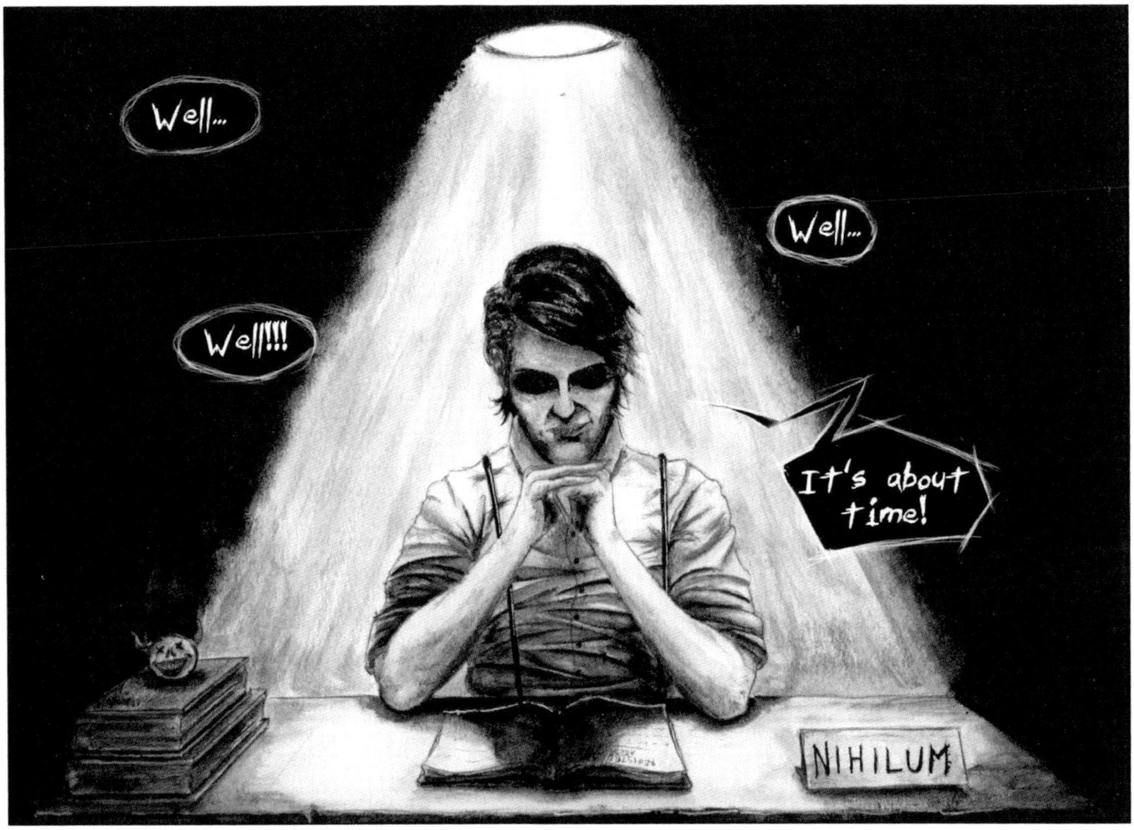
Well...
Well...
Well!!!
It's about time!
NIHILUM

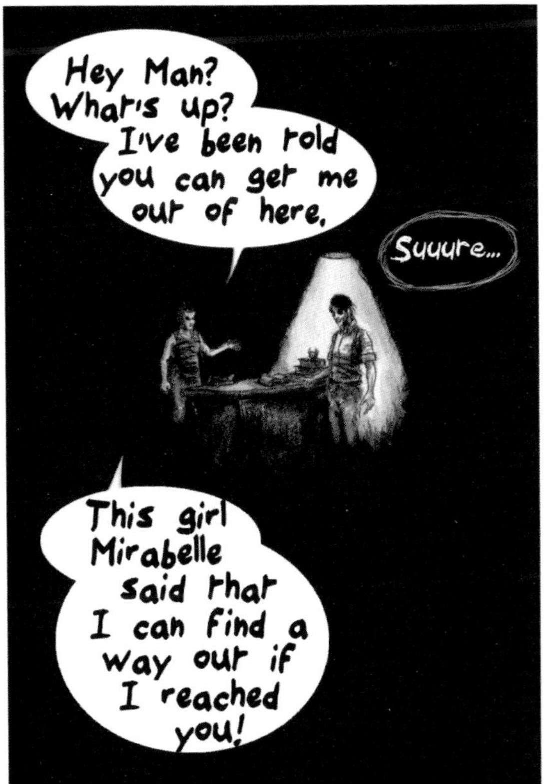
Hey Man? What's up? I've been told you can get me out of here.
Suuure...
This girl Mirabelle said that I can find a way out if I reached you!

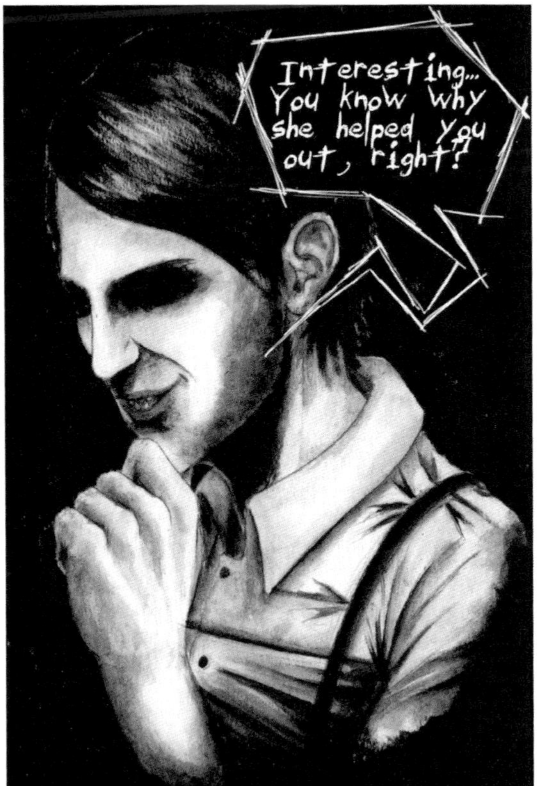
Interesting... You know why she helped you out, right?

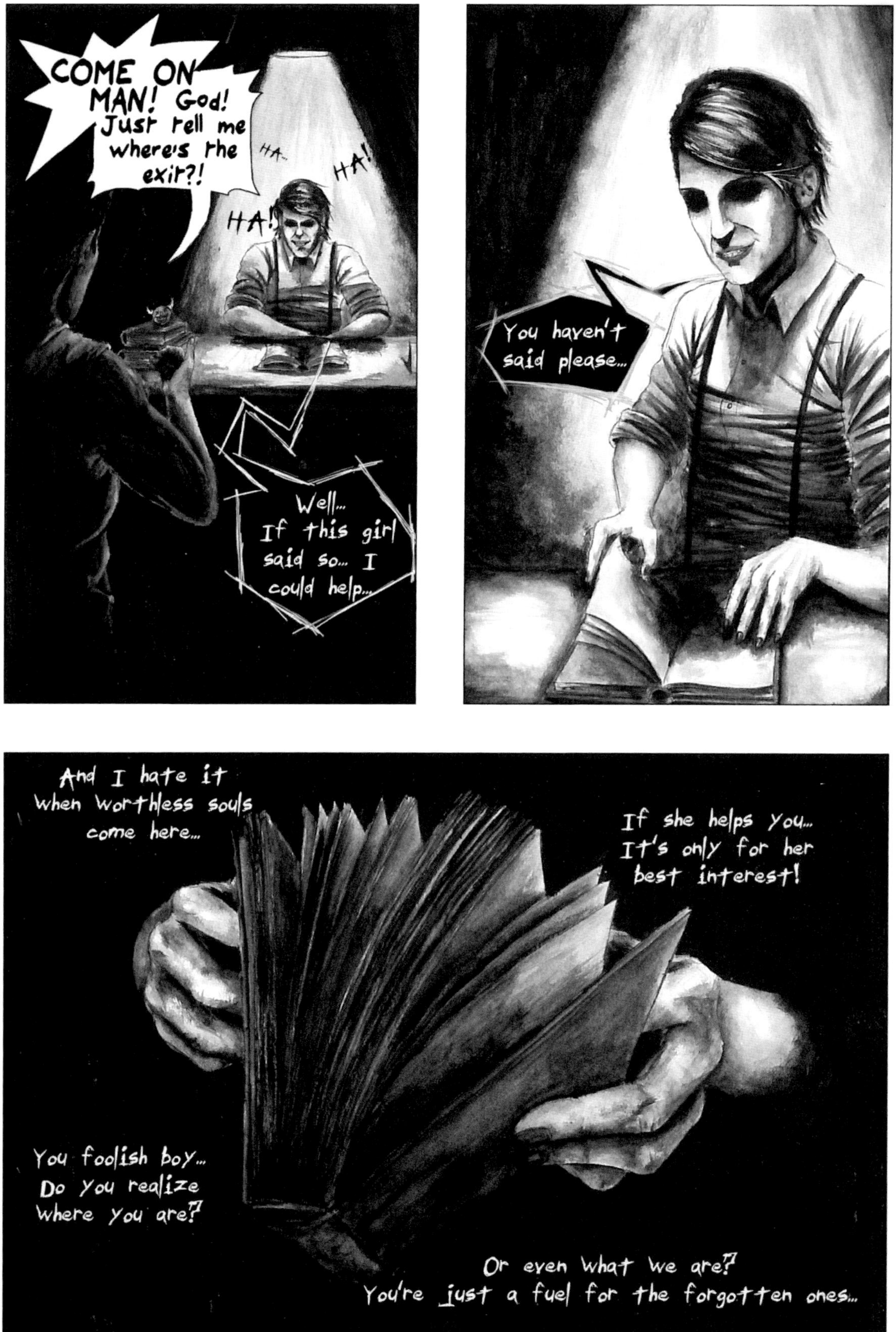
COME ON MAN! God! Just tell me where's the exit?!
HA...
HA!
HA!
Well... If this girl said so... I could help...
You haven't said please...
And I hate it when worthless souls come here...
If she helps you... It's only for her best interest!
You foolish boy... Do you realize where you are?!
Or even what we are?! You're just a fuel for the forgotten ones...

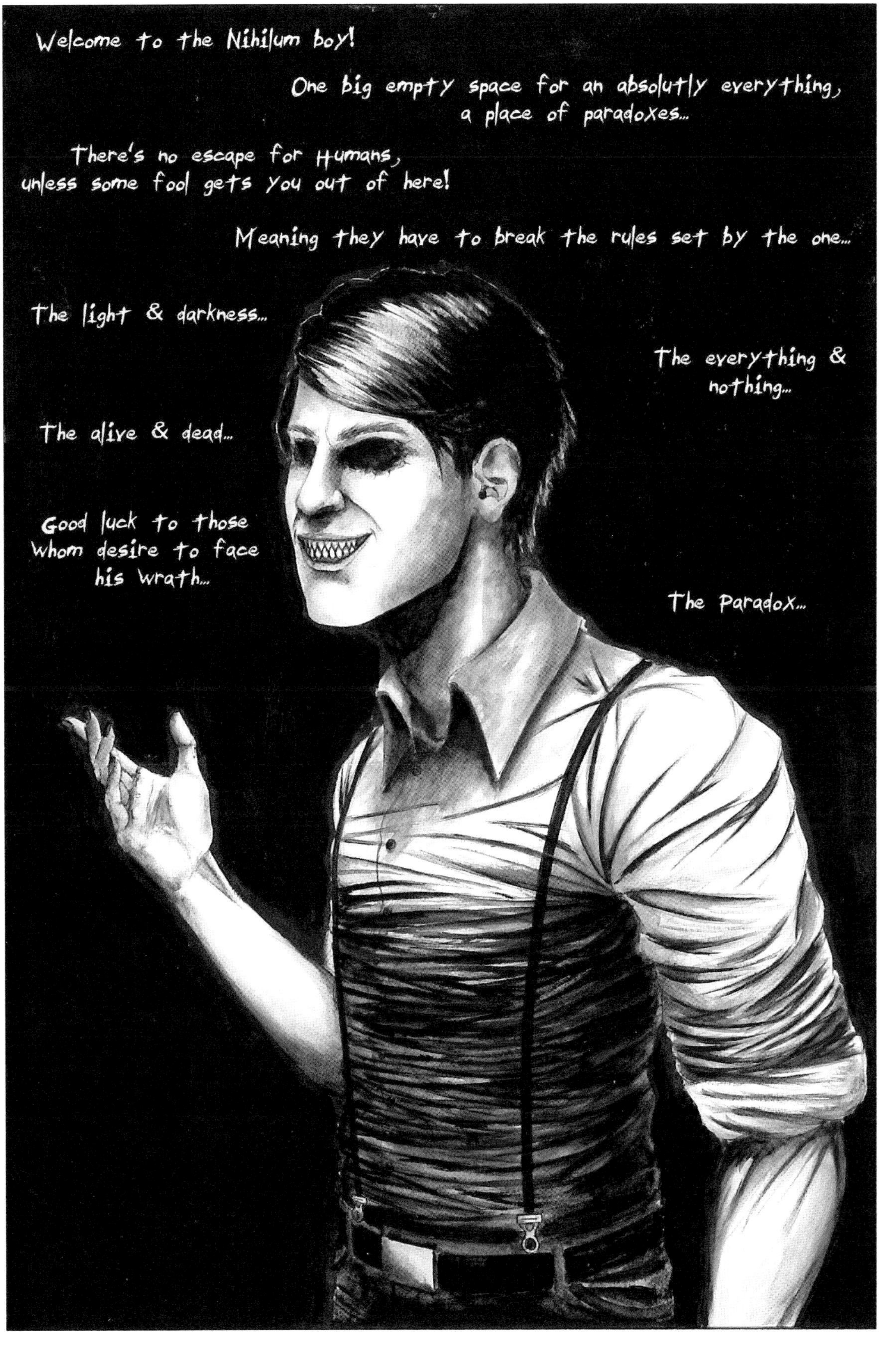
Welcome to the Nihilum boy!
One big empty space for an absolutly everything, a place of paradoxes...
There's no escape for Humans, unless some fool gets you out of here!
Meaning they have to break the rules set by the one...
The light & darkness...
The everything & nothing...
The alive & dead...
Good luck to those whom desire to face his wrath...
The Paradox...

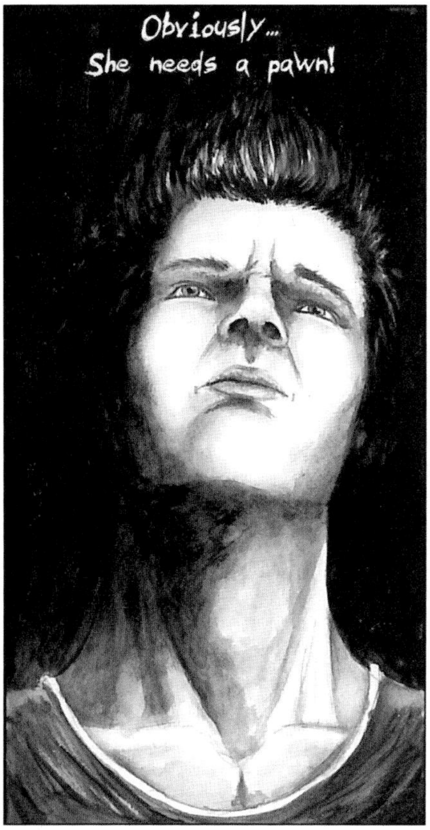
Obviously...
She needs a pawn!

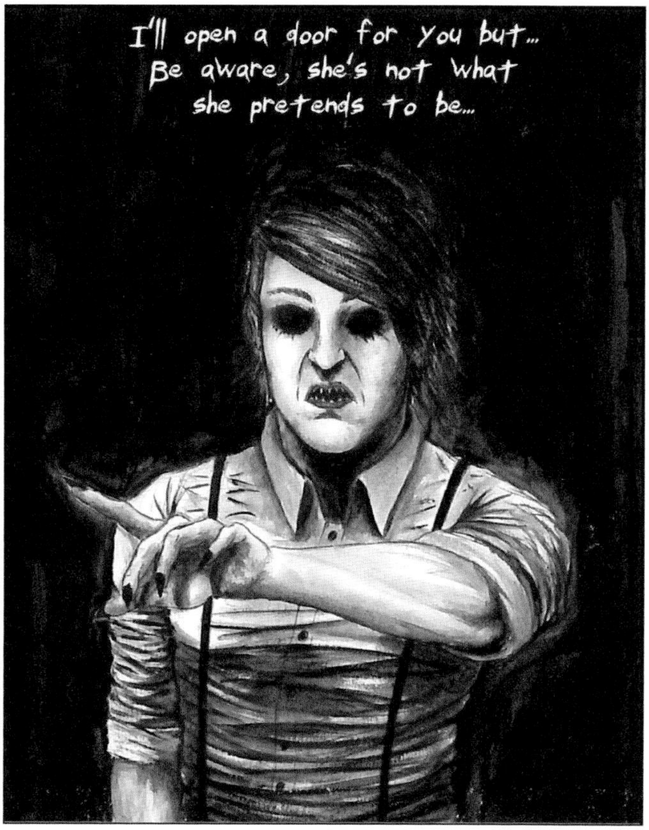
I'll open a door for you but...
Be aware, she's not what
she pretends to be...

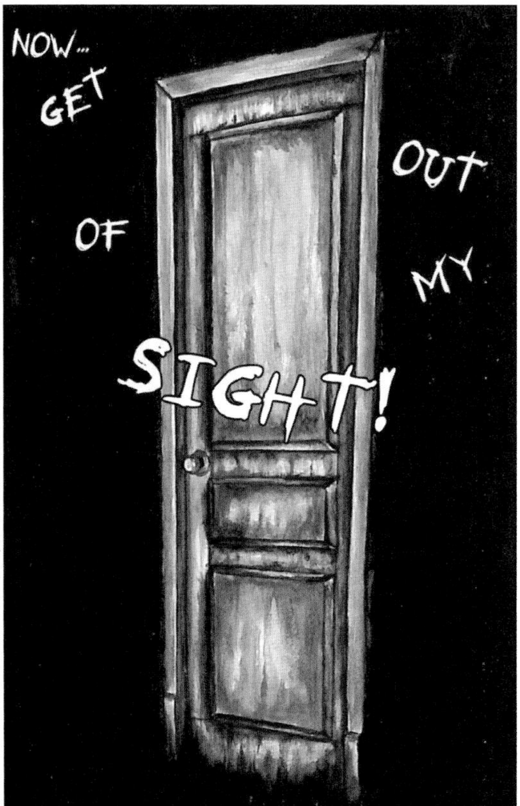
NOW...
GET
OUT
OF
MY
SIGHT!

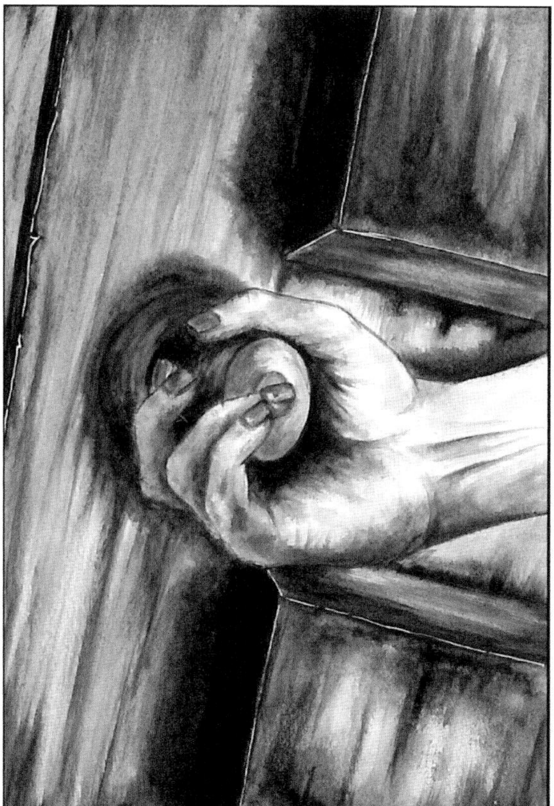

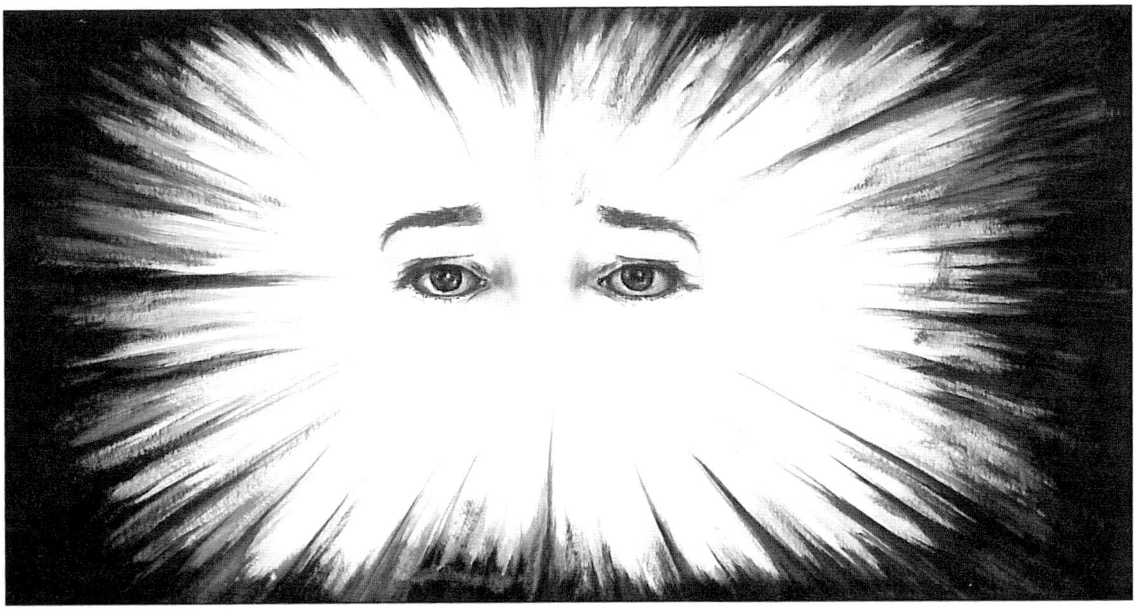

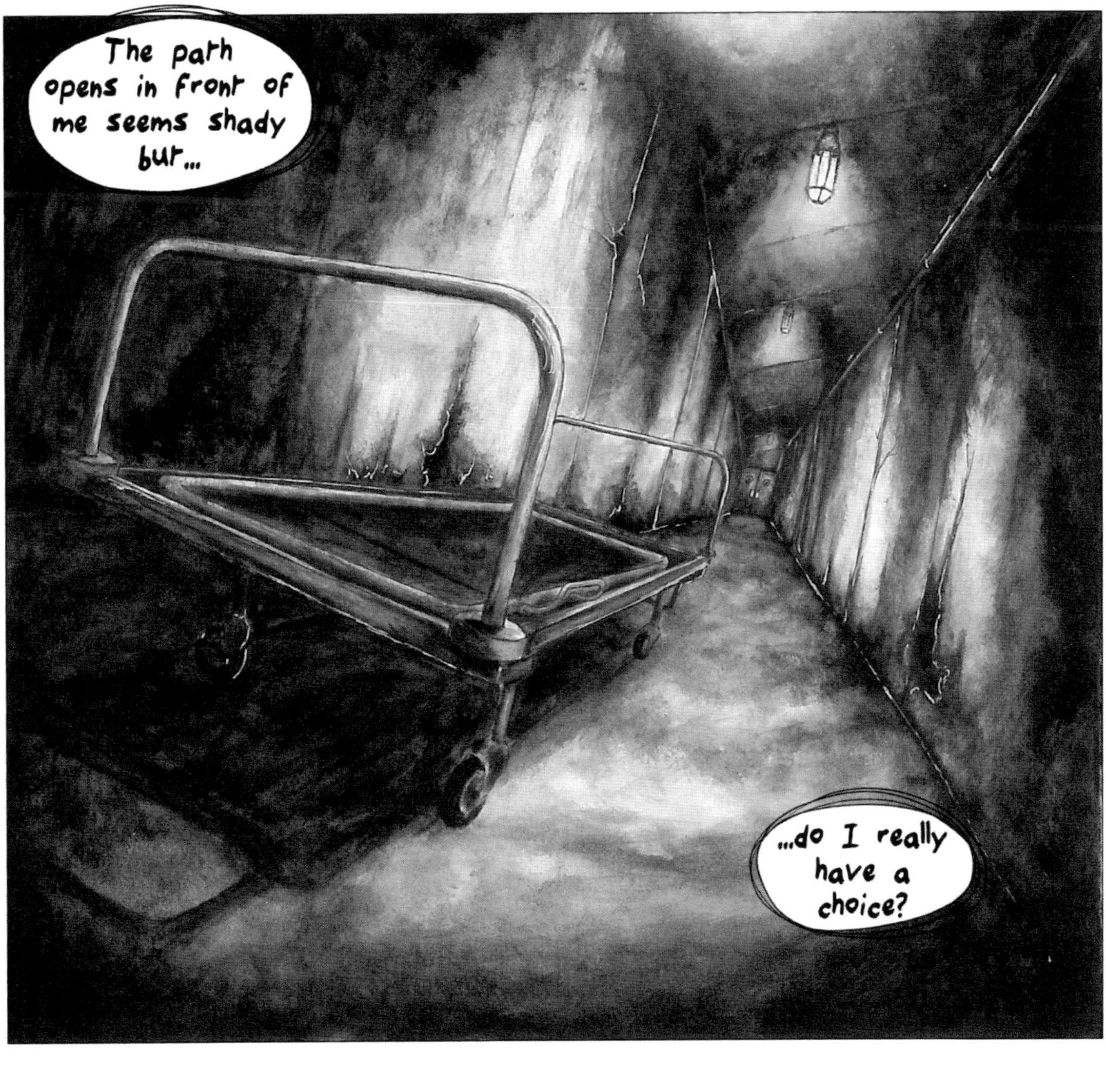
The path opens in front of me seems shady but...
...do I really have a choice?

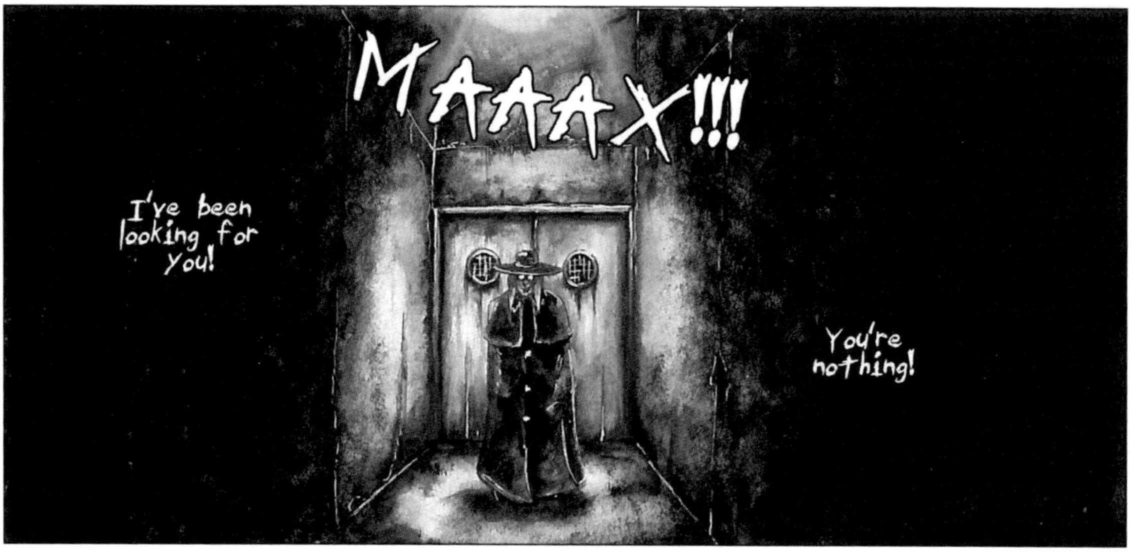
MAAAX!!!
I've been looking for you!
You're nothing!

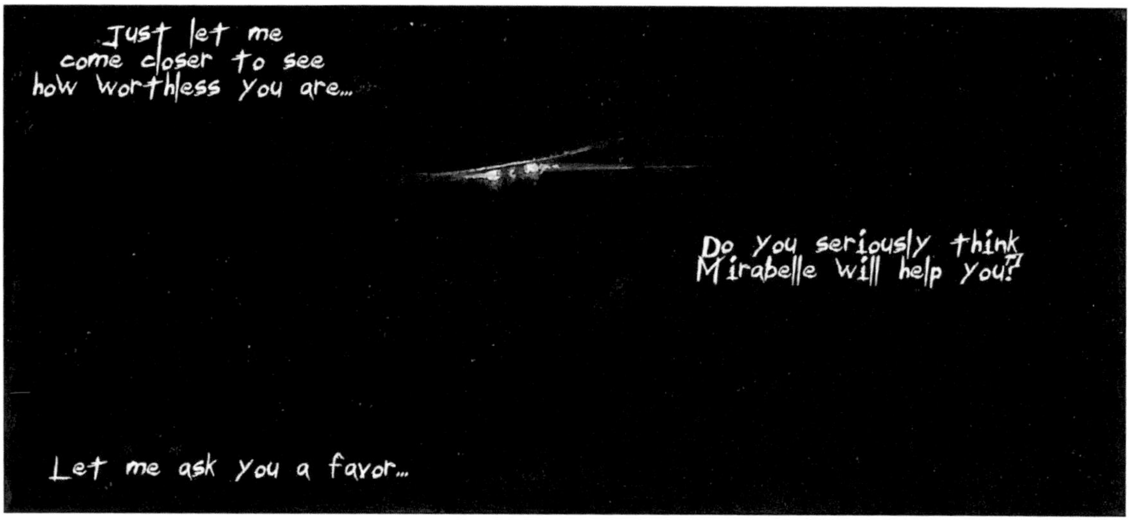
Just let me come closer to see how worthless you are...
Do you seriously think Mirabelle will help you?
Let me ask you a favor...

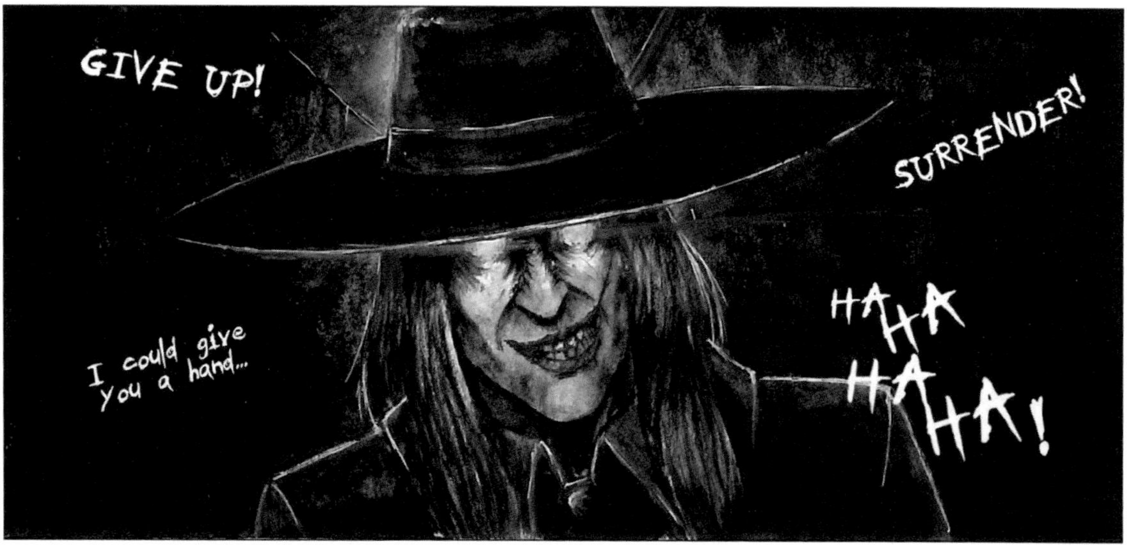
GIVE UP!
SURRENDER!
I could give you a hand...
HAHA HAHA HA!

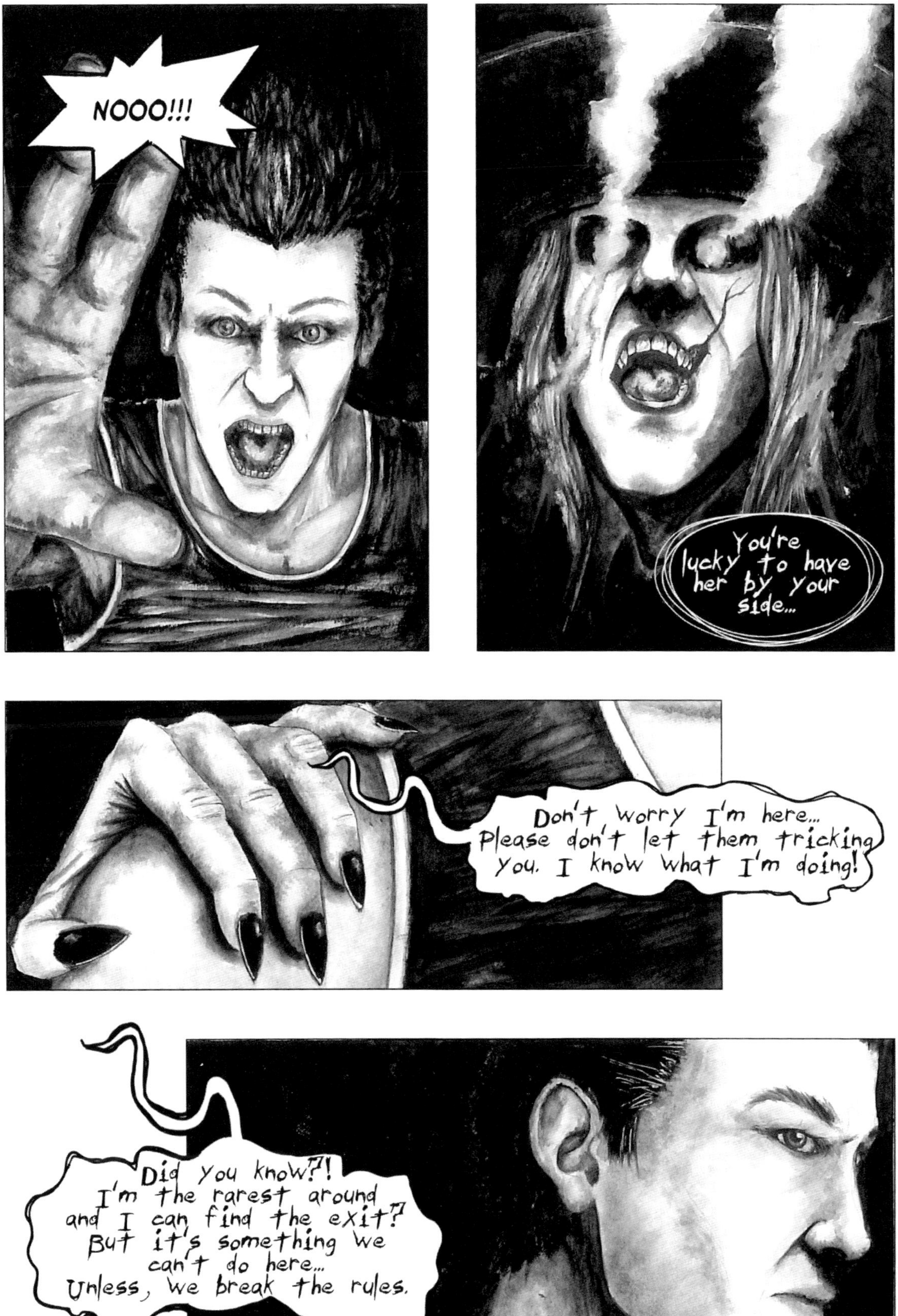
NOOO!!!
You're lucky to have her by your side...
Don't worry I'm here... Please don't let them tricking you. I know what I'm doing!
Did you know?!! I'm the rarest around and I can find the exit? But it's something we can't do here... Unless, we break the rules.

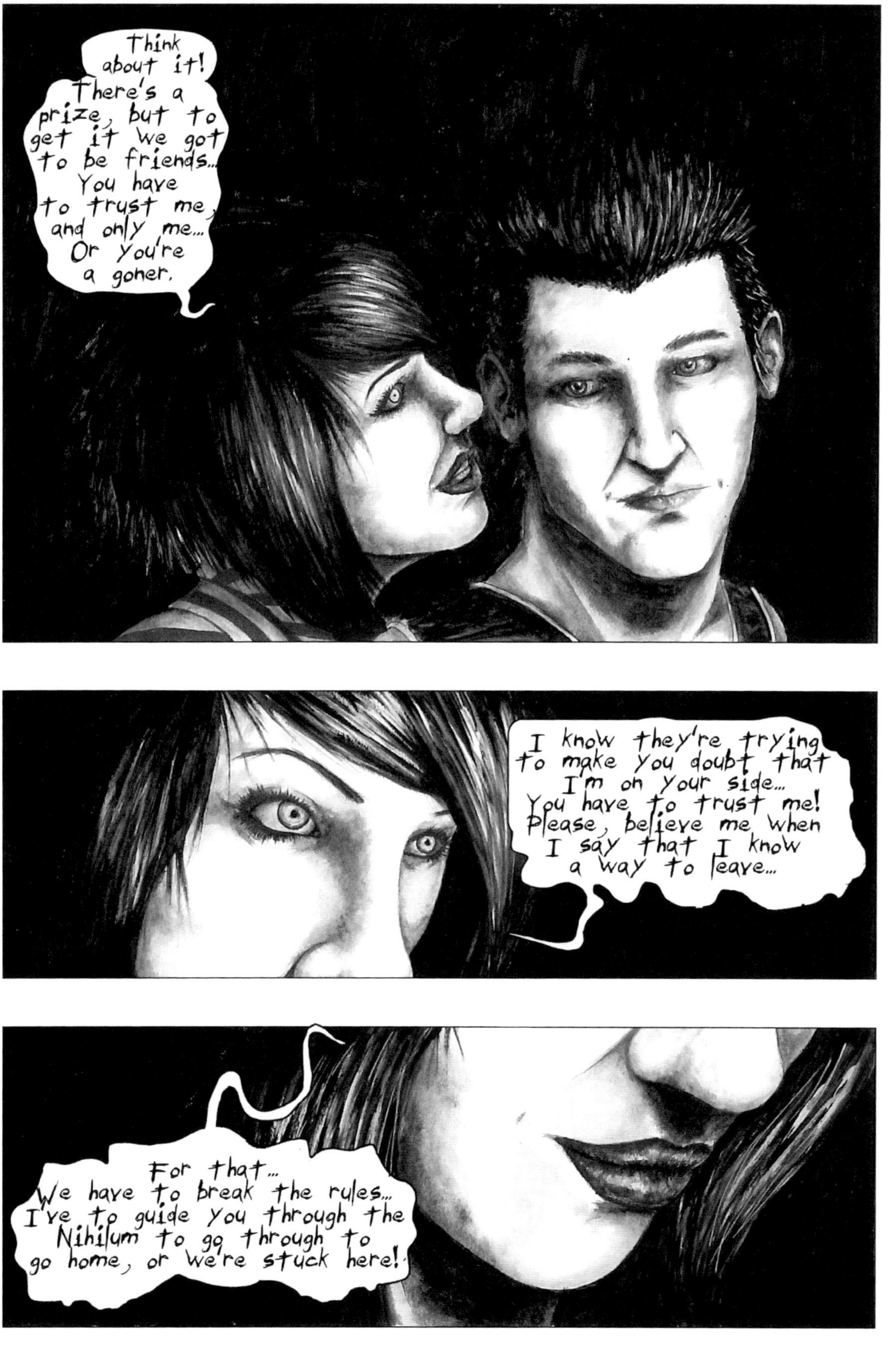
Think about it! There's a prize, but to get it we got to be friends... You have to trust me, and only me... Or you're a goner.
I know they're trying to make you doubt that I'm on your side... You have to trust me! Please, believe me when I say that I know a way to leave...
For that... We have to break the rules... I've to guide you through the Nihilum to go through to go home, or we're stuck here!

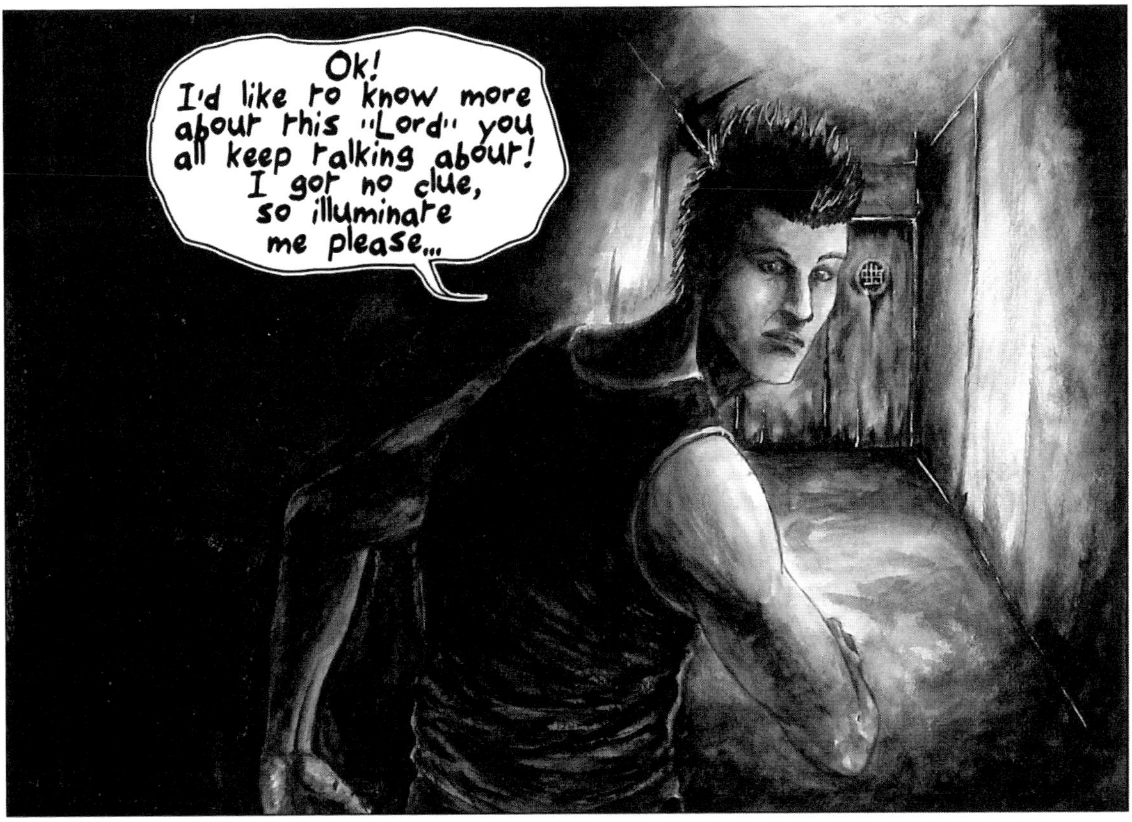
Ok! I'd like to know more about this "Lord" you all keep talking about! I got no clue, so illuminate me please...

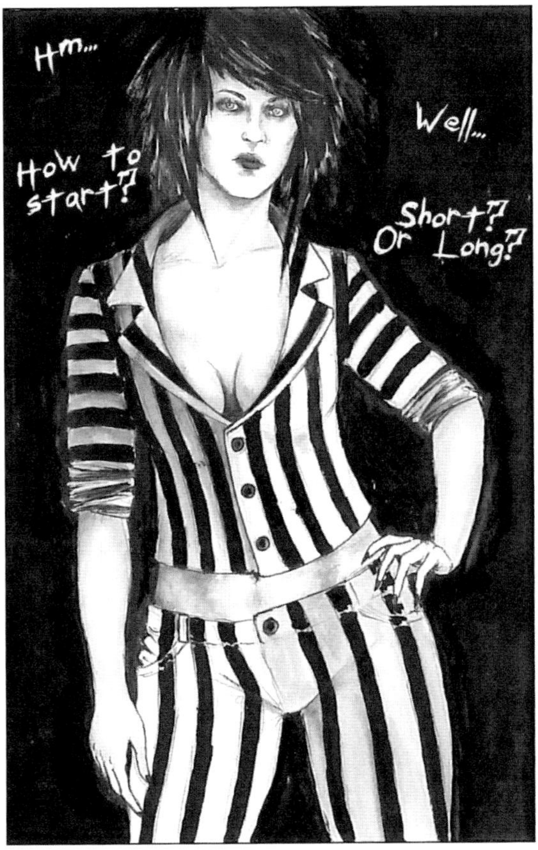
Hm...
Well...
How to start?!
Short?! Or Long?!

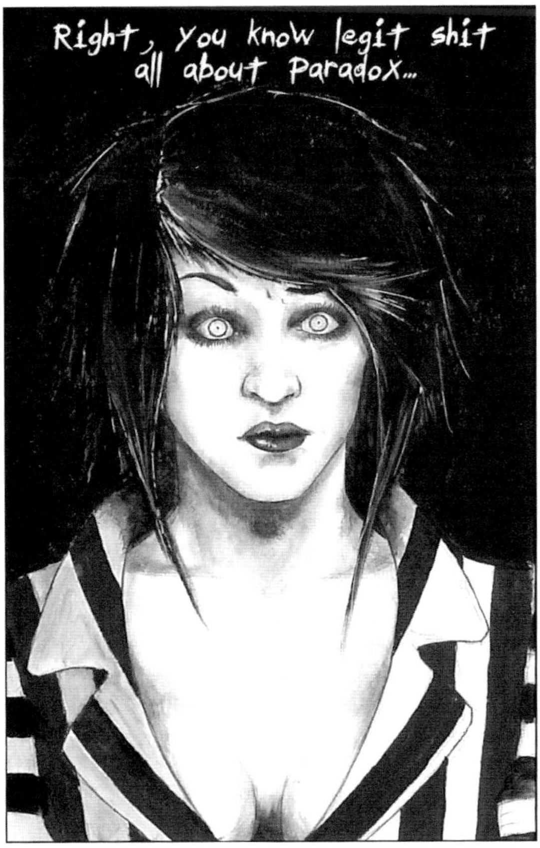
Right, you know legit shit all about Paradox...

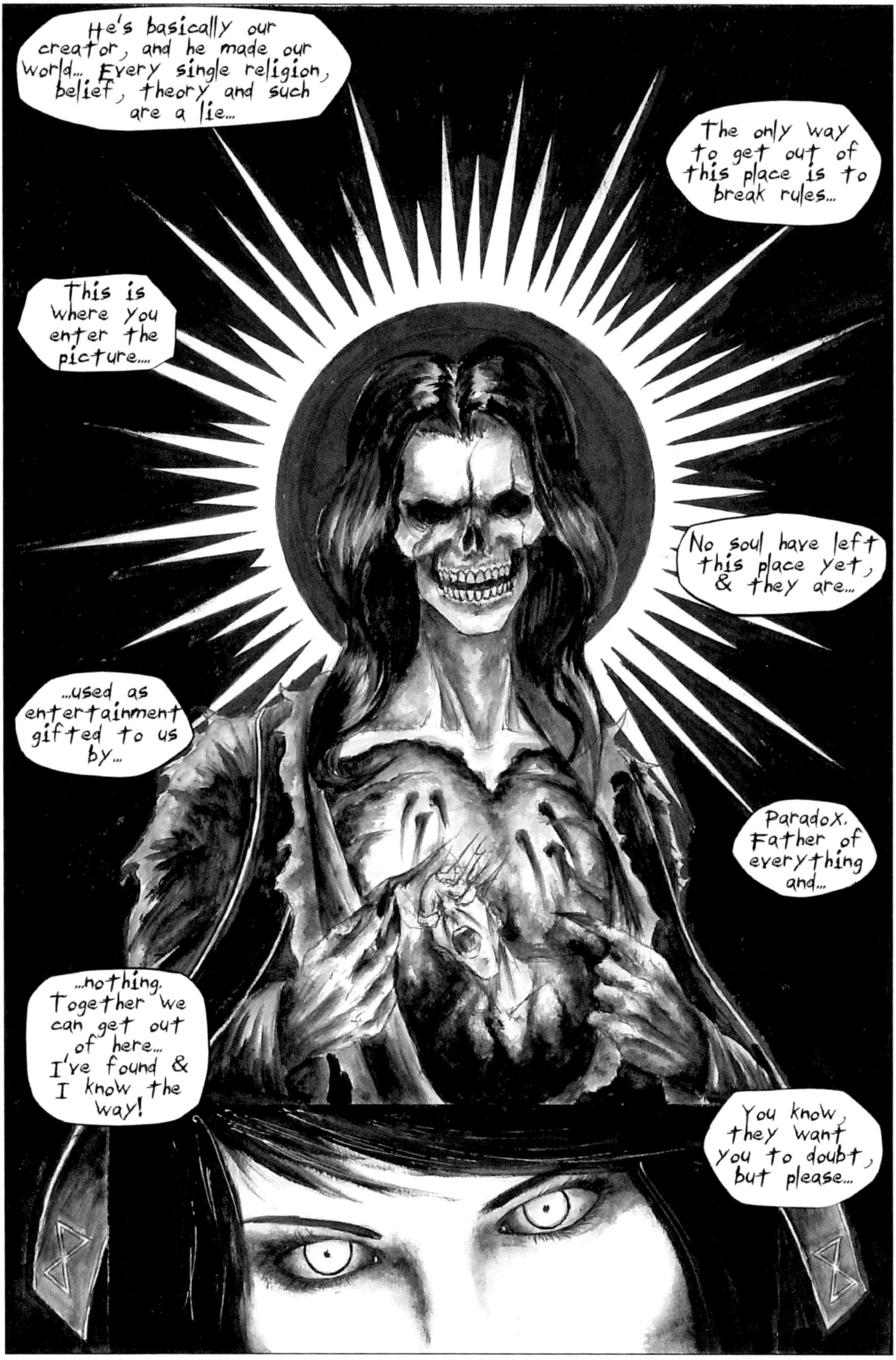
He's basically our creator, and he made our world... Every single religion, belief, theory and such are a lie...
The only way to get out of this place is to break rules...
This is where you enter the picture....
No soul have left this place yet, & they are...
...used as entertainment gifted to us by...
Paradox. Father of everything and...
...nothing. Together we can get out of here... I've found & I know the way!
You know, they want you to doubt, but please...

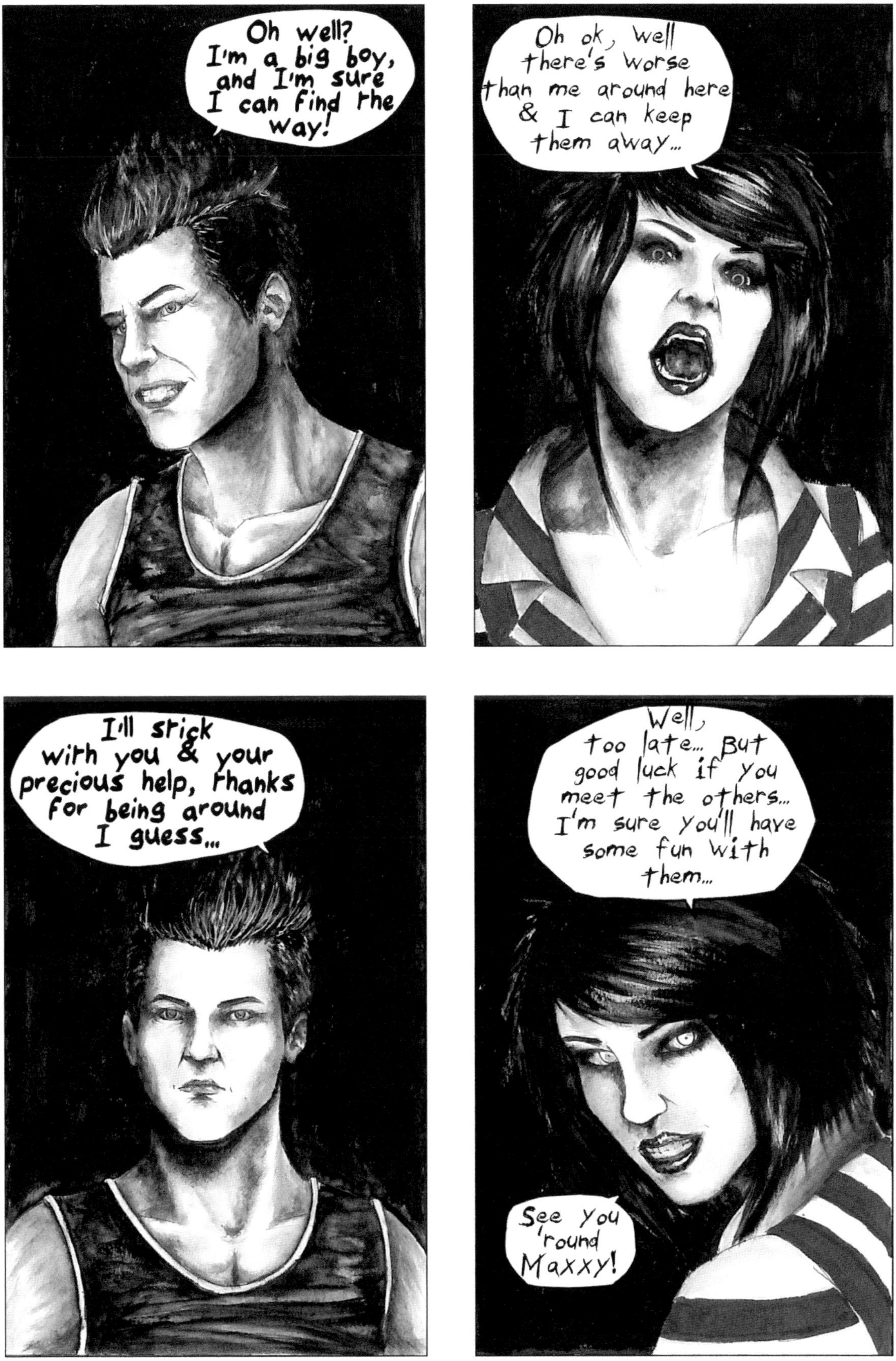
Oh well? I'm a big boy, and I'm sure I can find the way!
Oh ok, well there's worse than me around here & I can keep them away...
I'll stick with you & your precious help, thanks for being around I guess...
Well, too late... But good luck if you meet the others... I'm sure you'll have some fun with them...
See you 'round Maxxy!

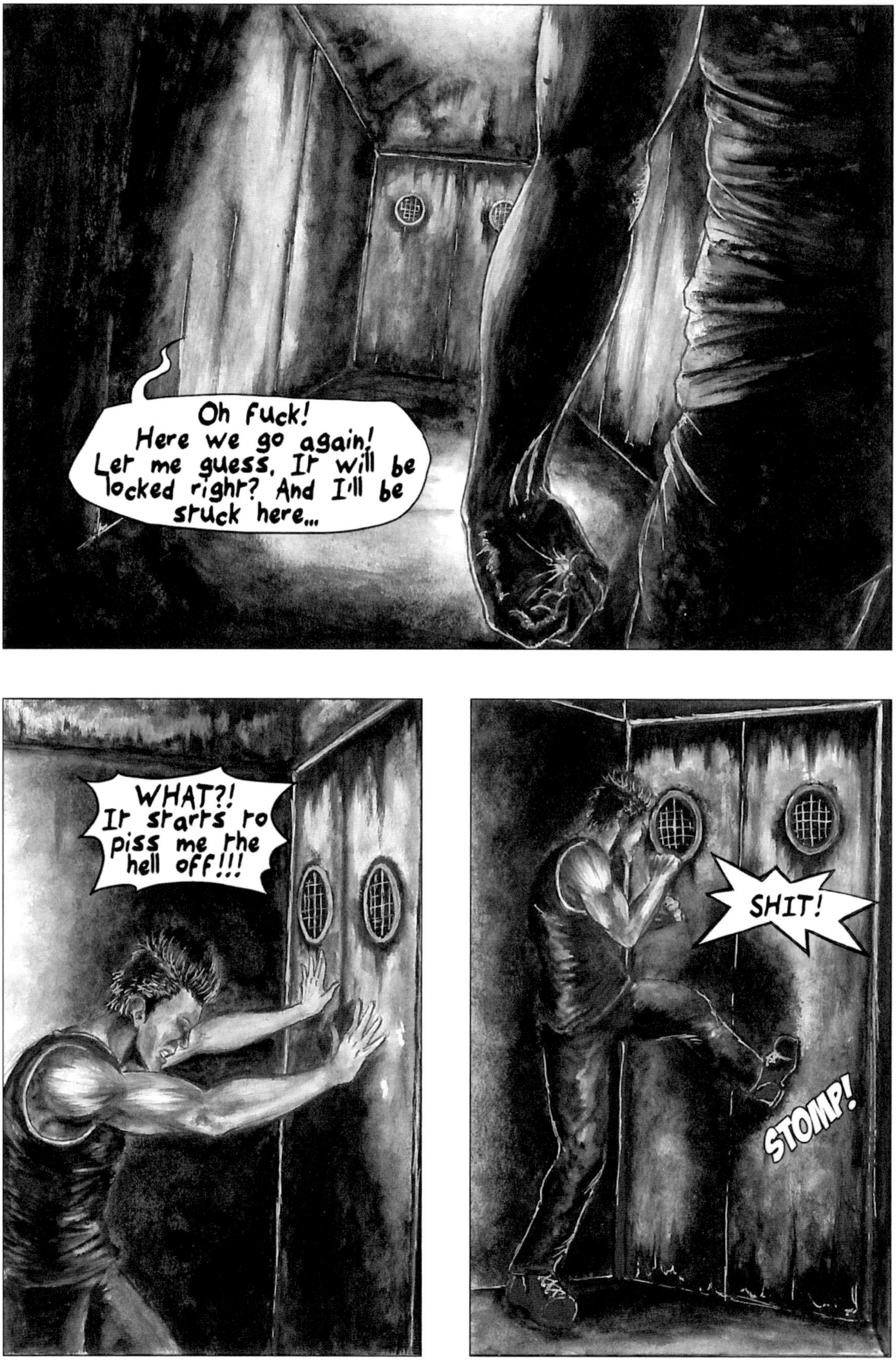
Oh fuck! Here we go again! Let me guess, It will be locked right? And I'll be stuck here...
WHAT?! It starts to piss me the hell off!!!
SHIT!
STOMP!

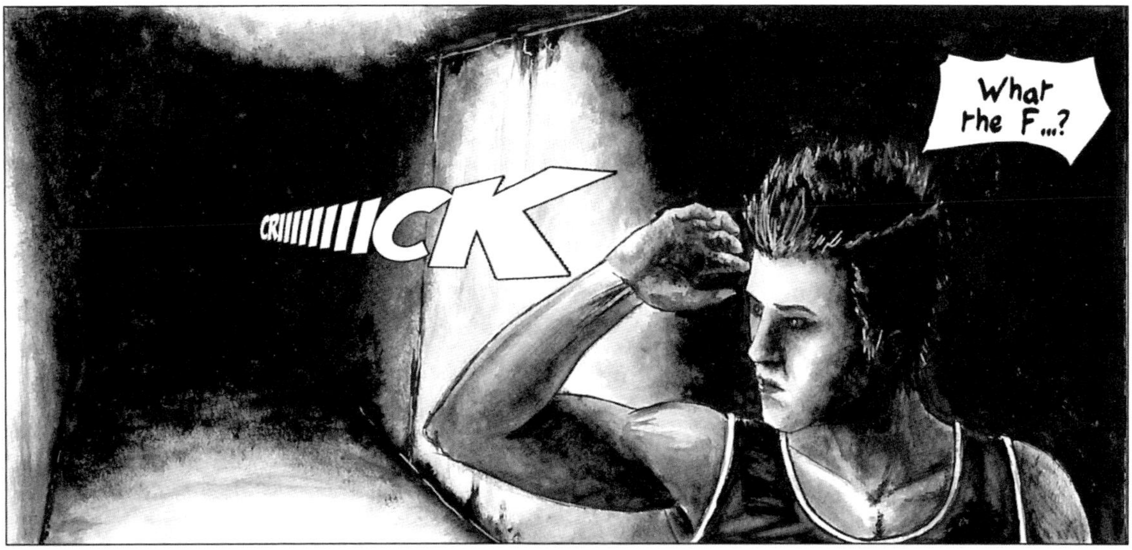
What the F...?
CRIIIIIIIICK

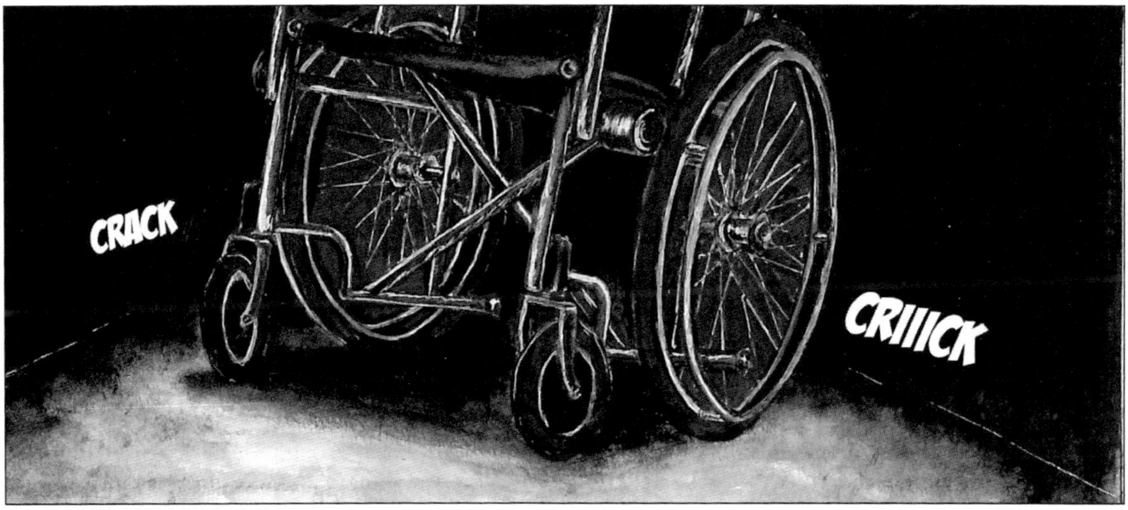
CRACK
CRIIICK

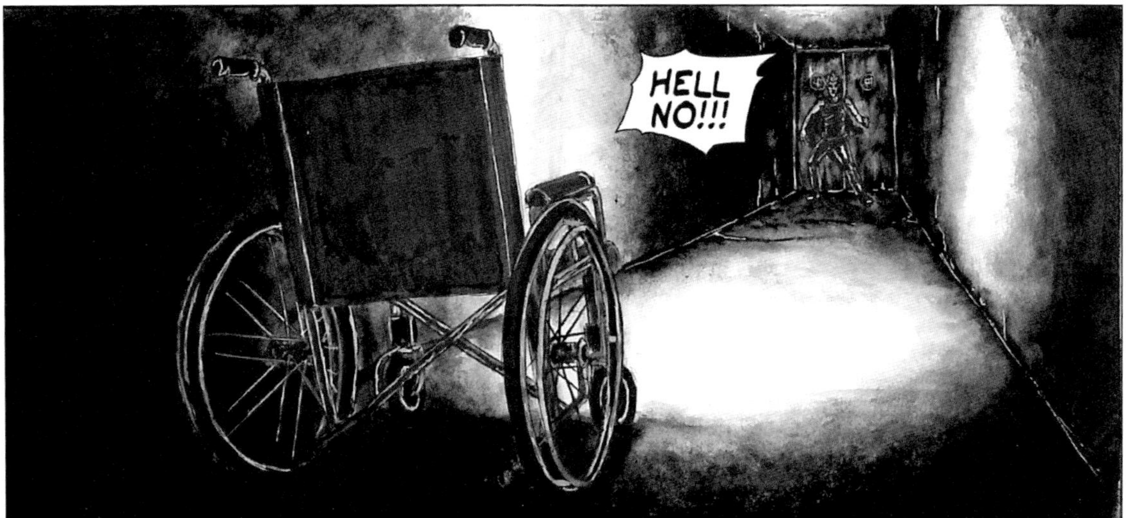
HELL NO!!!

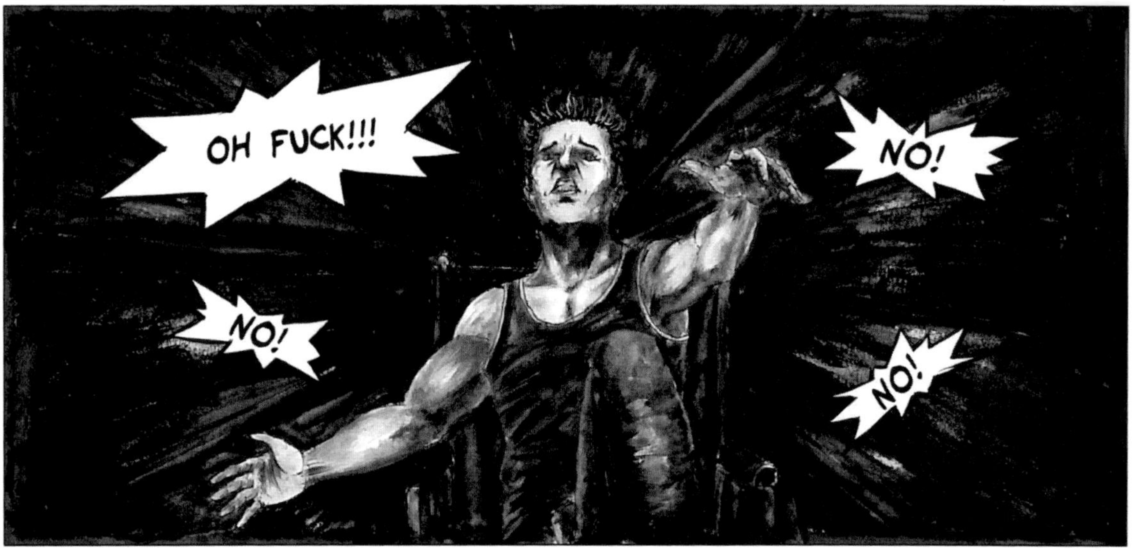
OH FUCK!!!
NO!
NO!
NO!

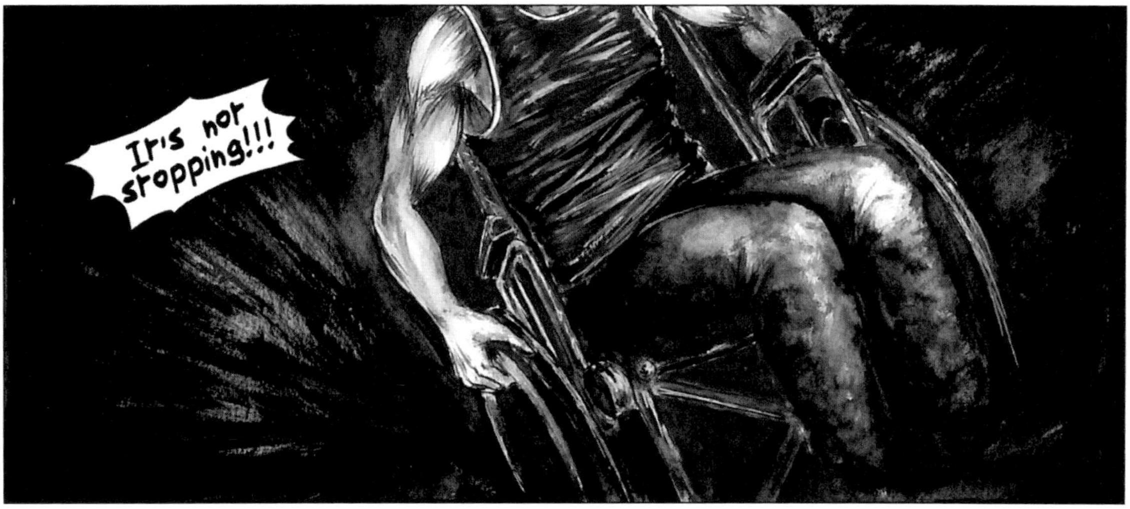
It's not stopping!!!

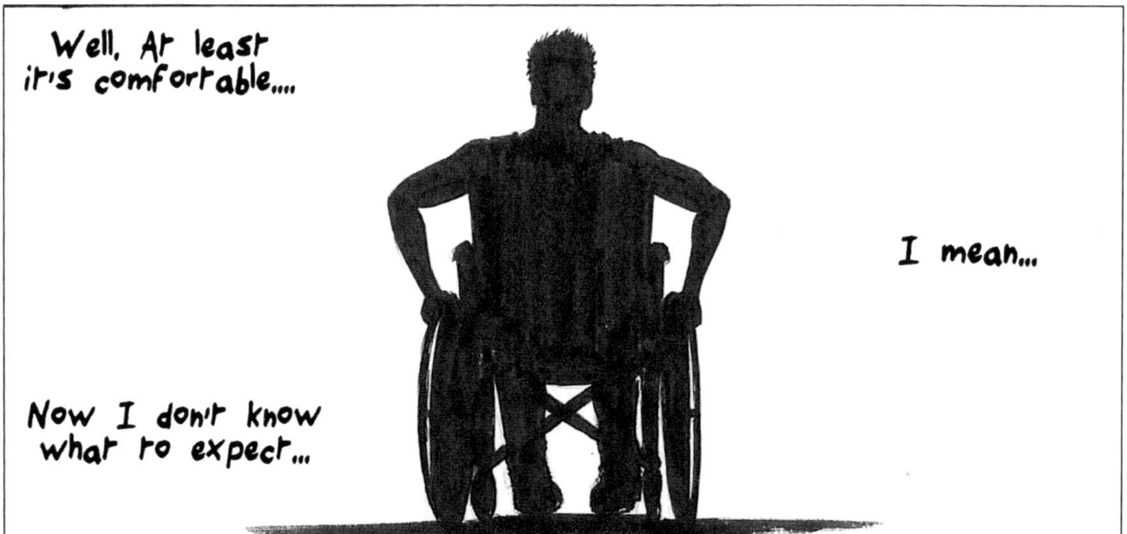
Well, At least it's comfortable....
I mean...
Now I don't know what to expect...

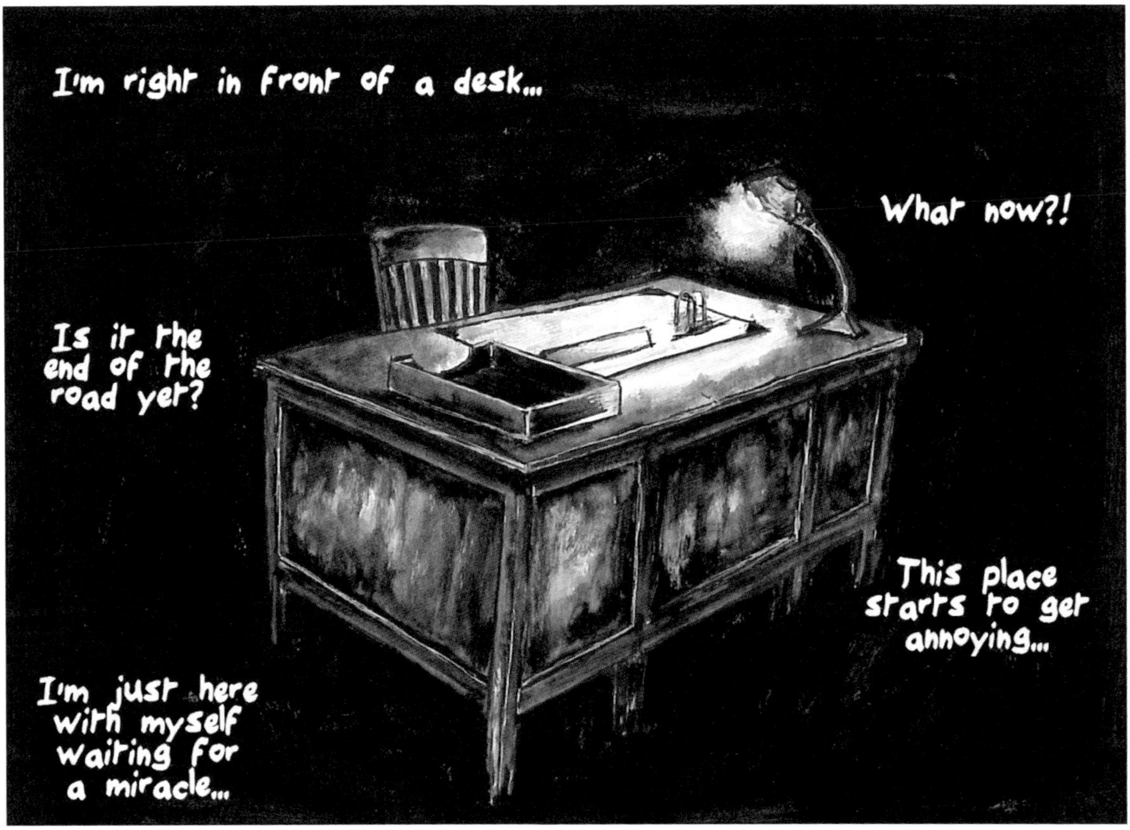
I'm right in front of a desk...
What now?!
Is it the end of the road yet?
This place starts to get annoying...
I'm just here with myself waiting for a miracle...

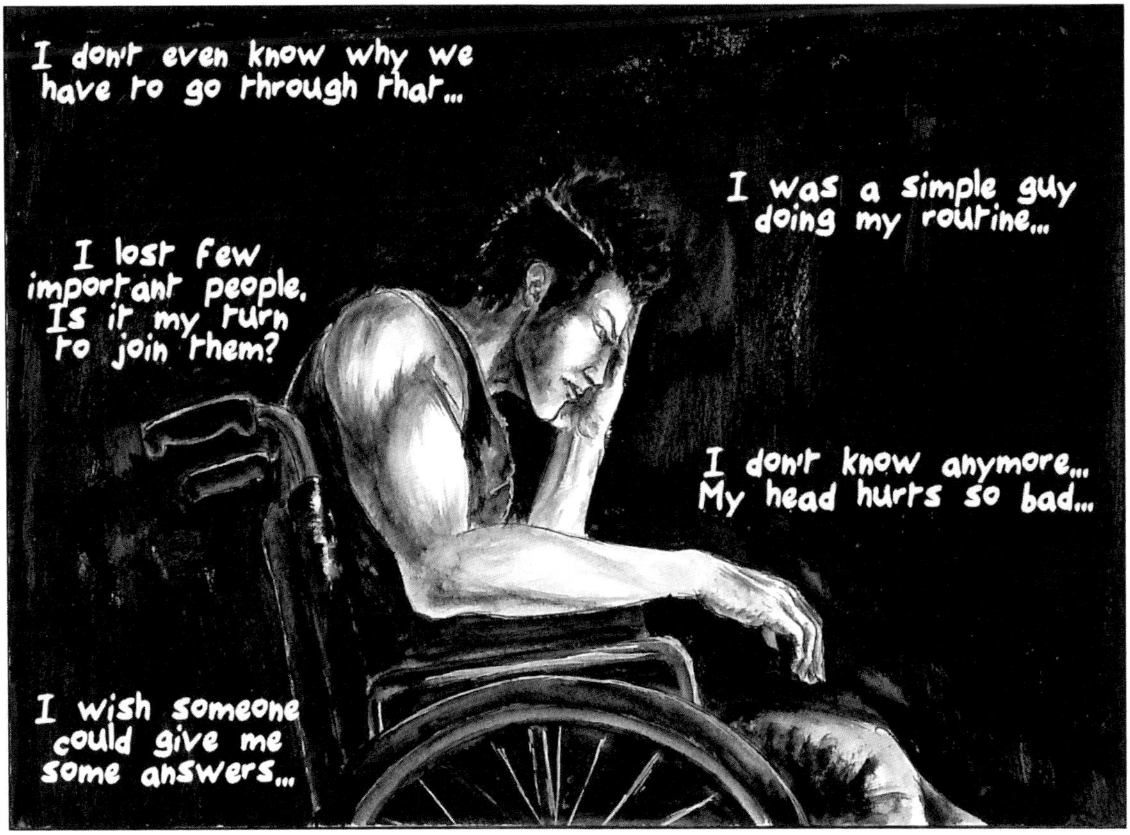
I don't even know why we have to go through that...
I was a simple guy doing my routine...
I lost few important people. Is it my turn to join them?
I don't know anymore... My head hurts so bad...
I wish someone could give me some answers...

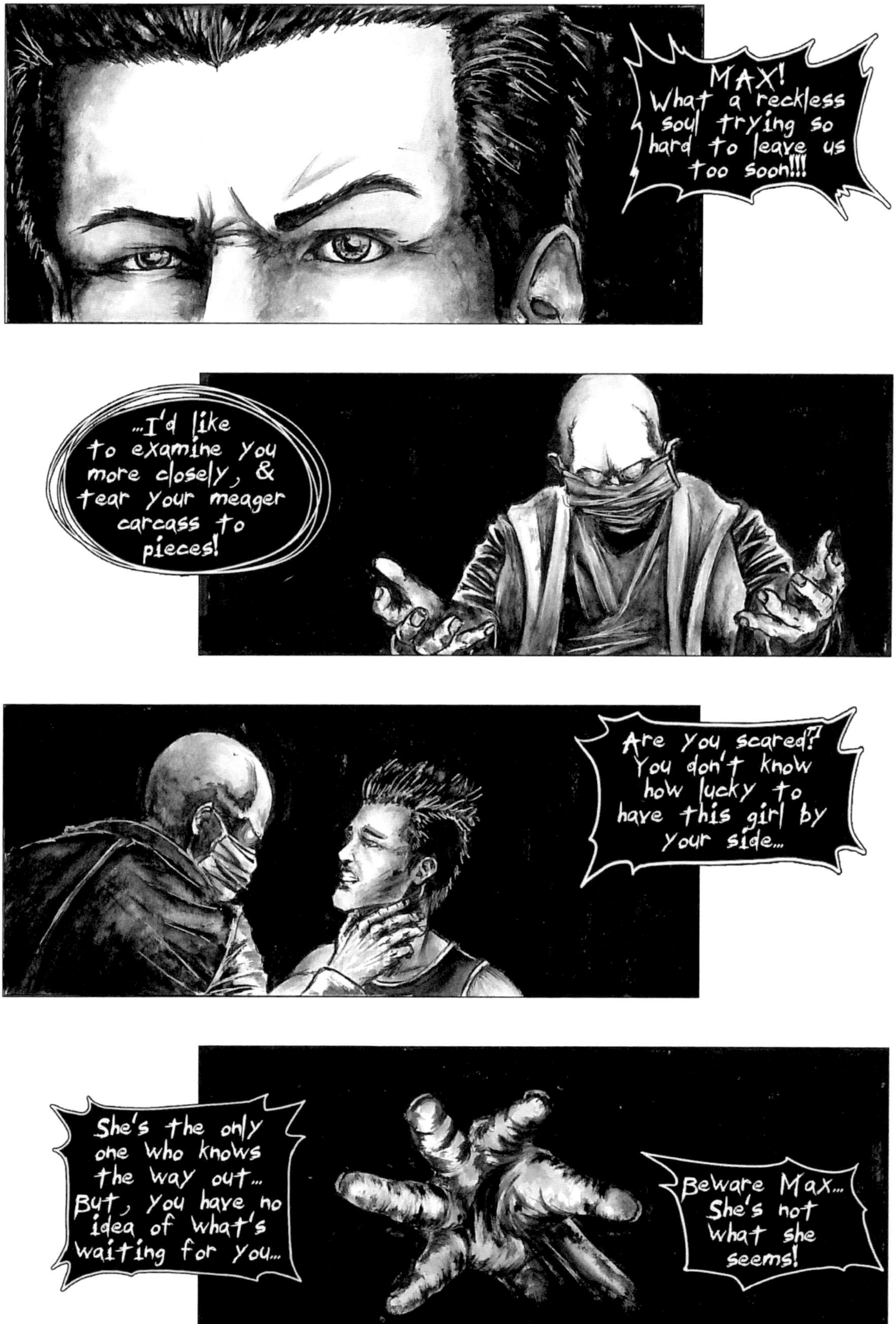
MAX! What a reckless soul trying so hard to leave us too soon!!!
...I'd like to examine you more closely, & tear your meager carcass to pieces!
Are you scared? You don't know how lucky to have this girl by your side...
She's the only one who knows the way out... But, you have no idea of what's waiting for you...
Beware Max... She's not what she seems!

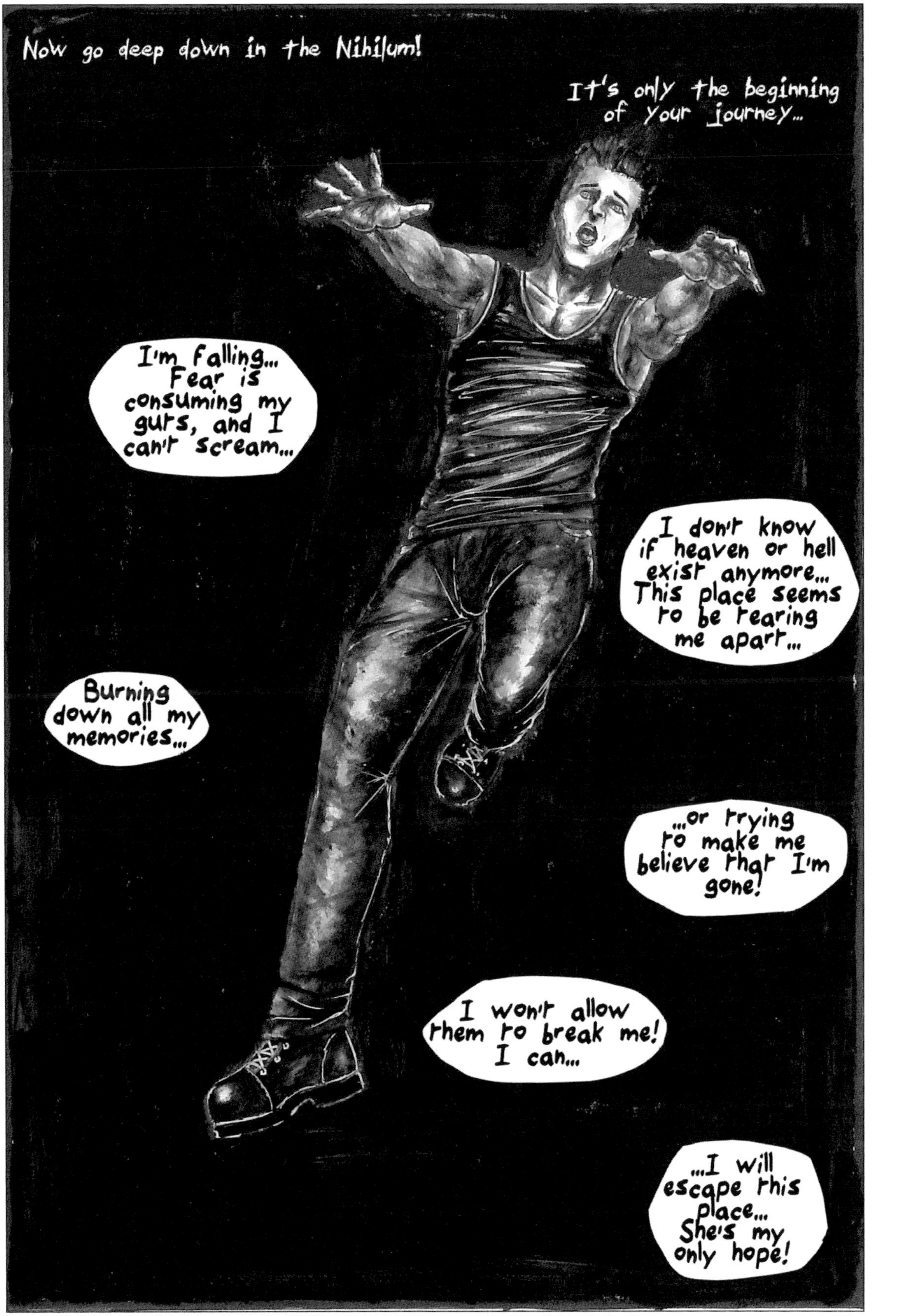

Now go deep down in the Nihilum!
It's only the beginning of your journey...
I'm falling... Fear is consuming my guts, and I can't scream...
I don't know if heaven or hell exist anymore... This place seems to be tearing me apart...
Burning down all my memories...
...or trying to make me believe that I'm gone!
I won't allow them to break me! I can...
...I will escape this place... She's my only hope!

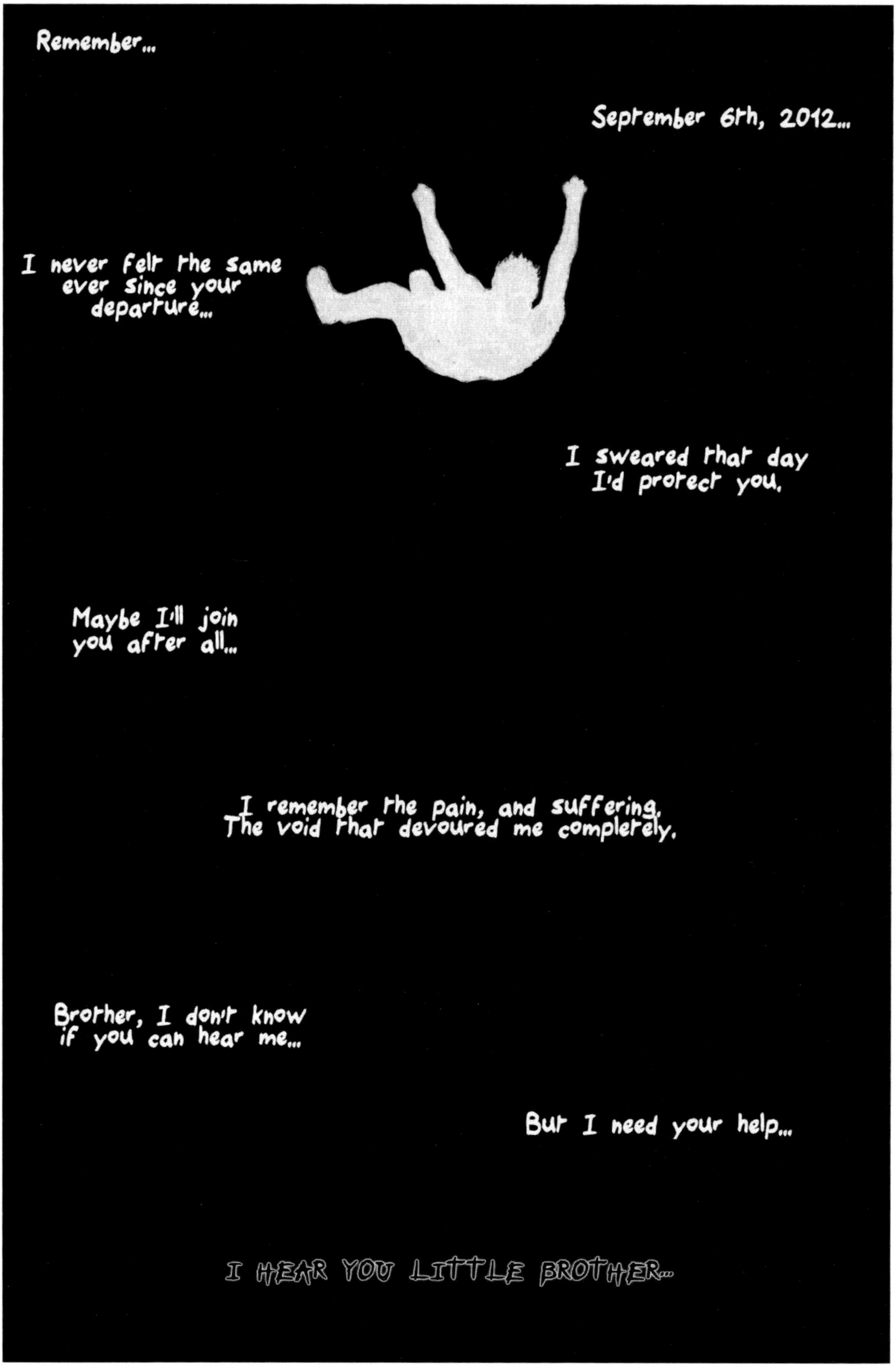
Remember...
September 6th, 2012...
I never felt the same ever since your departure...
I sweared that day I'd protect you.
Maybe I'll join you after all...
I remember the pain, and suffering.
The void that devoured me completely.
Brother, I don't know if you can hear me...
But I need your help...
I HEAR YOU LITTLE BROTHER...

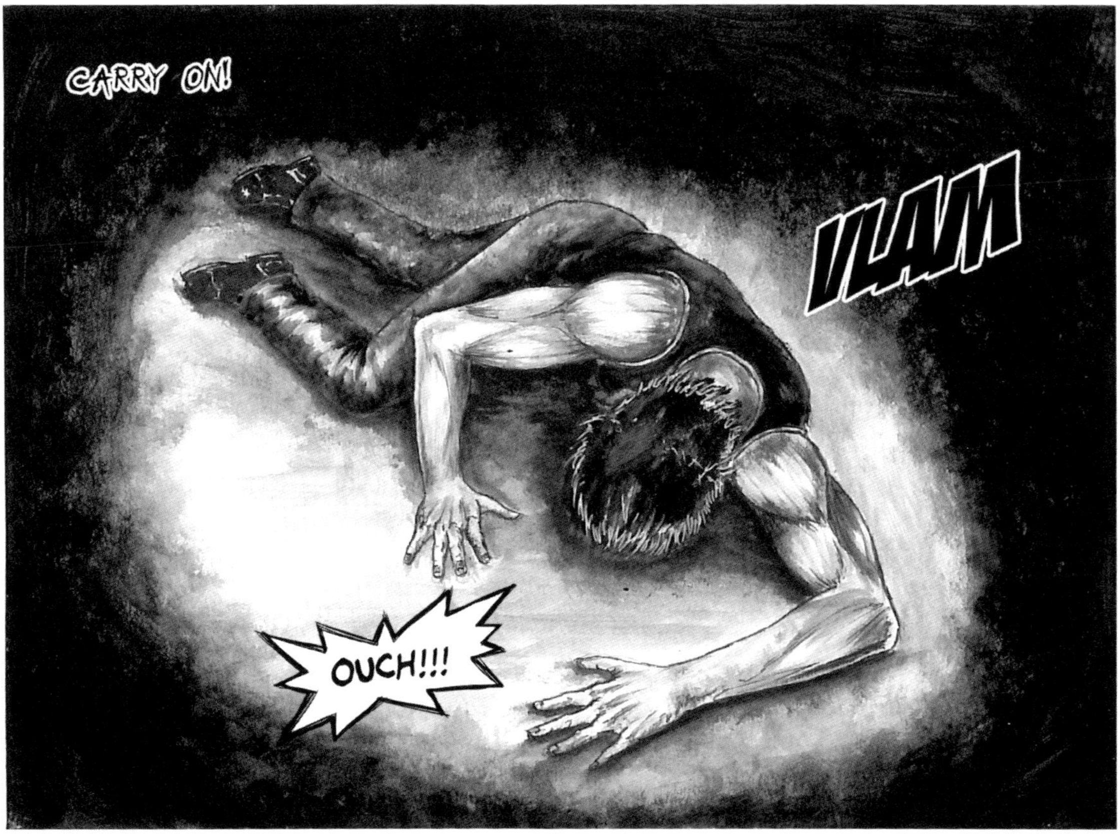
CARRY ON!
VLAM
OUCH!!!

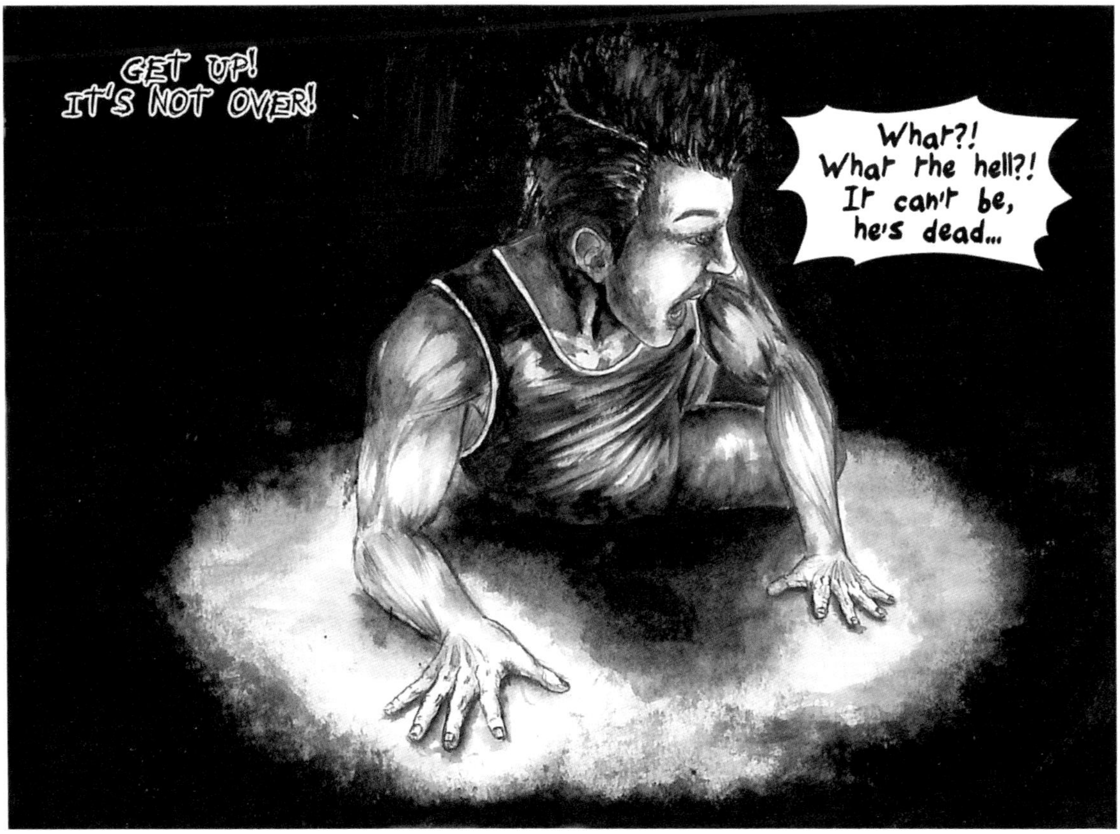
GET UP!
IT'S NOT OVER!
What?! What the hell?! It can't be, he's dead...

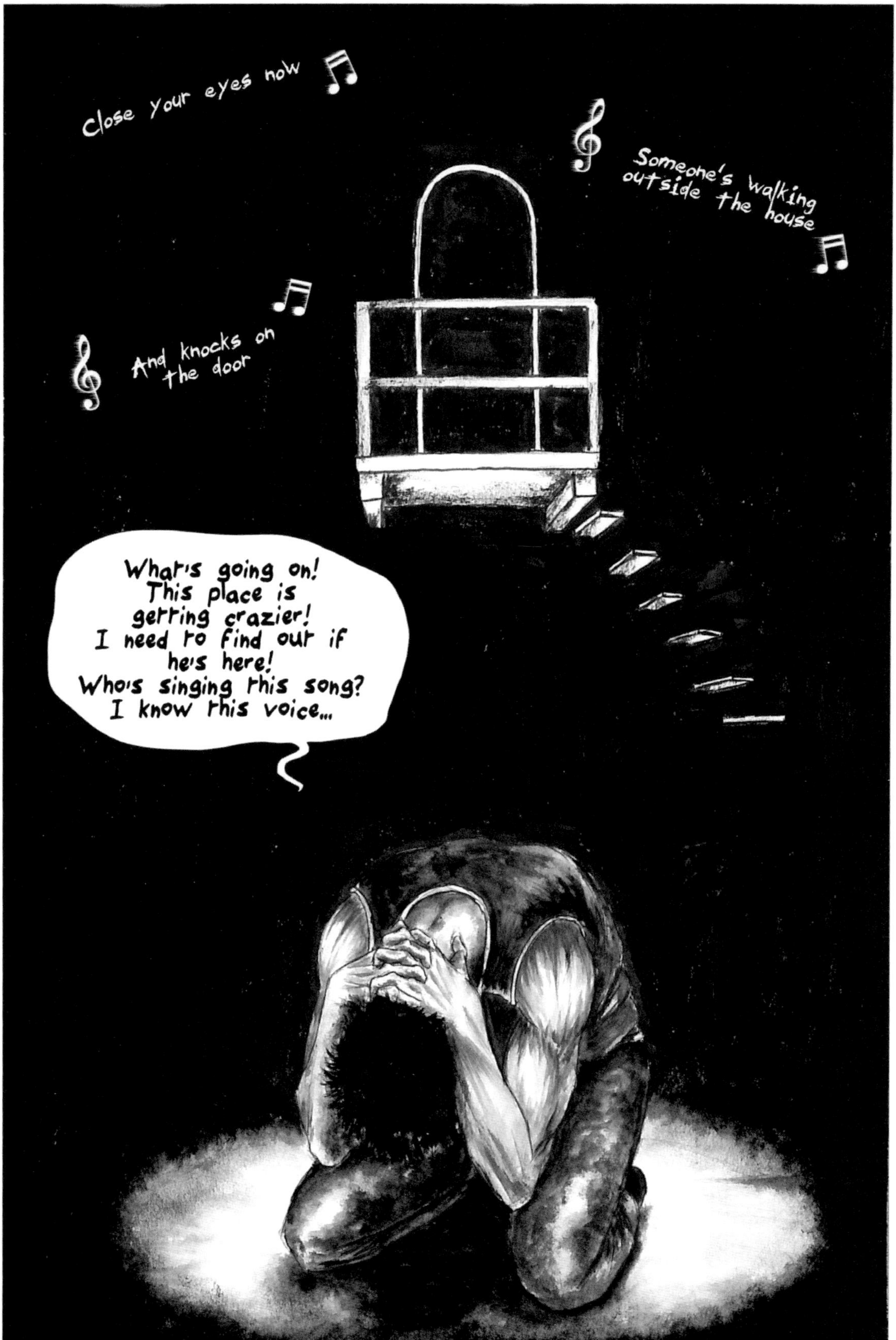
Close your eyes now
Someone's walking outside the house
And knocks on the door
What's going on! This place is getting crazier! I need to find out if he's here! Who's singing this song? I know this voice...

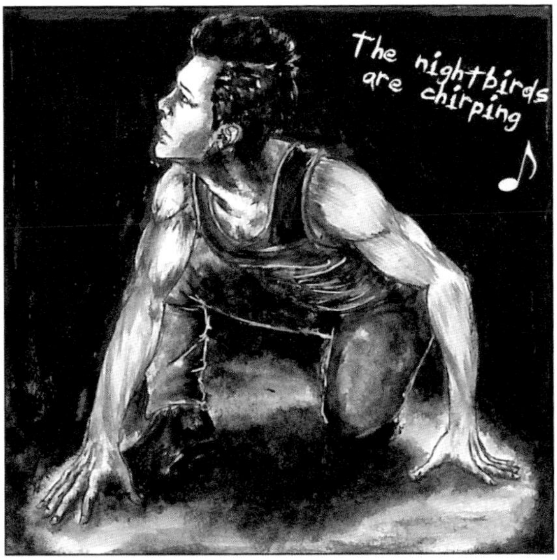
The nightbirds are chirping

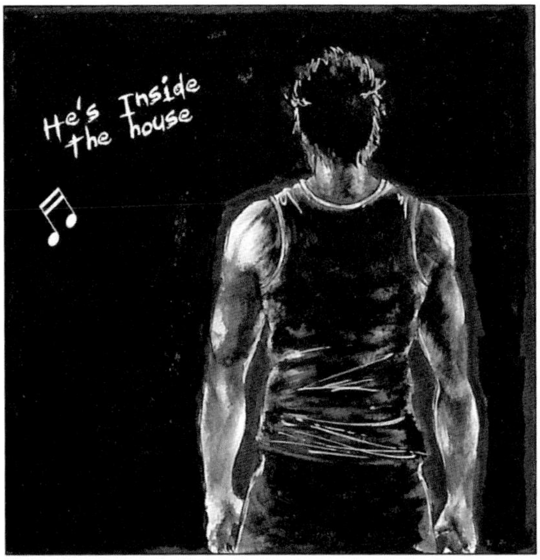
He's Inside the house

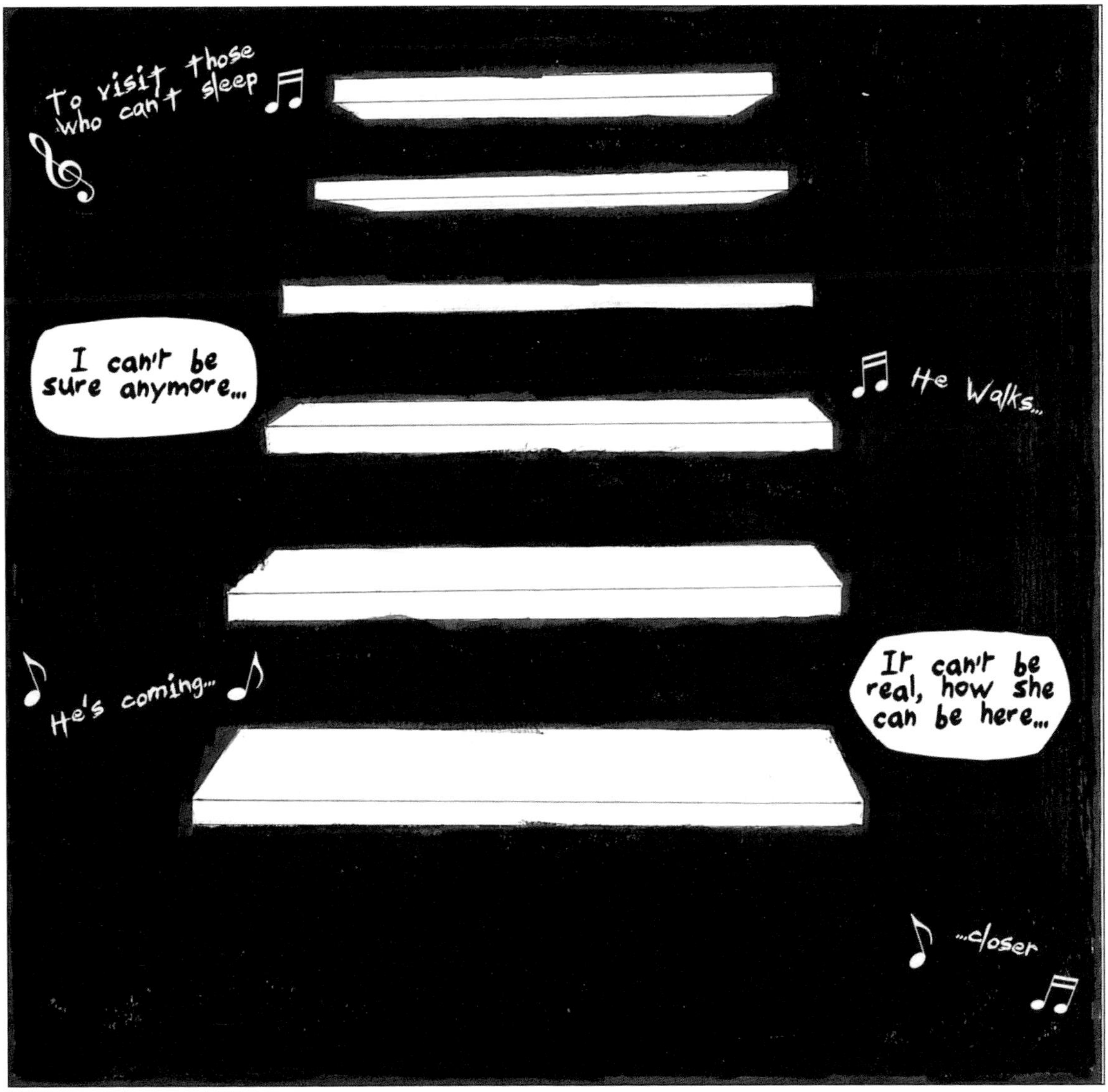
To visit those who can't sleep
I can't be sure anymore...
He Walks...
He's coming...
It can't be real, how she can be here...
...closer

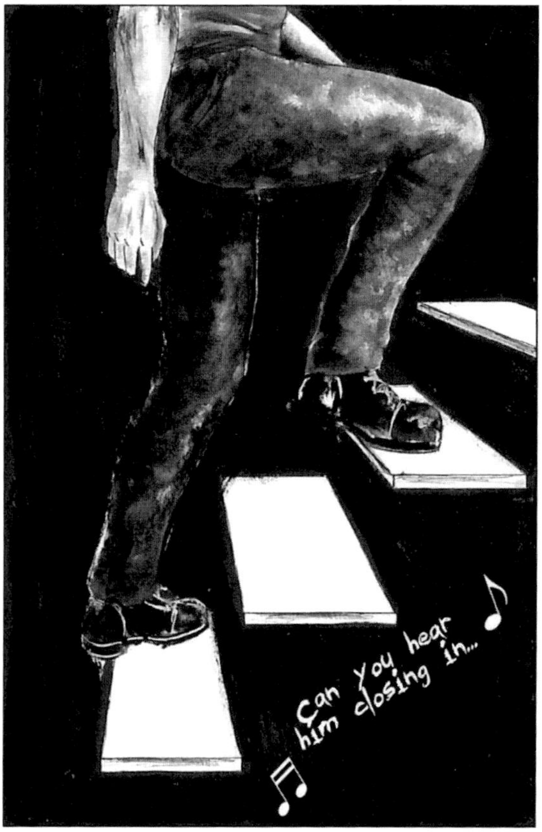
Can you hear him closing in...

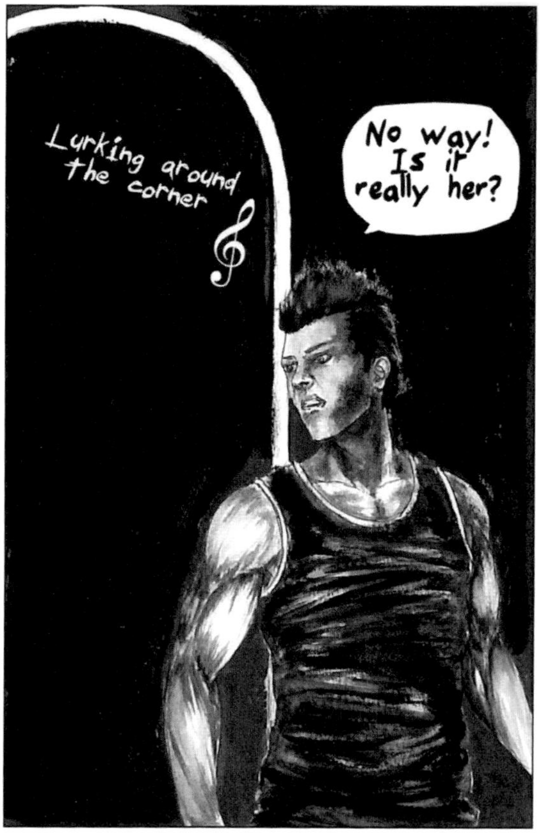
Lurking around the corner
No way! Is it really her?

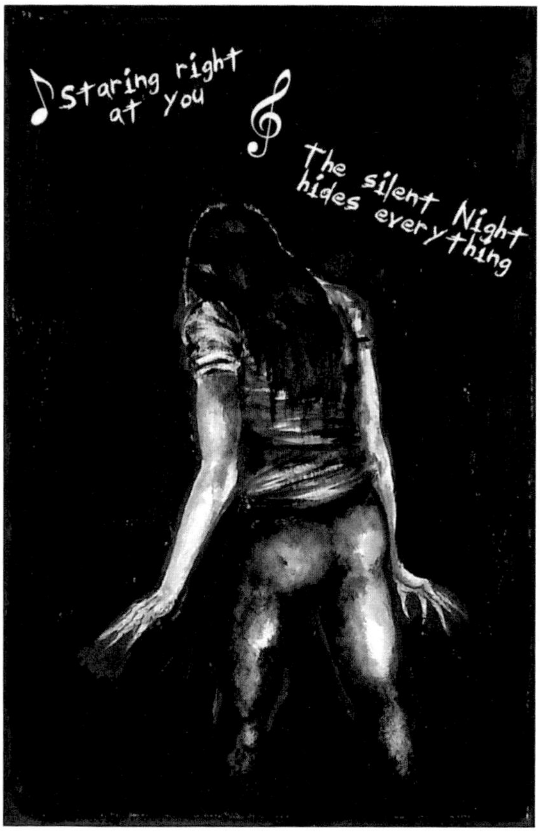
Staring right at you
The silent Night hides everything

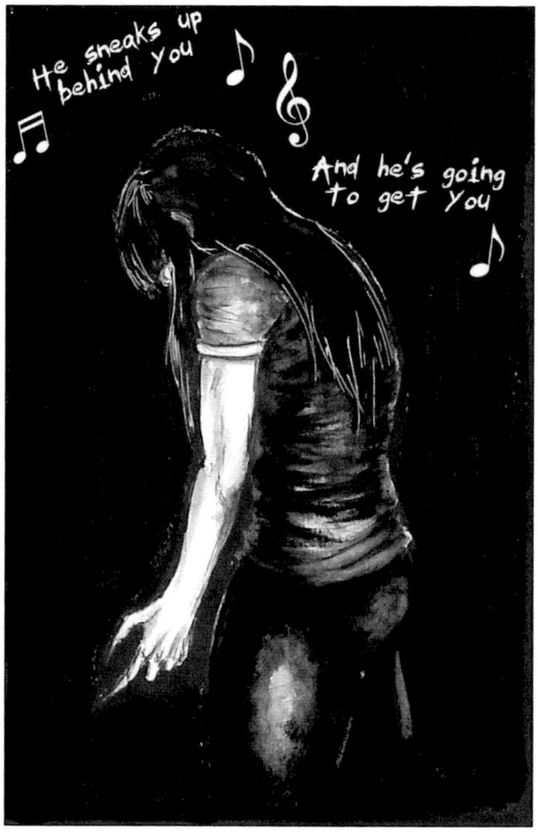
He sneaks up behind you
And he's going to get You

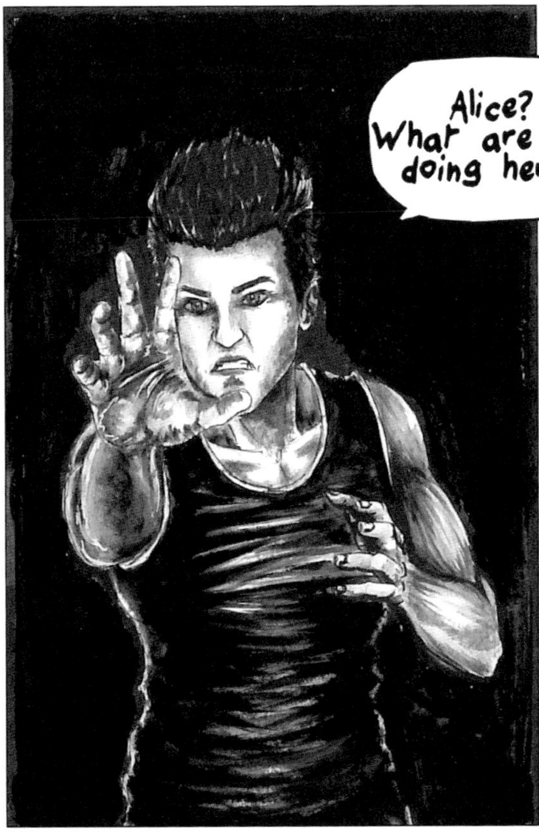
Alice? What are you doing here?

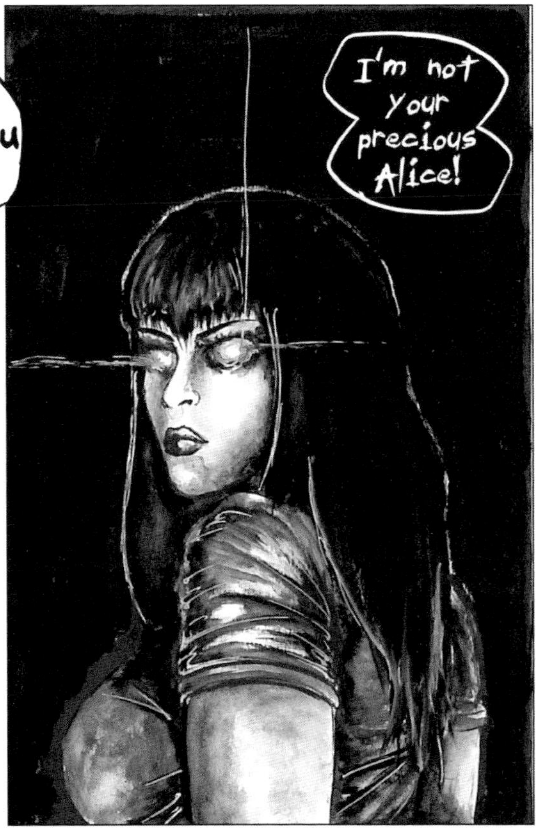
I'm not your precious Alice!

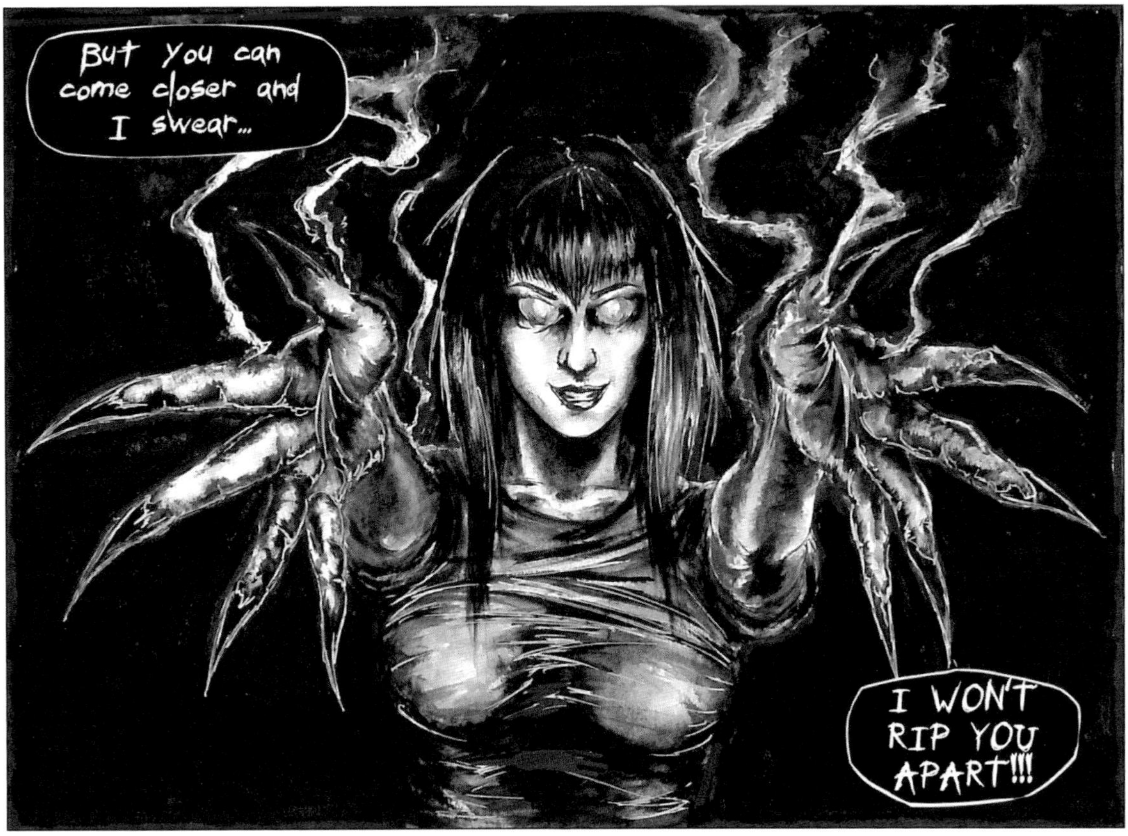
But you can come closer and I swear...
I WON'T RIP YOU APART!!!

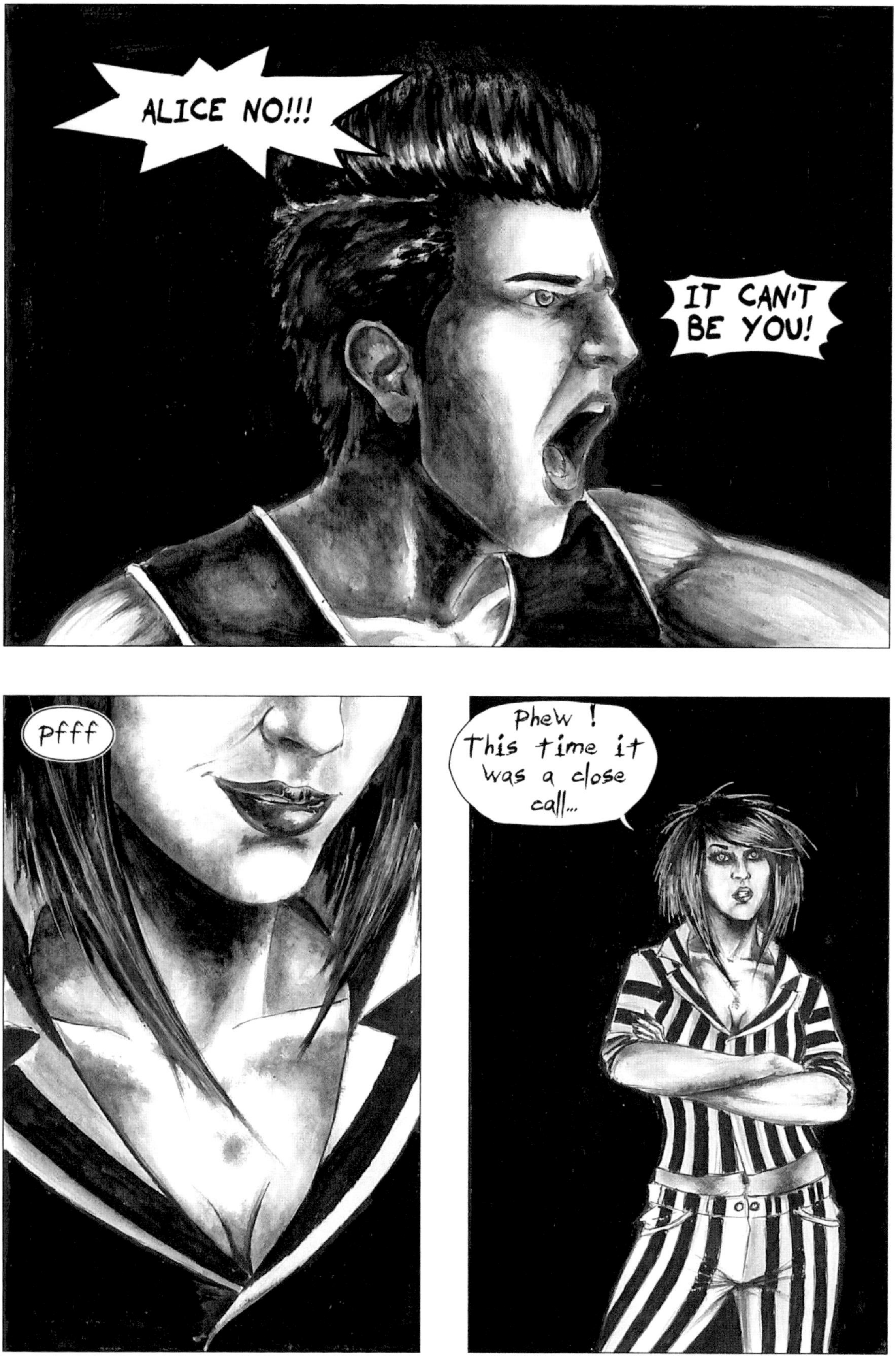
ALICE NO!!!
IT CAN'T BE YOU!
pfff
Phew ! This time it was a close call...

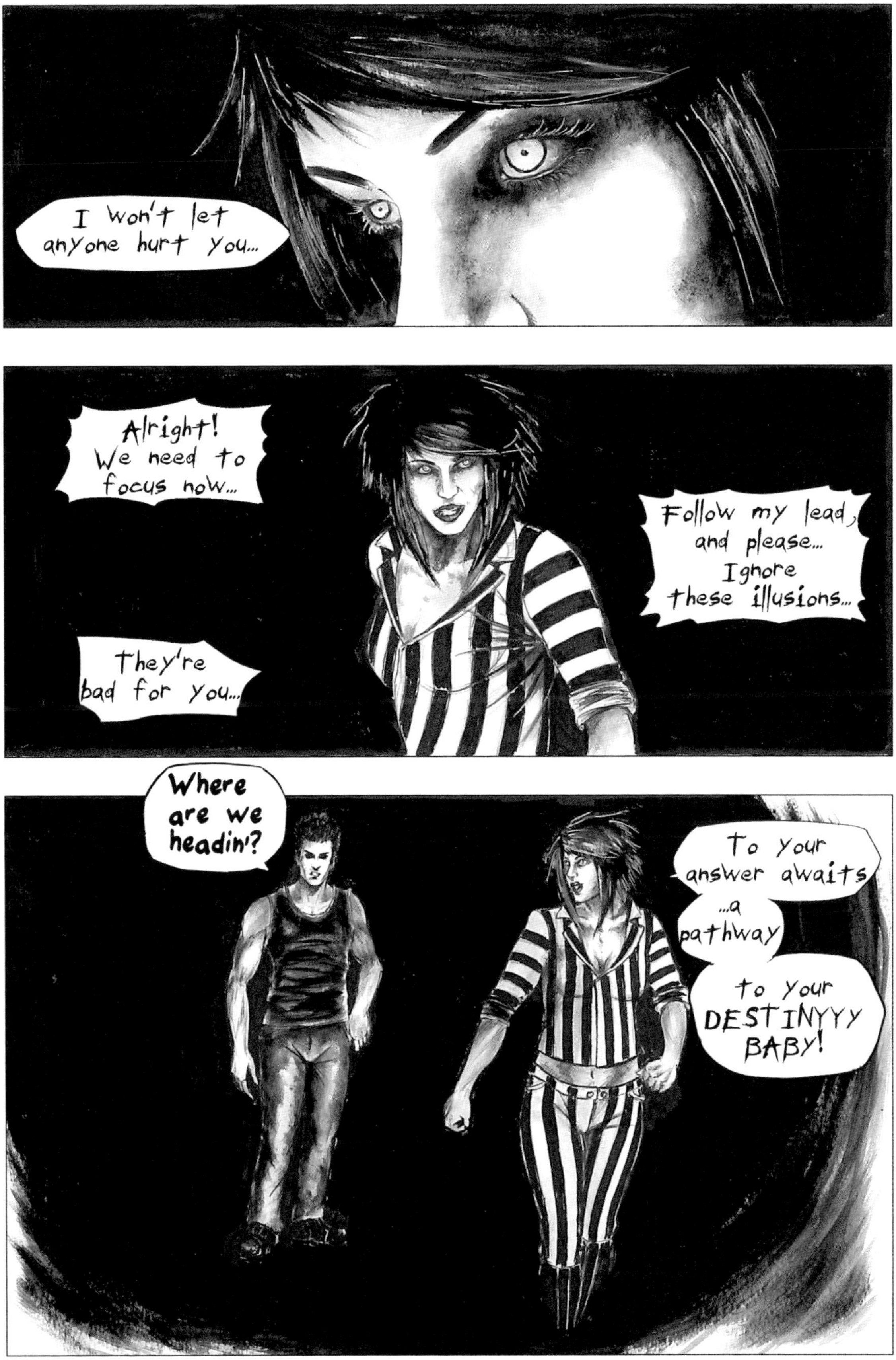
I won't let anyone hurt you...
Alright! We need to focus now...
Follow my lead, and please... Ignore these illusions...
They're bad for you...
Where are we headin'?
To your answer awaits
...a pathway
to your DESTINYYY BABY!

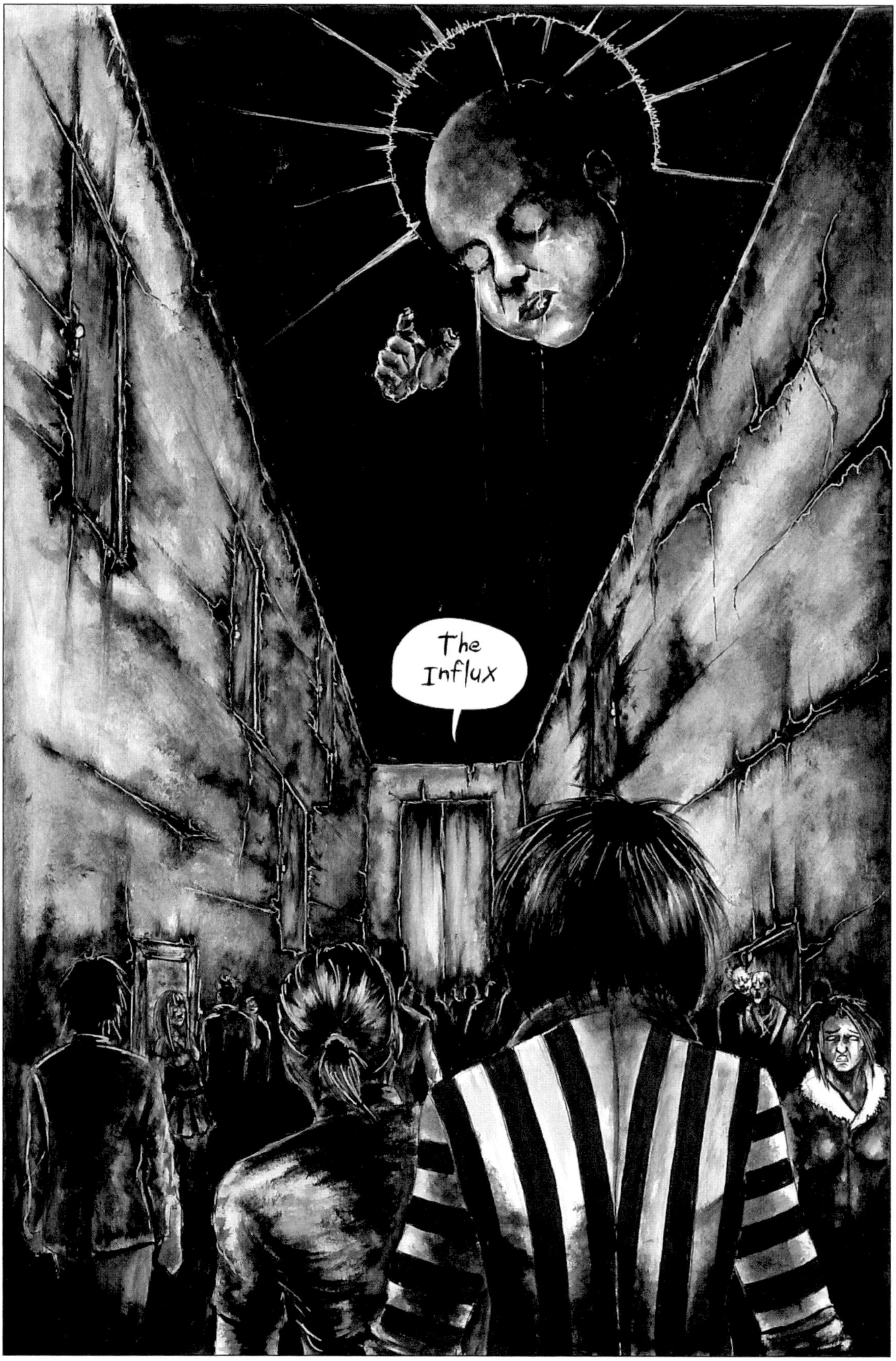
The Influx

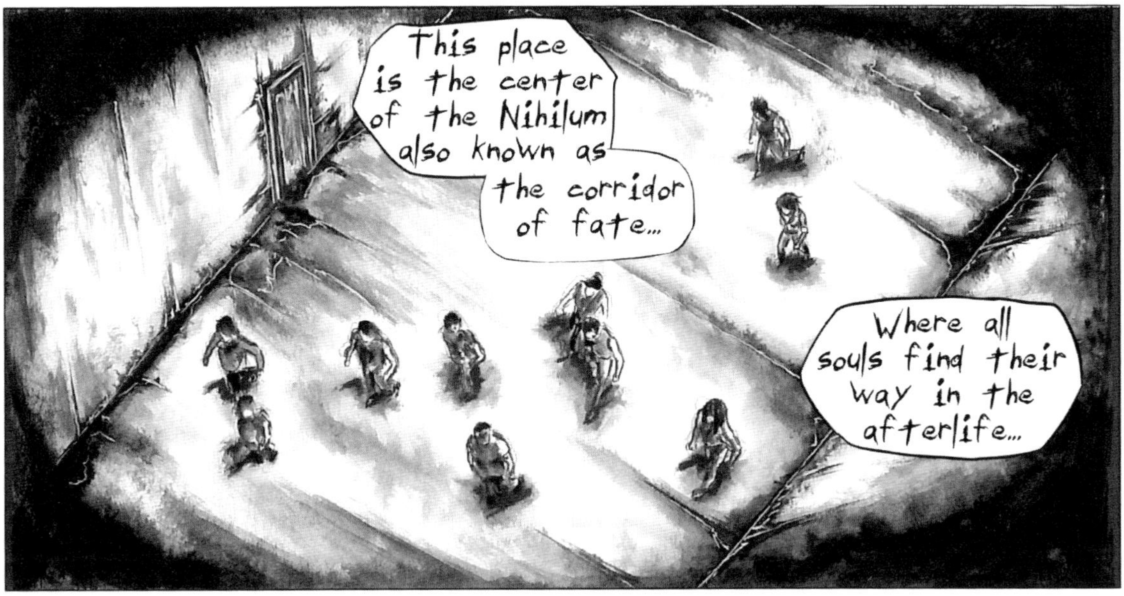
This place is the center of the Nihilum also known as the corridor of fate...
Where all souls find their way in the afterlife...

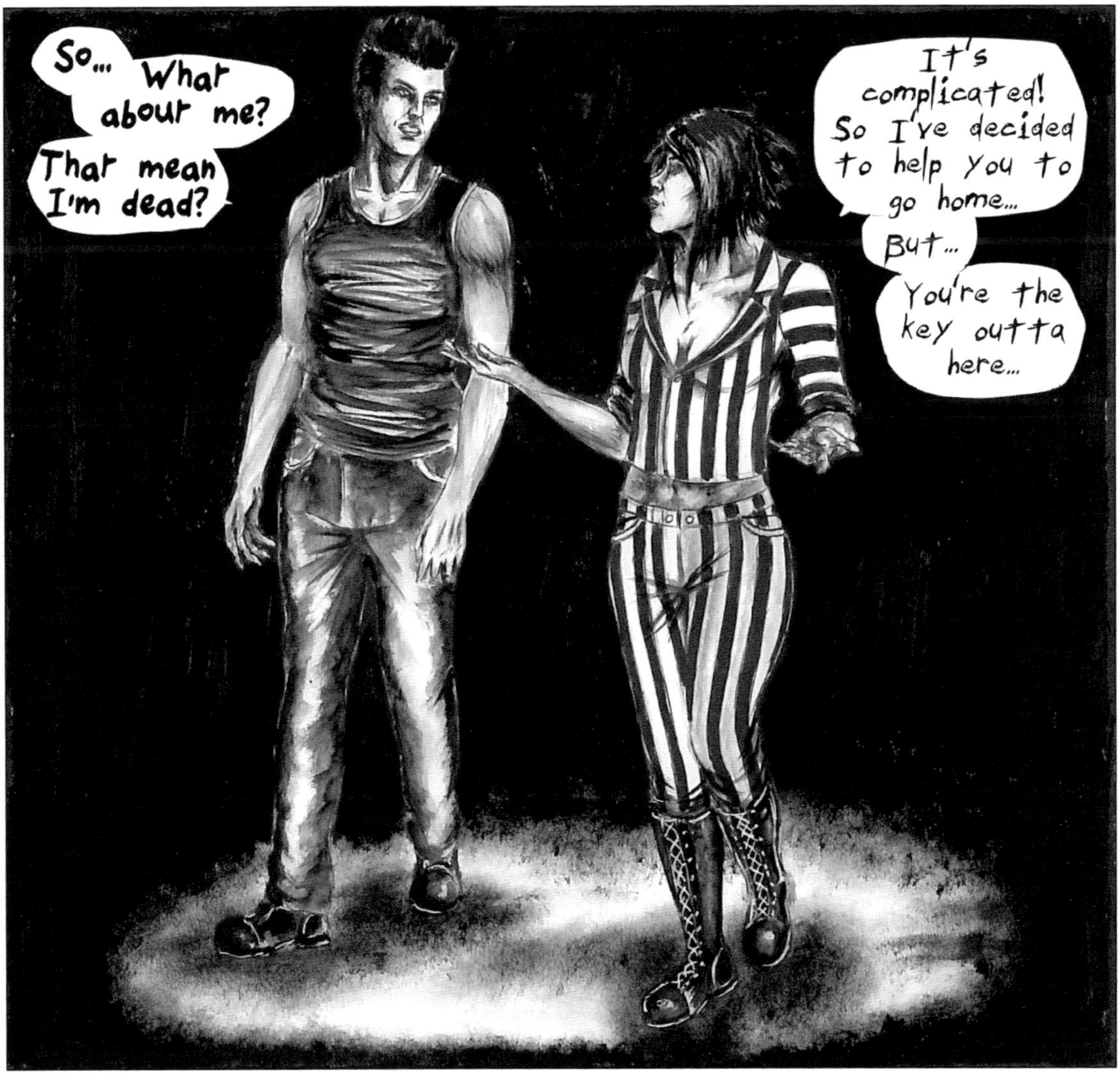
So... What about me?
That mean I'm dead?
It's complicated! So I've decided to help you to go home...
But...
You're the key outta here...

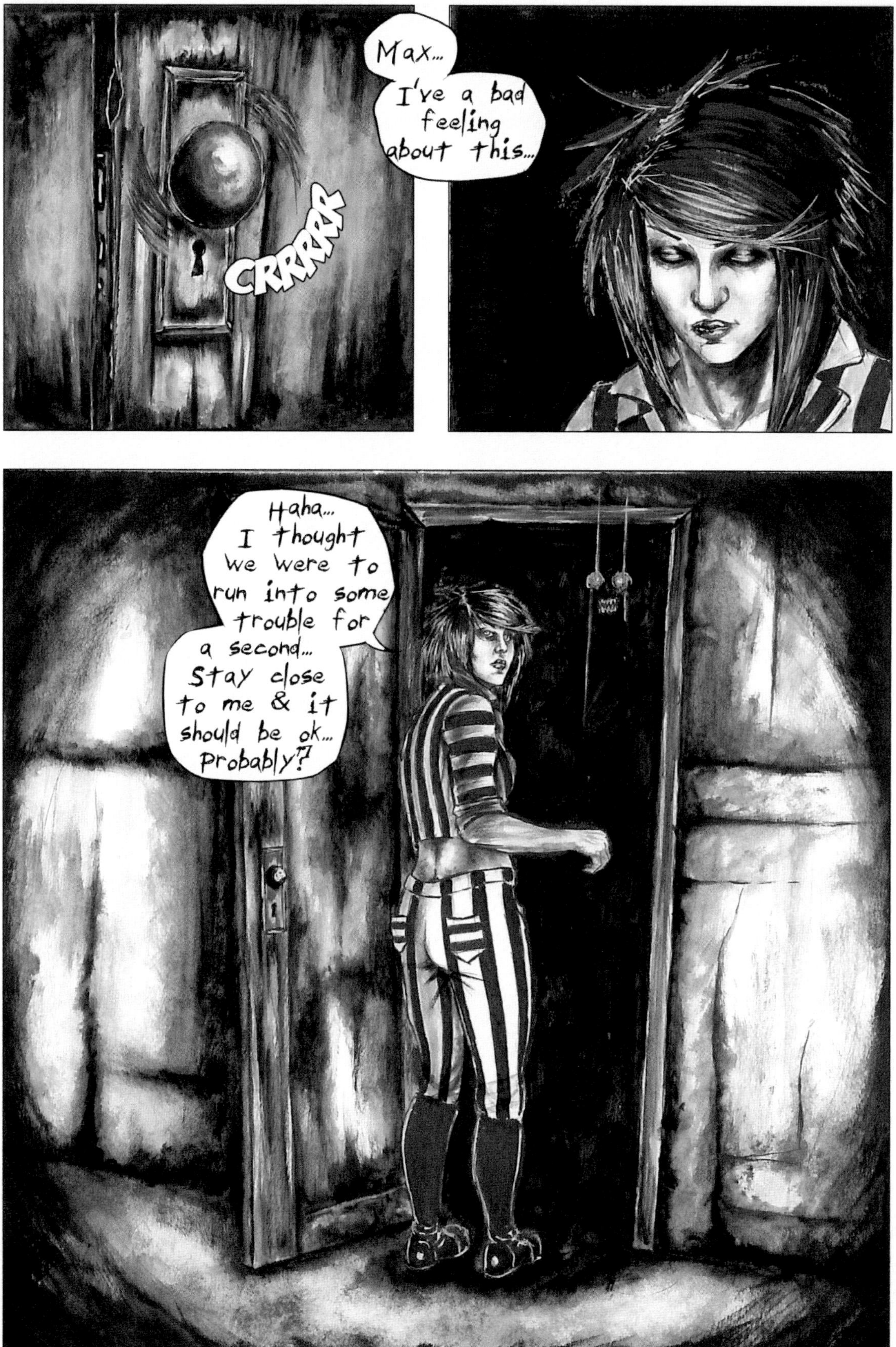
CRRRRR
Max... I've a bad feeling about this...
Haha... I thought we were to run into some trouble for a second... Stay close to me & it should be ok... probably?!

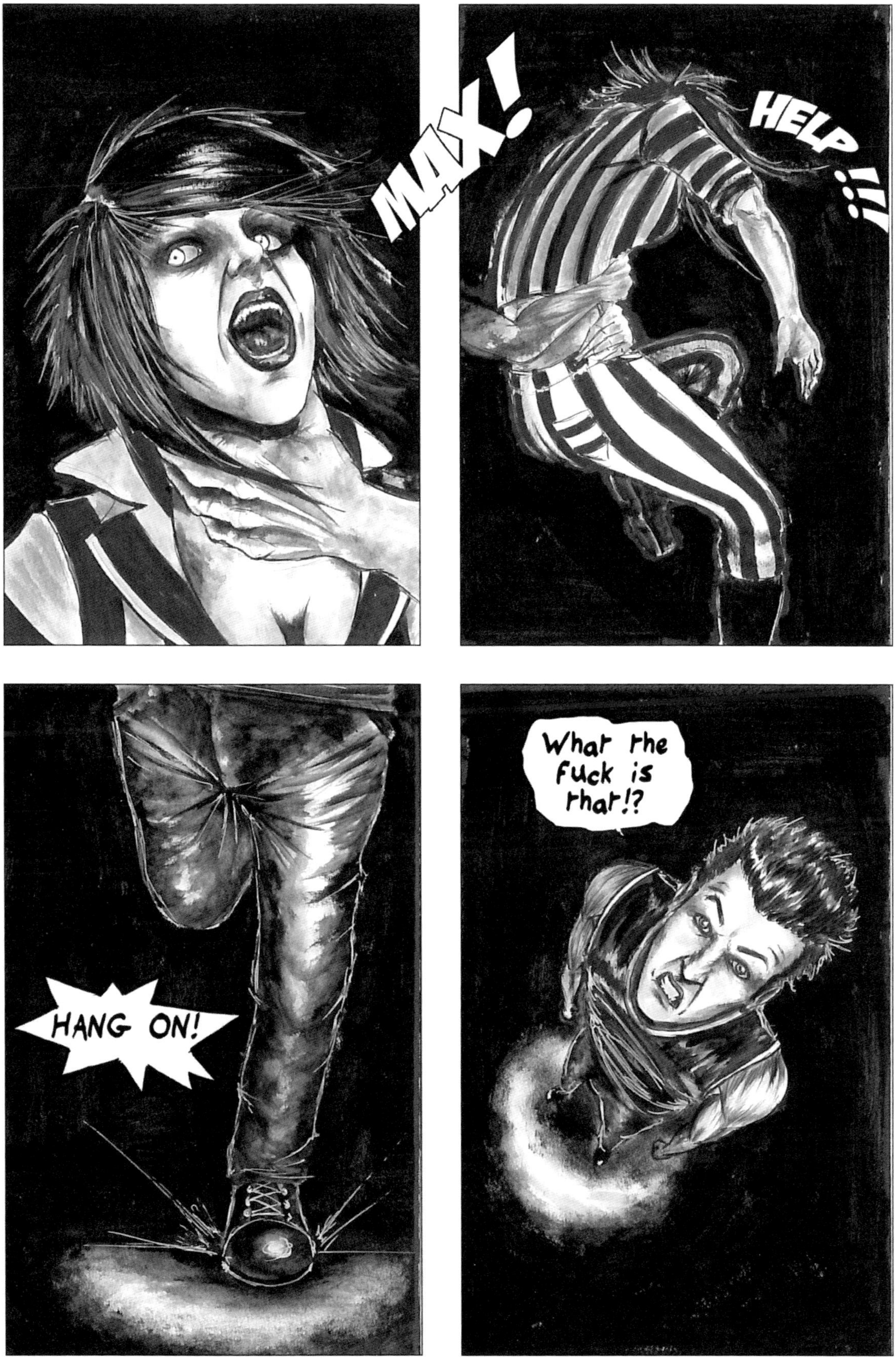
MAX!
HELP !!!
HANG ON!
What the fuck is that!?

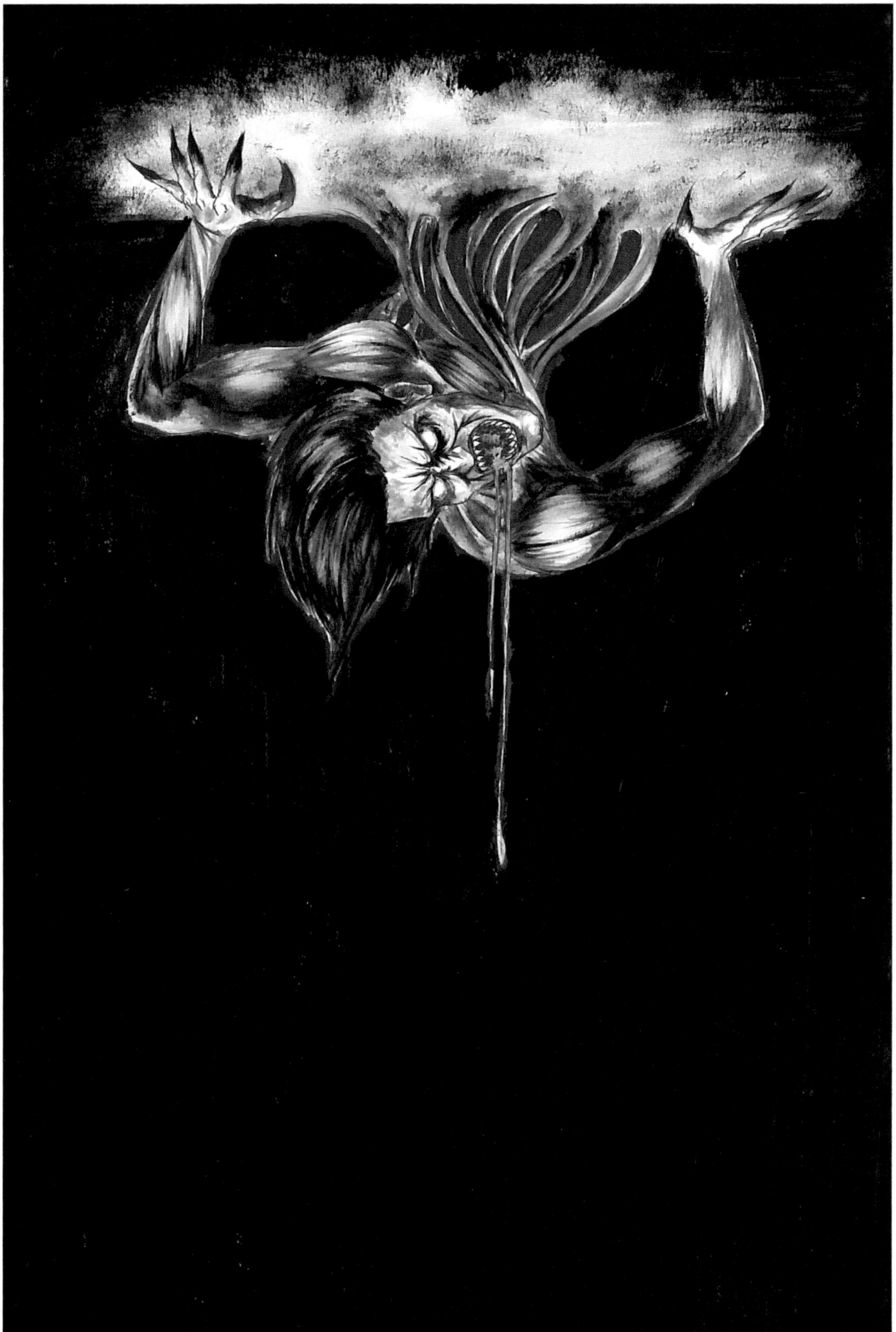

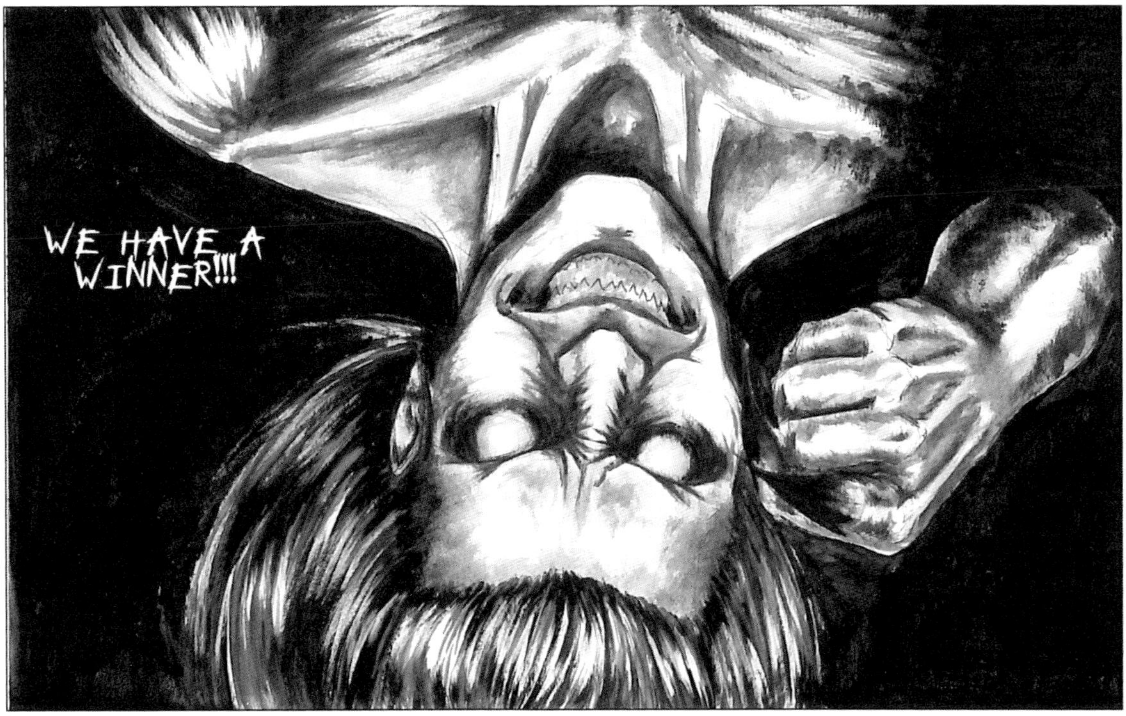
WE HAVE A WINNER!!!

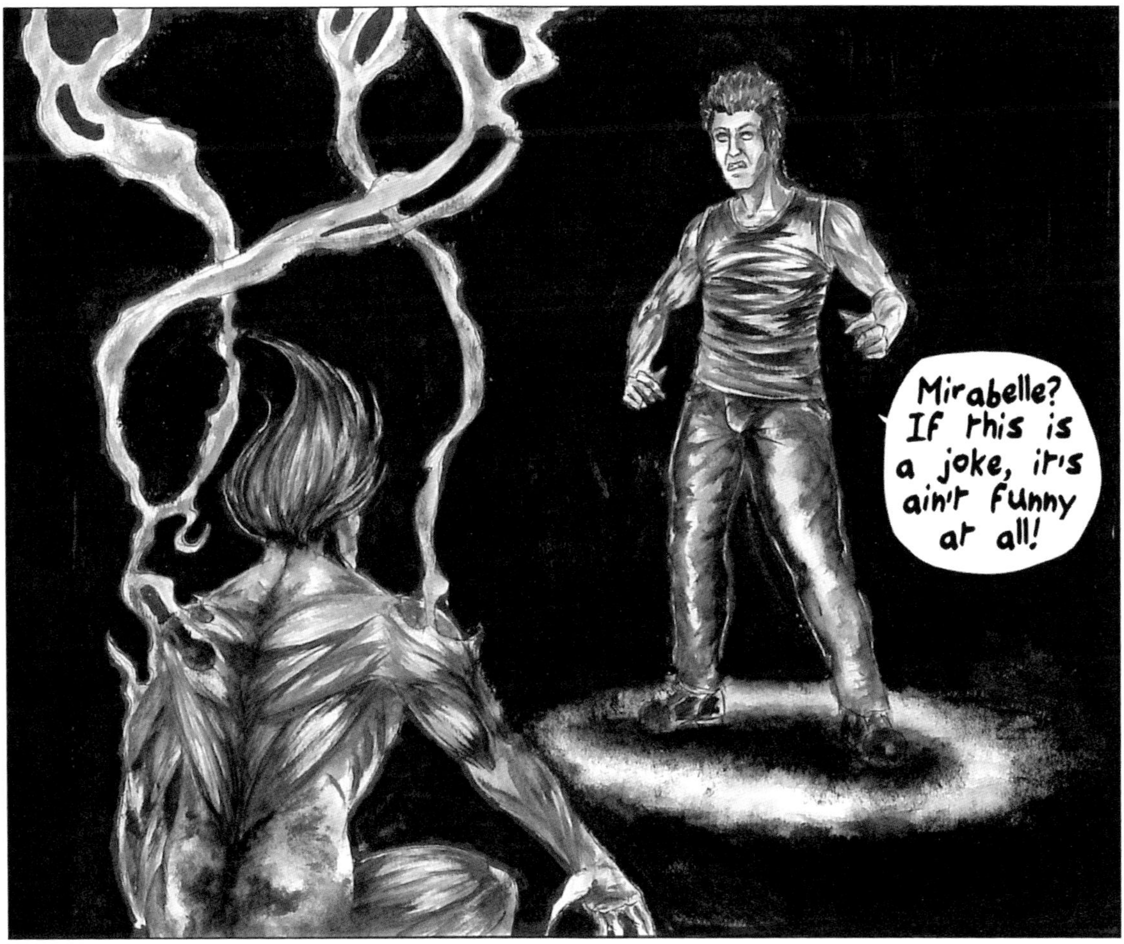
Mirabelle? If this is a joke, it's ain't funny at all!

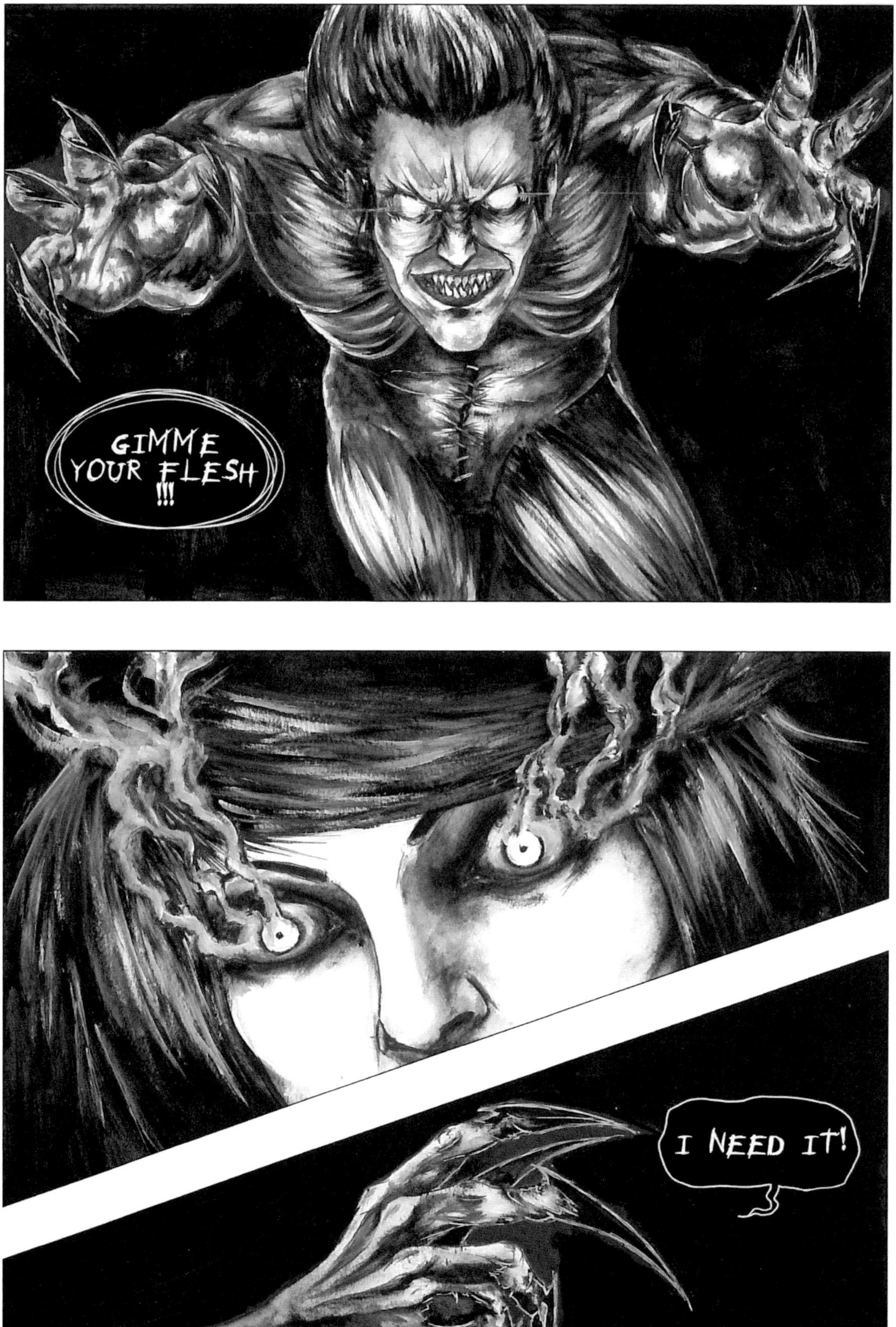
GIMME YOUR FLESH !!!
I NEED IT!

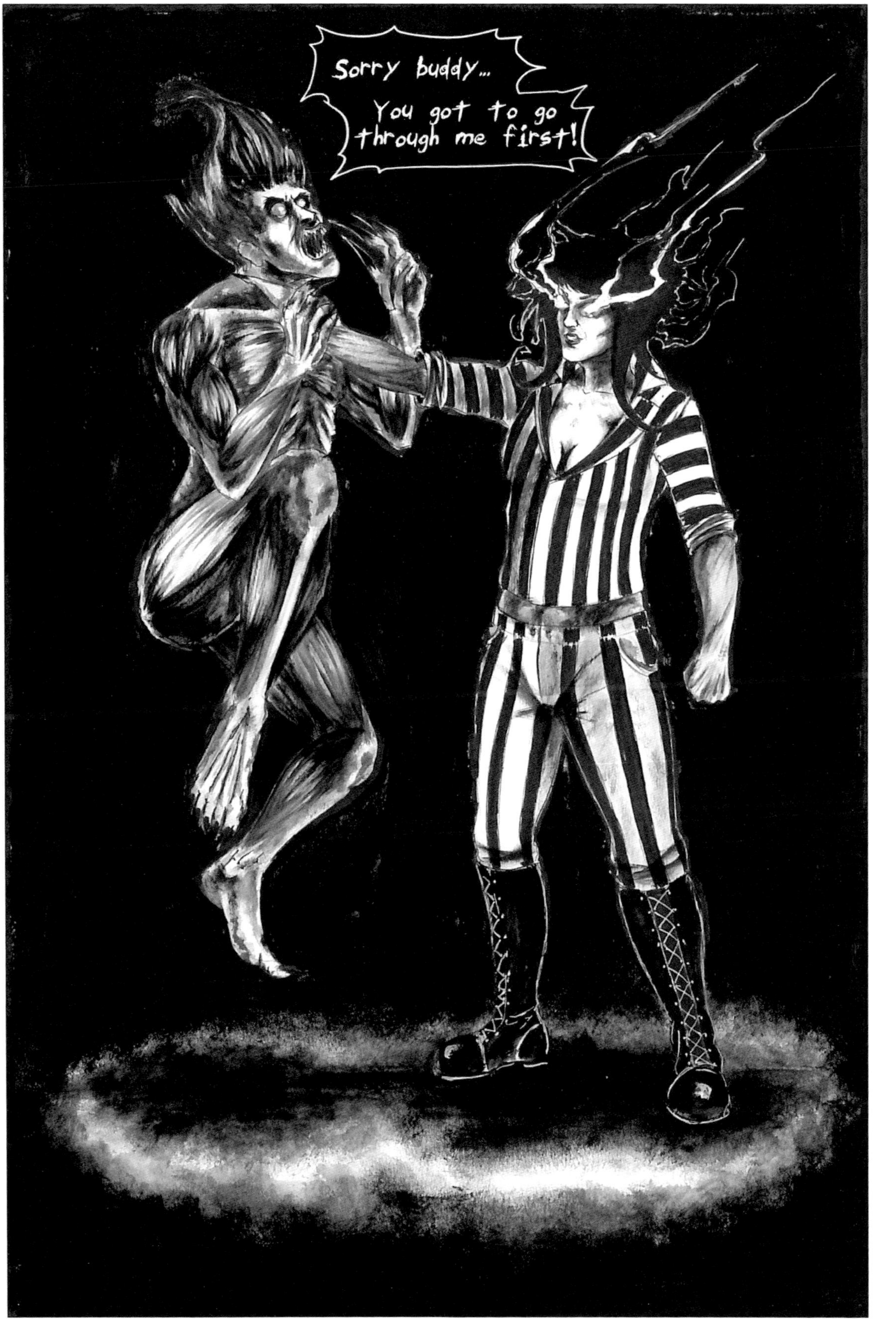
Sorry buddy... You got to go through me first!

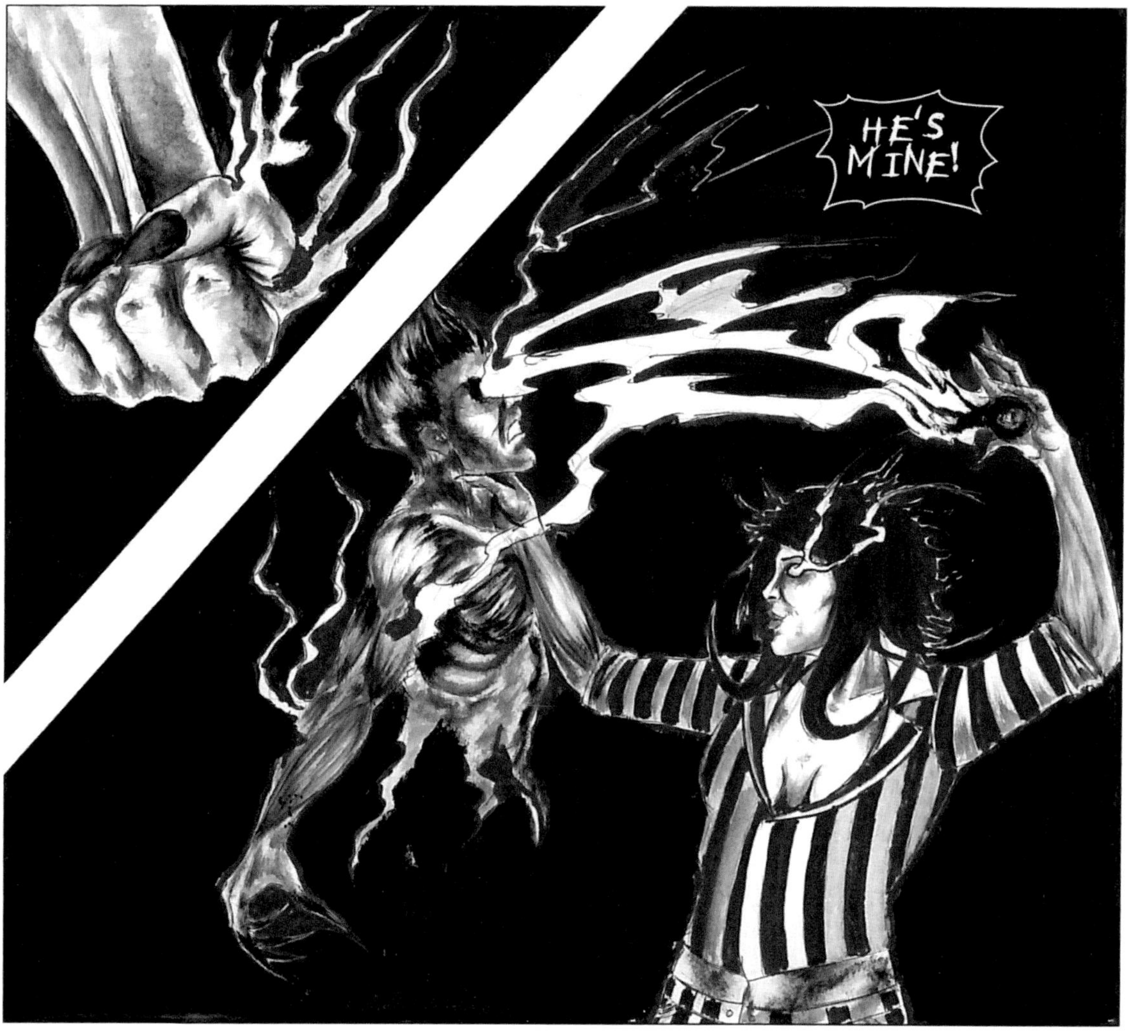
HE'S MINE!

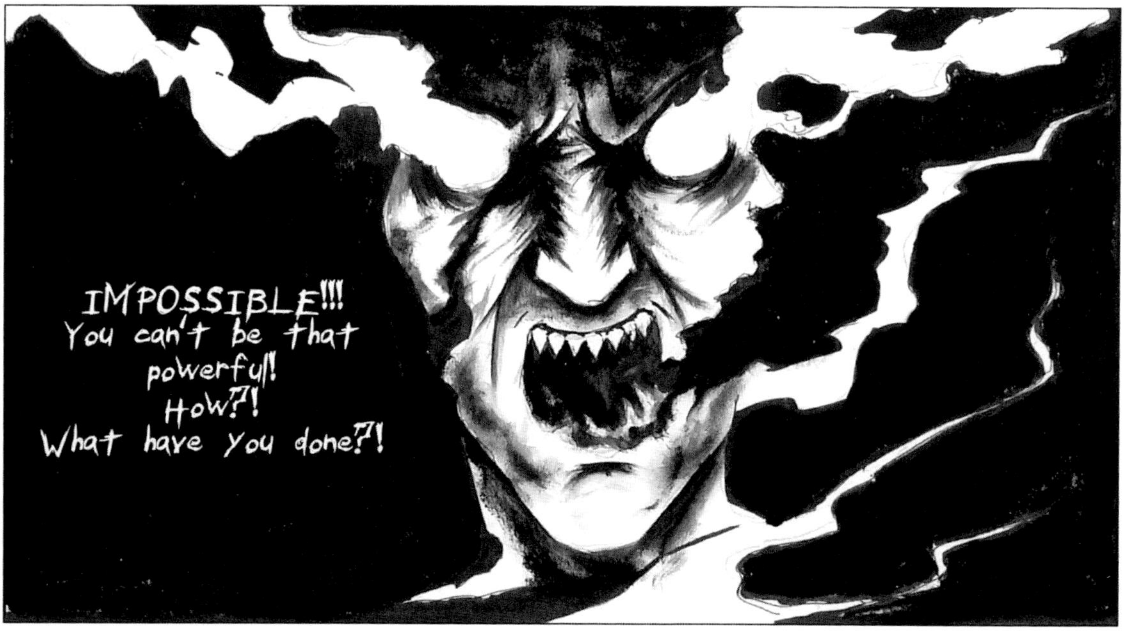
IMPOSSIBLE!!!
You can't be that
powerful!
HOW?!
What have you done?!

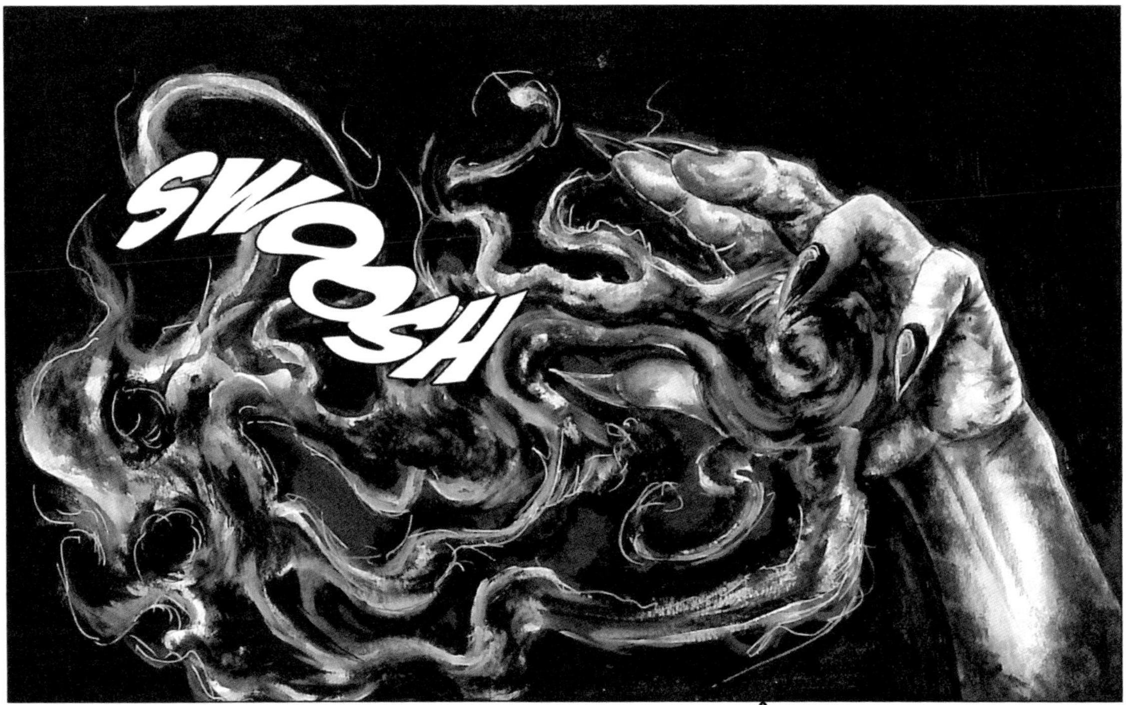
SWOOSH
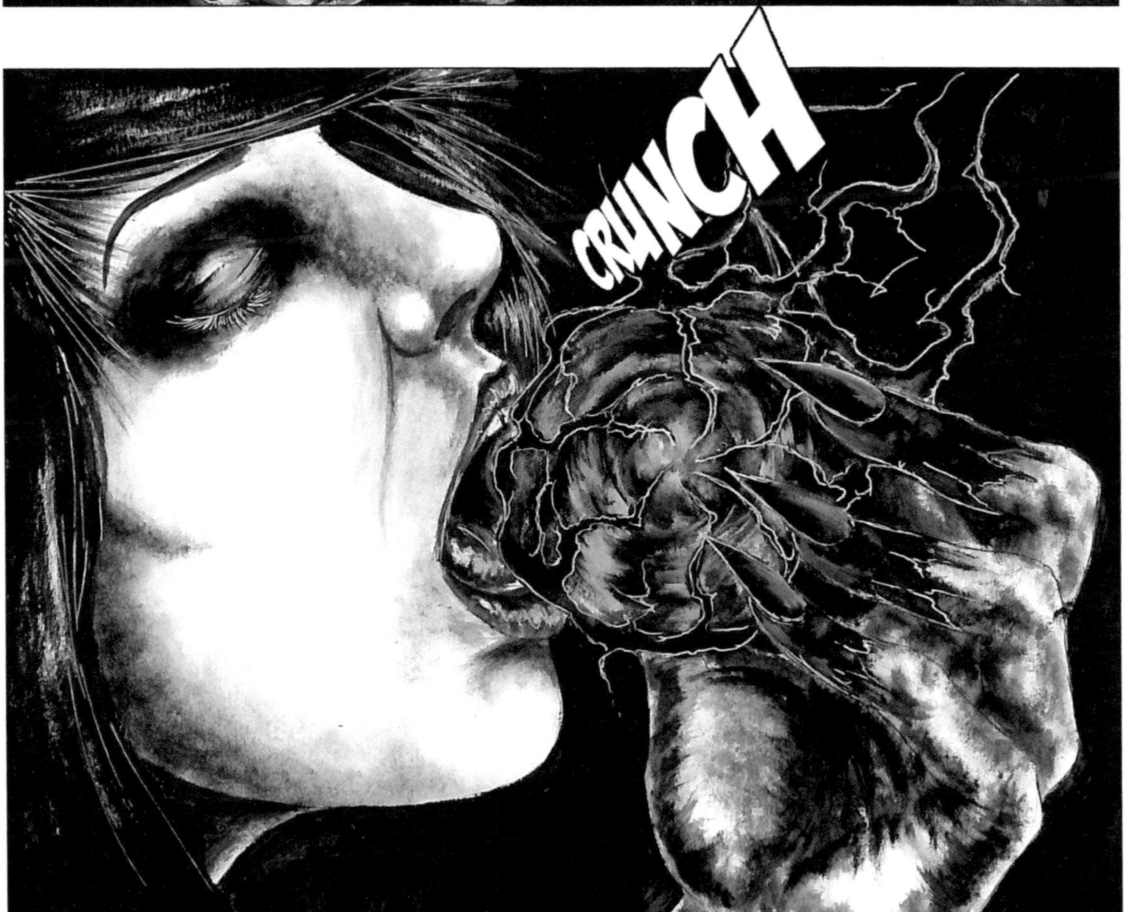
CRUNCH

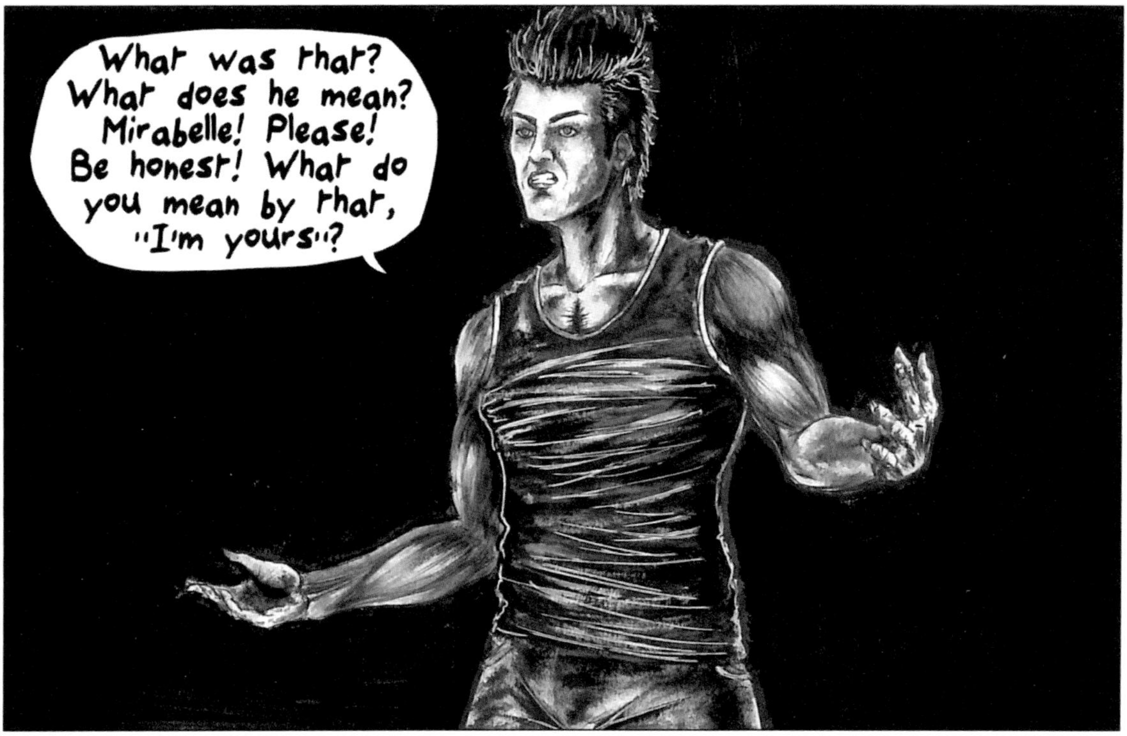
What was that? What does he mean? Mirabelle! Please! Be honest! What do you mean by that, "I'm yours"?

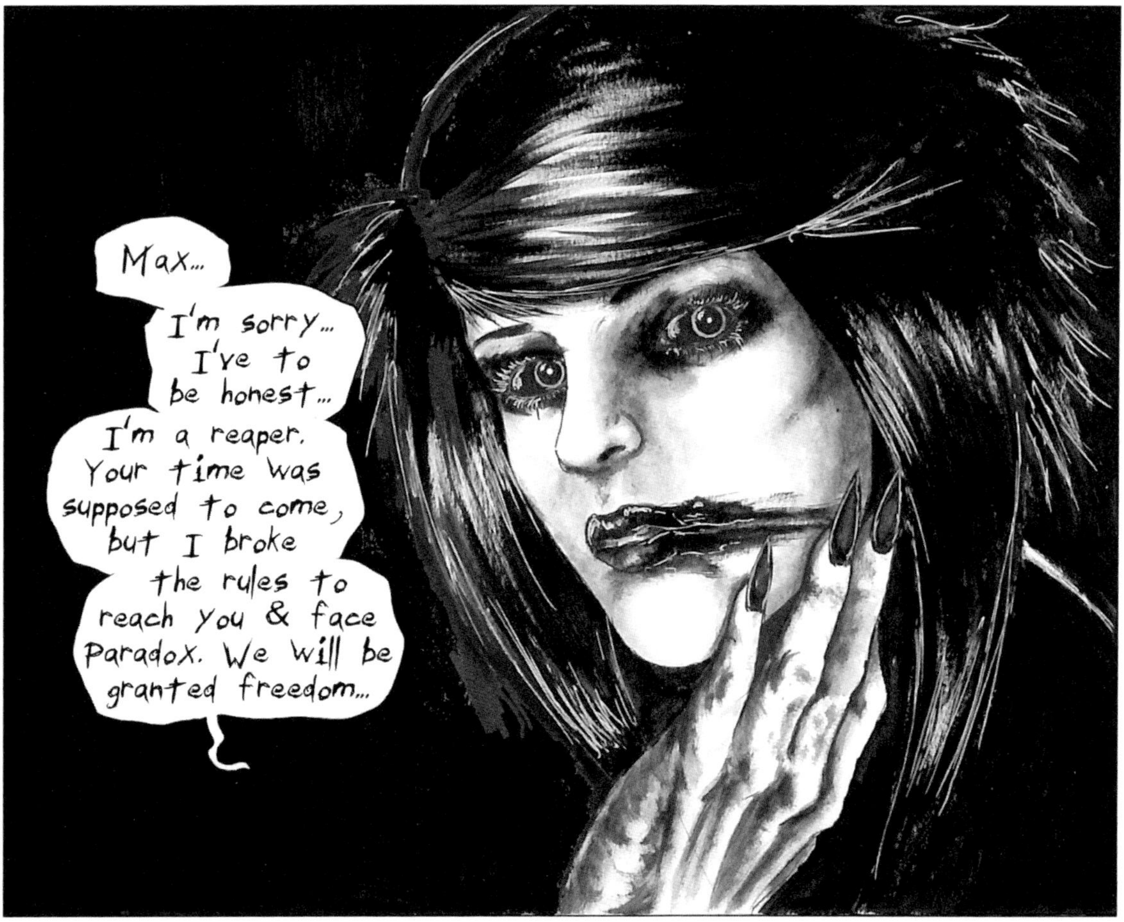
Max...
I'm sorry... I've to be honest...
I'm a reaper. Your time was supposed to come, but I broke the rules to reach you & face paradox. We will be granted freedom...

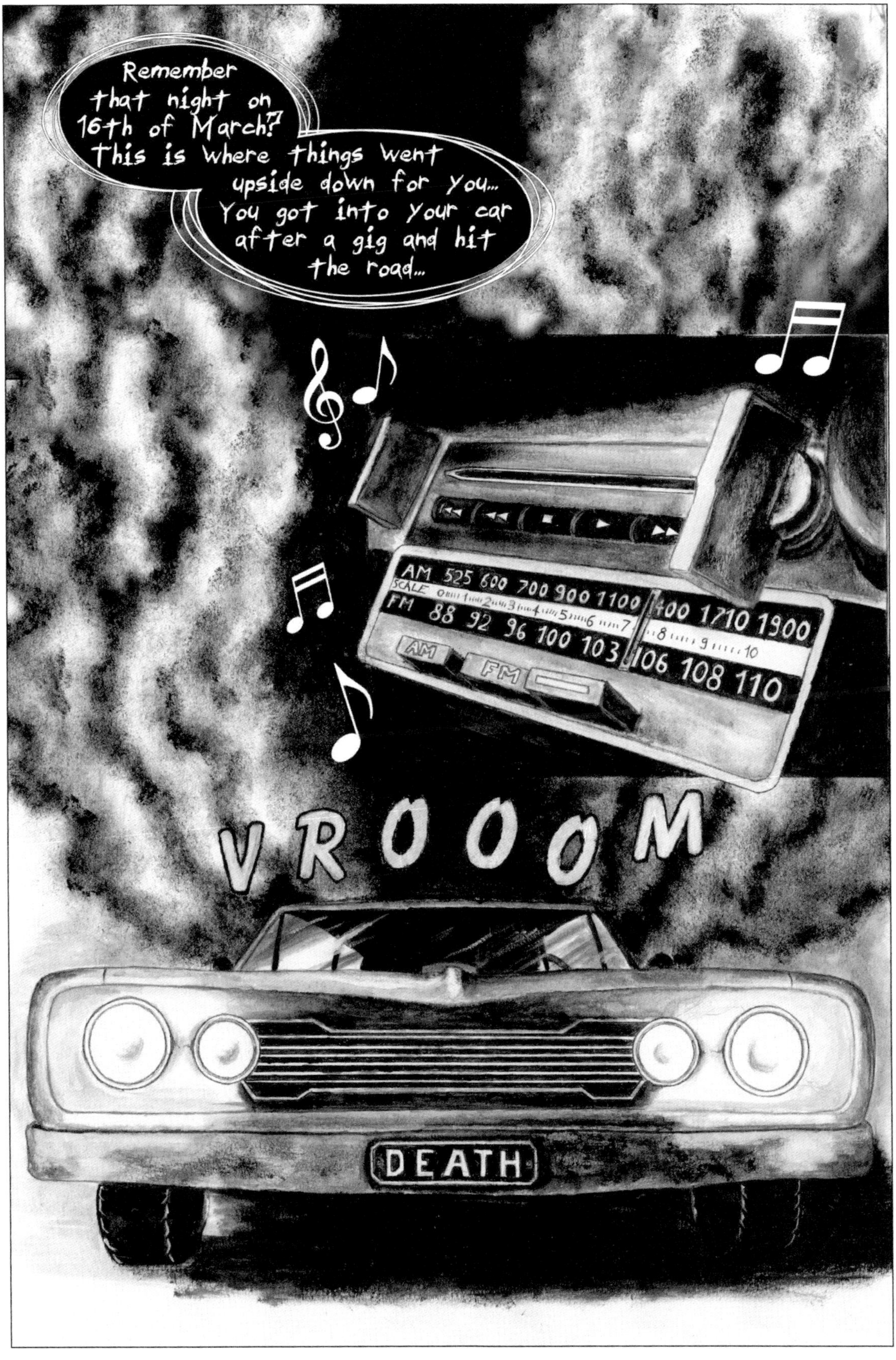
Remember that night on 16th of March? This is where things went upside down for you... You got into your car after a gig and hit the road...
AM 525 600 700 900 1100 1400 1710 1900
SCALE 0 1 2 3 4 5 6 7 8 9 10
FM 88 92 96 100 103 106 108 110
AM
FM
VROOOM
DEATH

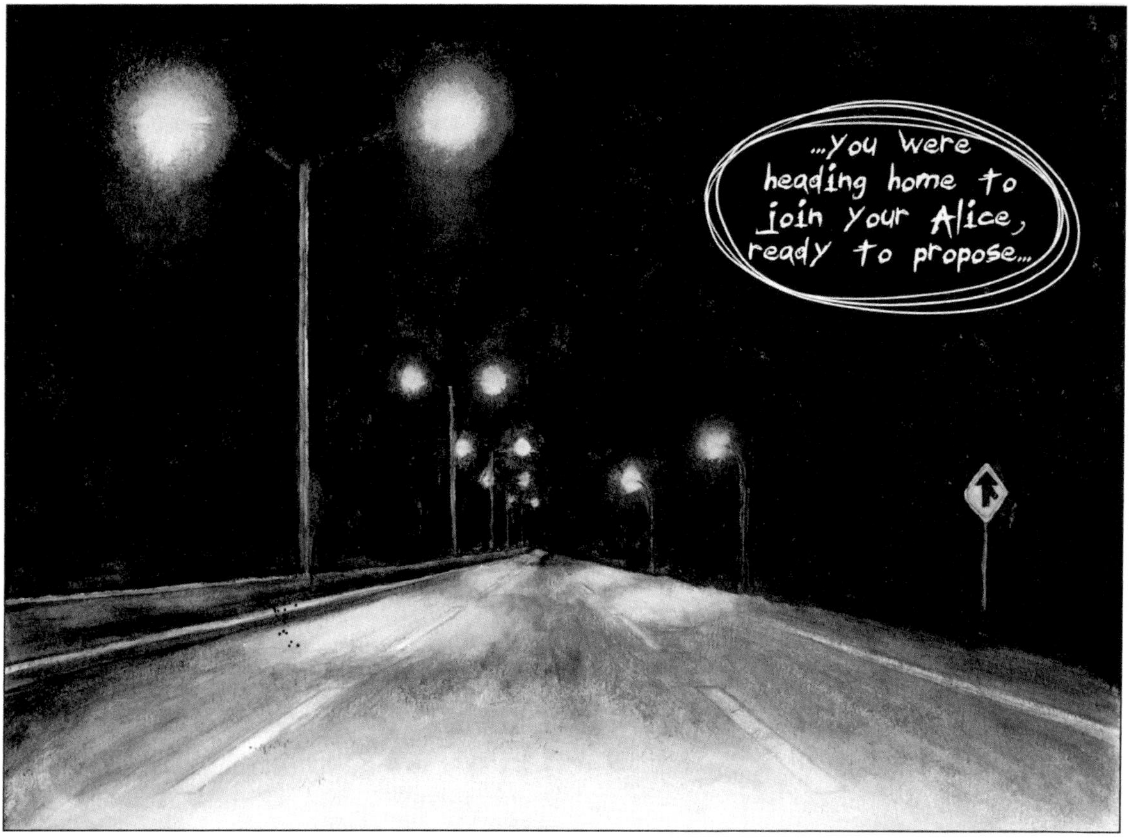
...You were heading home to join your Alice, ready to propose...

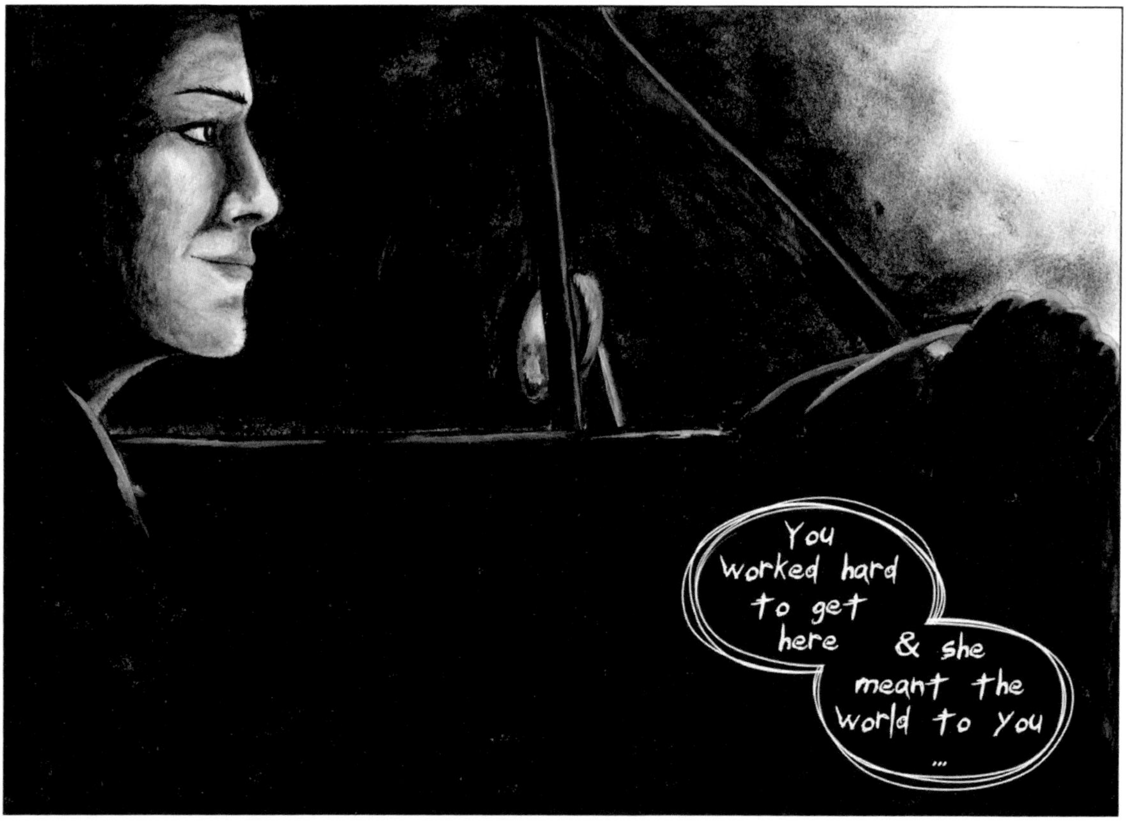
You worked hard to get here
& she meant the world to you ...

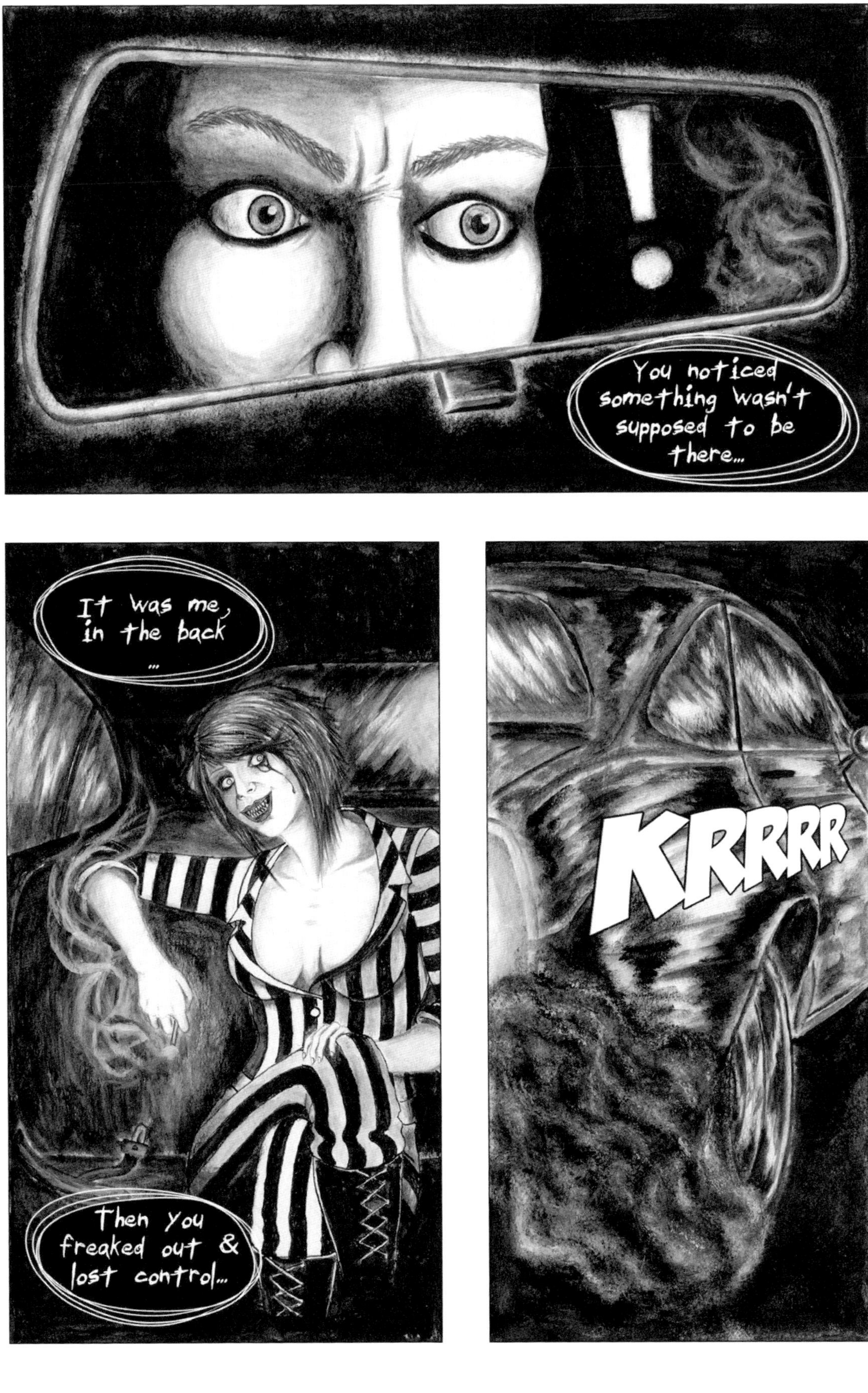
!
You noticed something wasn't supposed to be there...
It was me, in the back ...
Then you freaked out & lost control...
KRRRR

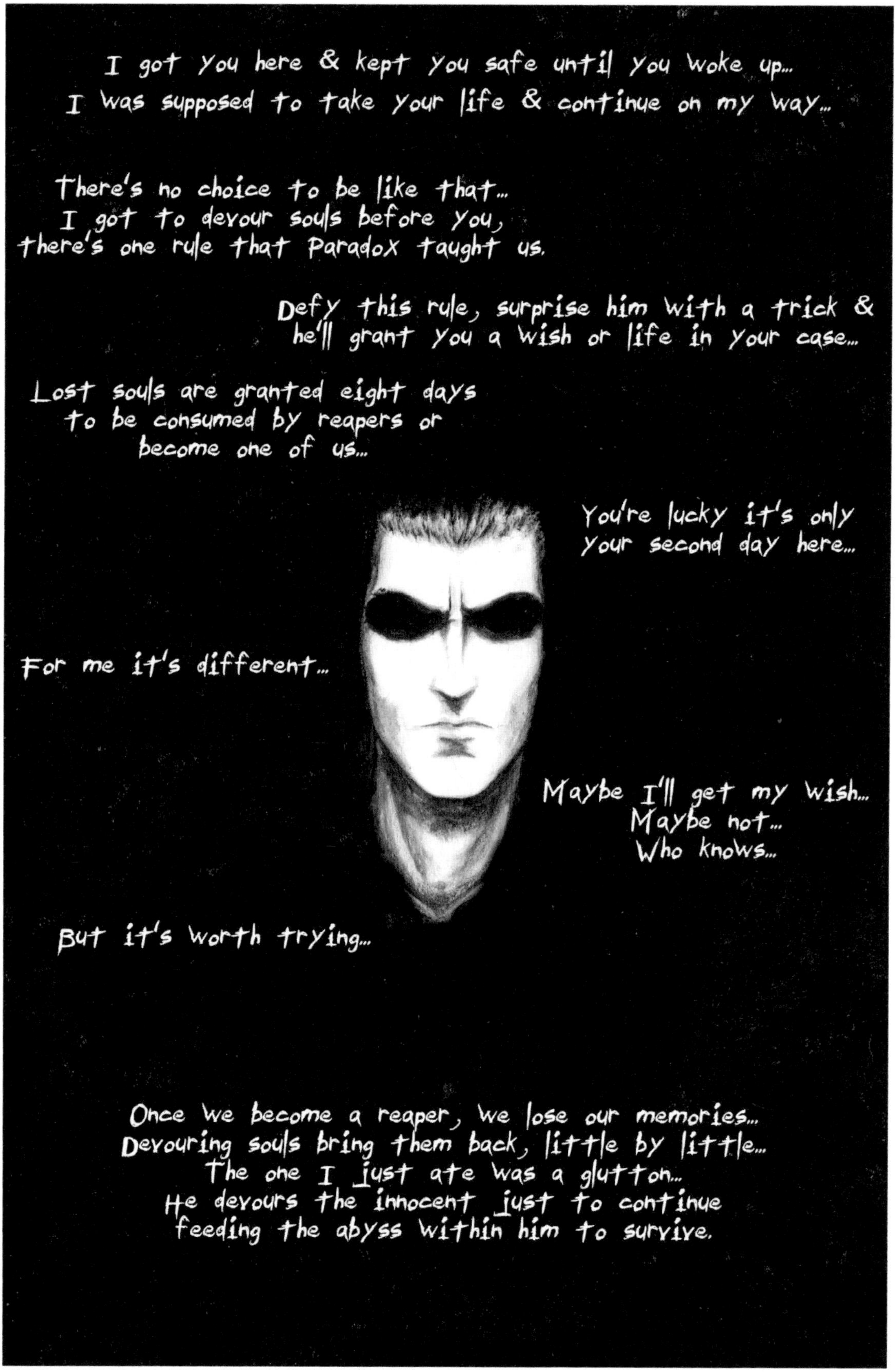
I got you here & kept you safe until you woke up...
I was supposed to take your life & continue on my way...
There's no choice to be like that...
I got to devour souls before you,
there's one rule that Paradox taught us.
Defy this rule, surprise him with a trick &
he'll grant you a wish or life in your case...
Lost souls are granted eight days
to be consumed by reapers or
become one of us...
You're lucky it's only
your second day here...
For me it's different...
Maybe I'll get my wish...
Maybe not...
Who knows...
But it's worth trying...
Once we become a reaper, we lose our memories...
Devouring souls bring them back, little by little...
The one I just ate was a glutton...
He devours the innocent just to continue
feeding the abyss within him to survive.

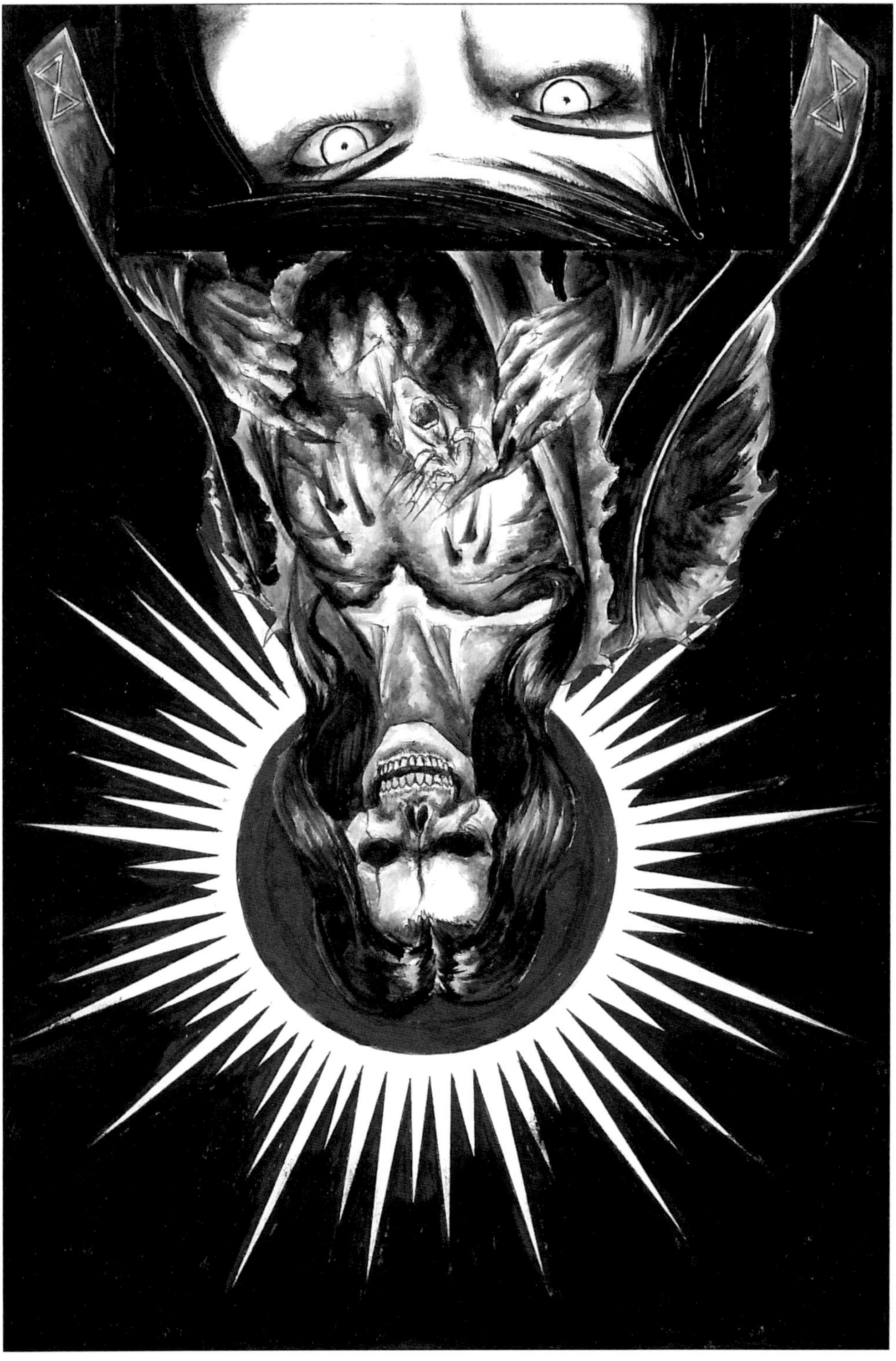

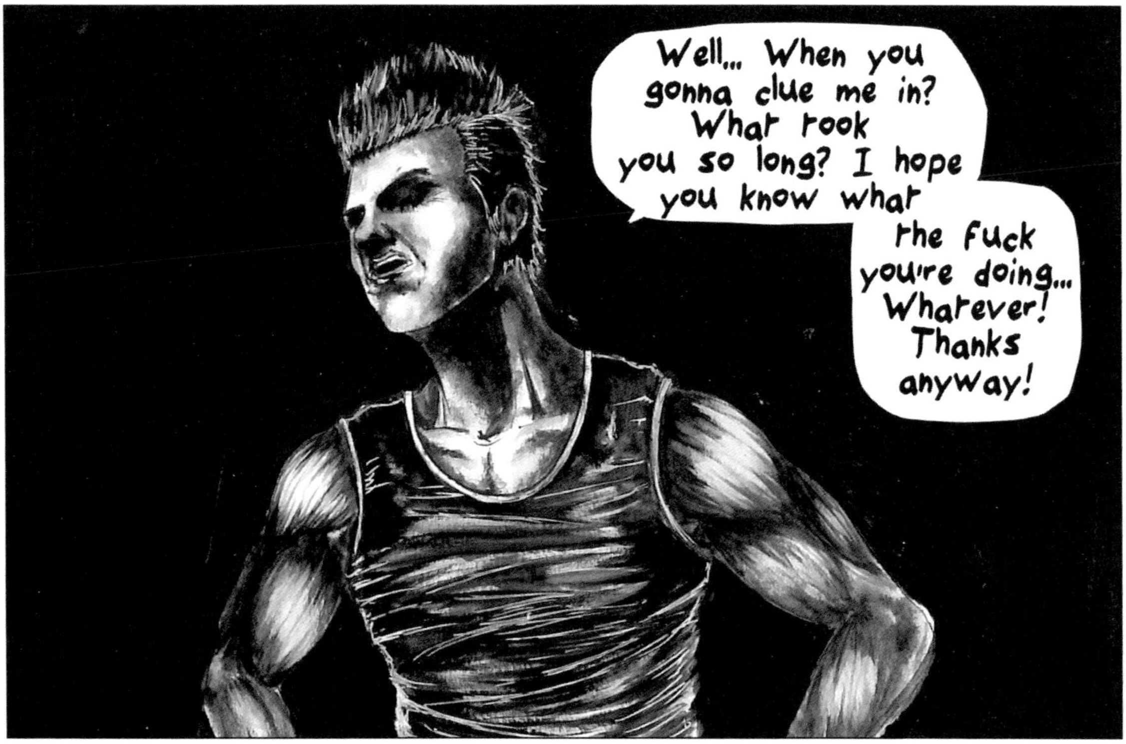
Well... When you gonna clue me in? What took you so long? I hope you know what the fuck you're doing... Whatever! Thanks anyway!

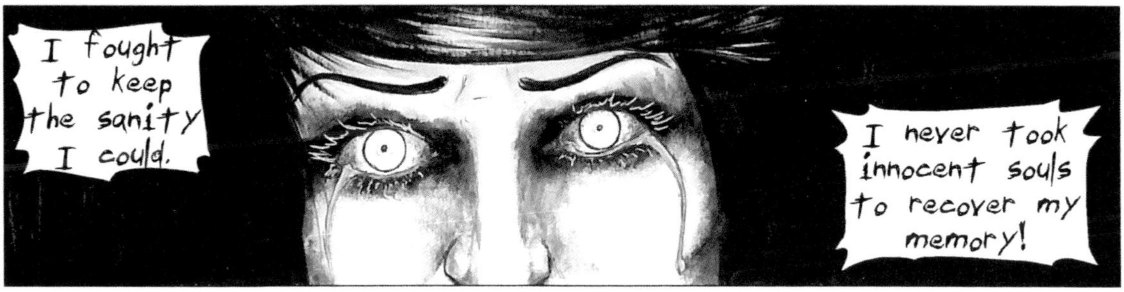
I fought to keep the sanity I could.
I never took innocent souls to recover my memory!

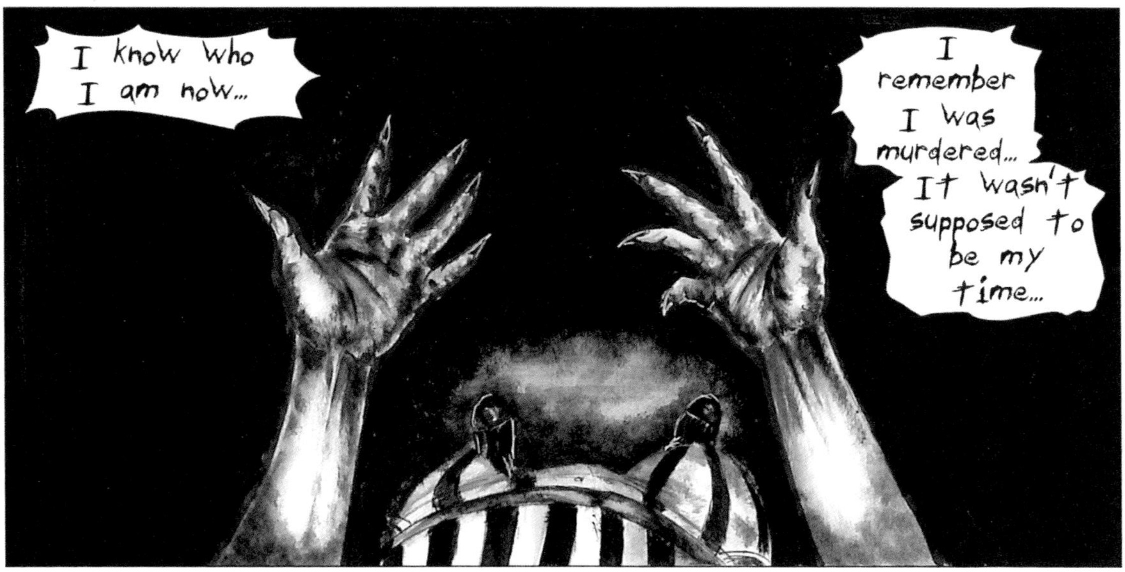
I know who I am now...
I remember I was murdered...
It wasn't supposed to be my time...

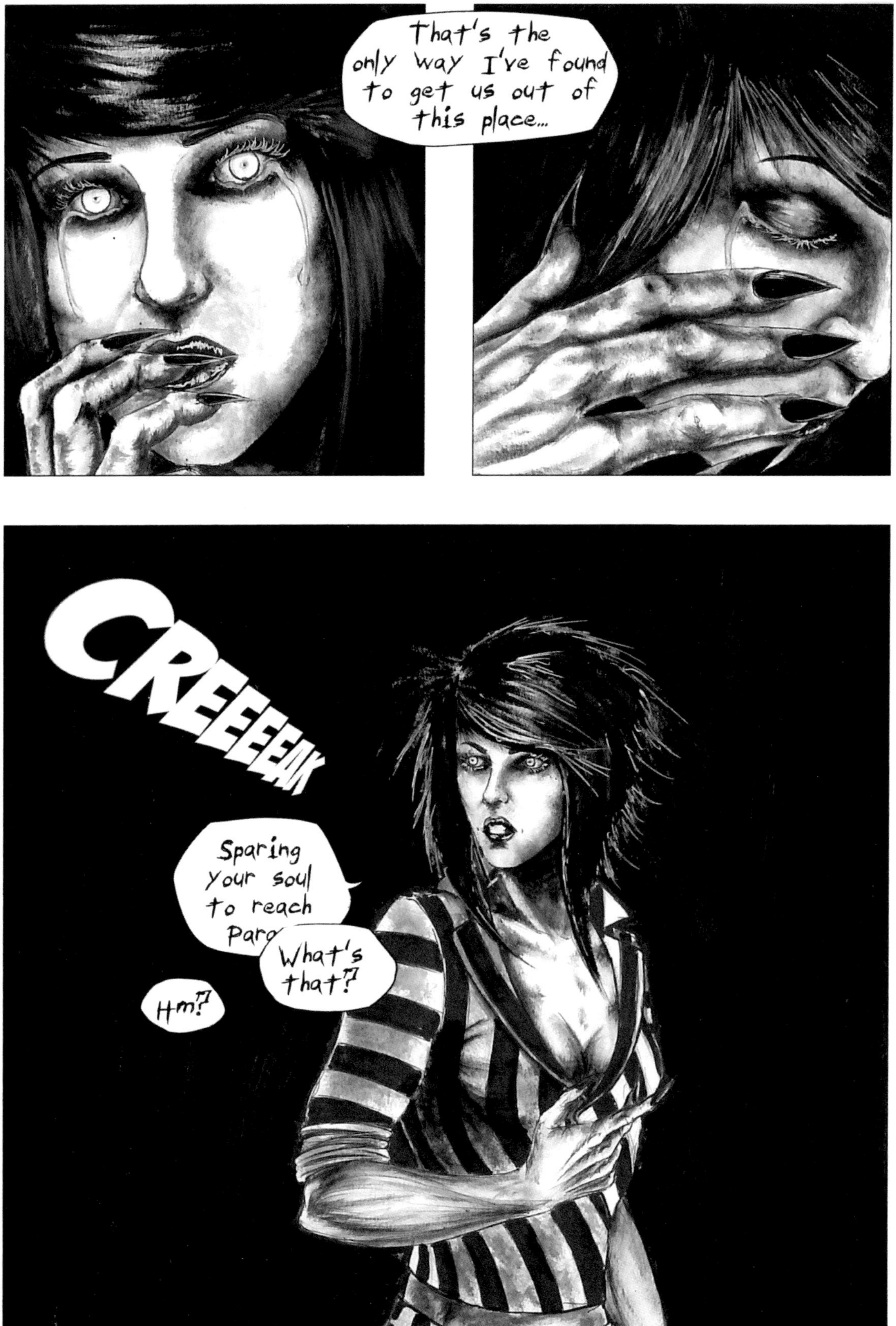
That's the only way I've found to get us out of this place...
CREEEEAK
Sparing your soul to reach Par
What's that?
Hm?!

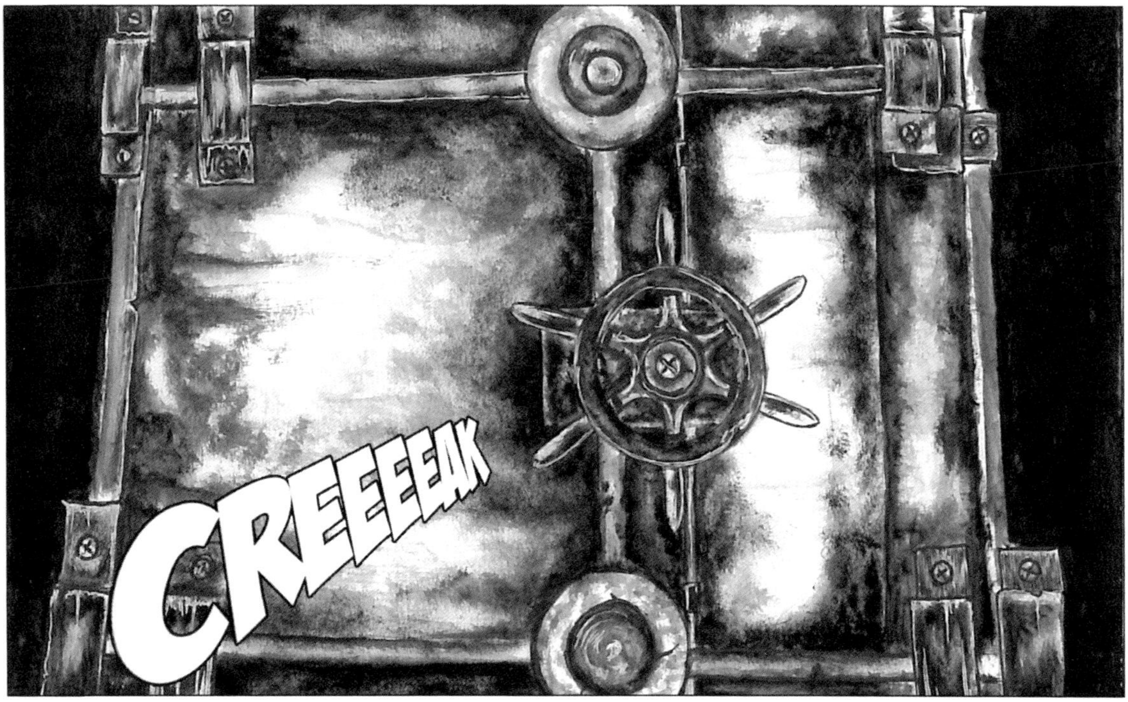
CREEEEAK

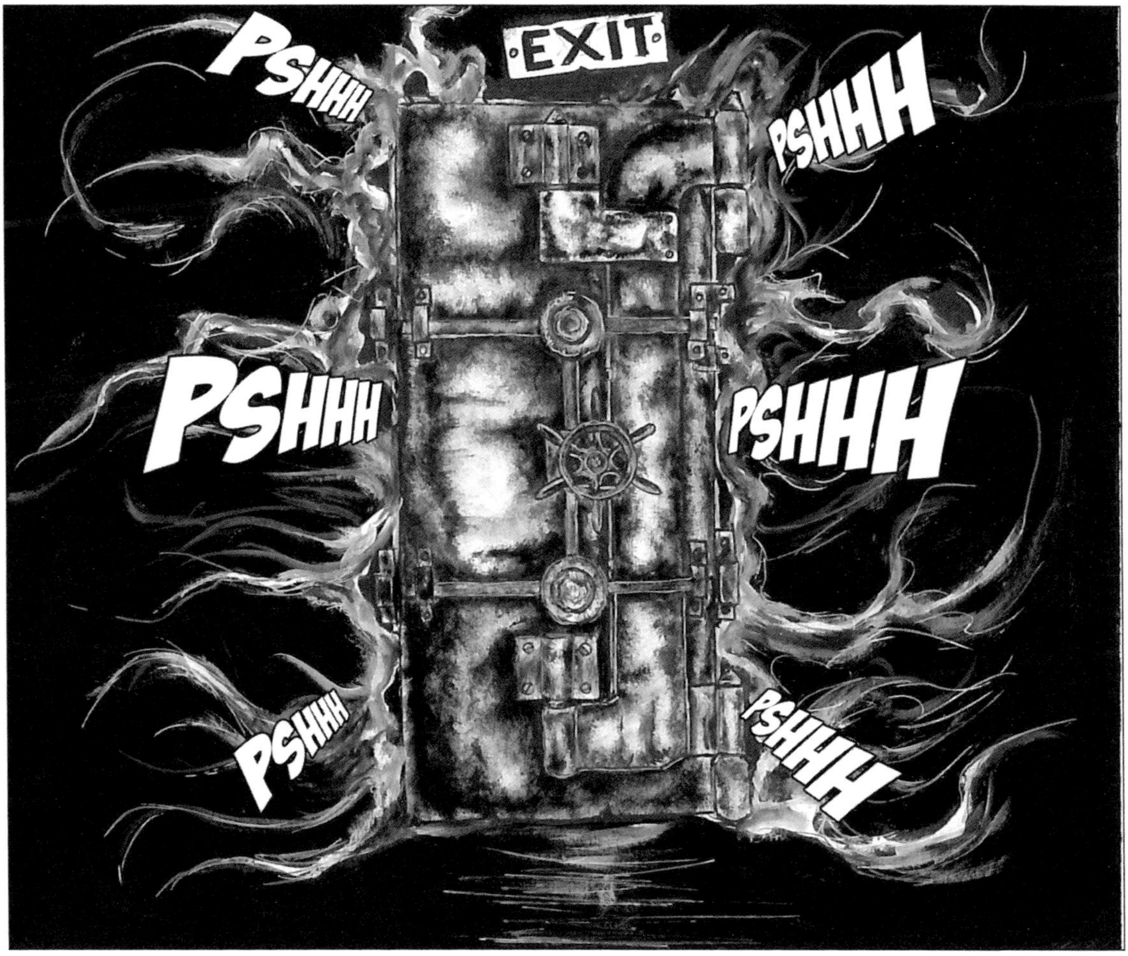
EXIT
PSHHH
PSHHH
PSHHH
PSHHH
PSHHH
PSHHH

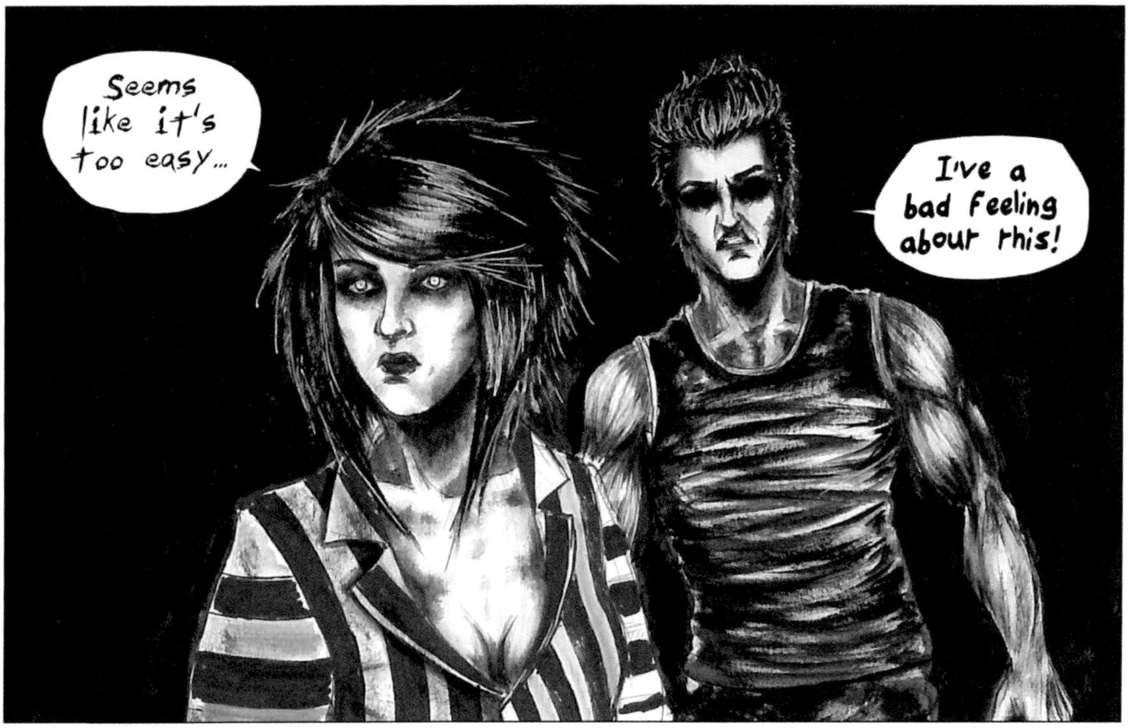
Seems like it's too easy...
I've a bad feeling about this!

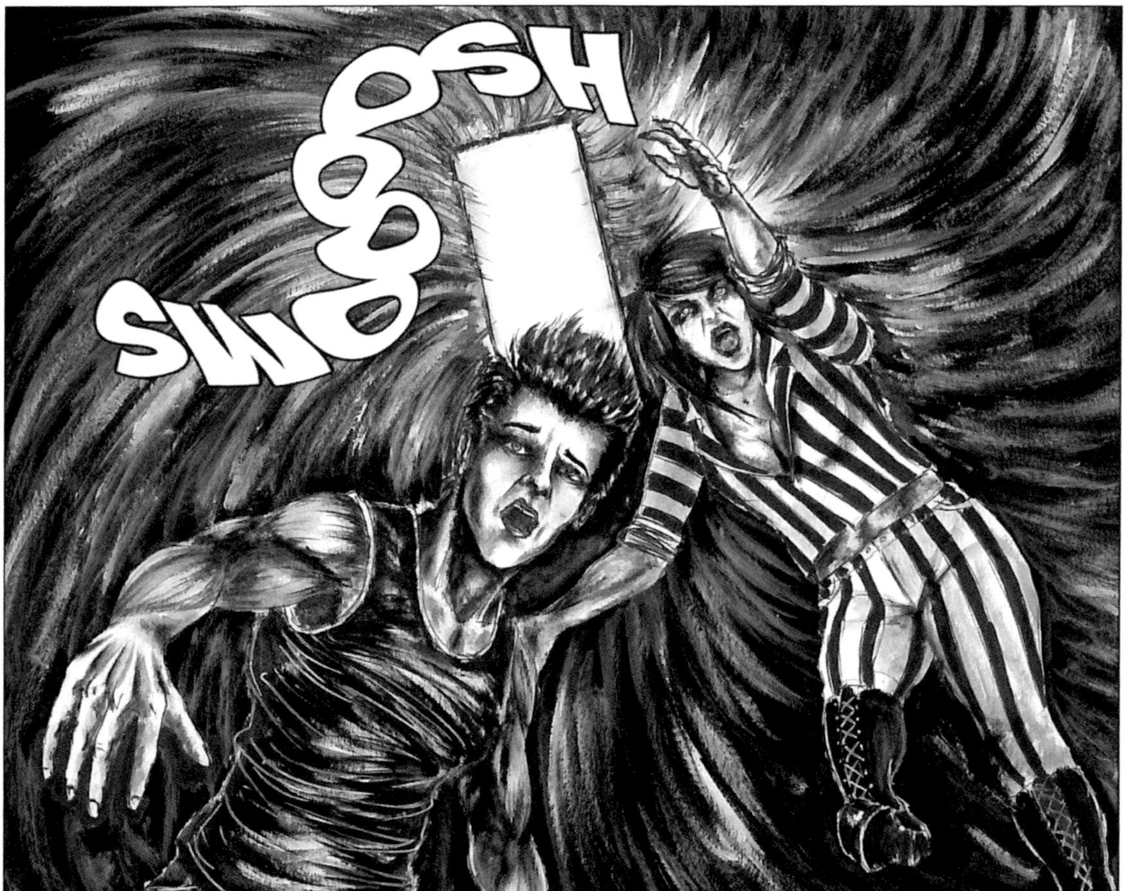
SWOOOOSH

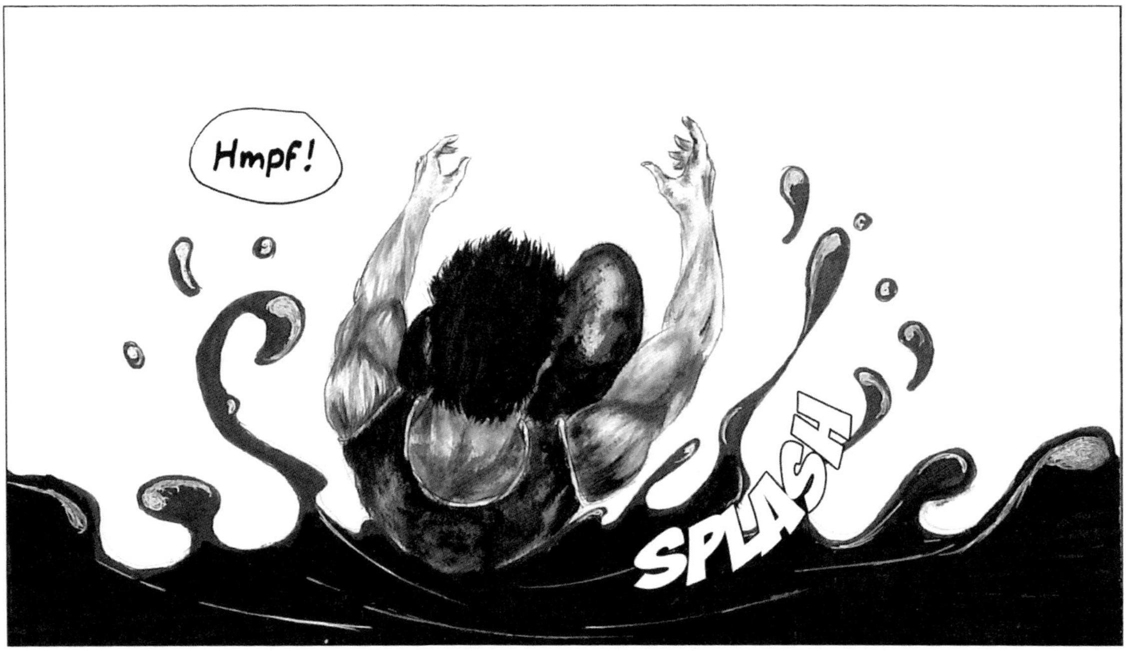
Hmpf!
SPLASH

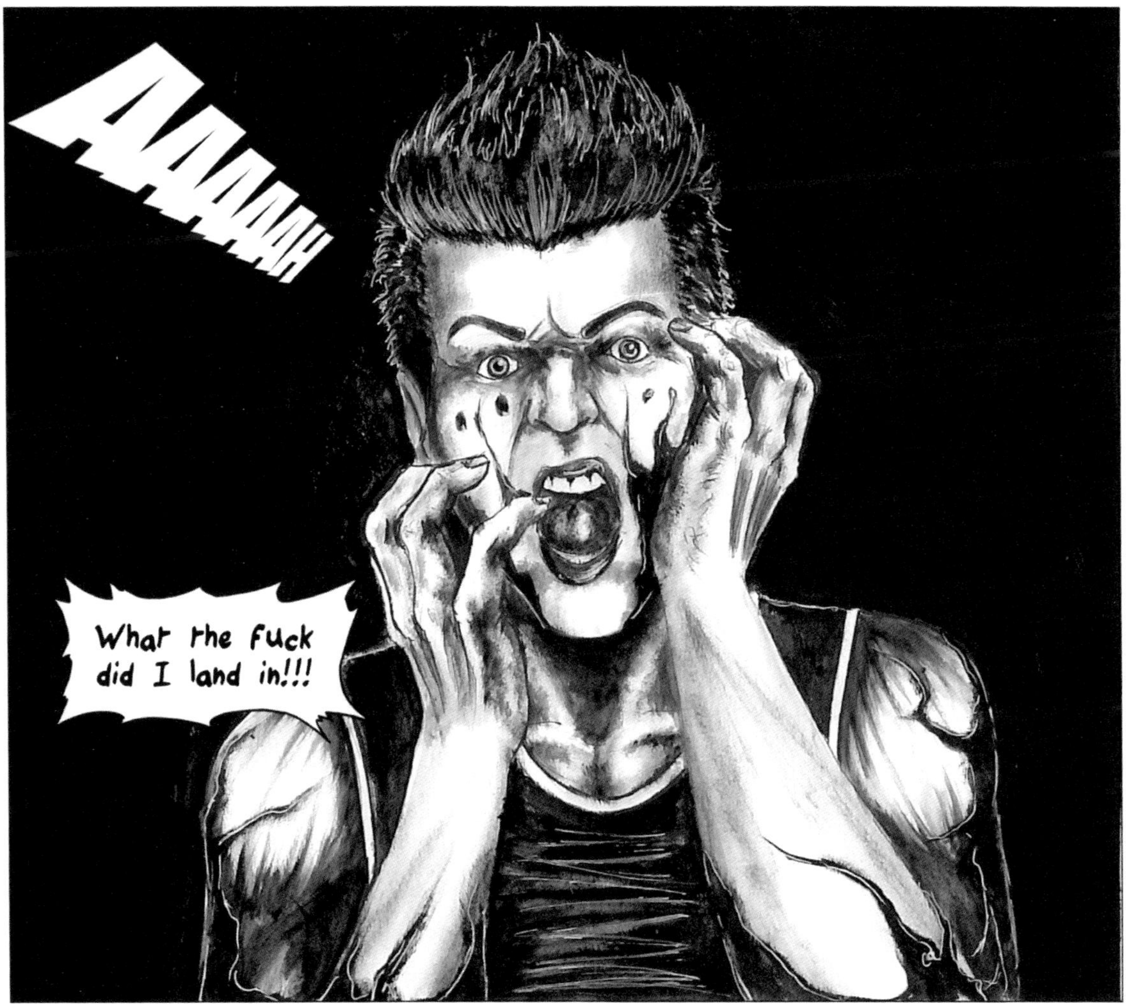
AAAAAAH
What the fuck did I land in!!!

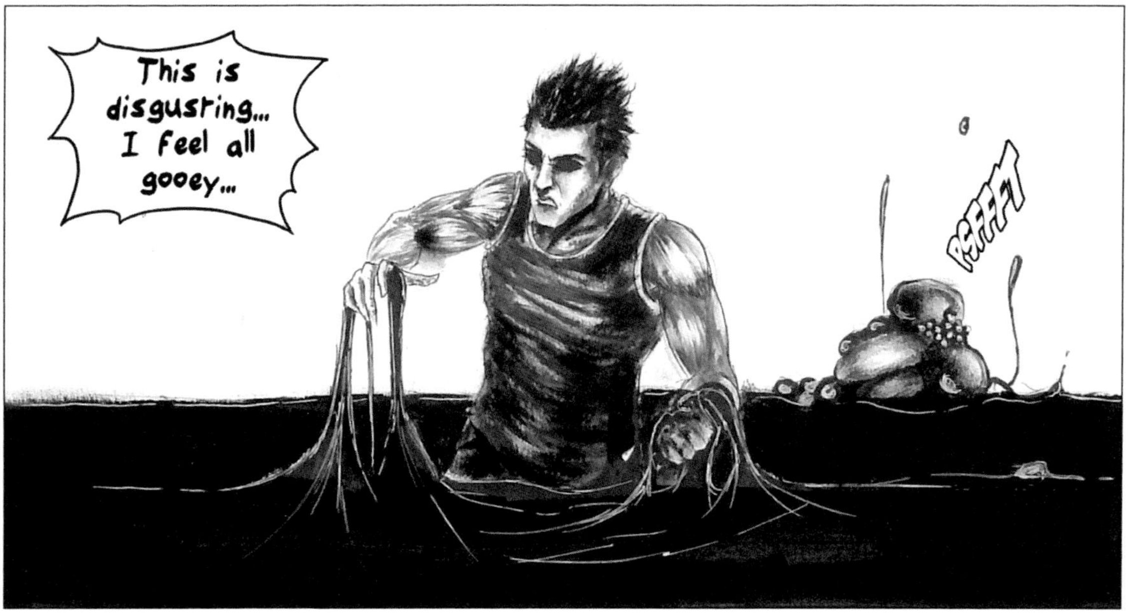
This is disgusting... I feel all gooey...
PSFFFT

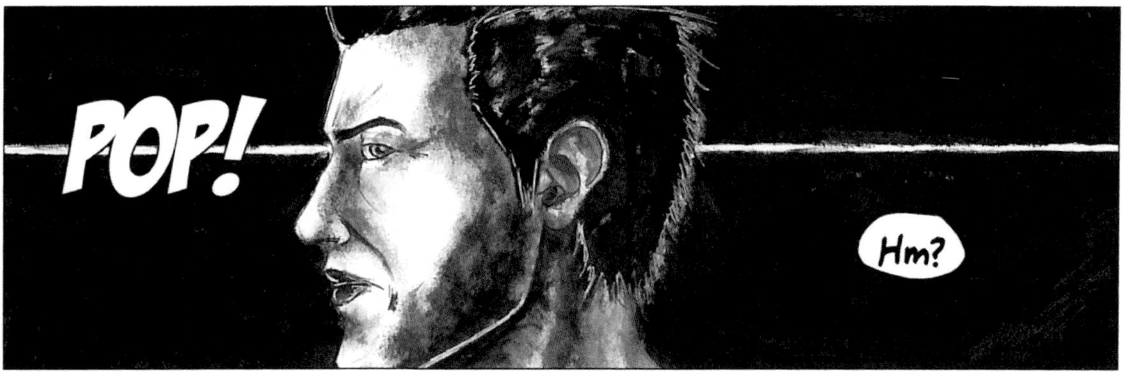
POP!
Hm?

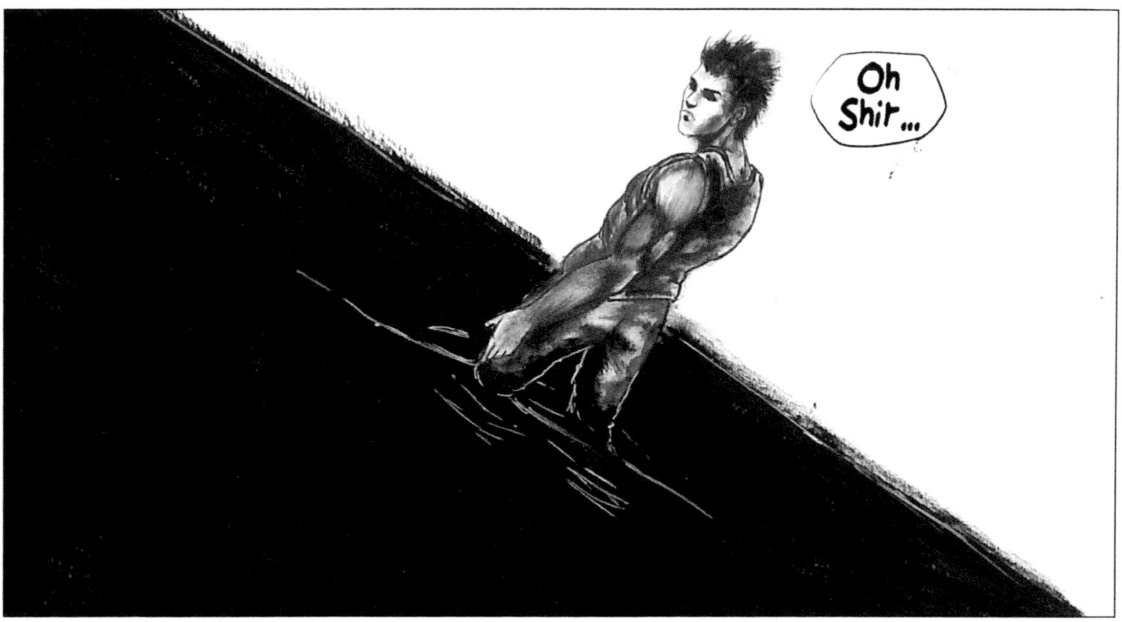
Oh Shit...

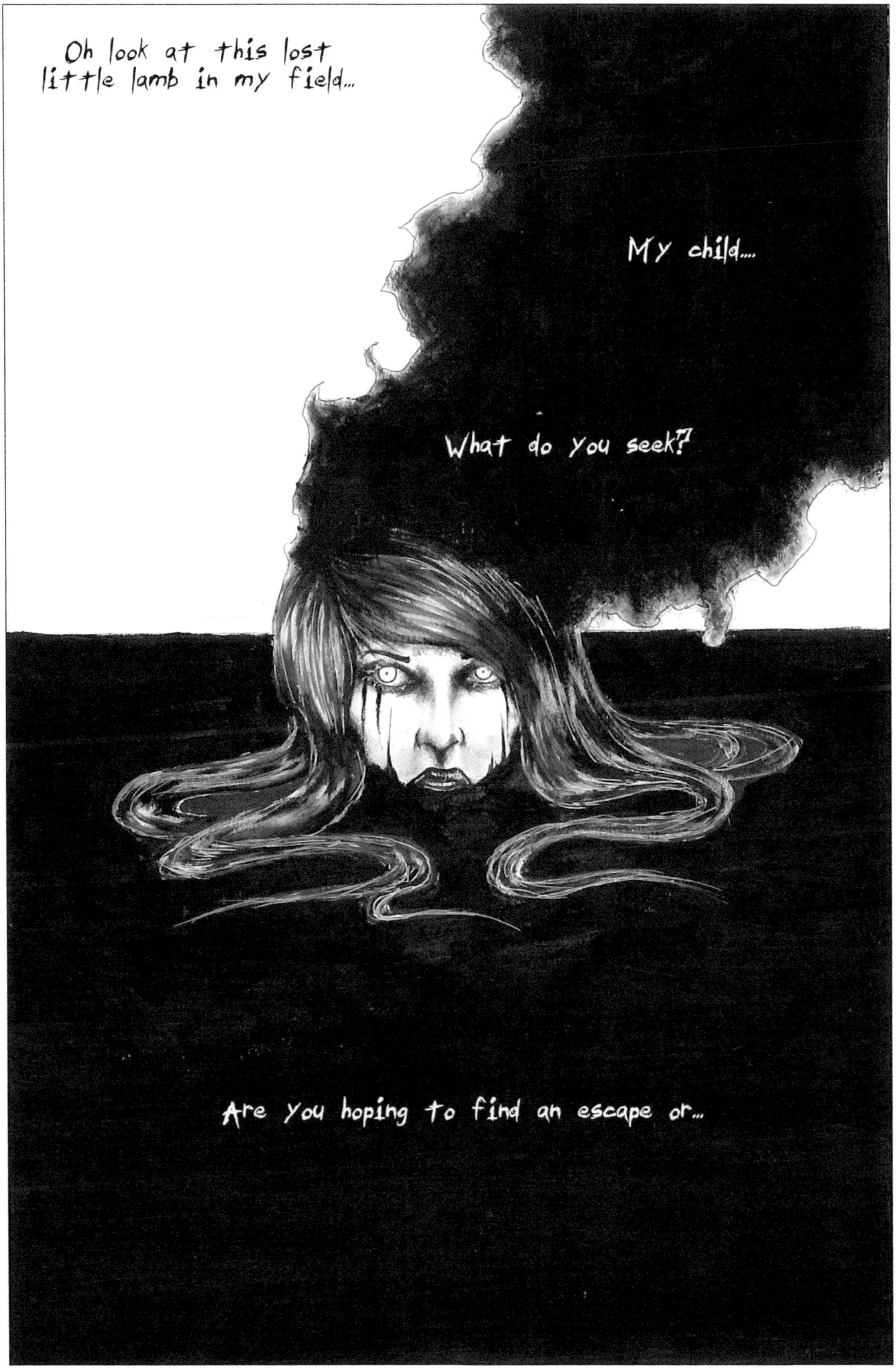
Oh look at this lost little lamb in my field...
My child....
What do you seek??
Are you hoping to find an escape or...

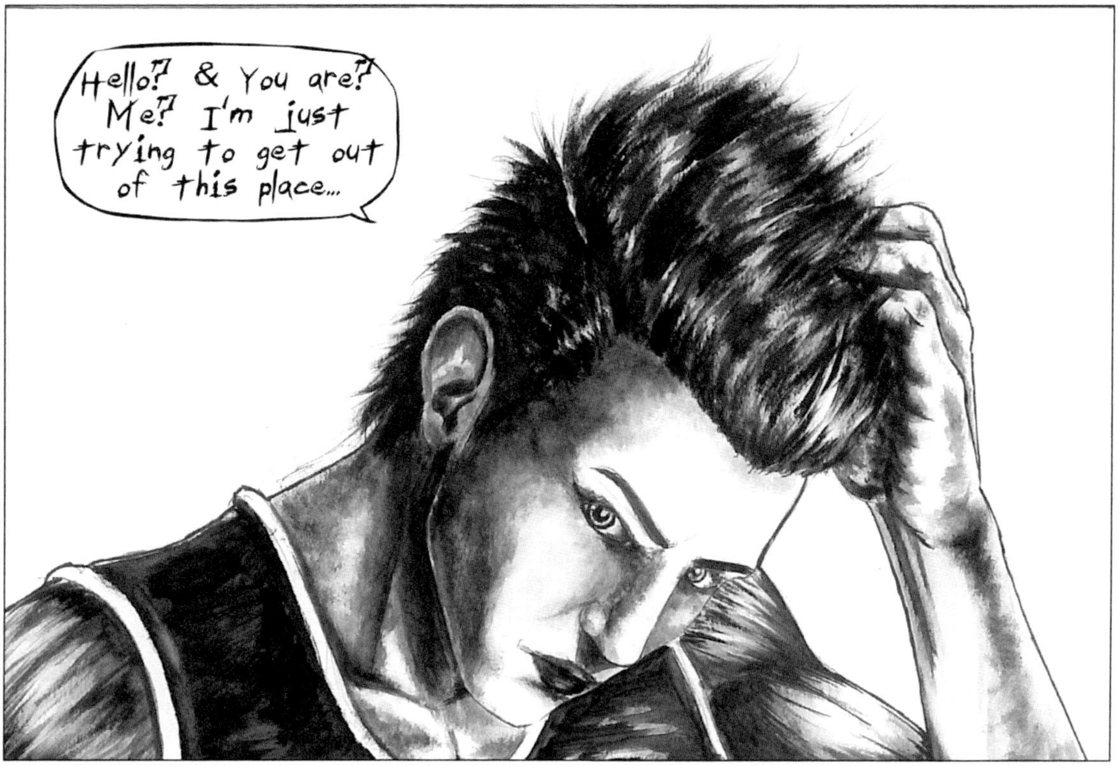
Hello?? & You are?? Me?? I'm just trying to get out of this place...

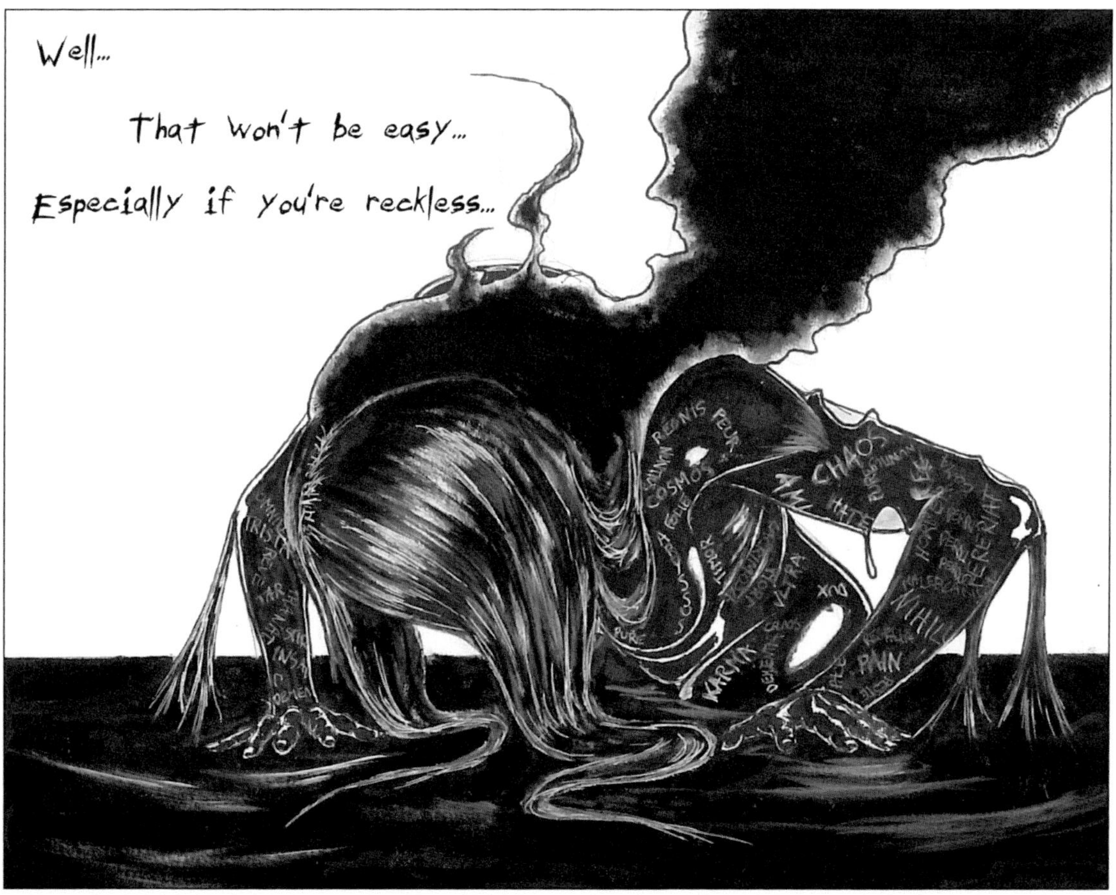
Well...
That won't be easy...
Especially if you're reckless...
CHAOS
COSMOS
KARMA
PAIN

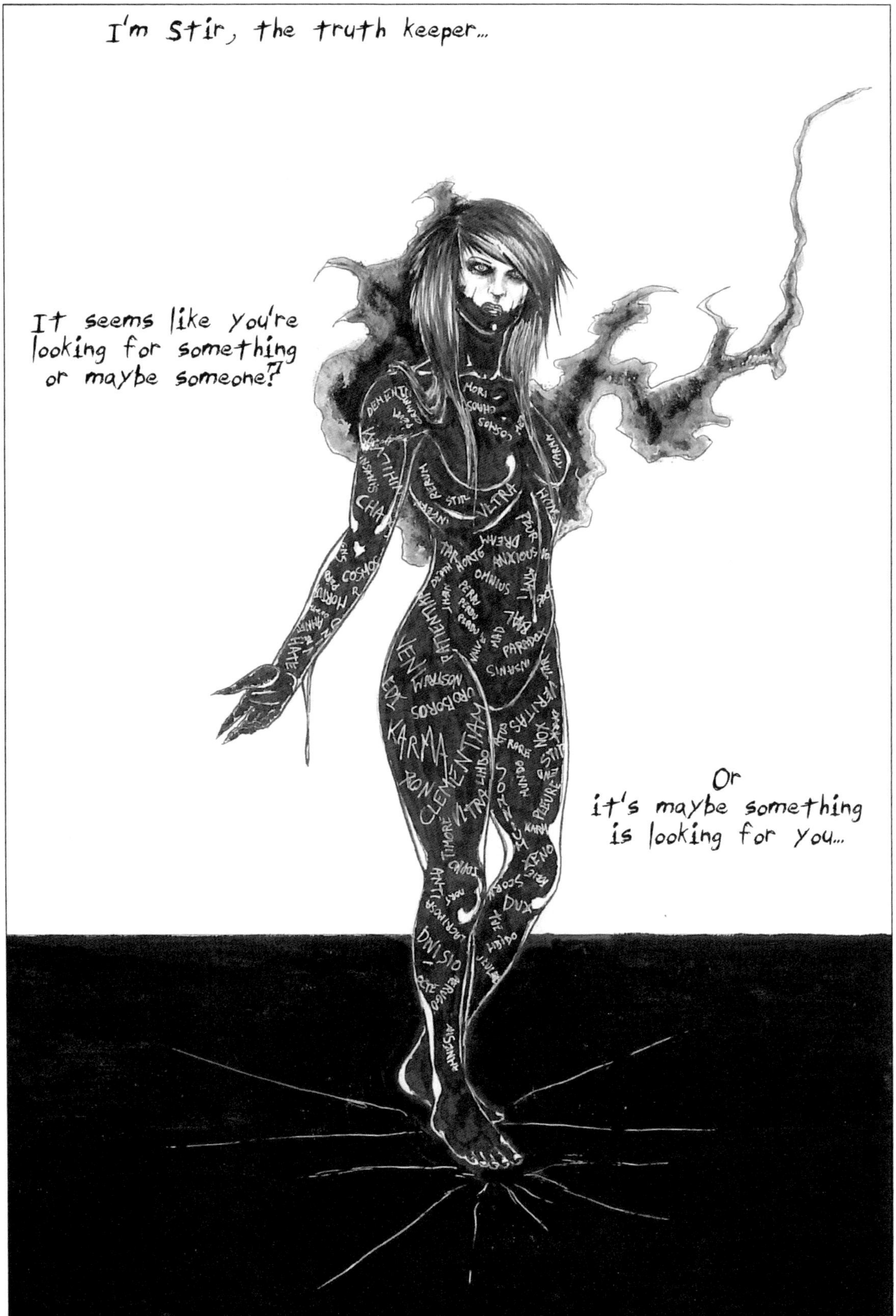
I'm Stir, the truth keeper...
It seems like you're looking for something or maybe someone??
Or it's maybe something is looking for you...

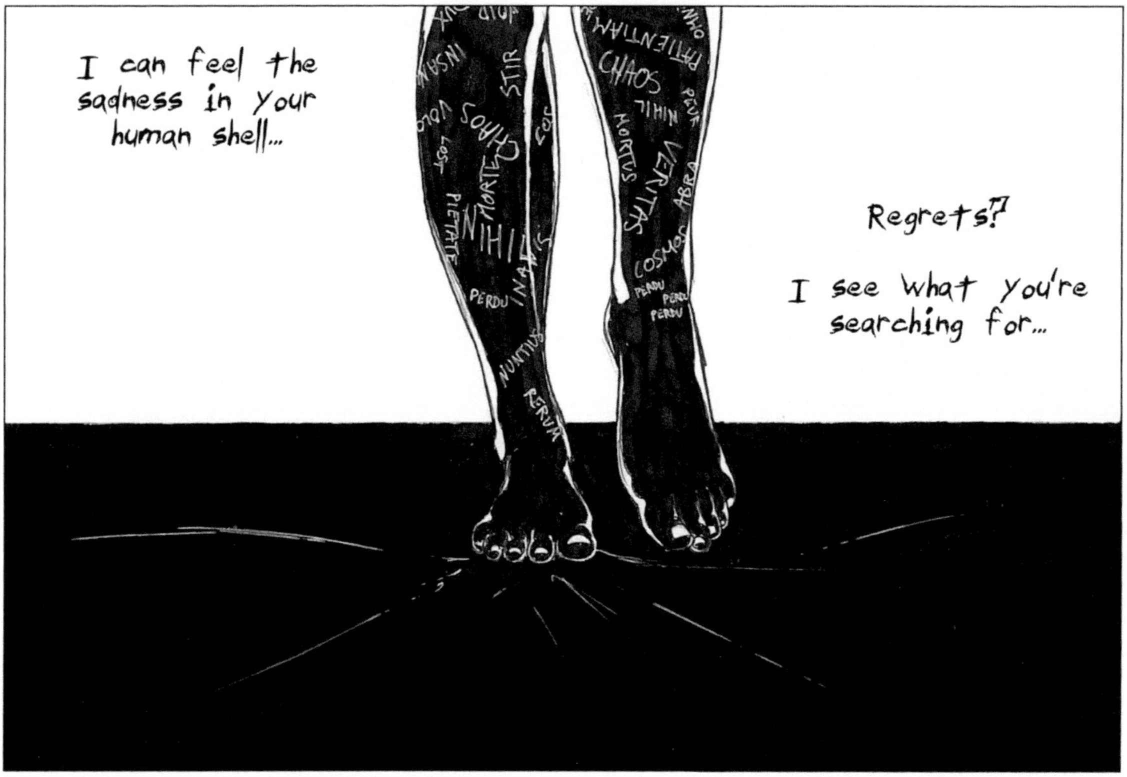
I can feel the sadness in your human shell...
Regrets?
I see what you're searching for...

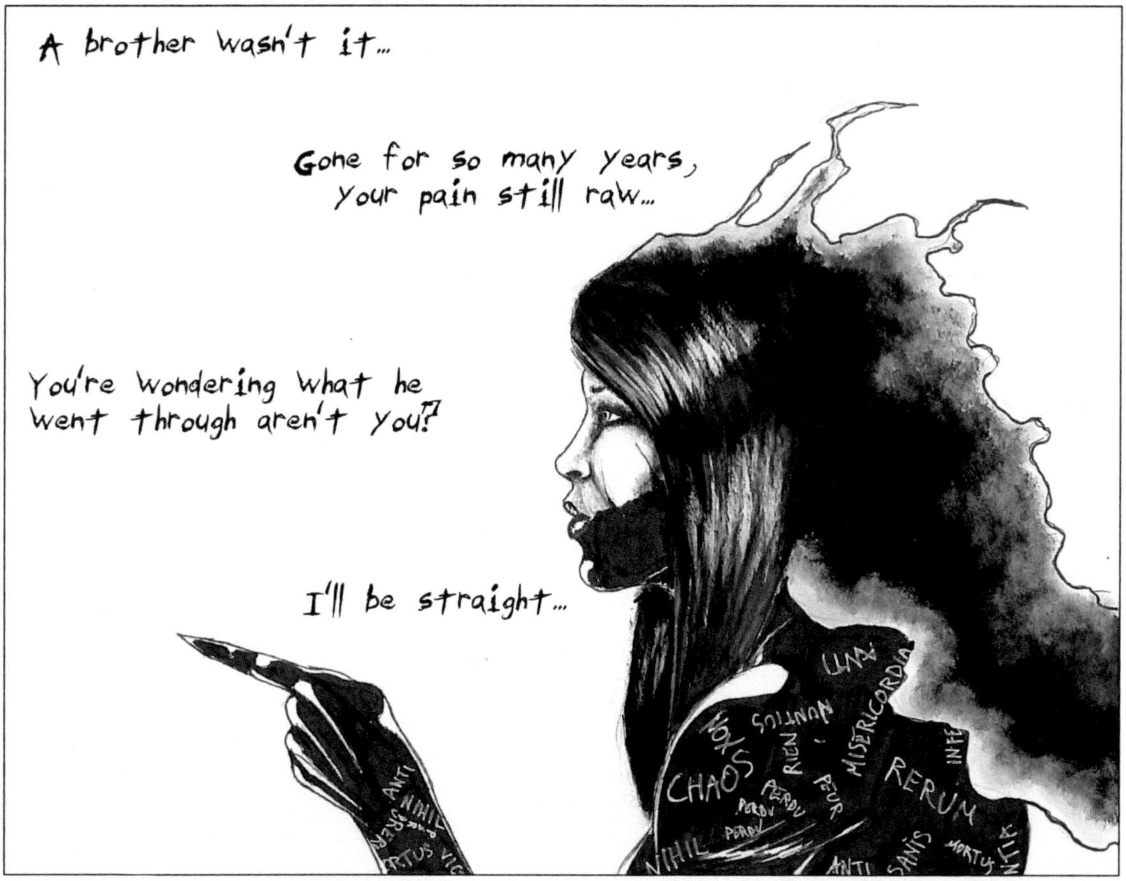
A brother wasn't it...
Gone for so many years, your pain still raw...
You're wondering what he went through aren't you?
I'll be straight...

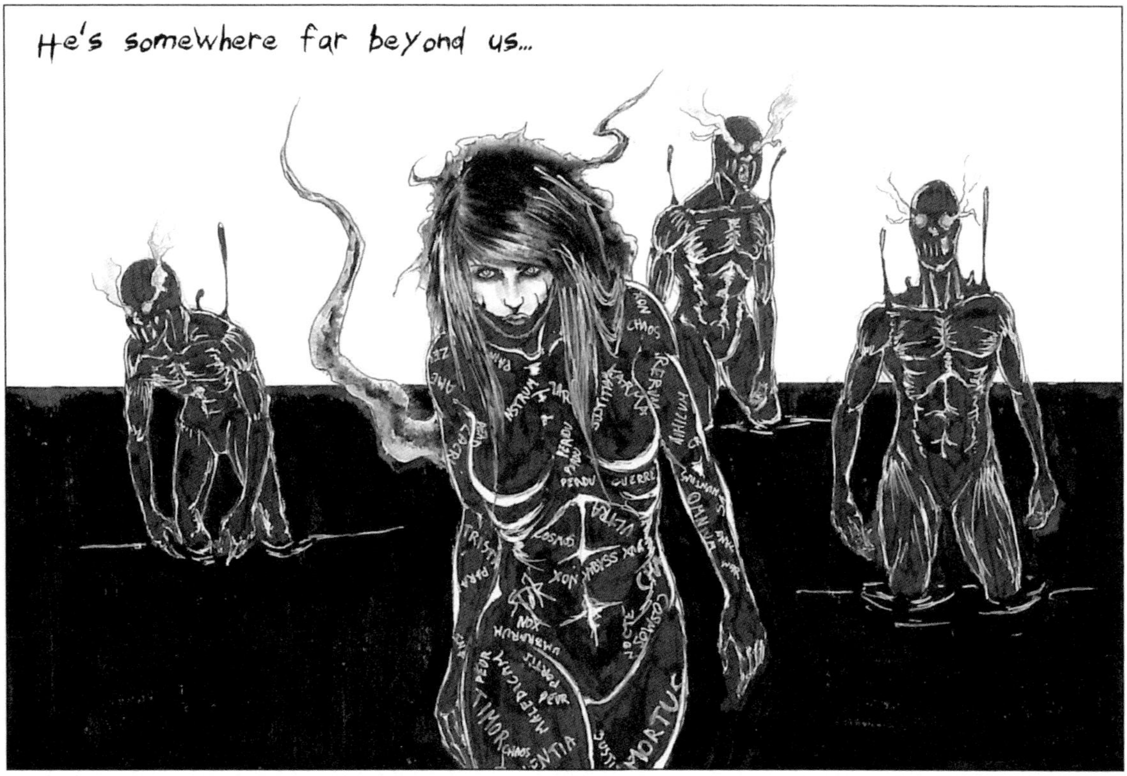
He's somewhere far beyond us...

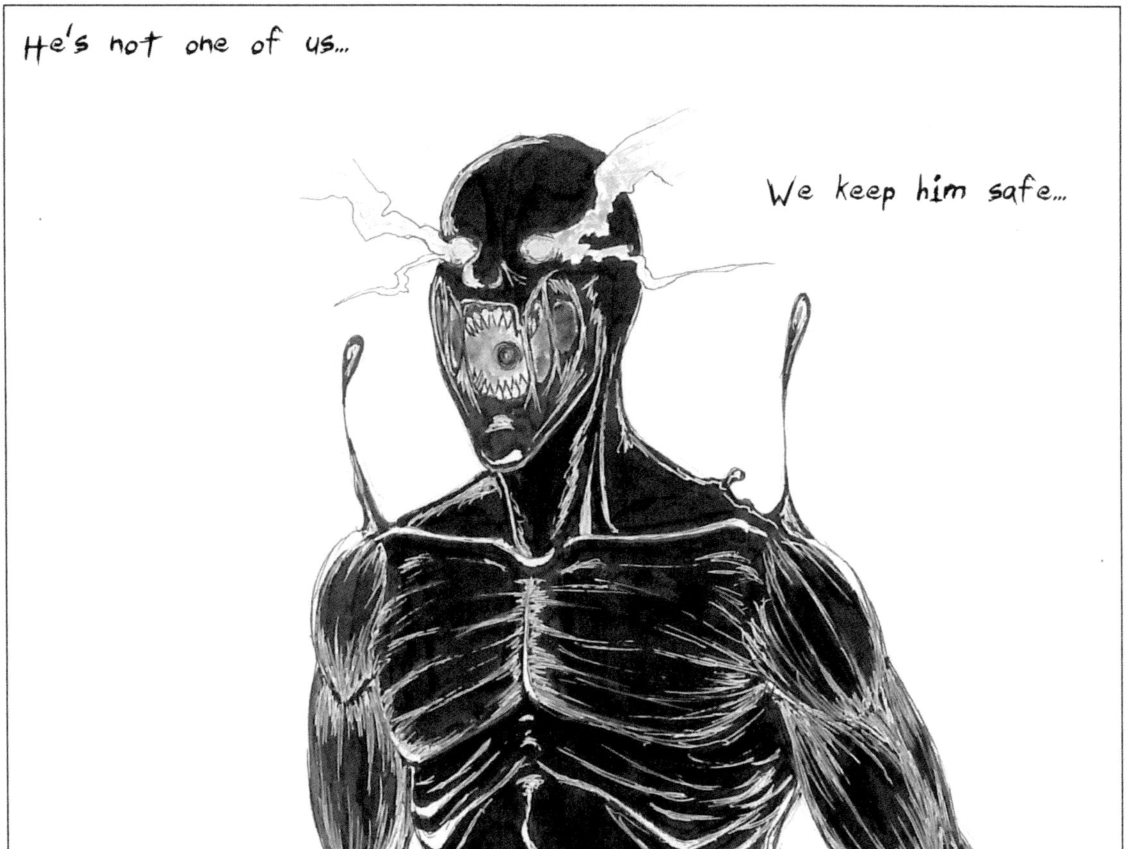
He's not one of us...
We keep him safe...

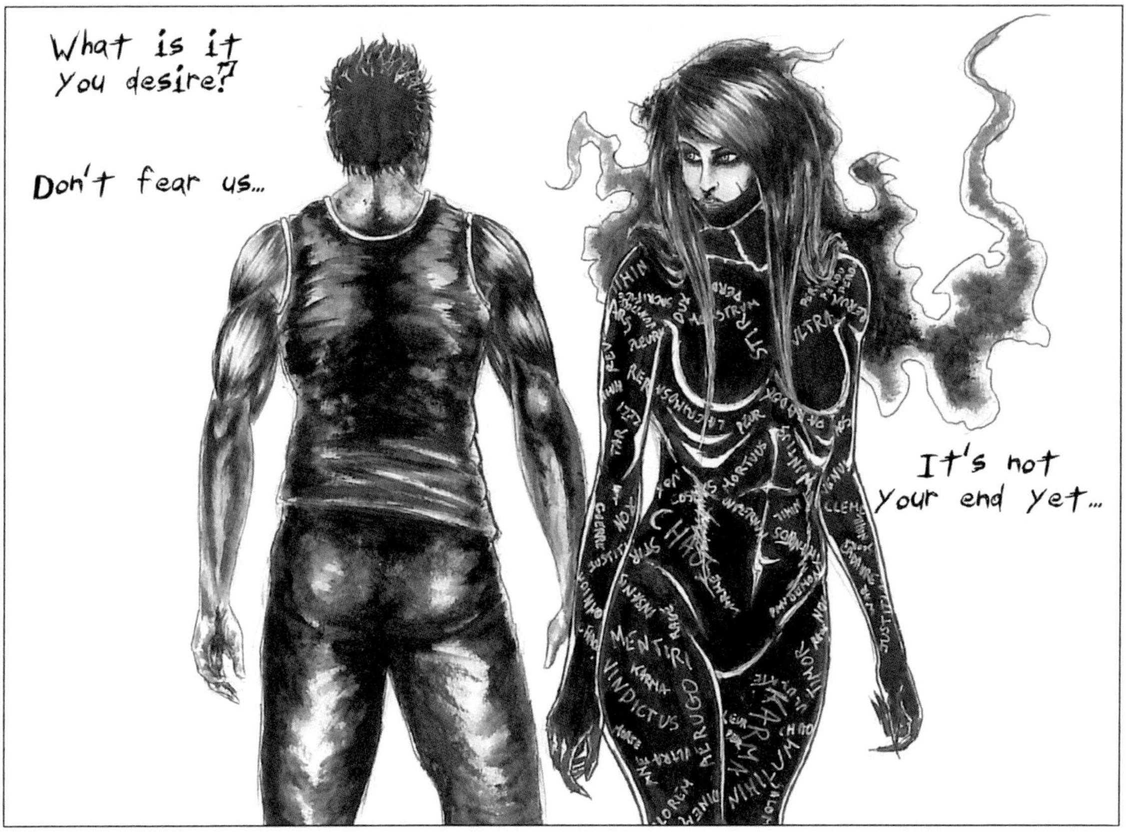
What is it you desire?
Don't fear us...
It's not your end yet...

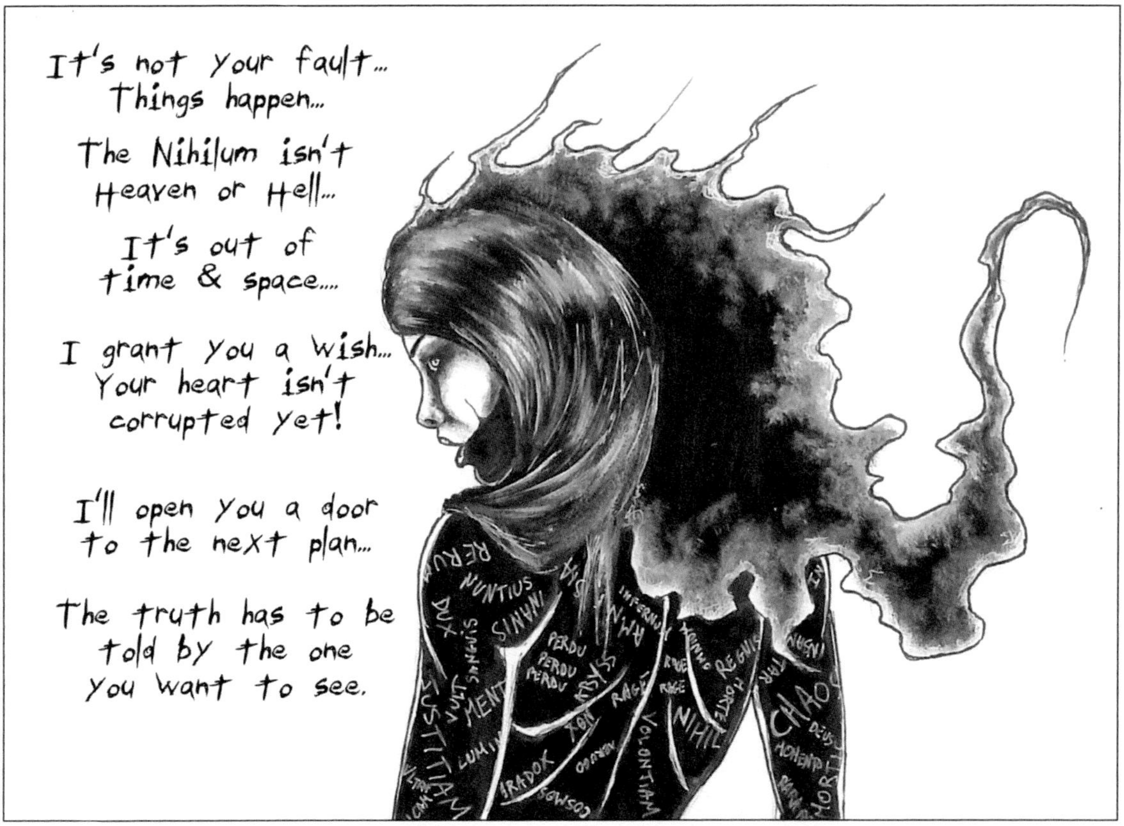
It's not your fault... Things happen...
The Nihilum isn't Heaven or Hell...
It's out of time & space....
I grant you a wish... Your heart isn't corrupted yet!
I'll open you a door to the next plan...
The truth has to be told by the one you want to see.

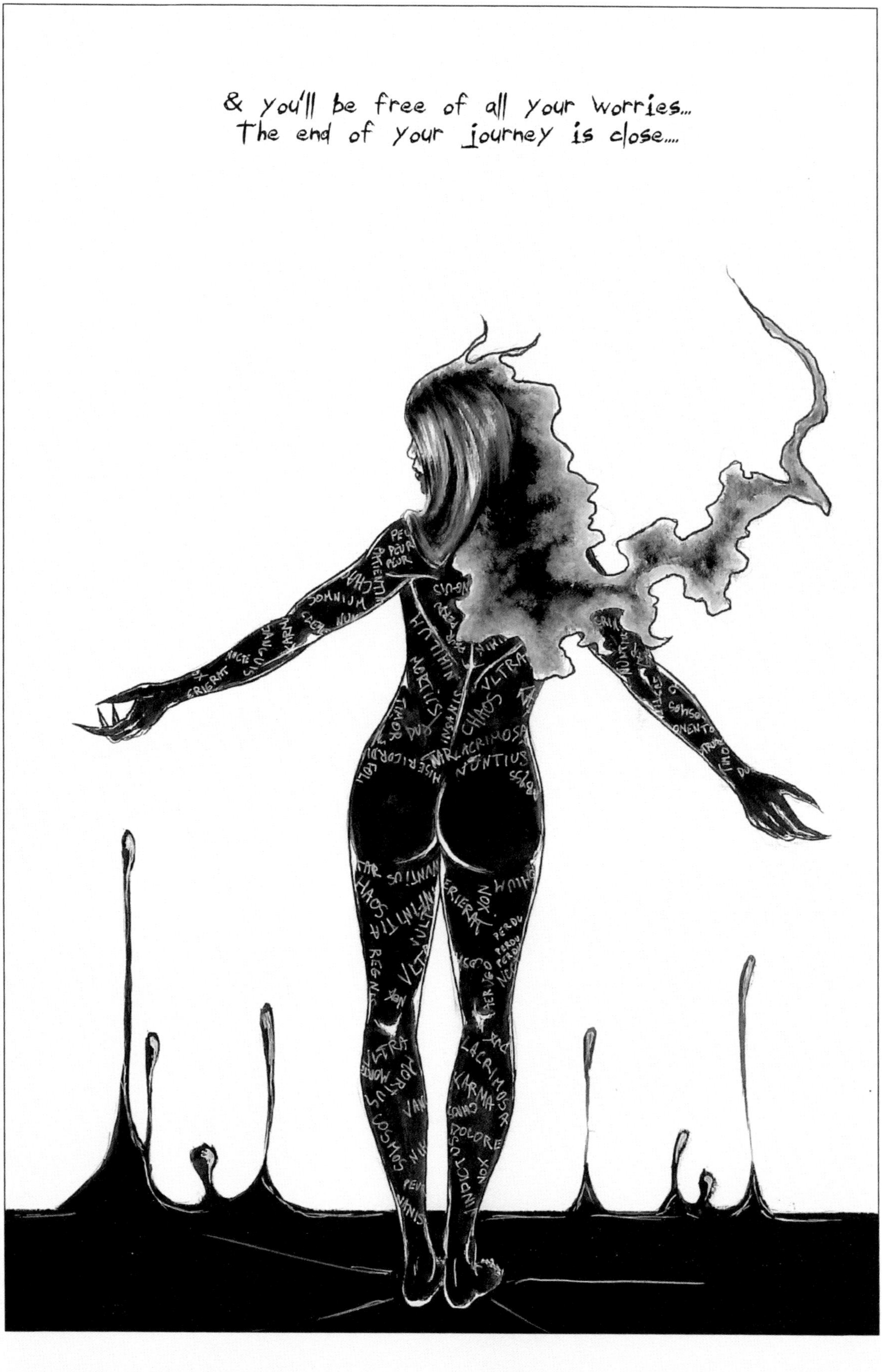
& you'll be free of all your worries...
The end of your journey is close....

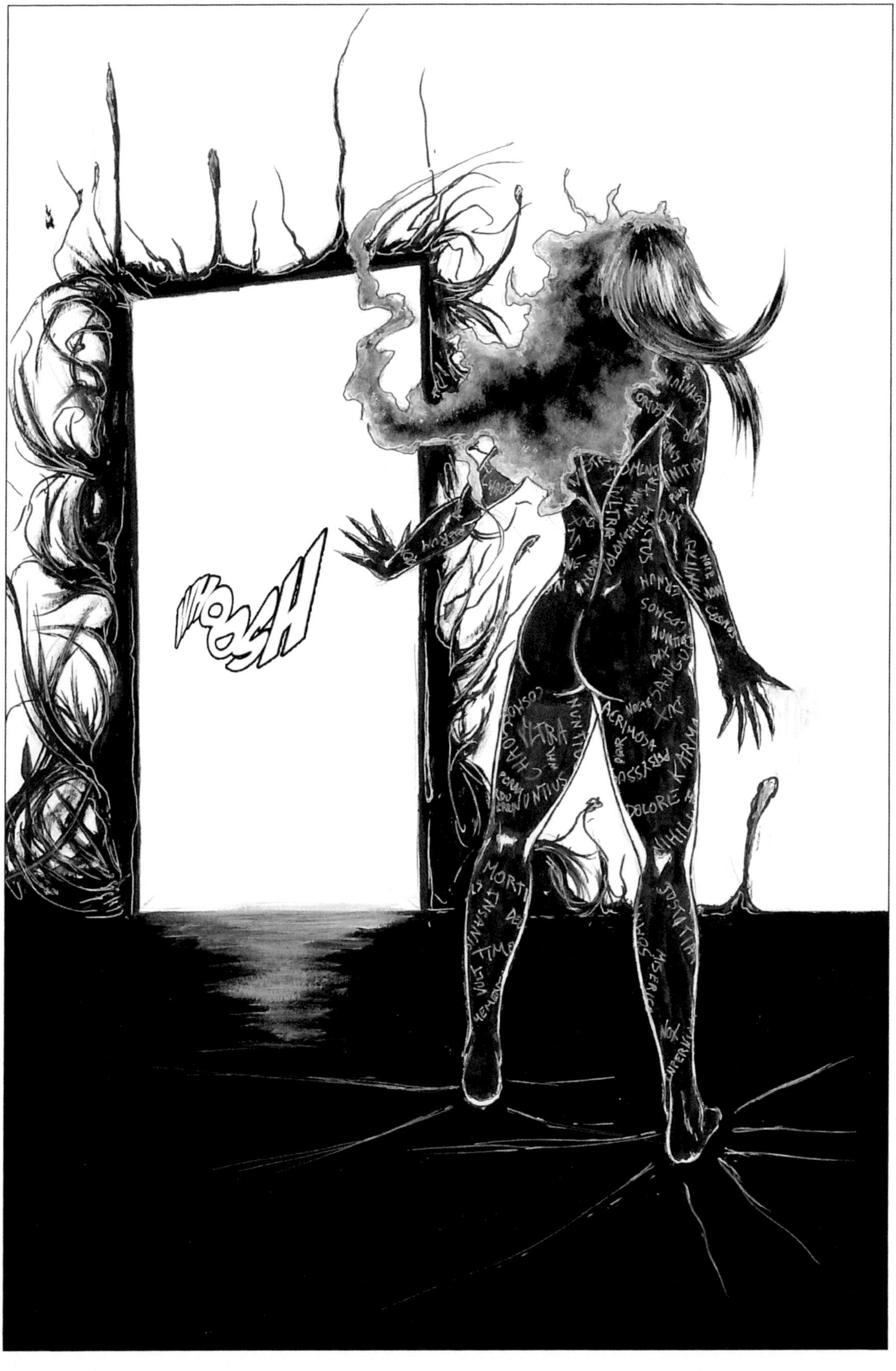
WHOOSH

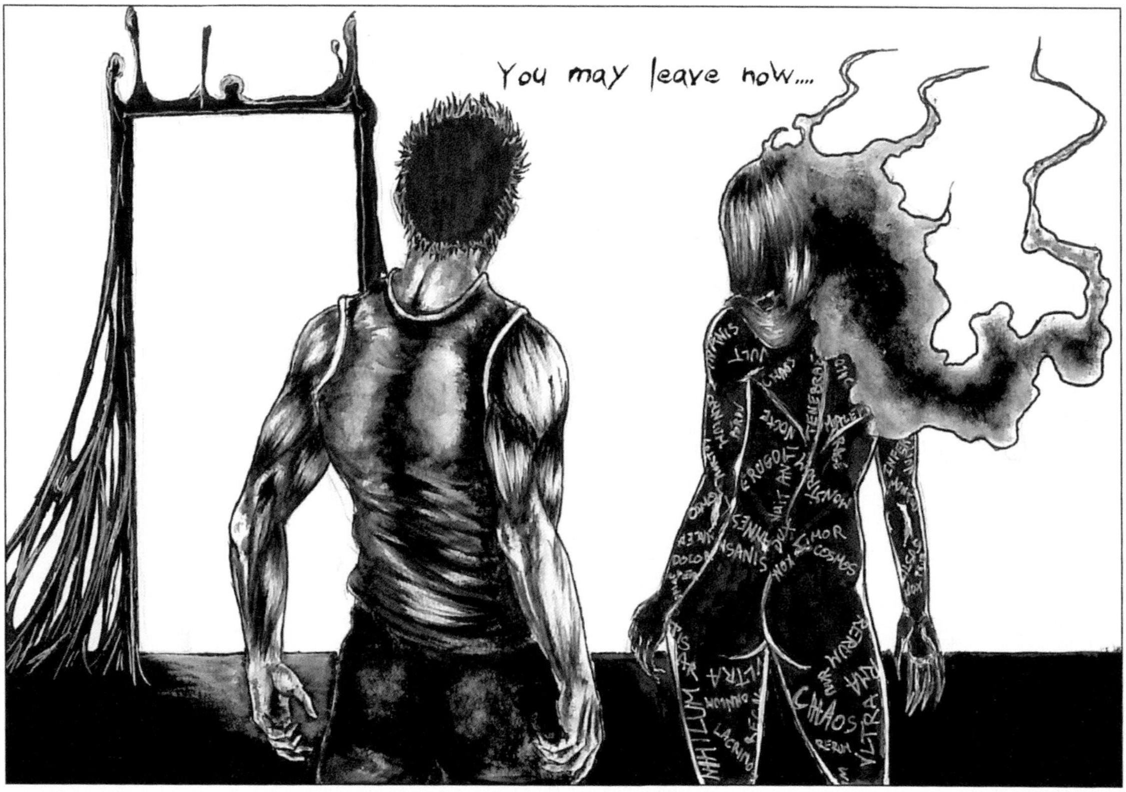
You may leave now....

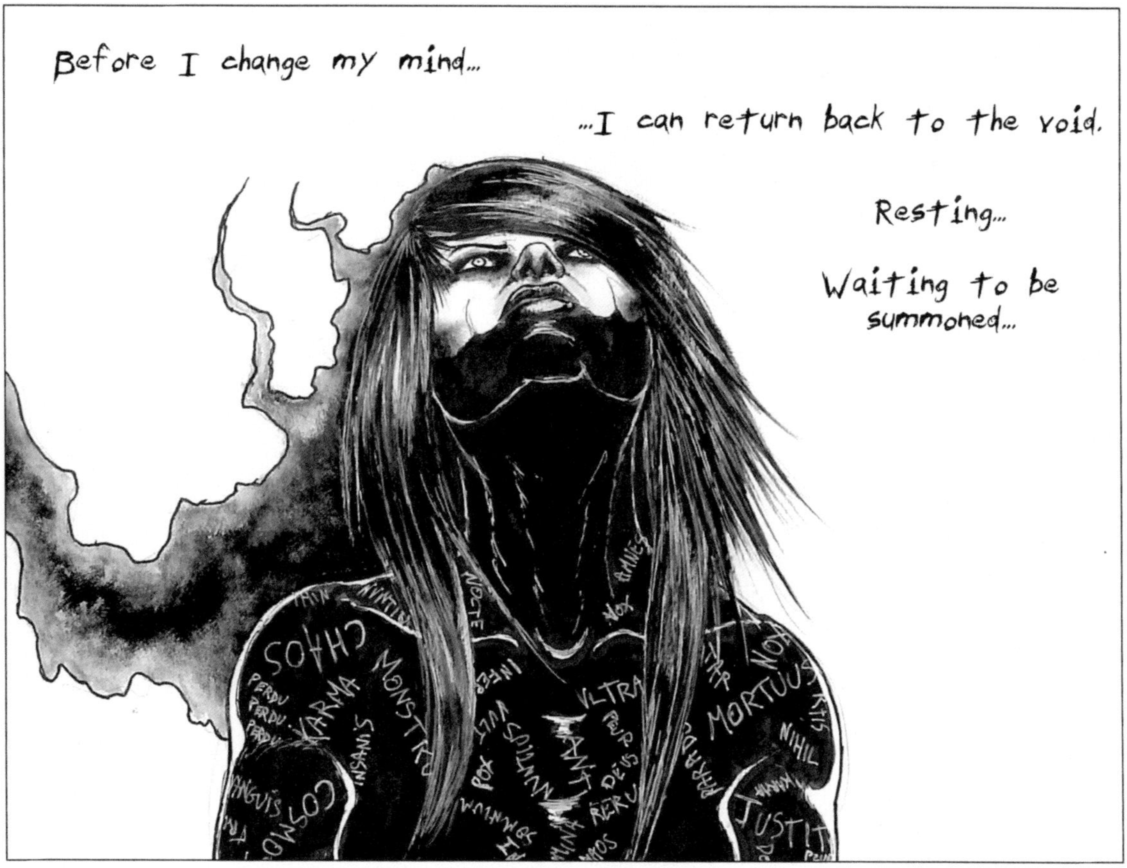
Before I change my mind...
...I can return back to the void.
Resting...
Waiting to be summoned...

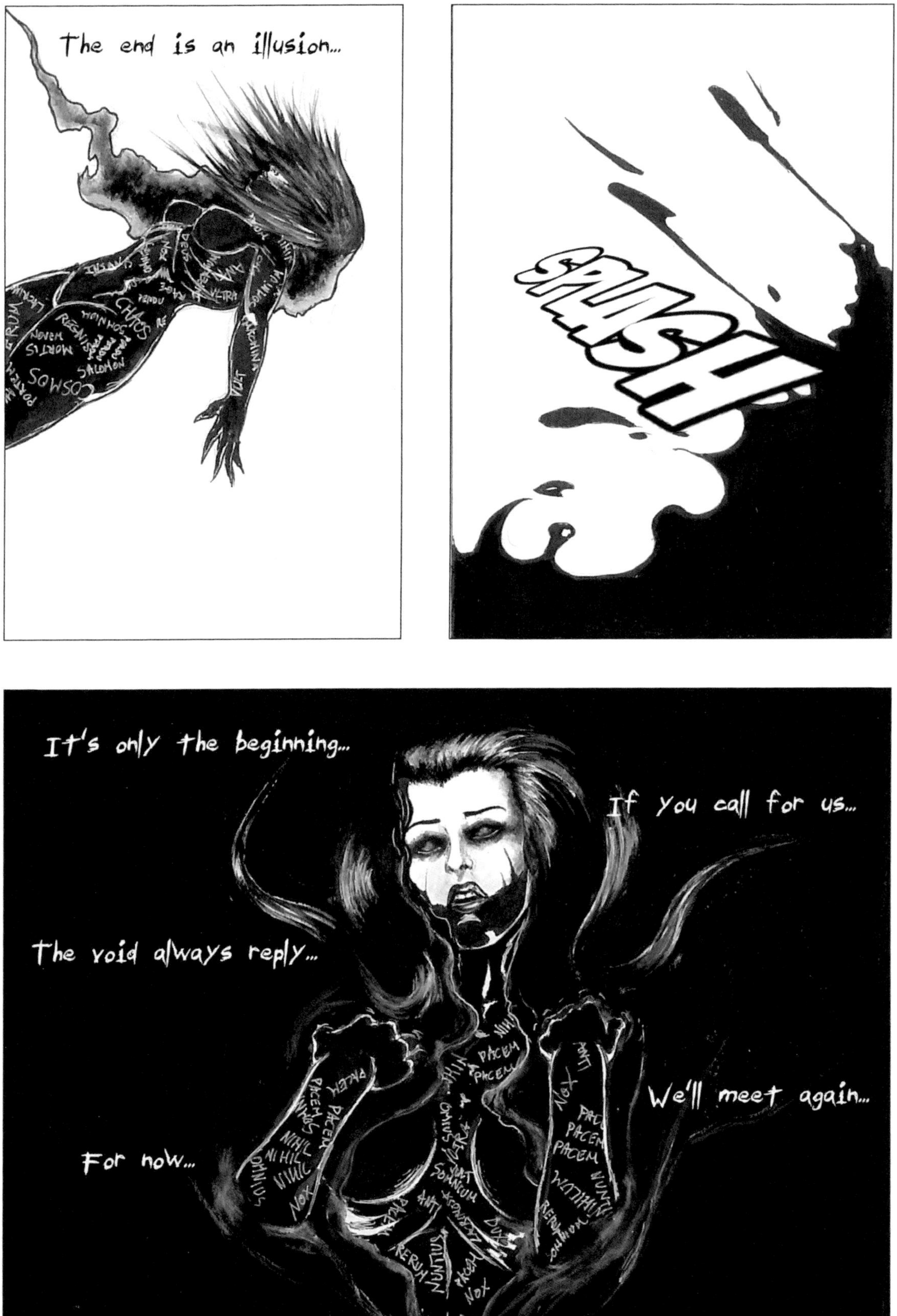
The end is an illusion...
SPLASH
It's only the beginning...
If you call for us...
The void always reply...
We'll meet again...
For now...

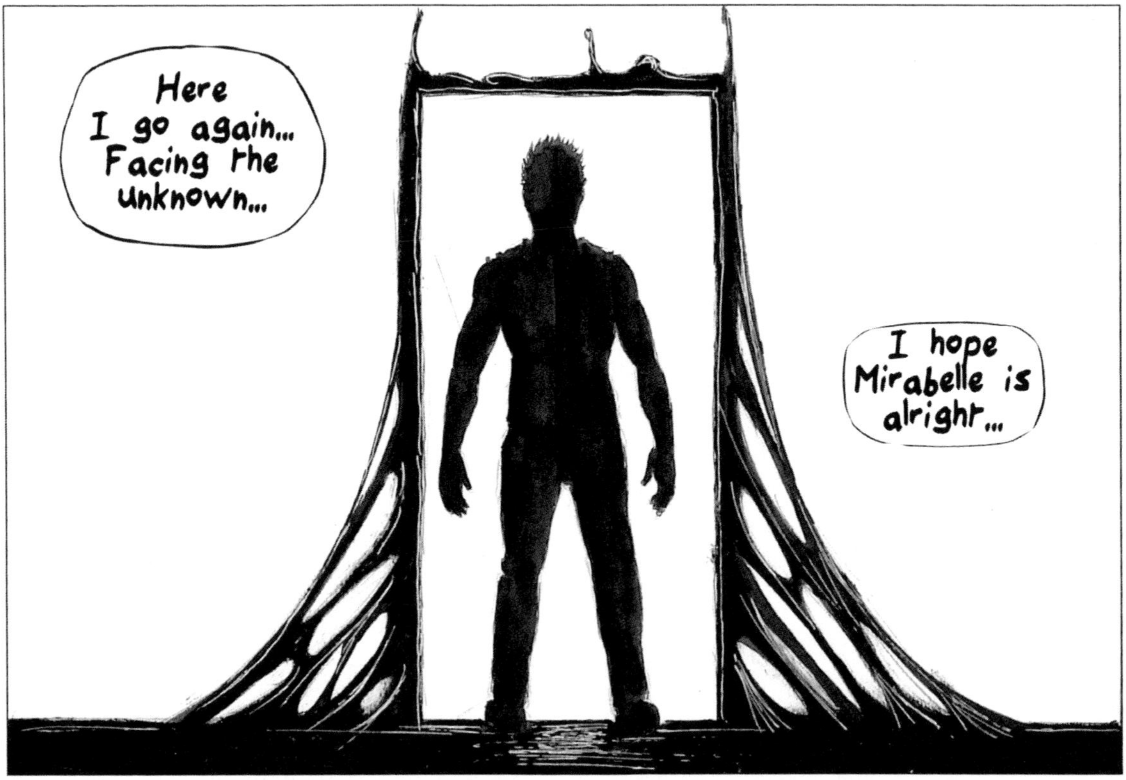
Here I go again... Facing the unknown...
I hope Mirabelle is alright...

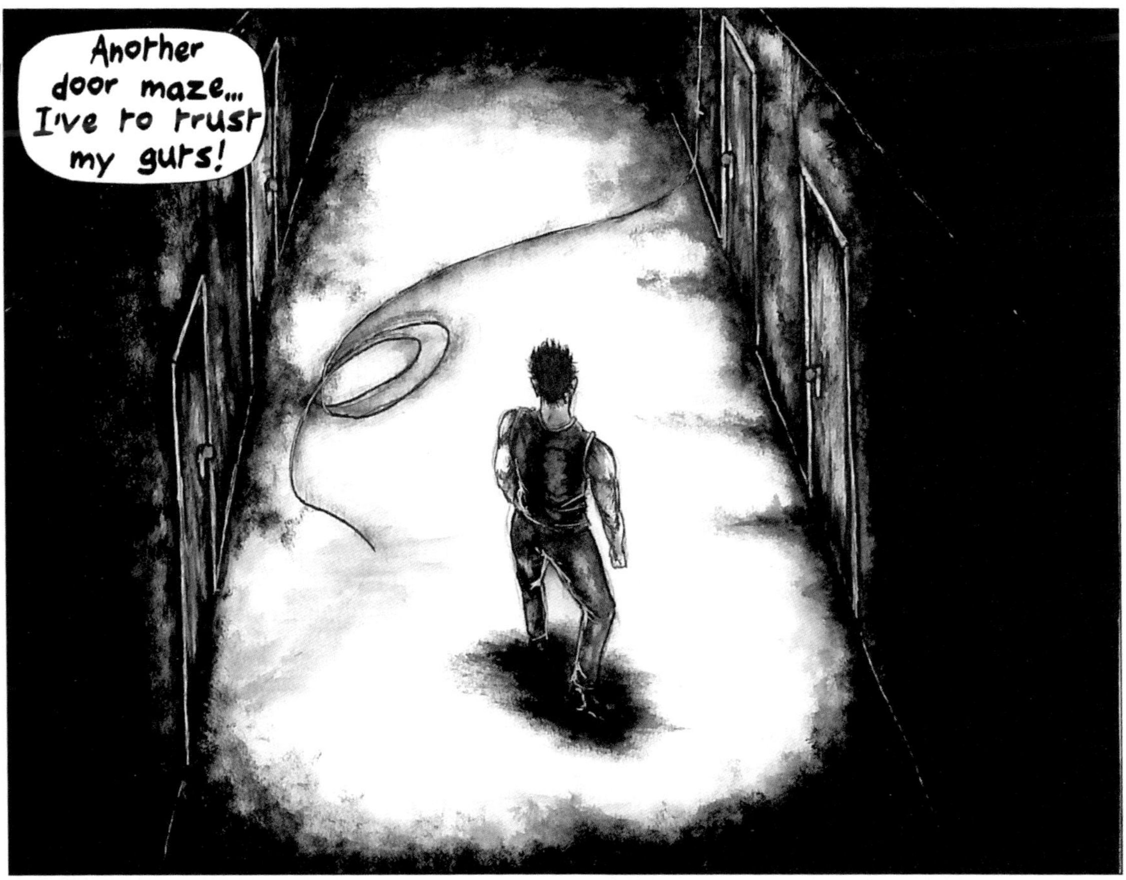
Another door maze... I've to trust my guts!

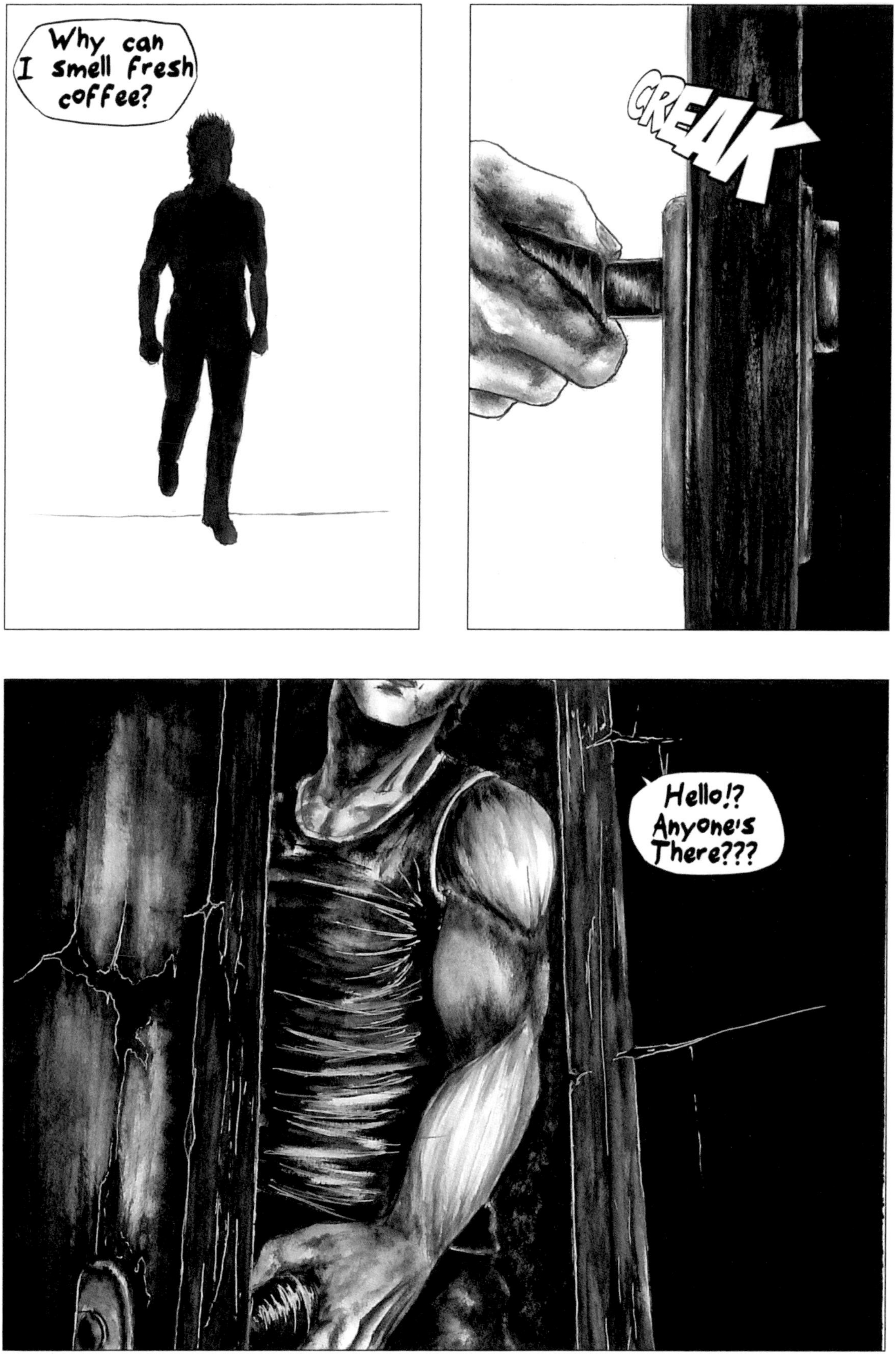
Why can I smell fresh coffee?
CREAK
Hello!? Anyone's There???

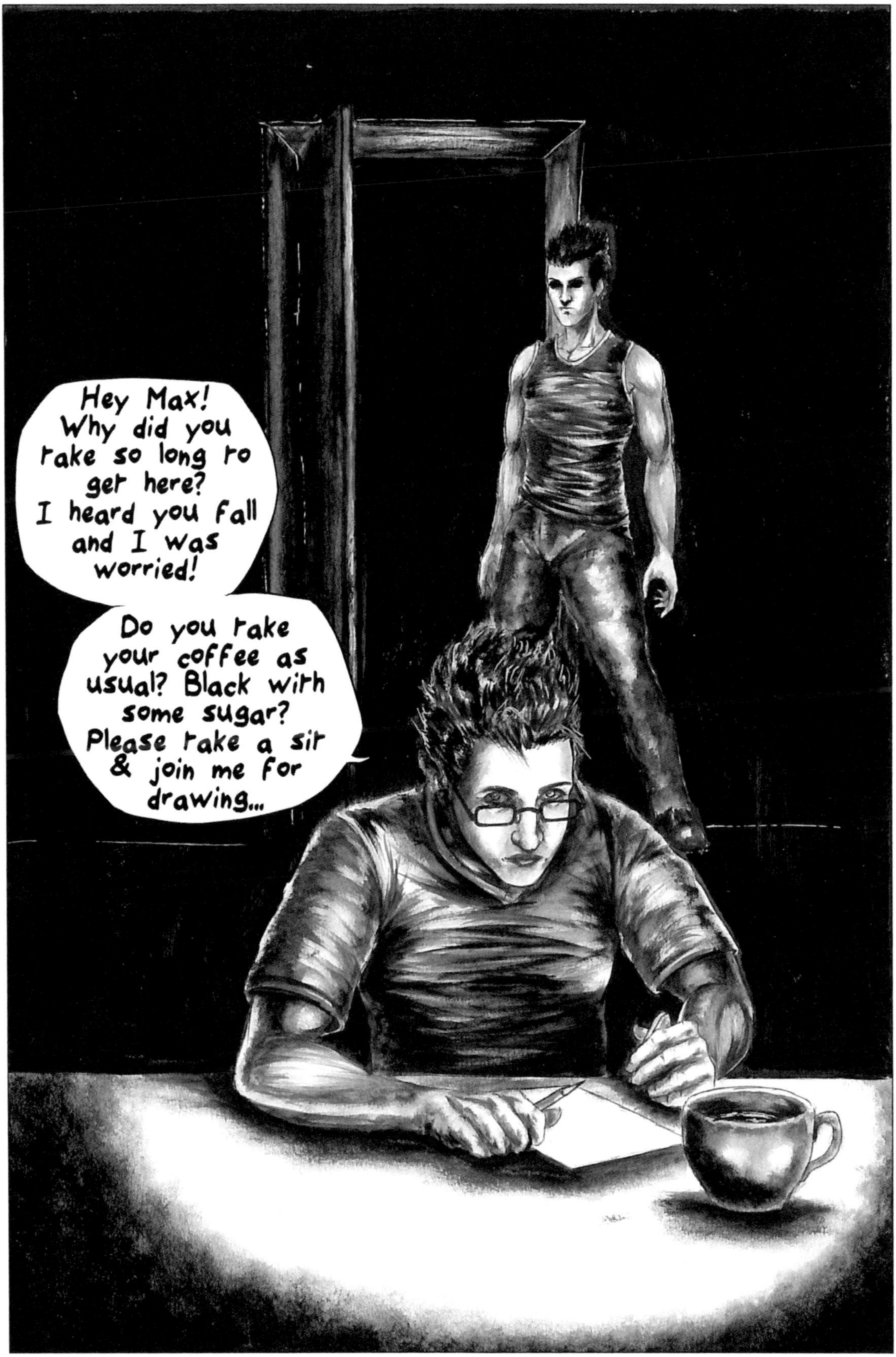
Hey Max! Why did you take so long to get here? I heard you fall and I was worried!
Do you take your coffee as usual? Black with some sugar? Please take a sit & join me for drawing...

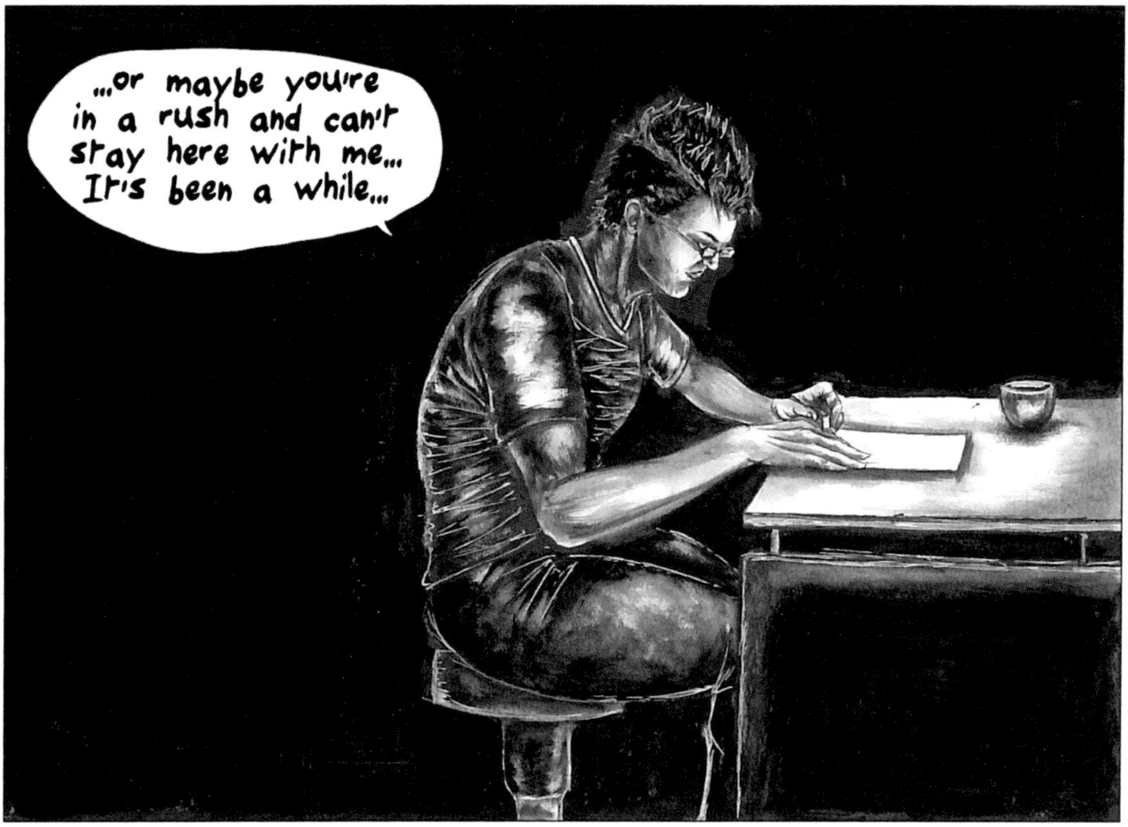
...or maybe you're in a rush and can't stay here with me... It's been a while...

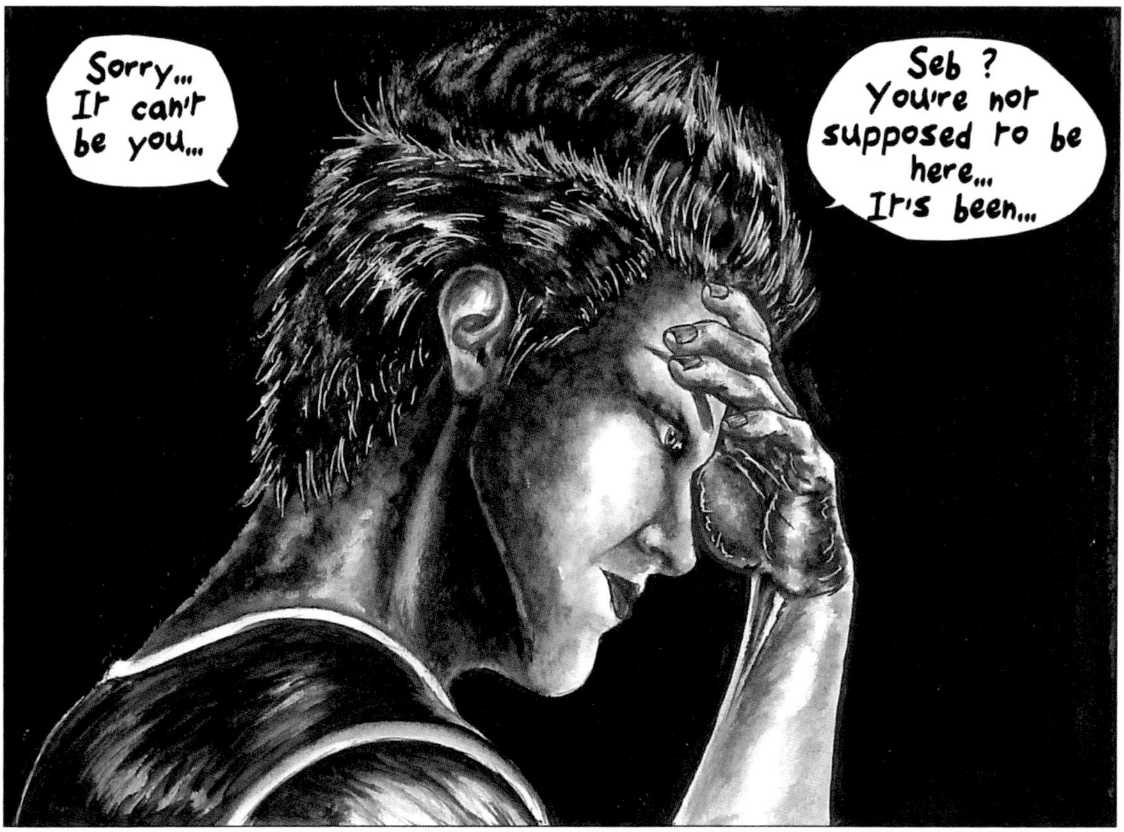
Sorry... It can't be you...
Seb ? You're not supposed to be here... It's been...

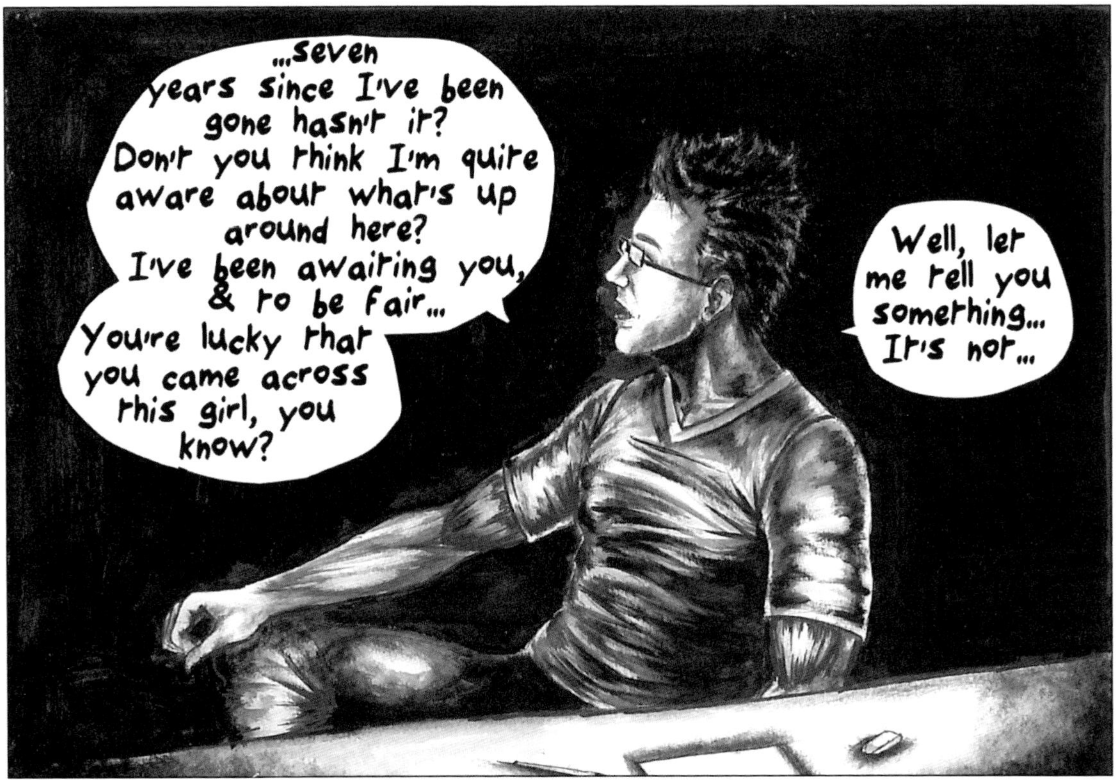
...seven years since I've been gone hasn't it? Don't you think I'm quite aware about what's up around here? I've been awaiting you, & to be fair...
You're lucky that you came across this girl, you know?
Well, let me tell you something... It's not...

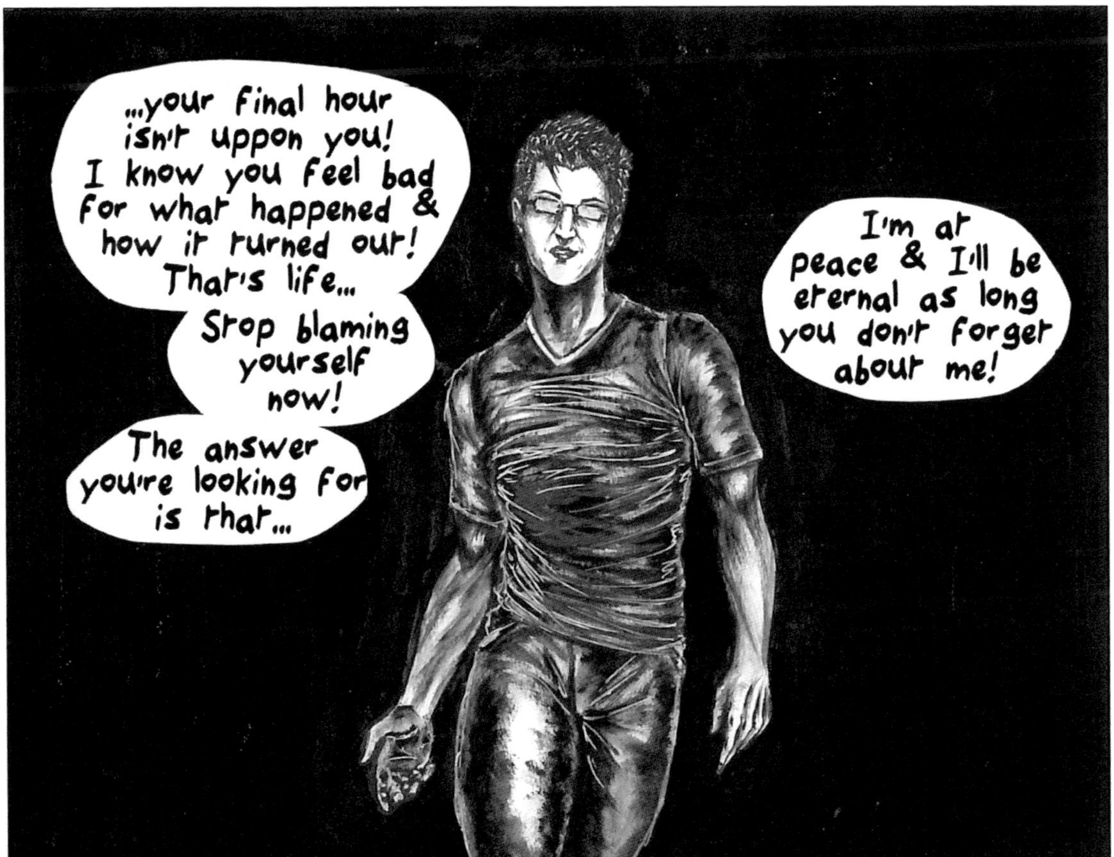
...your final hour isn't uppon you! I know you feel bad for what happened & how it turned out! That's life...
Stop blaming yourself now!
The answer you're looking for is that...
I'm at peace & I'll be eternal as long you don't forget about me!

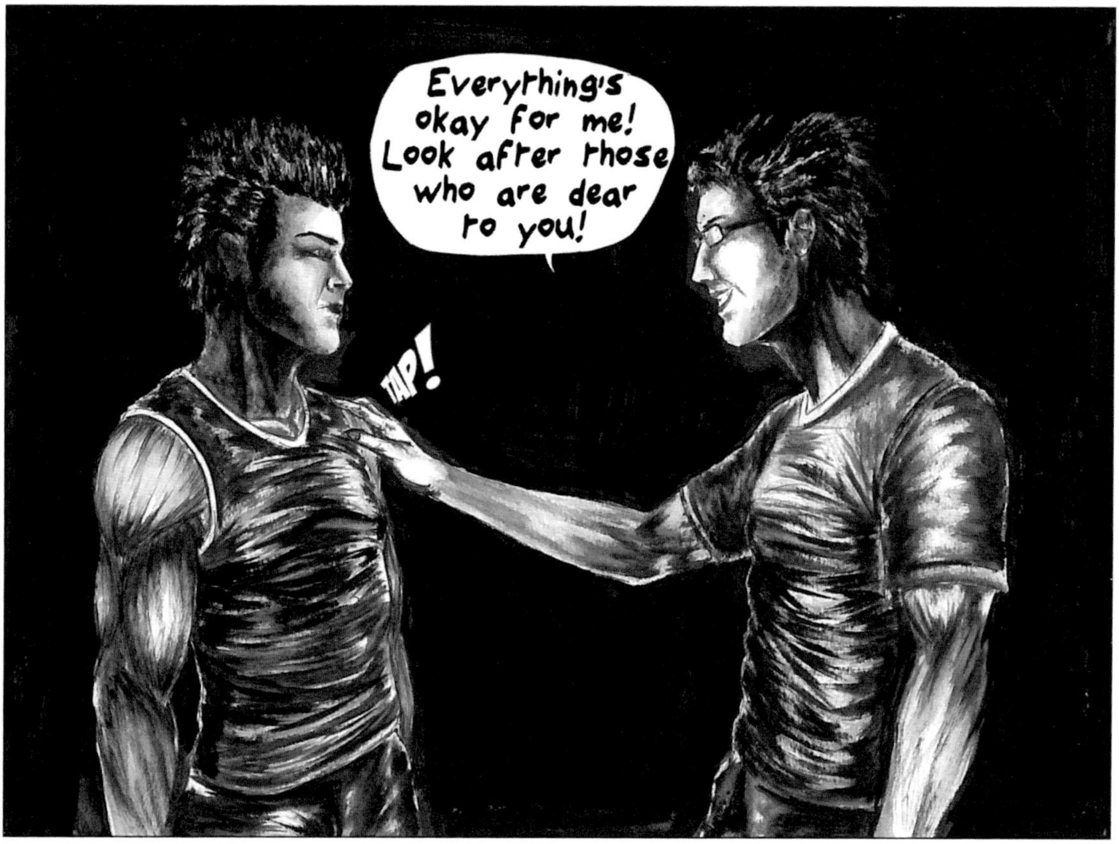
Everything's okay for me! Look after those who are dear to you!
TAP!

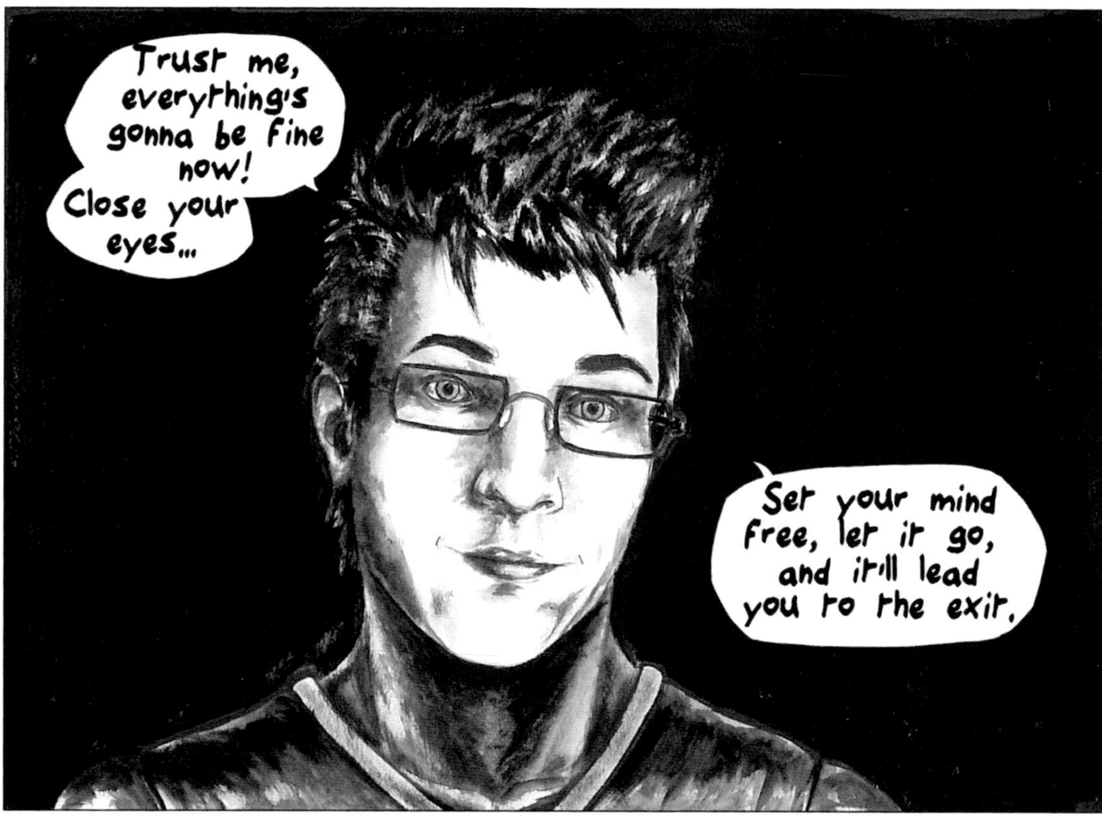
Trust me, everything's gonna be fine now!
Close your eyes...
Set your mind free, let it go, and it'll lead you to the exit.

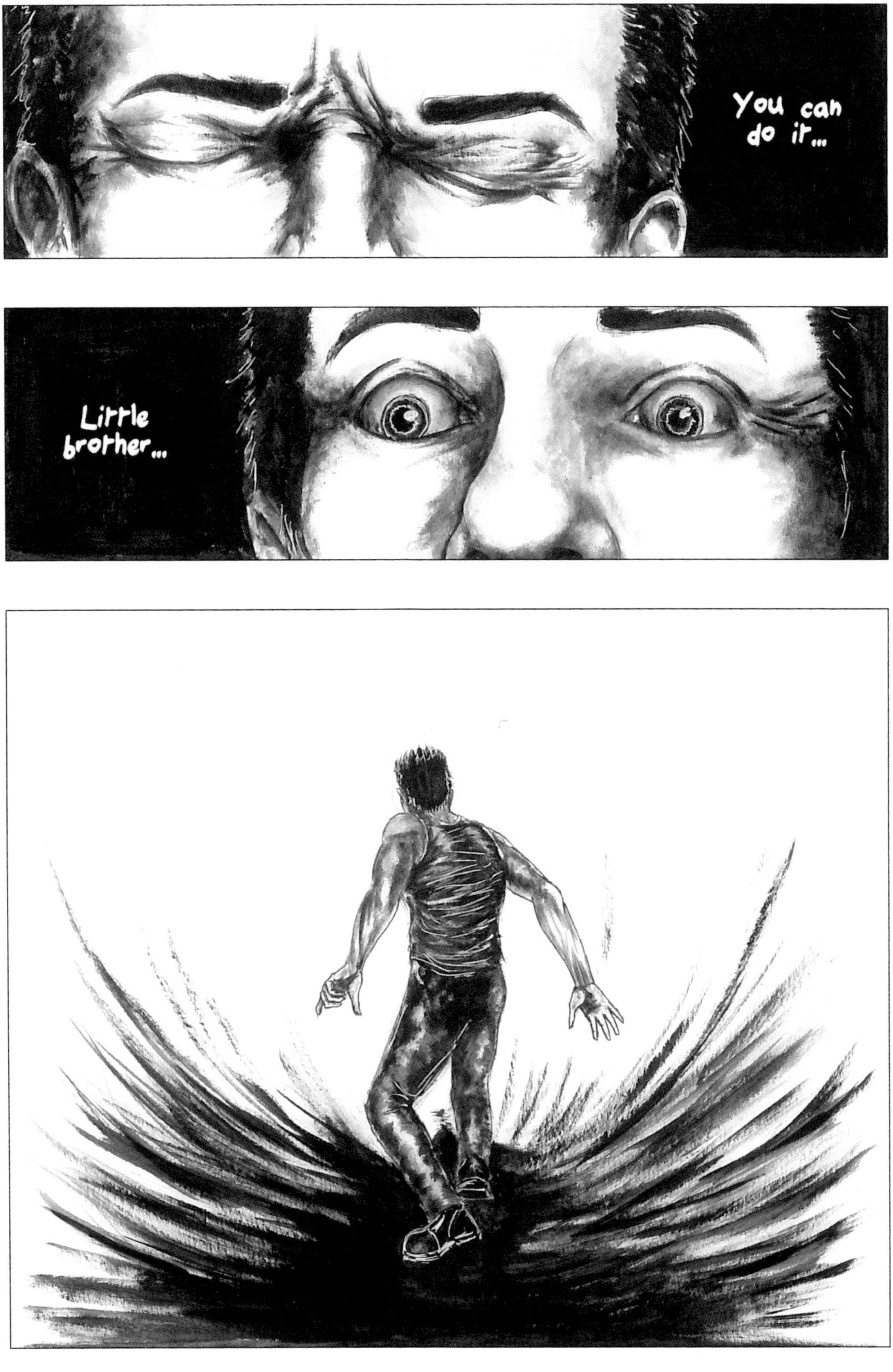
You can do it...
Little brother...

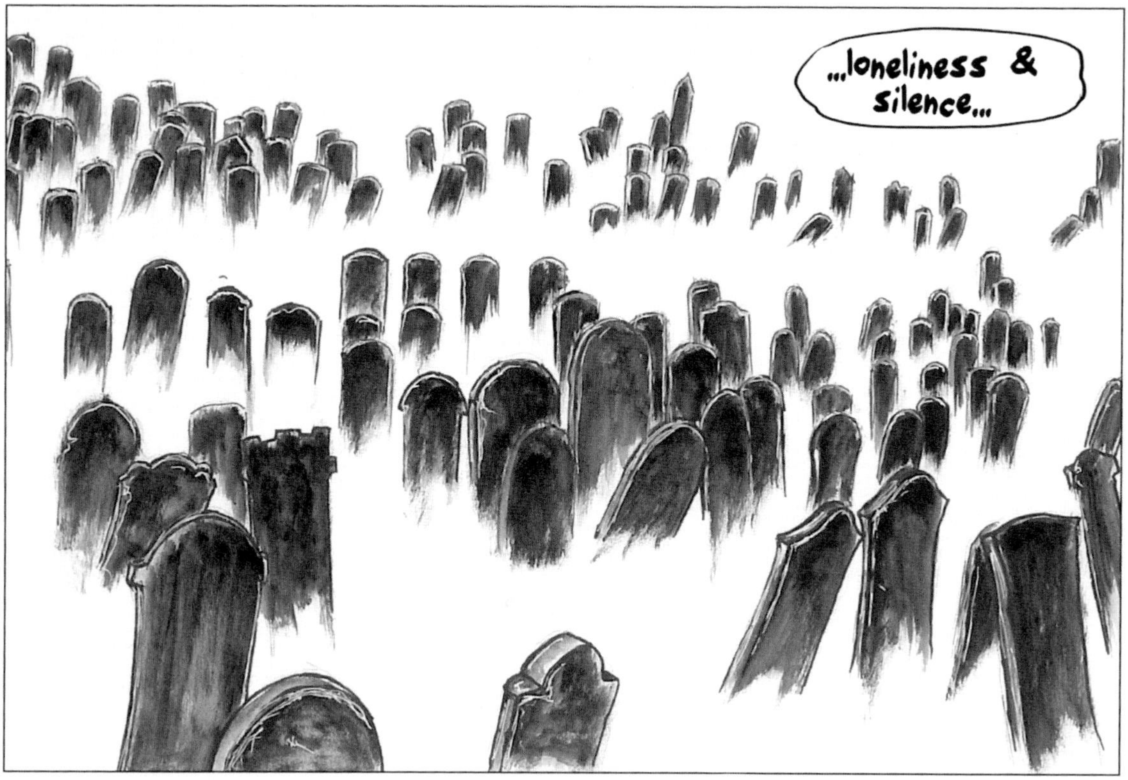
...loneliness & silence...

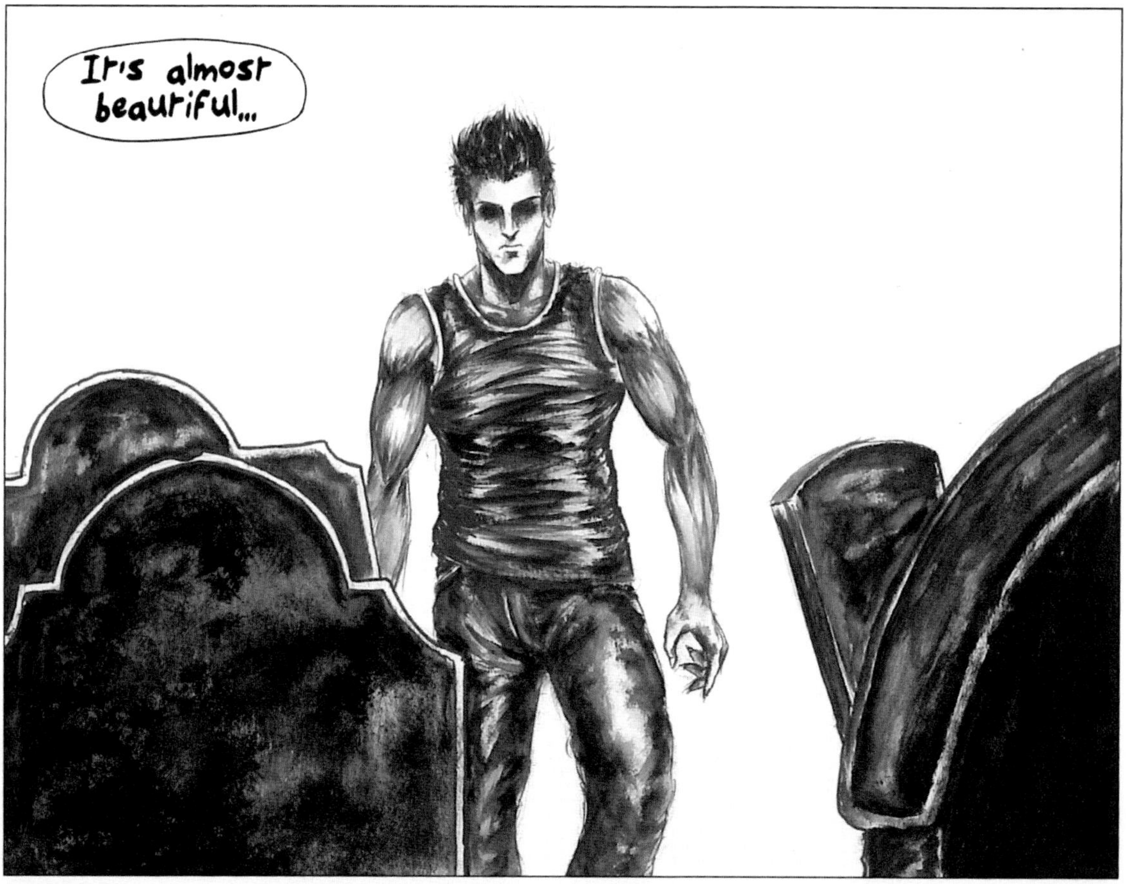
It's almost beautiful...

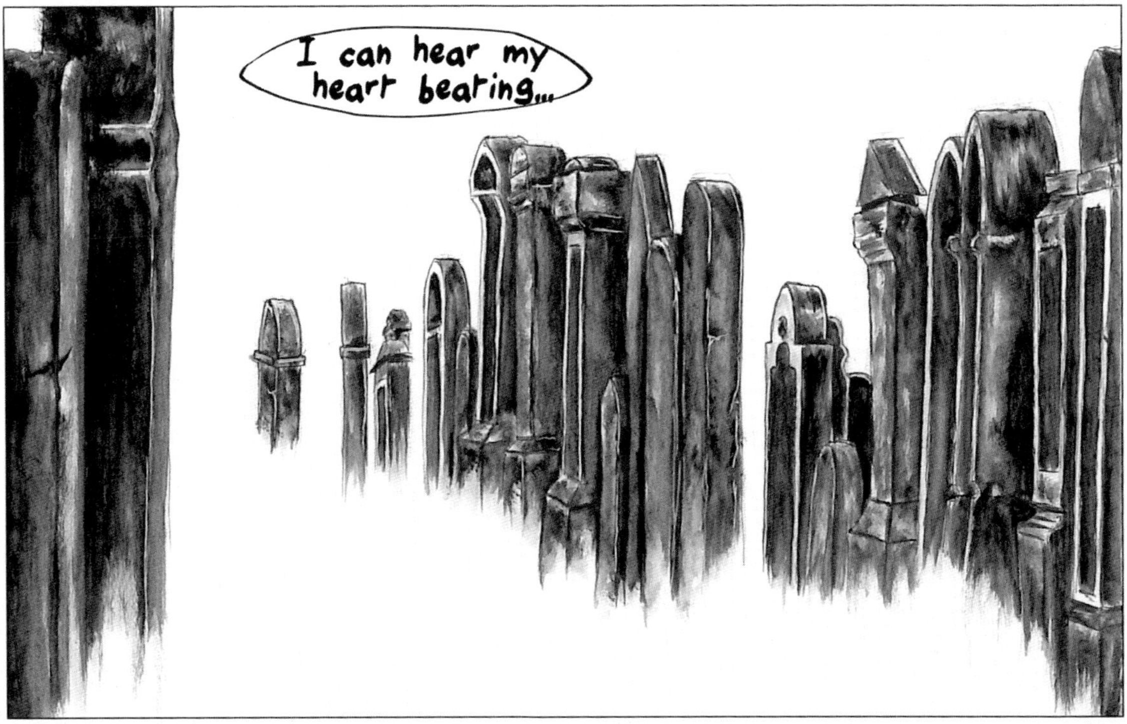
I can hear my heart beating...

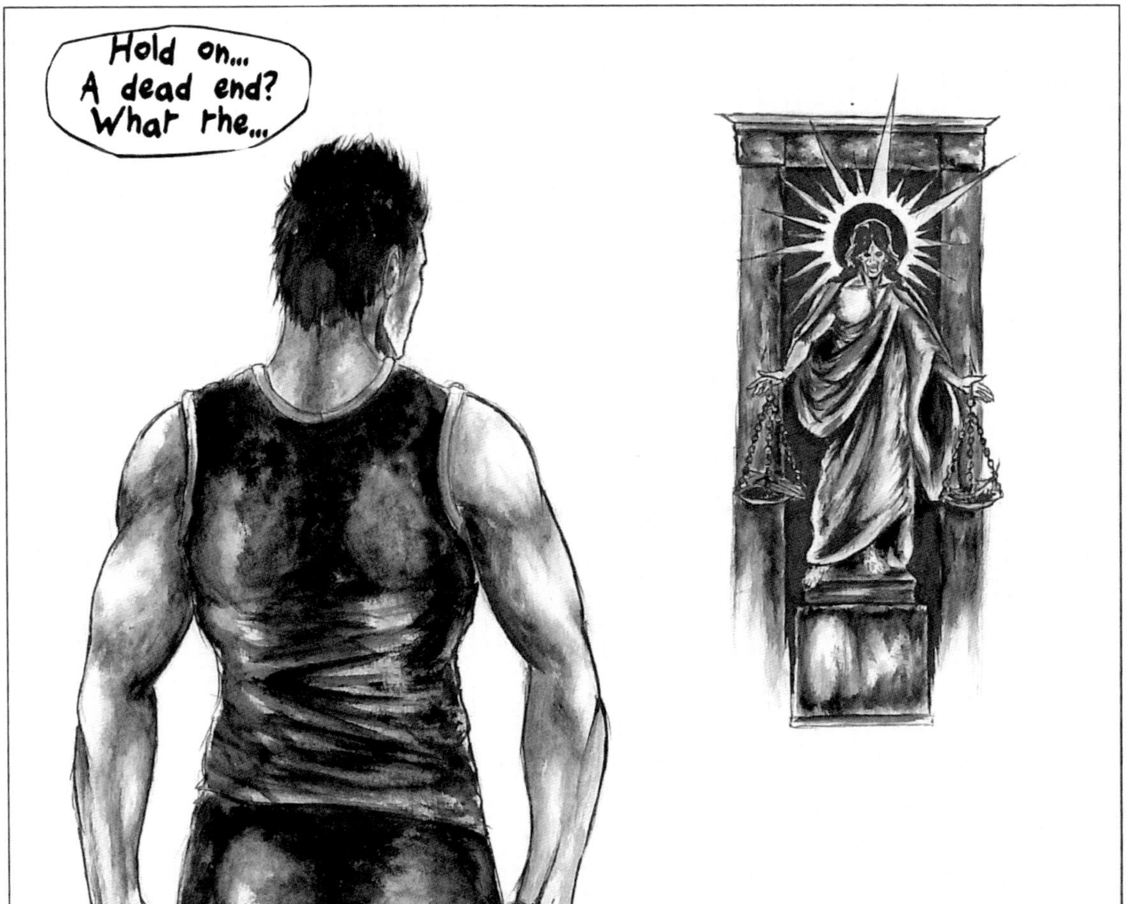
Hold on... A dead end? What the...

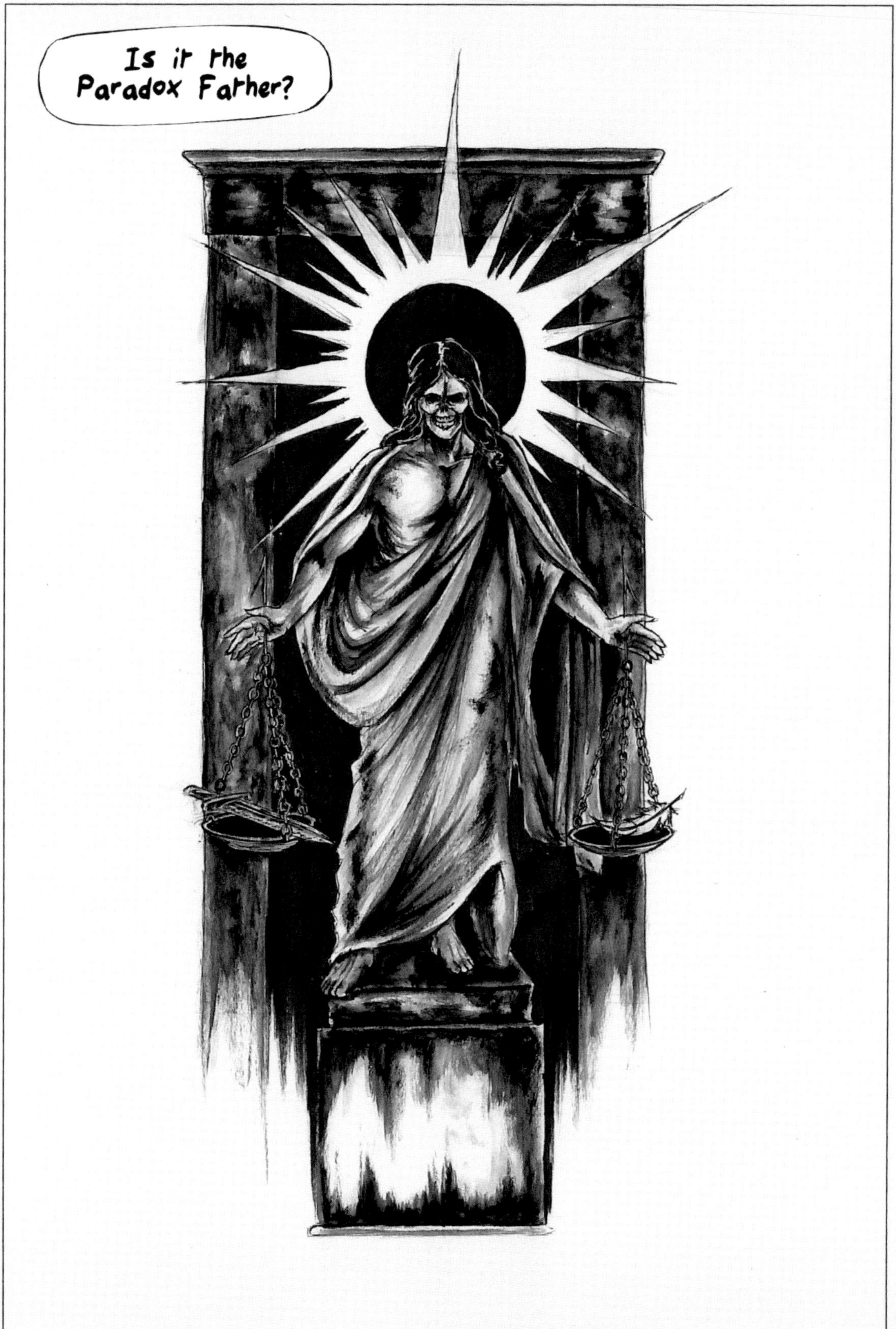
Is it the Paradox Father?

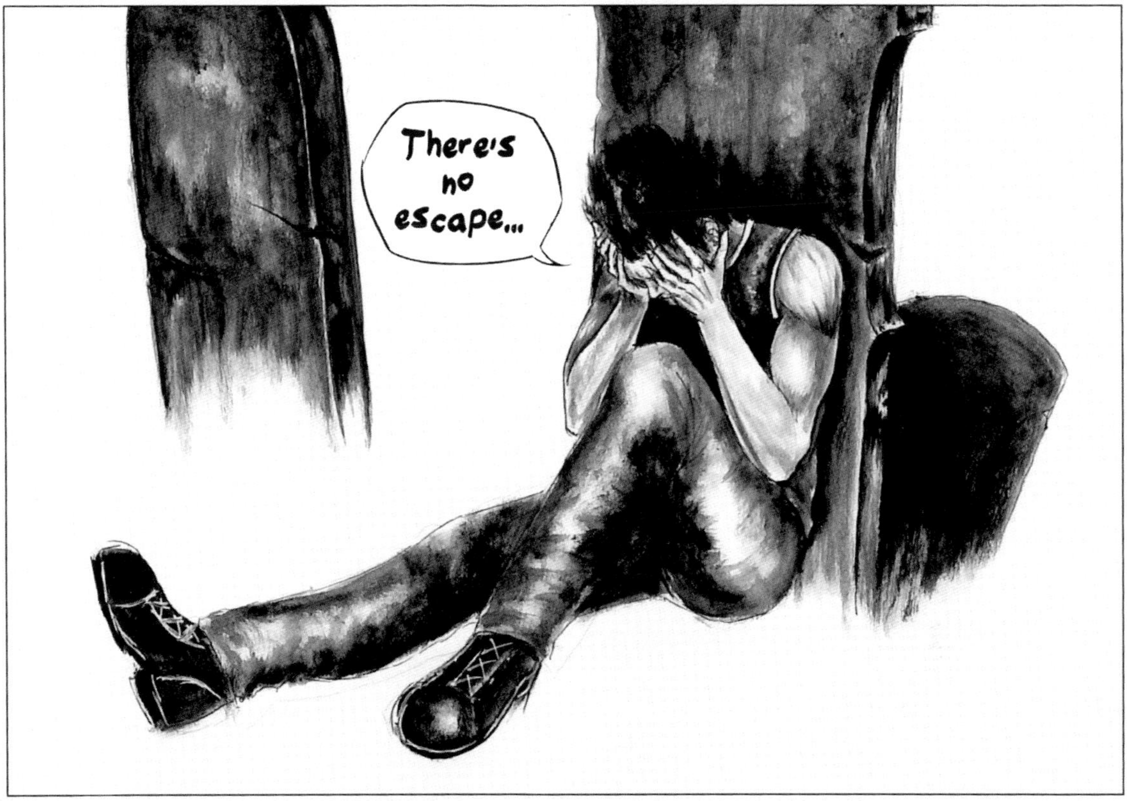
There's no escape...

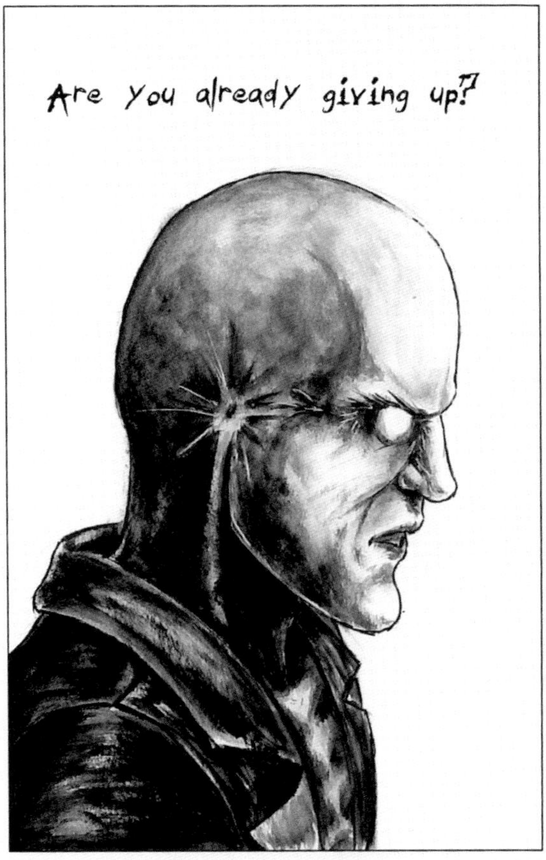
Are you already giving up??

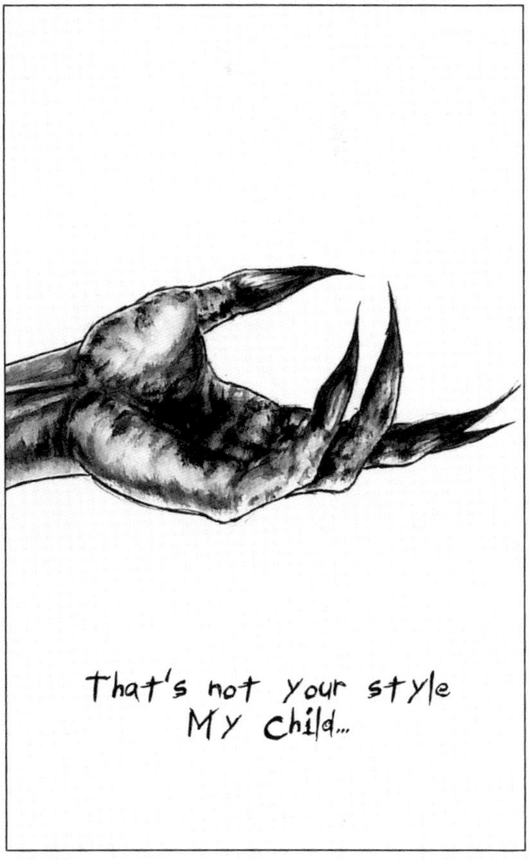
That's not your style
My Child...

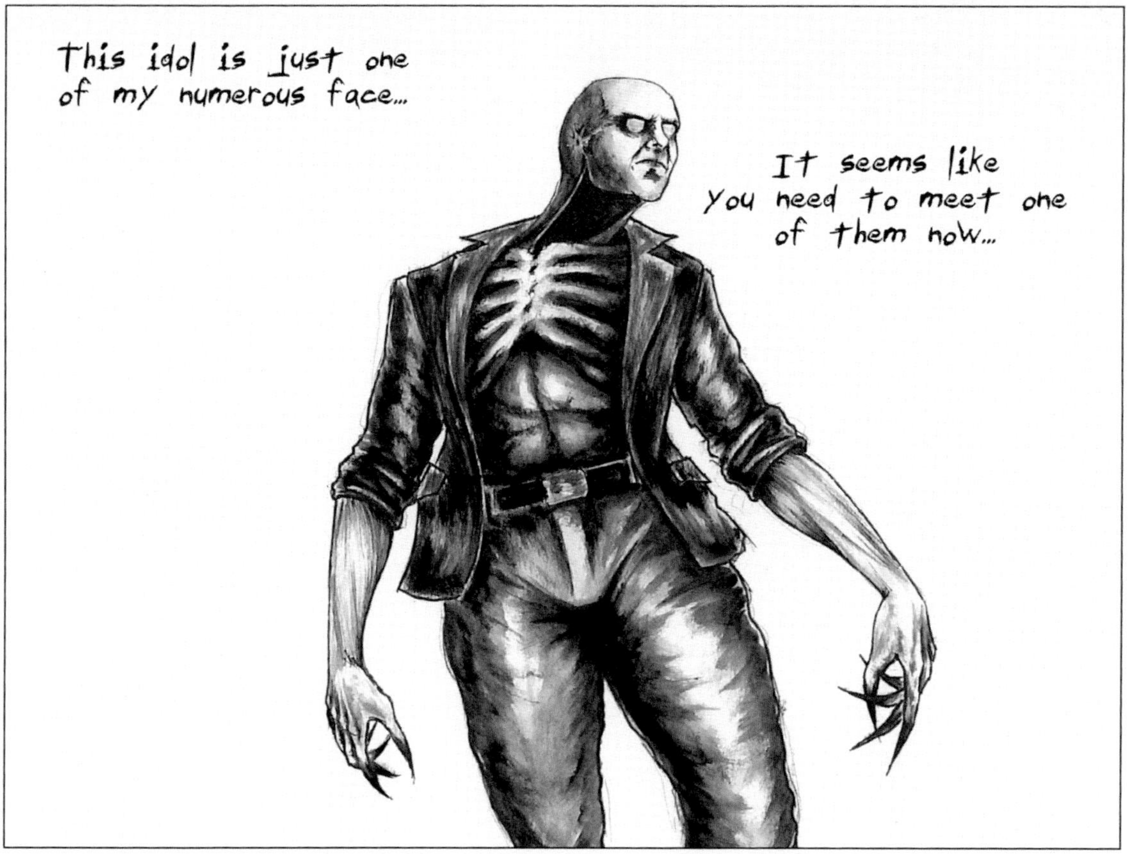
This idol is just one of my numerous face...
It seems like you need to meet one of them now...

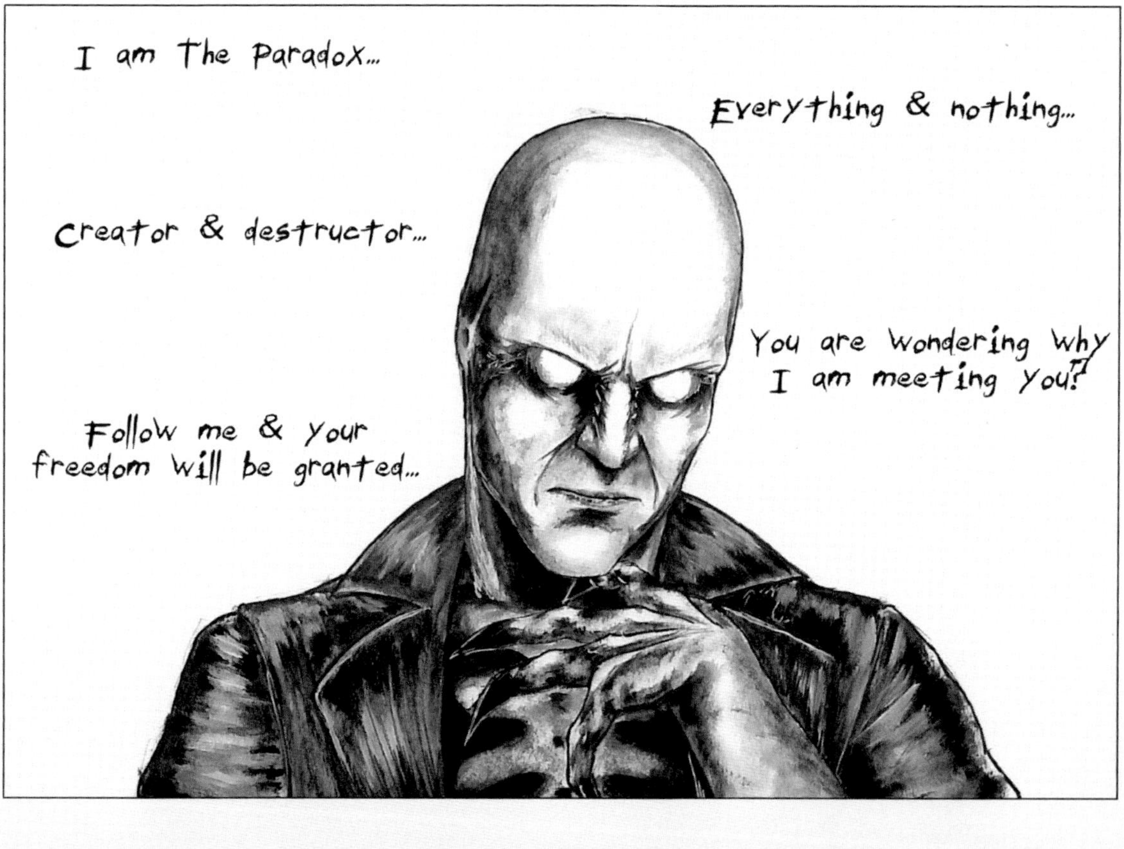
I am the paradox...
Everything & nothing...
Creator & destructor...
You are wondering why I am meeting you?
Follow me & your freedom will be granted...

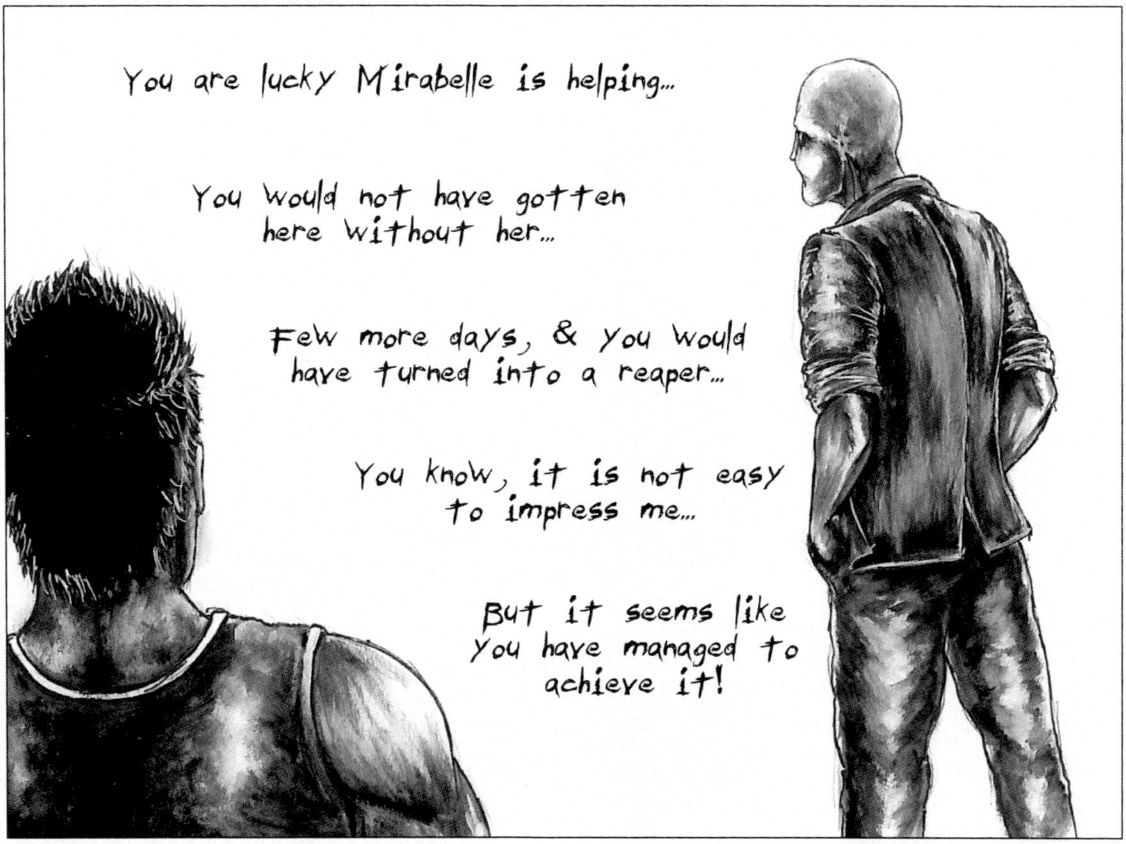
You are lucky Mirabelle is helping...
You would not have gotten here without her...
Few more days, & you would have turned into a reaper...
You know, it is not easy to impress me...
But it seems like you have managed to achieve it!

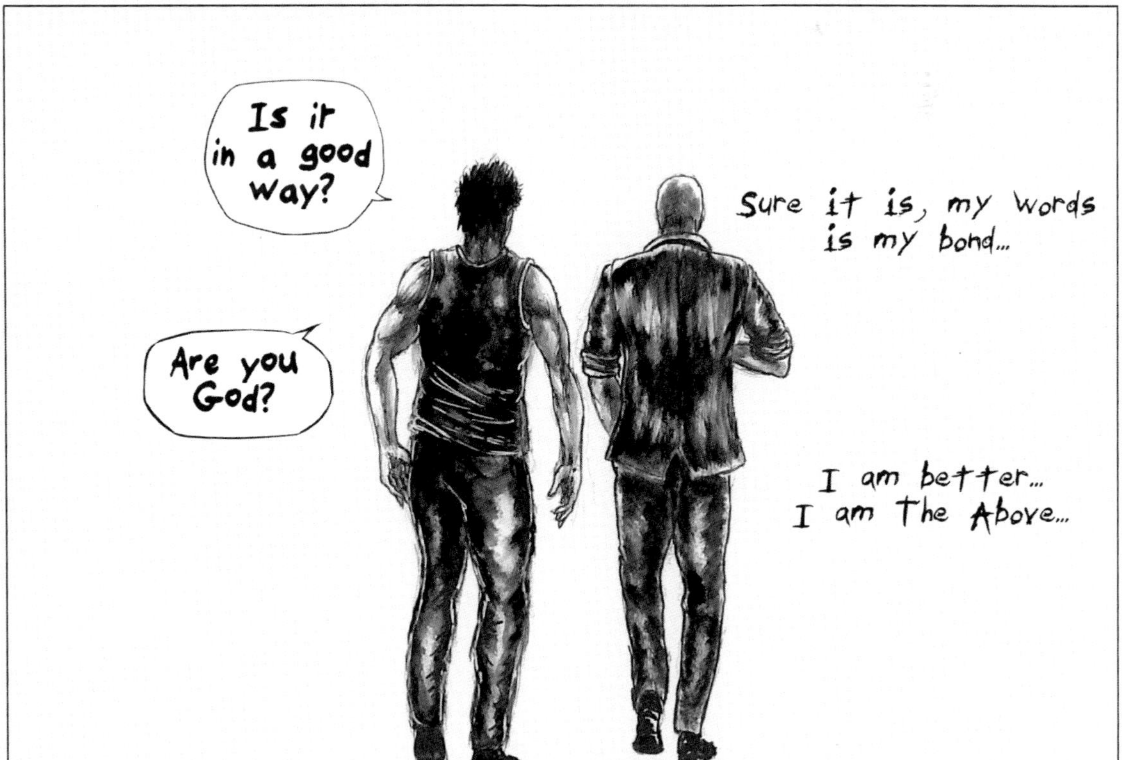
Is it in a good way?
Sure it is, my words is my bond...
Are you God?
I am better...
I am The Above...

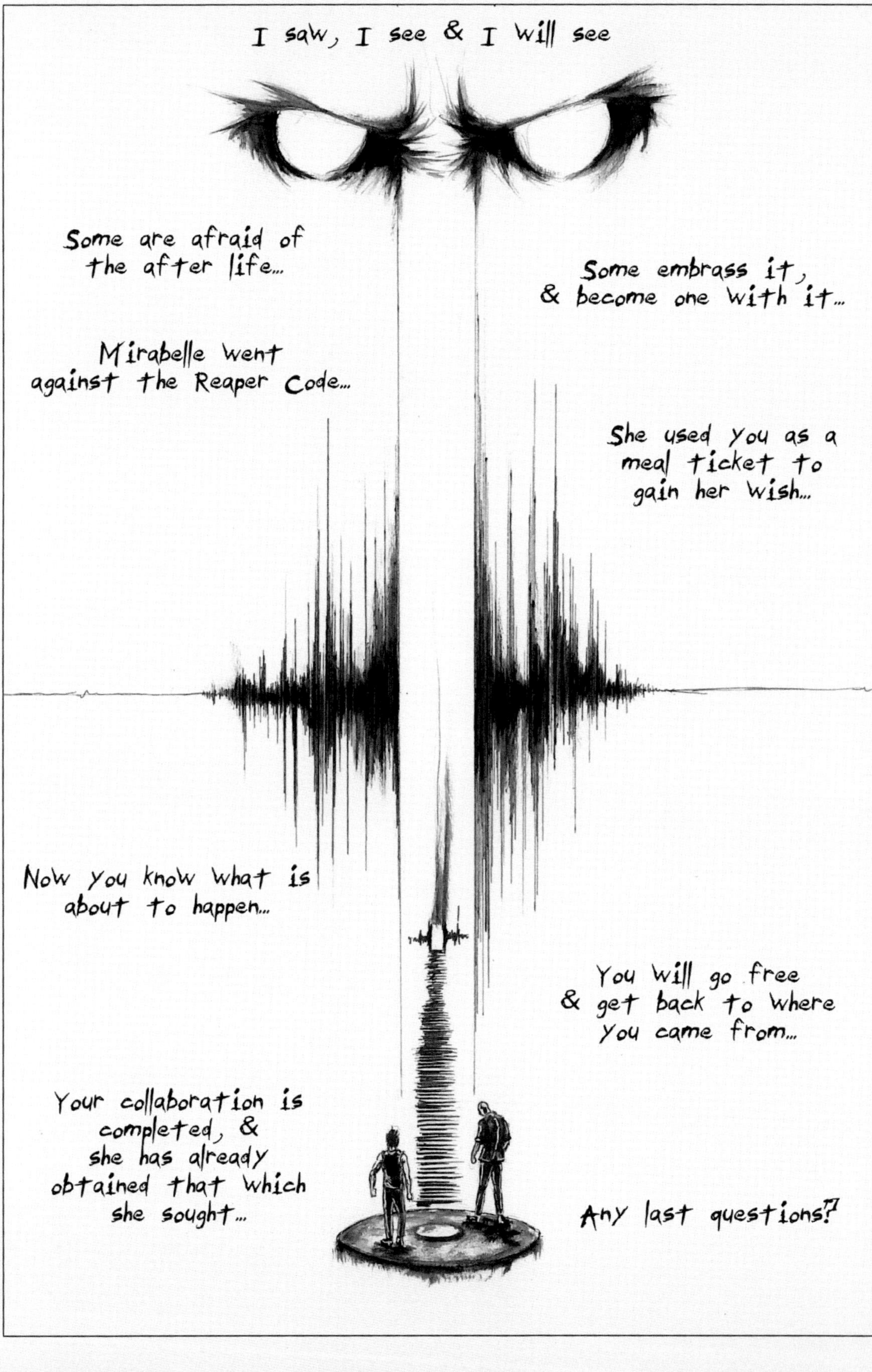
I saw, I see & I will see
Some are afraid of the after life...
Some embrass it, & become one with it...
Mirabelle went against the Reaper Code...
She used you as a meal ticket to gain her wish...
Now you know what is about to happen...
You will go free & get back to where you came from...
Your collaboration is completed, & she has already obtained that which she sought...
Any last questions?!

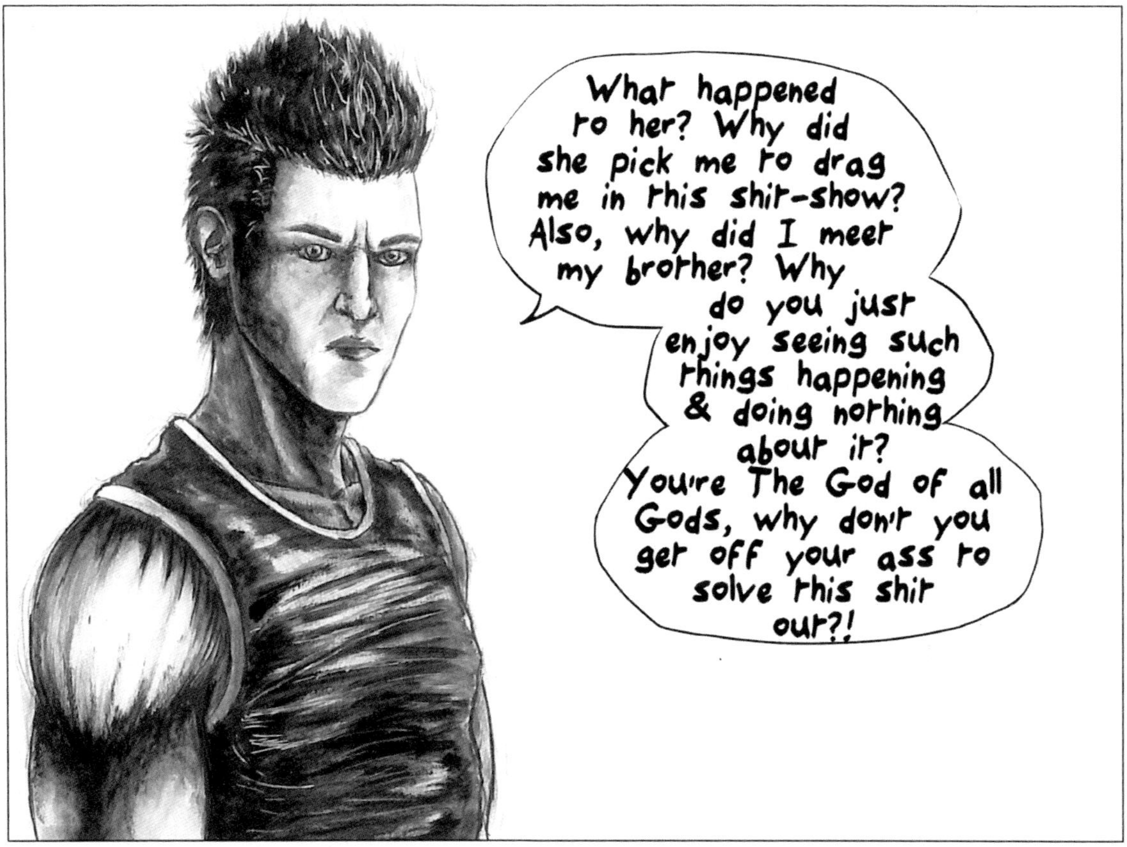
What happened to her? Why did she pick me to drag me in this shit-show? Also, why did I meet my brother? Why do you just enjoy seeing such things happening & doing nothing about it? You're The God of all Gods, why don't you get off your ass to solve this shit out?!

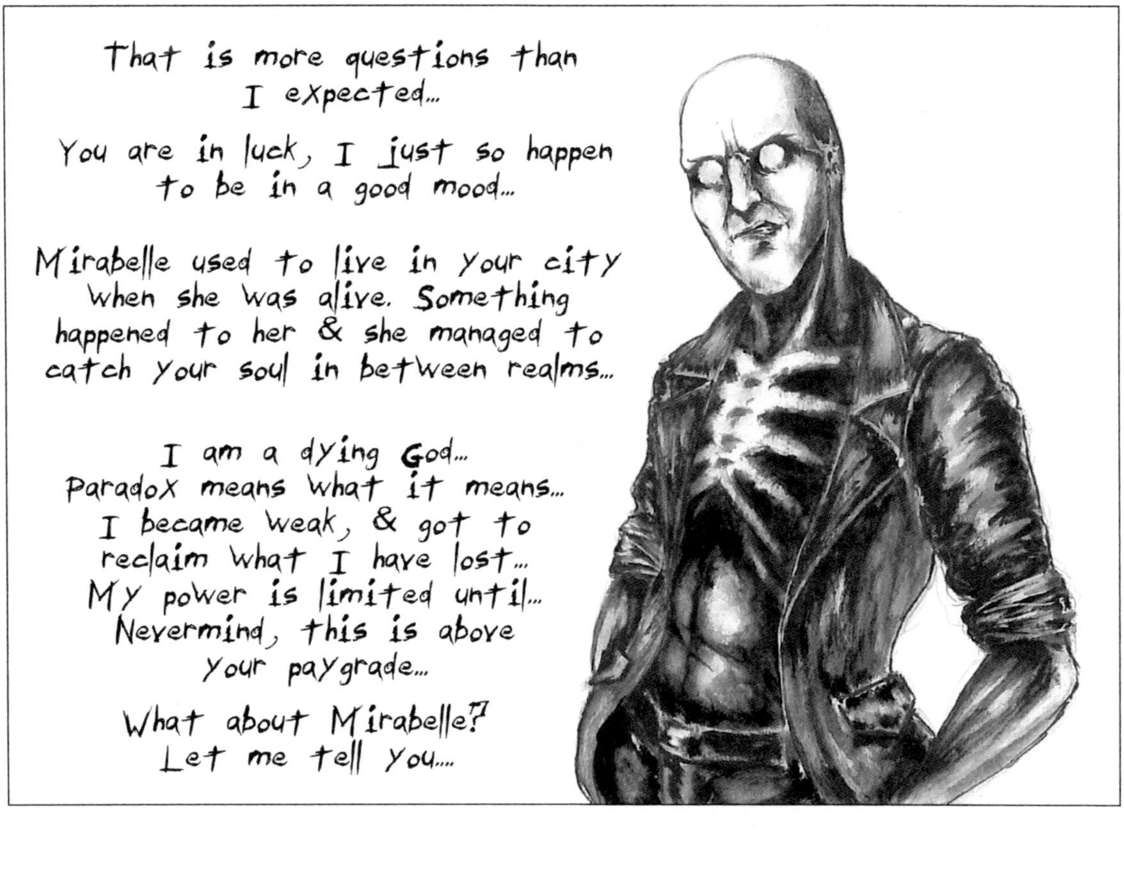
That is more questions than I expected...
You are in luck, I just so happen to be in a good mood...
Mirabelle used to live in your city when she was alive. Something happened to her & she managed to catch your soul in between realms...
I am a dying God... Paradox means what it means... I became weak, & got to reclaim what I have lost... My power is limited until... Nevermind, this is above your paygrade...
What about Mirabelle? Let me tell you....

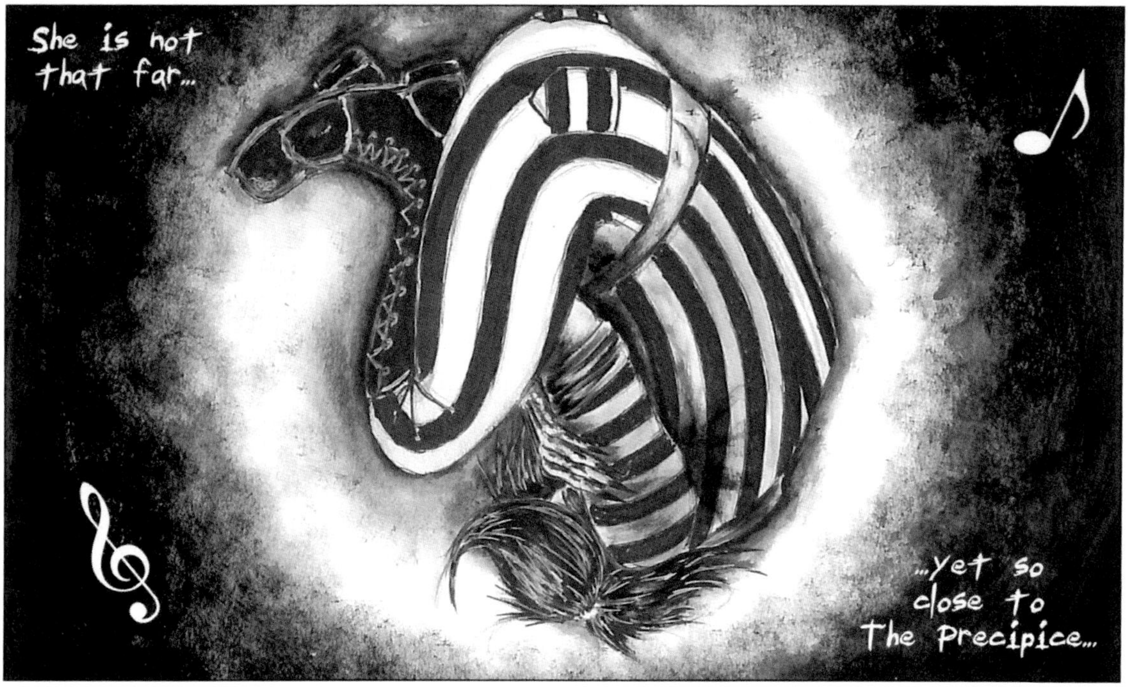
She is not that far...
...yet so close to The precipice...

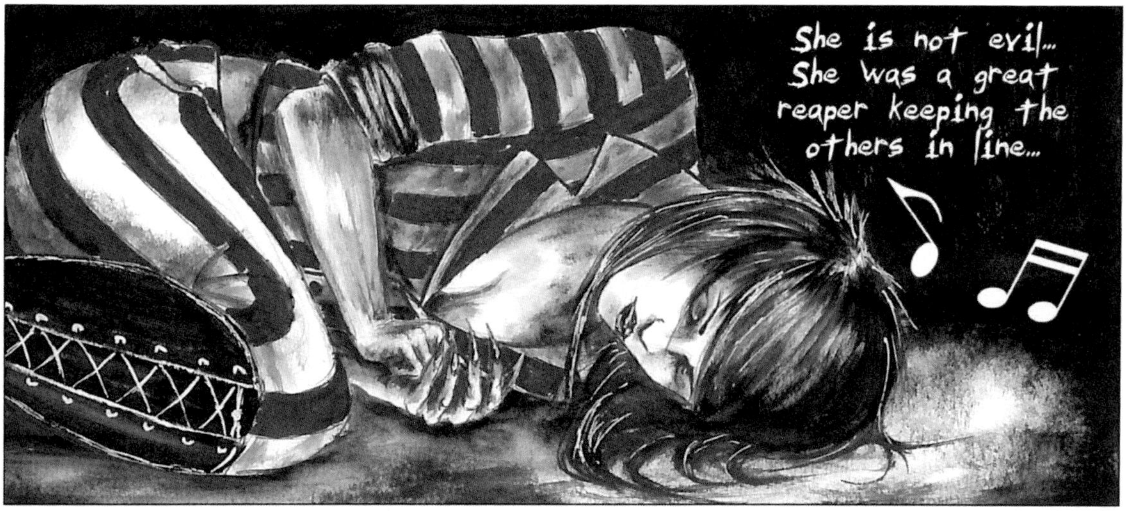
She is not evil... She was a great reaper keeping the others in line...

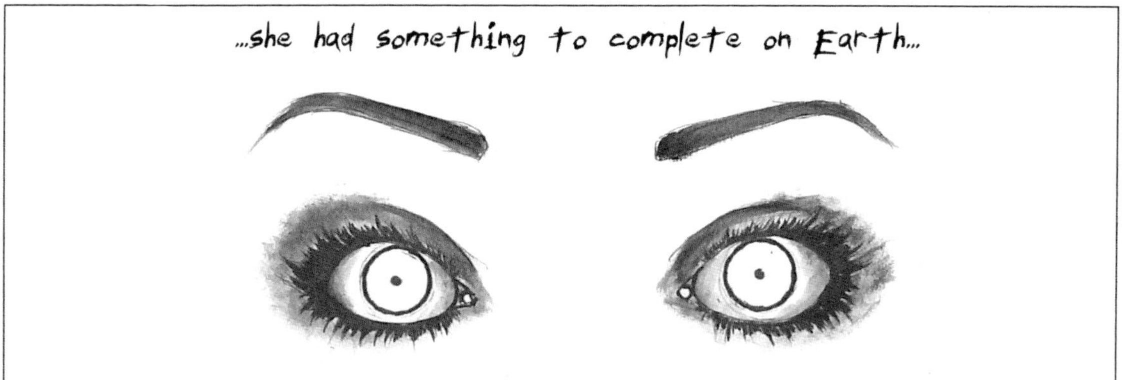
...she had something to complete on Earth...

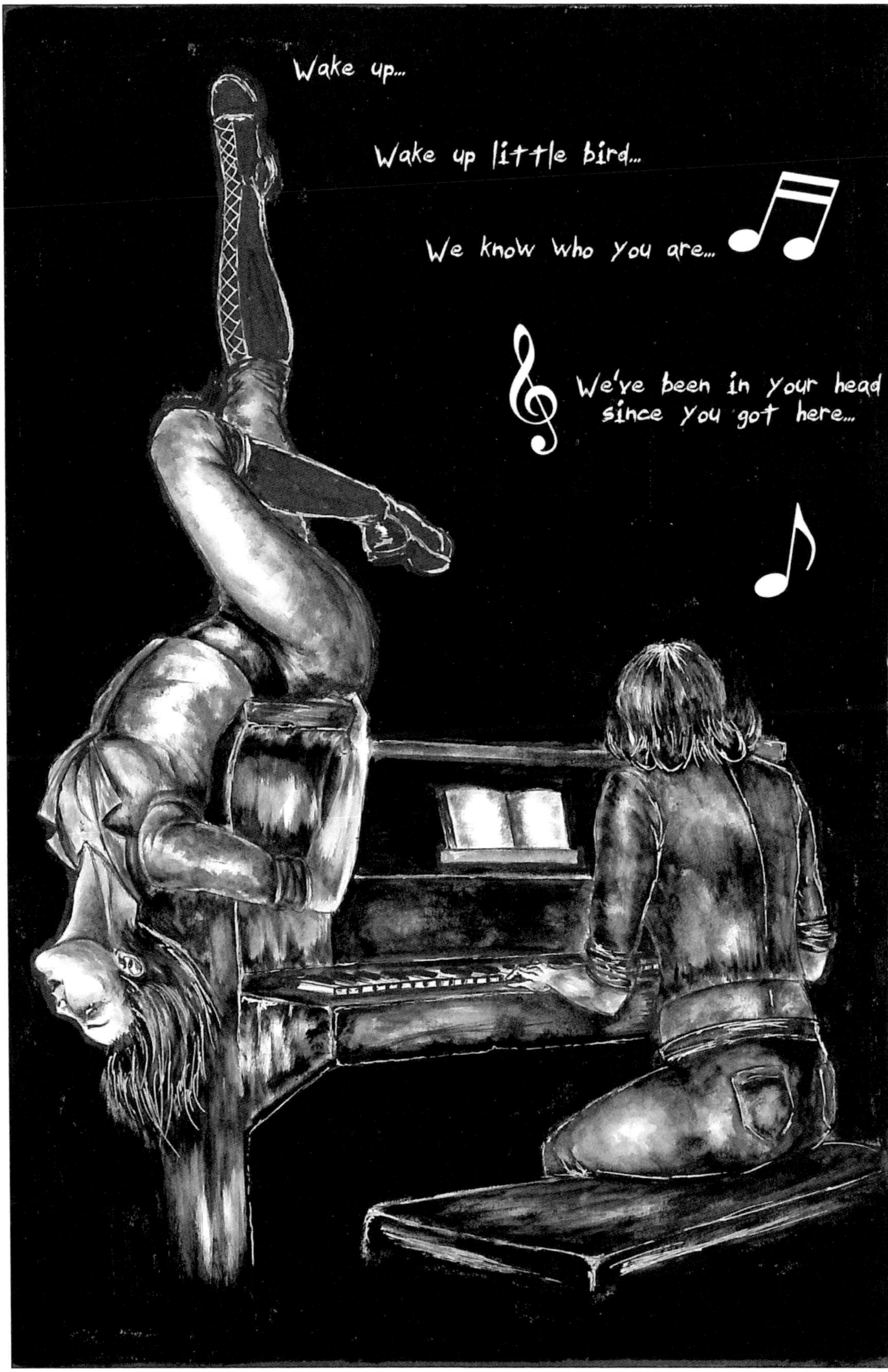

Wake up...
Wake up little bird...
We know who you are...
We've been in your head since you got here...

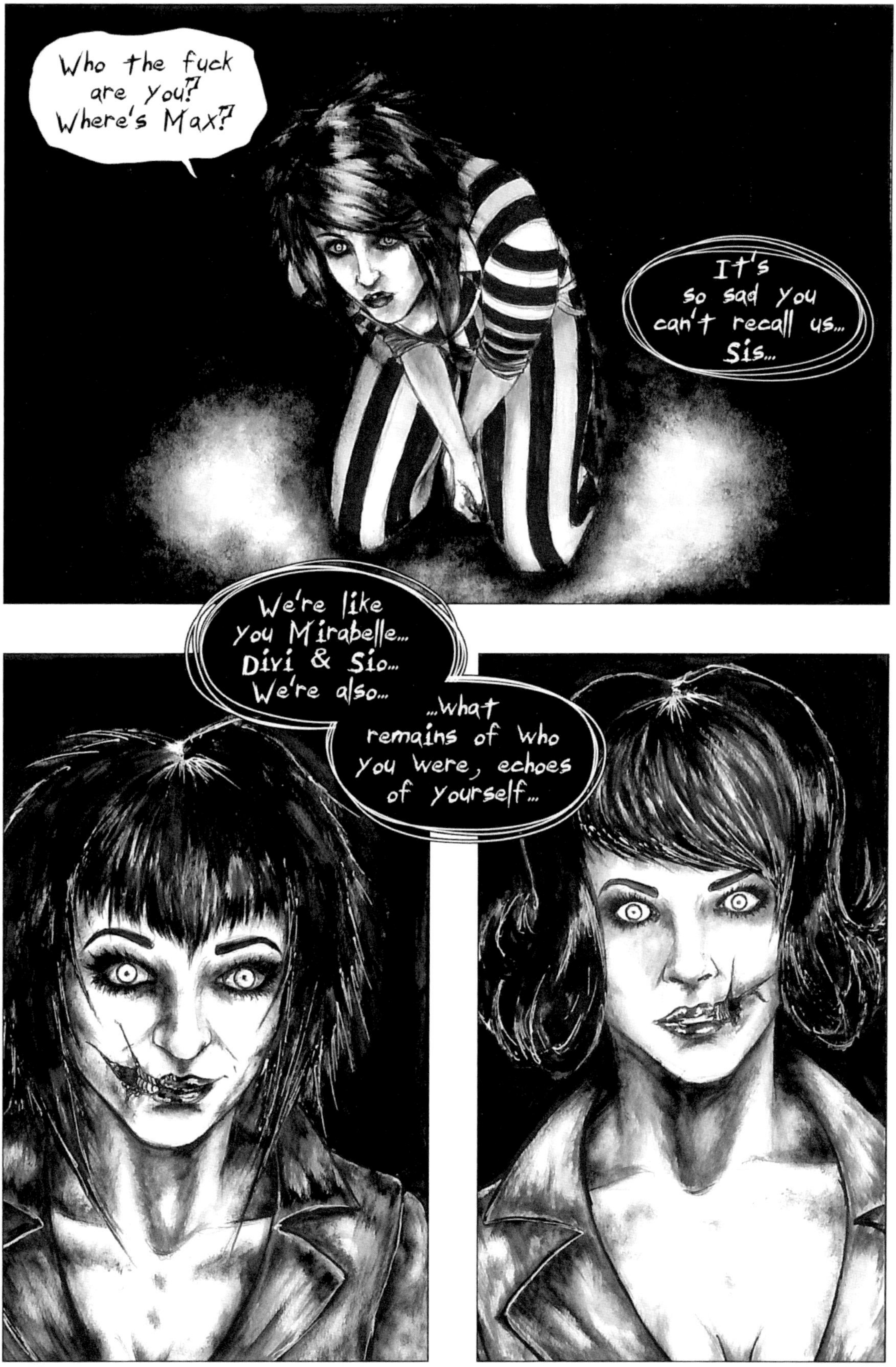
Who the fuck are you?! Where's Max?!
It's so sad you can't recall us... Sis...
We're like you Mirabelle... Divi & Sio... We're also...
...what remains of who you were, echoes of yourself...

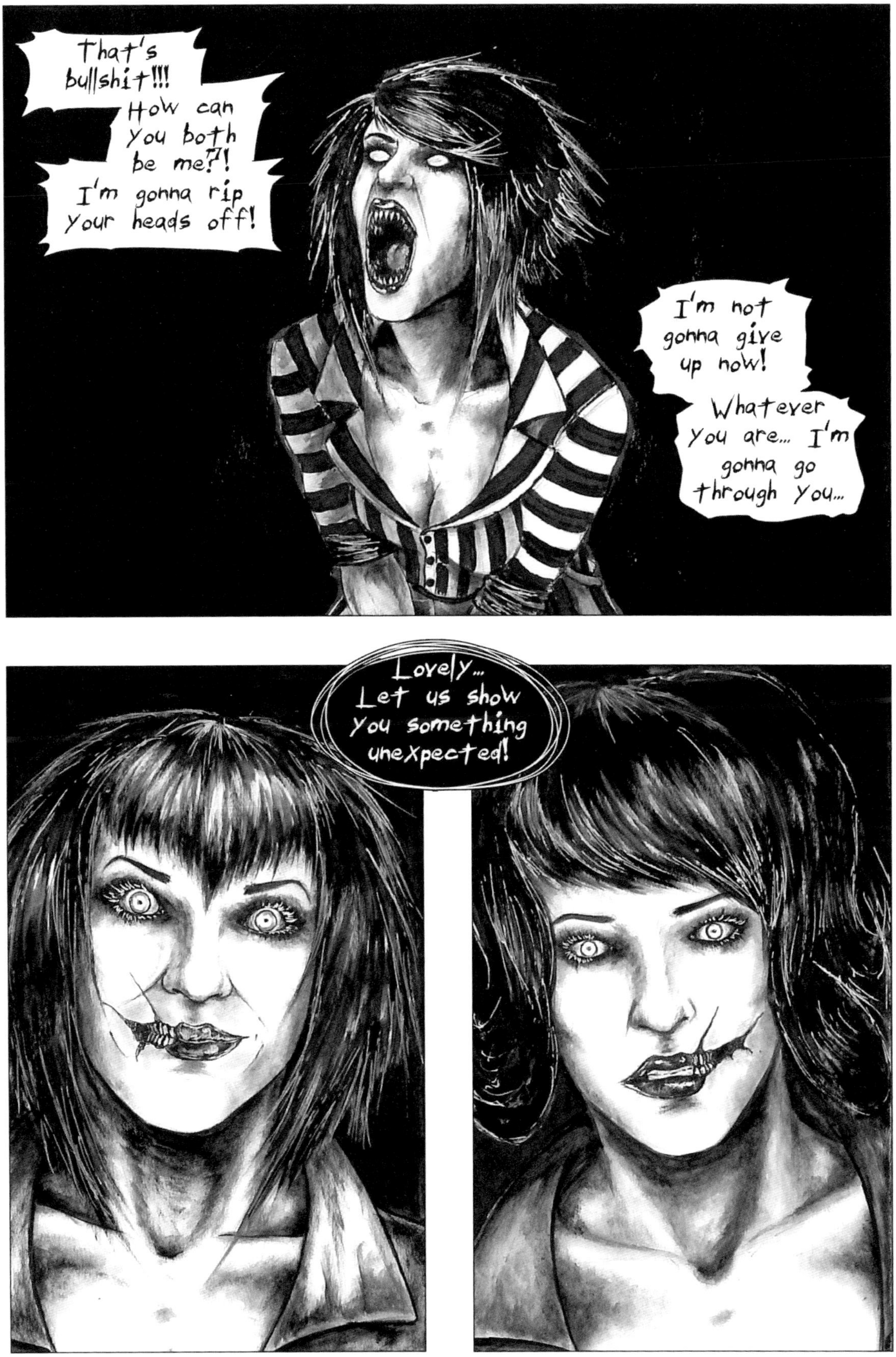
That's bullshit!!!
How can you both be me?!
I'm gonna rip your heads off!
I'm not gonna give up now!
Whatever you are... I'm gonna go through you...
Lovely... Let us show you something unexpected!

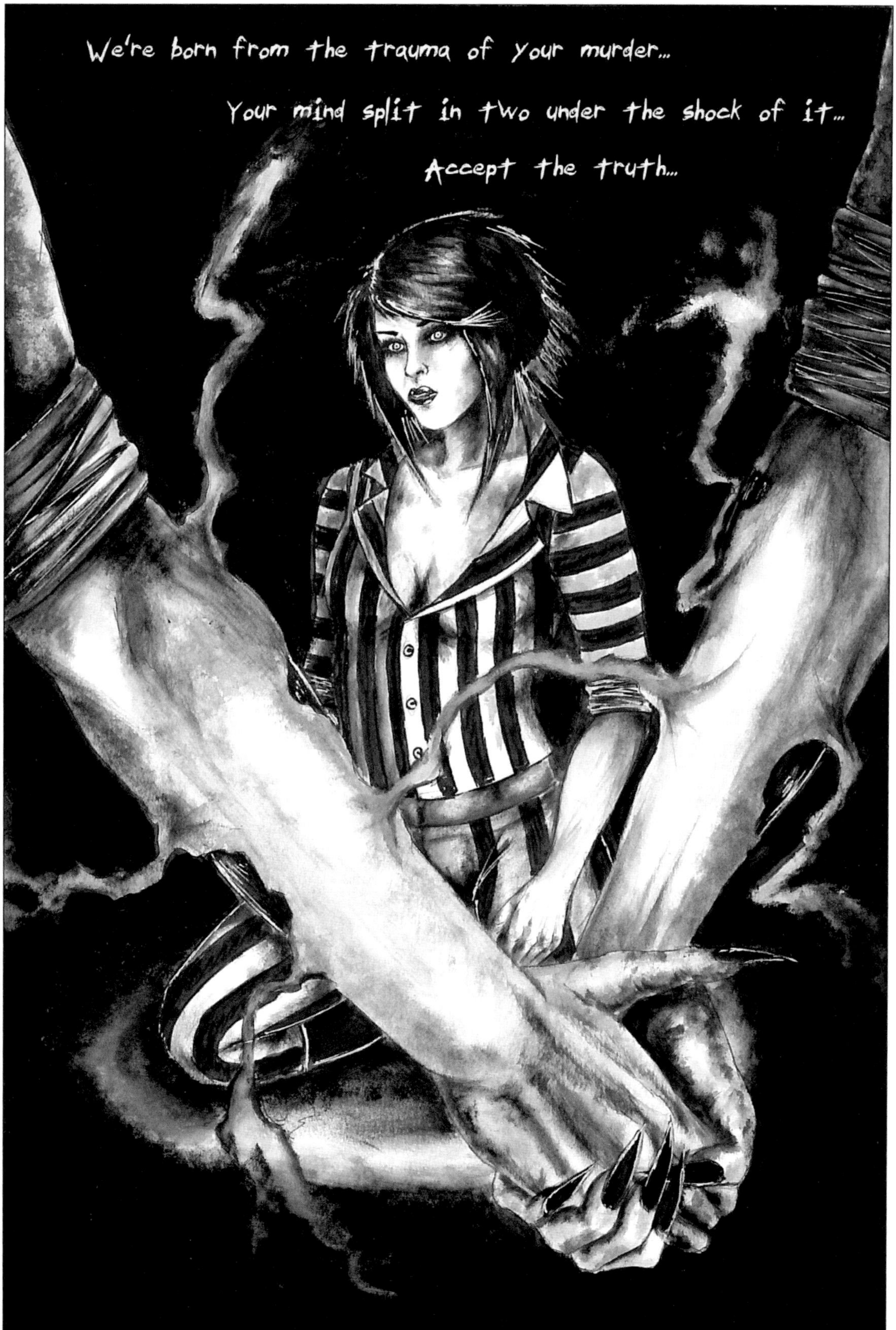
We're born from the trauma of your murder...
Your mind split in two under the shock of it...
Accept the truth...

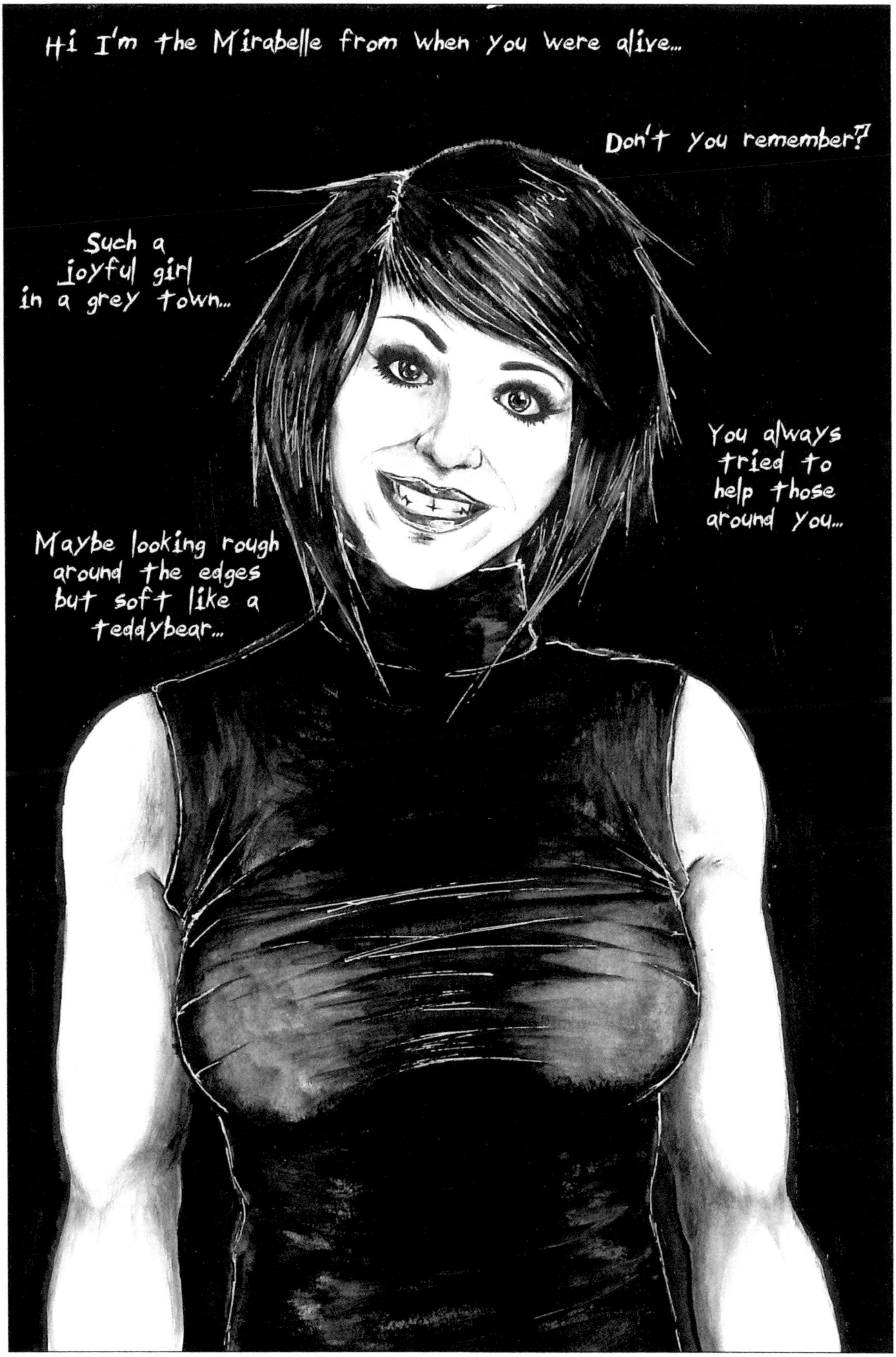
Hi I'm the Mirabelle from when you were alive...
Don't you remember?
Such a joyful girl in a grey town...
You always tried to help those around you...
Maybe looking rough around the edges but soft like a teddybear...

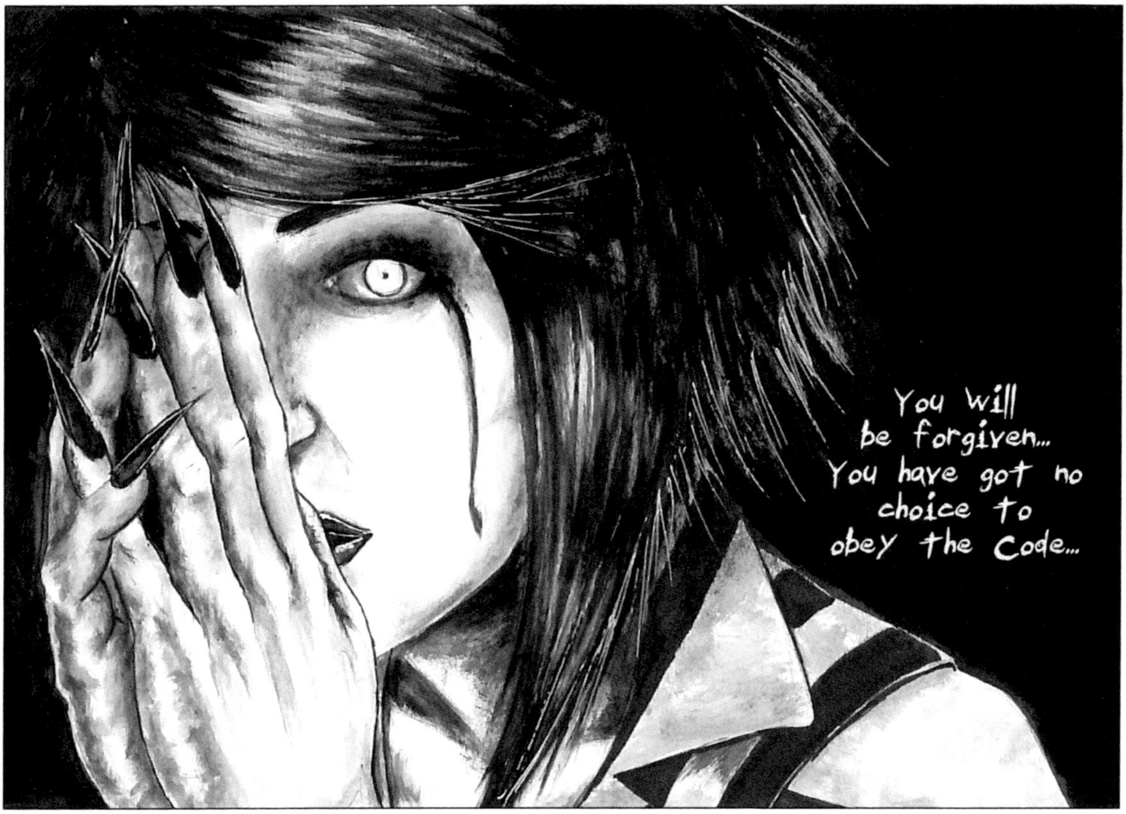
You will
be forgiven...
You have got no
choice to
obey the Code...

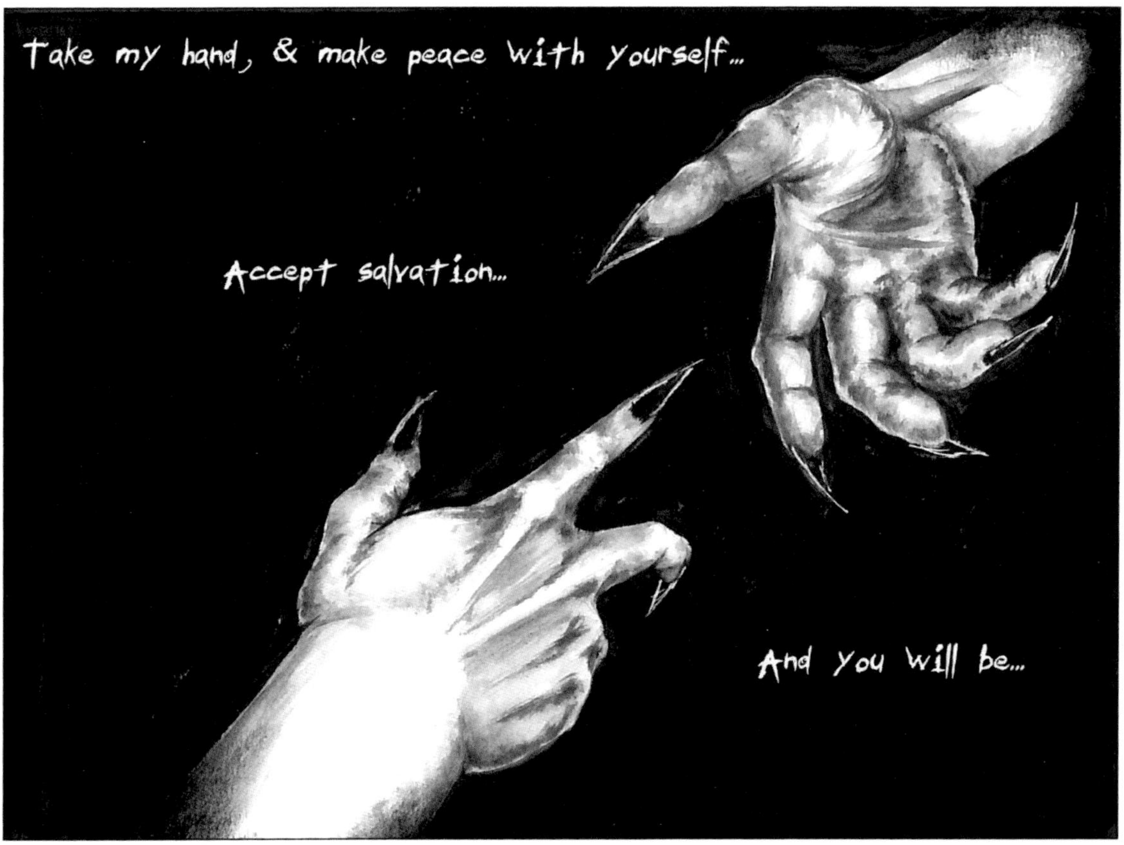
Take my hand, & make peace with yourself...
Accept salvation...
And you will be...

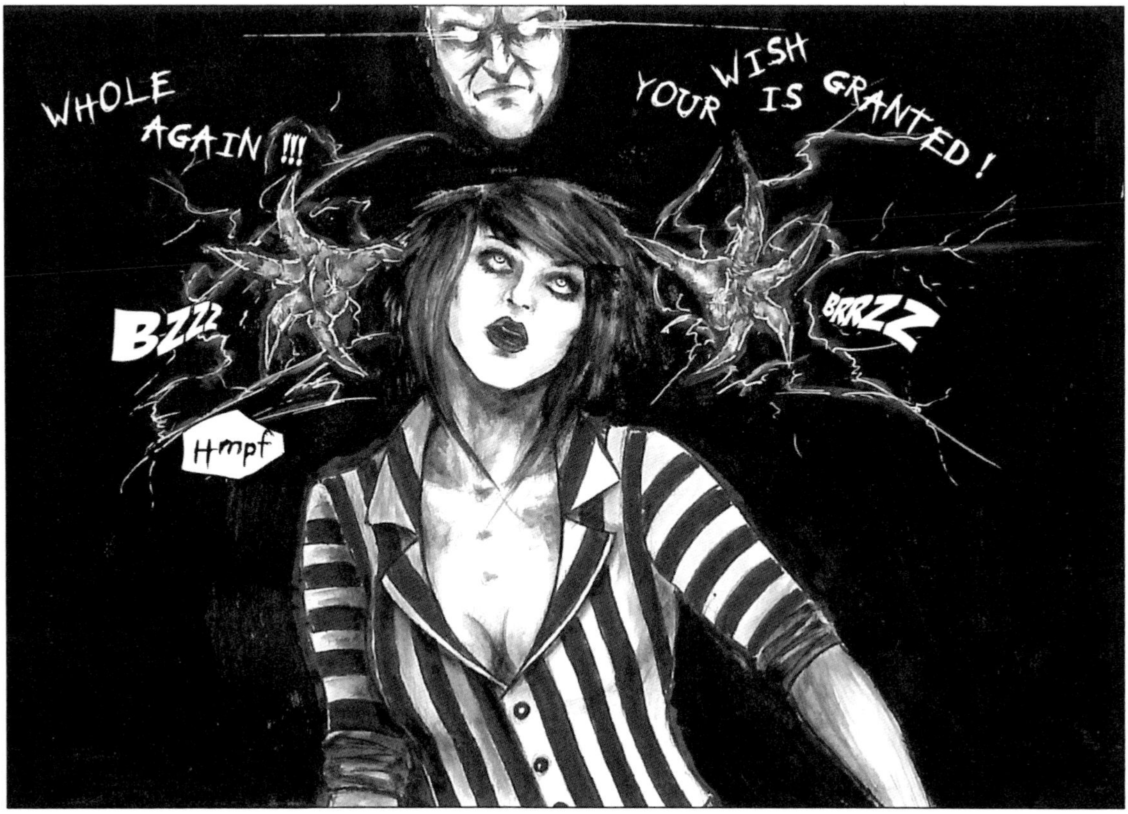
WHOLE AGAIN !!!
YOUR WISH IS GRANTED!
BZZZ
BRRZZ
Hmpf

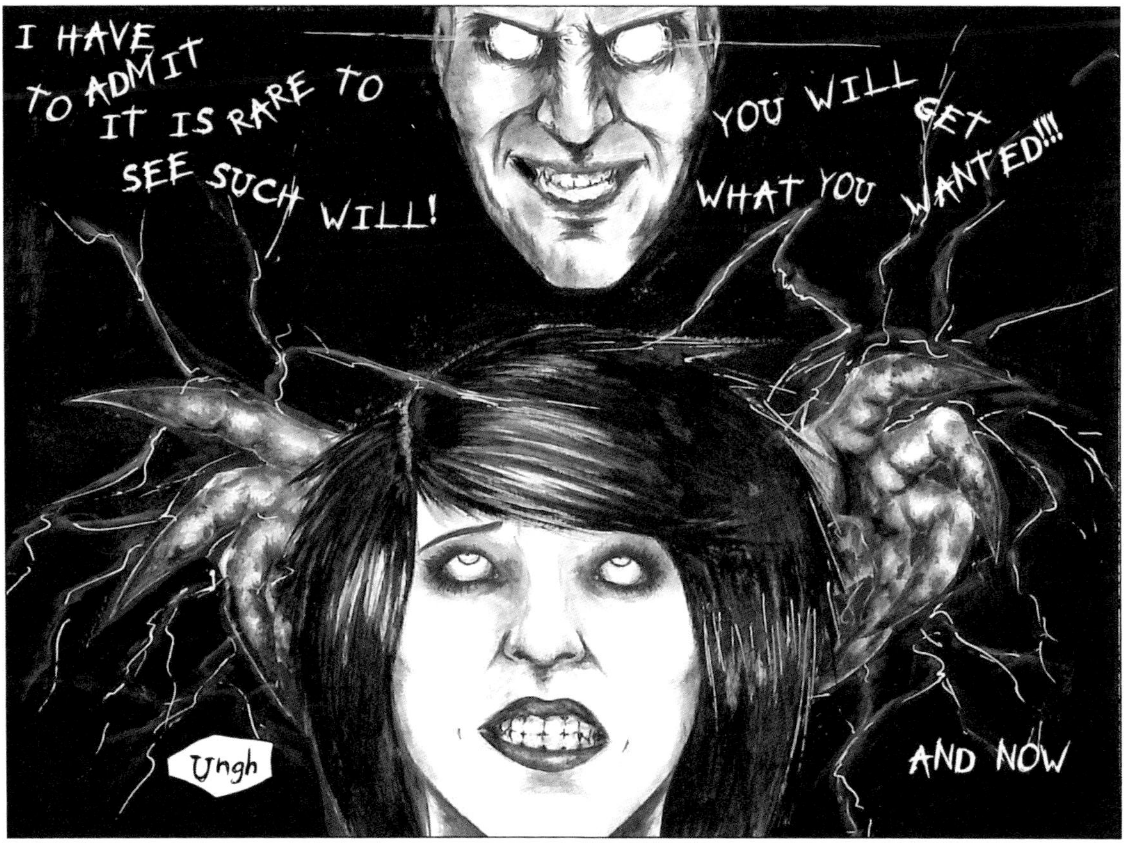
I HAVE TO ADMIT IT IS RARE TO SEE SUCH WILL!
YOU WILL GET WHAT YOU WANTED!!!
Ungh
AND NOW

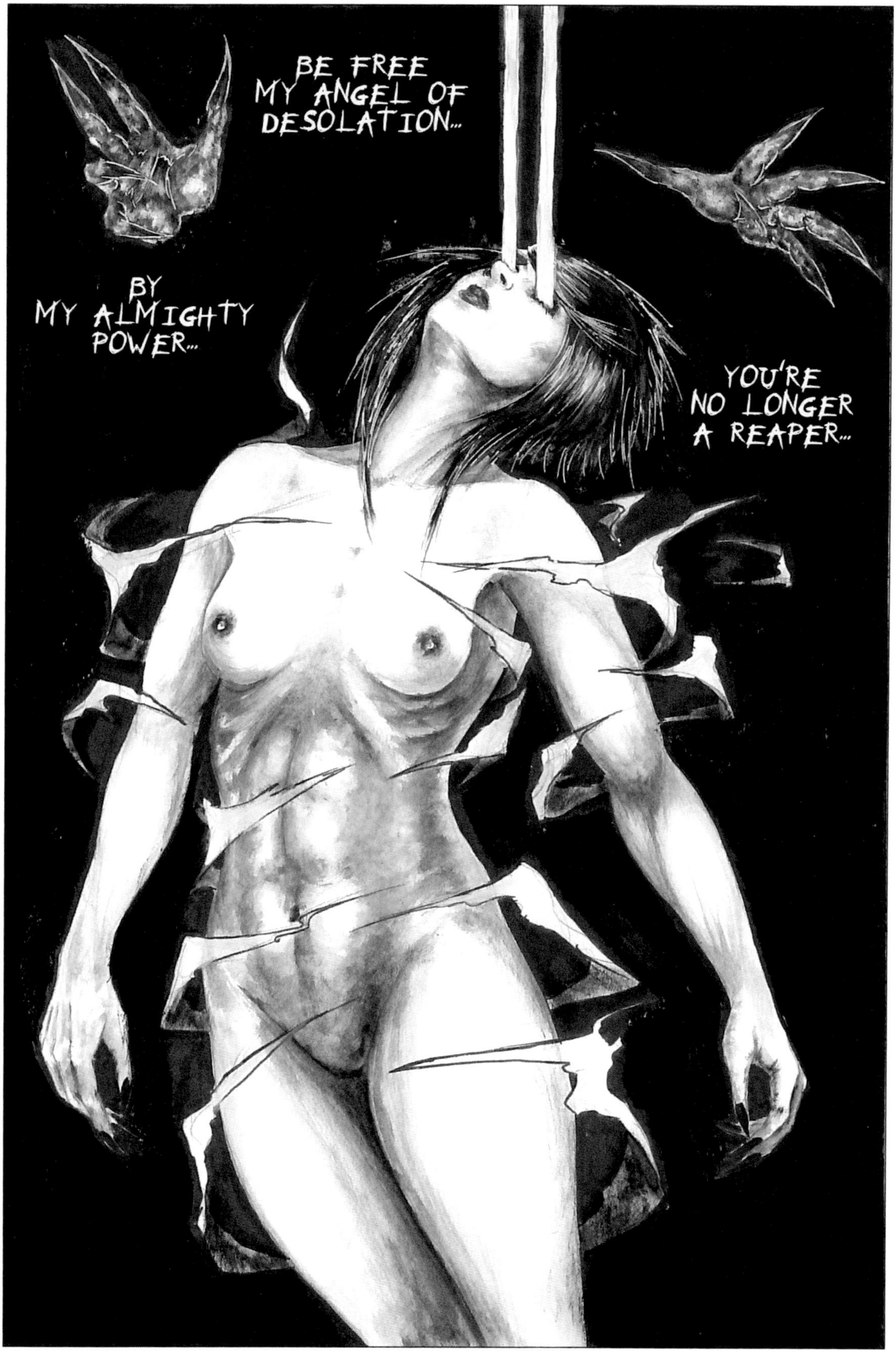
BE FREE MY ANGEL OF DESOLATION...
BY MY ALMIGHTY POWER...
YOU'RE NO LONGER A REAPER...

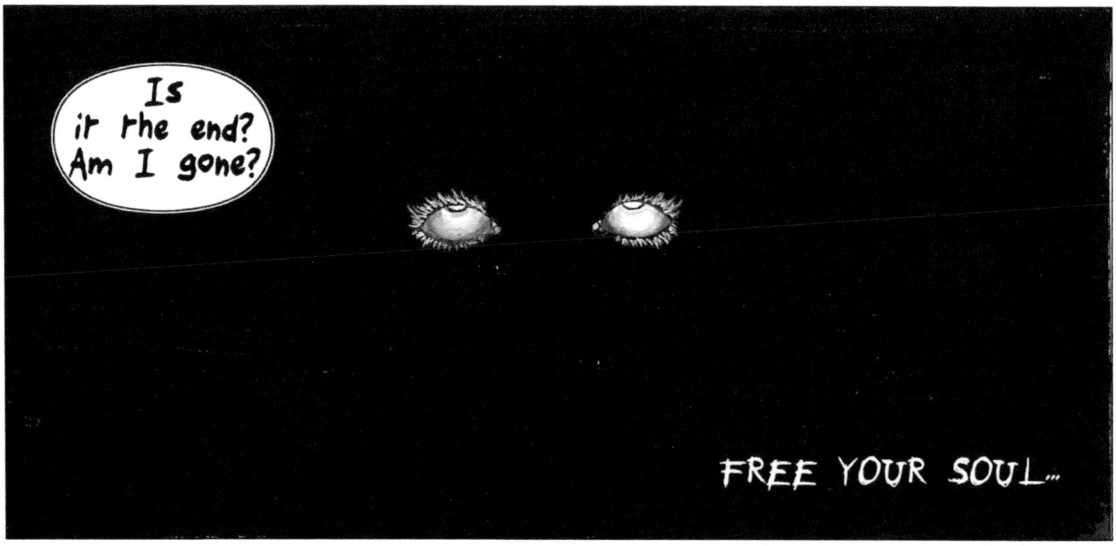
Is it the end? Am I gone?
FREE YOUR SOUL...

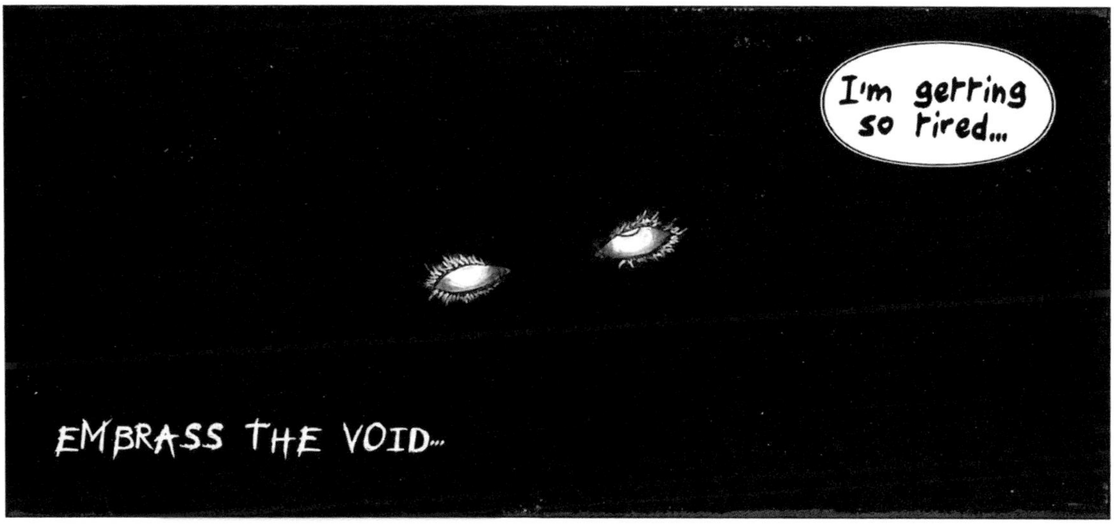
I'm getting so tired...
EMBRASS THE VOID...

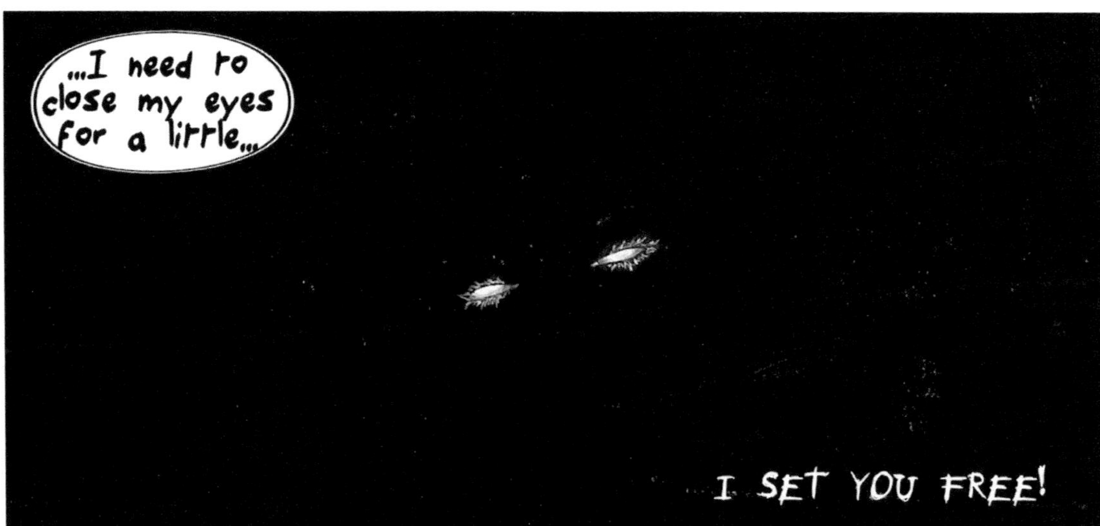
...I need to close my eyes for a little...
...I SET YOU FREE!

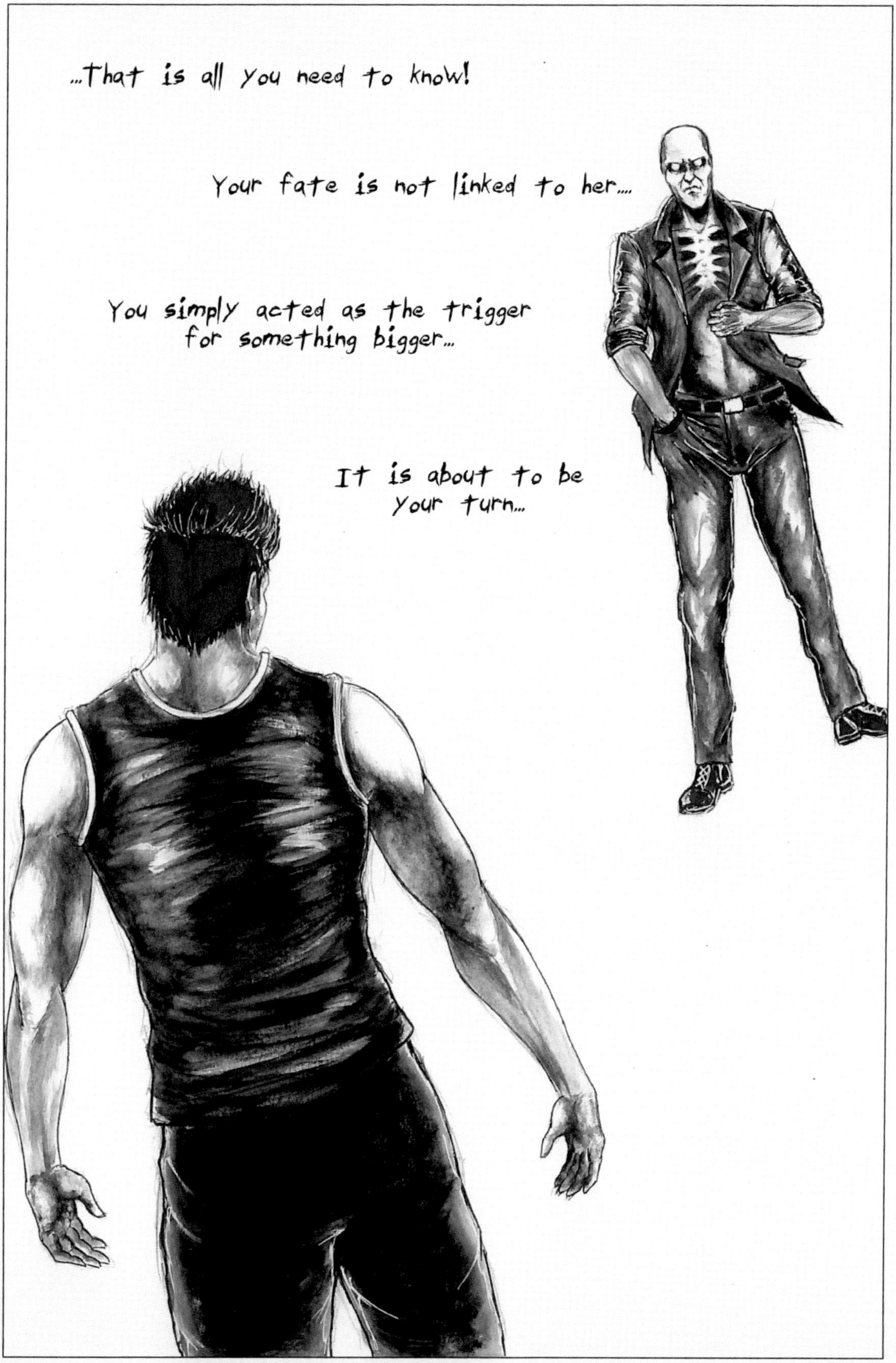
...That is all you need to know!
Your fate is not linked to her....
You simply acted as the trigger for something bigger...
It is about to be your turn...

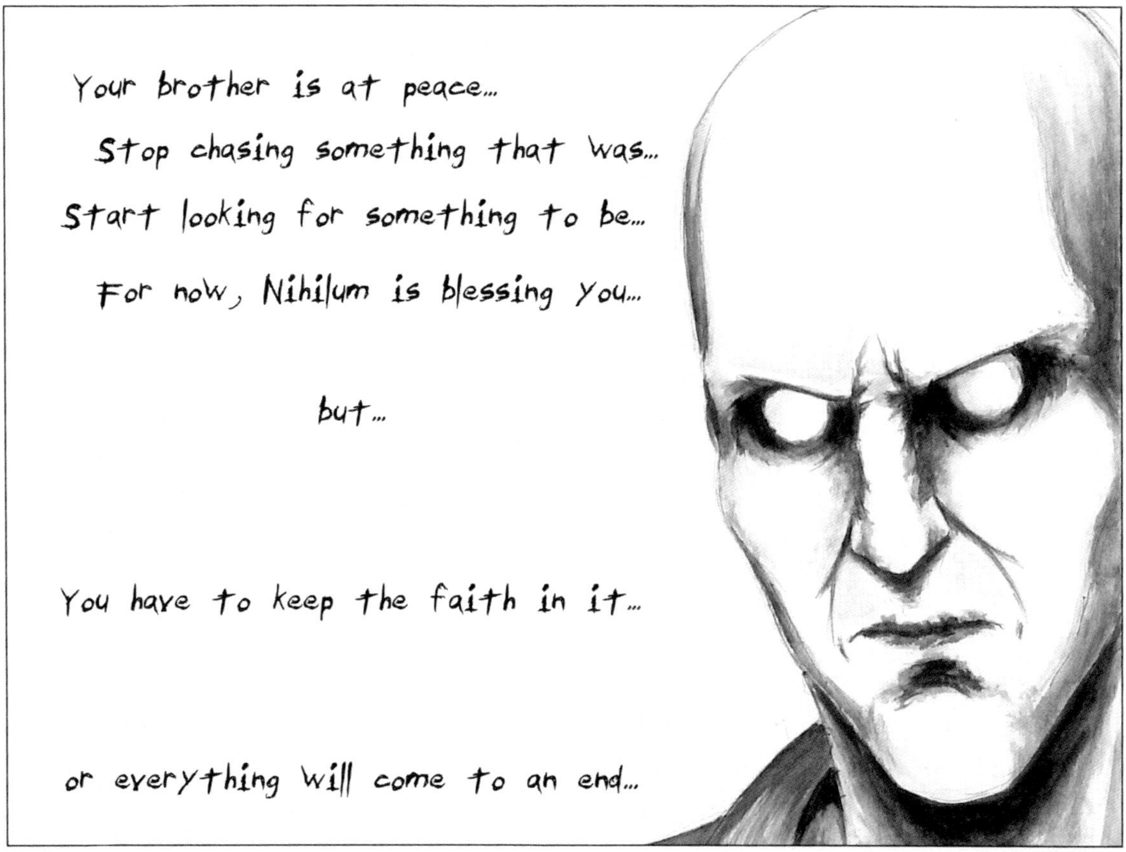
Your brother is at peace...
Stop chasing something that was...
Start looking for something to be...
For now, Nihilum is blessing you...
but...
You have to keep the faith in it...
or everything will come to an end...

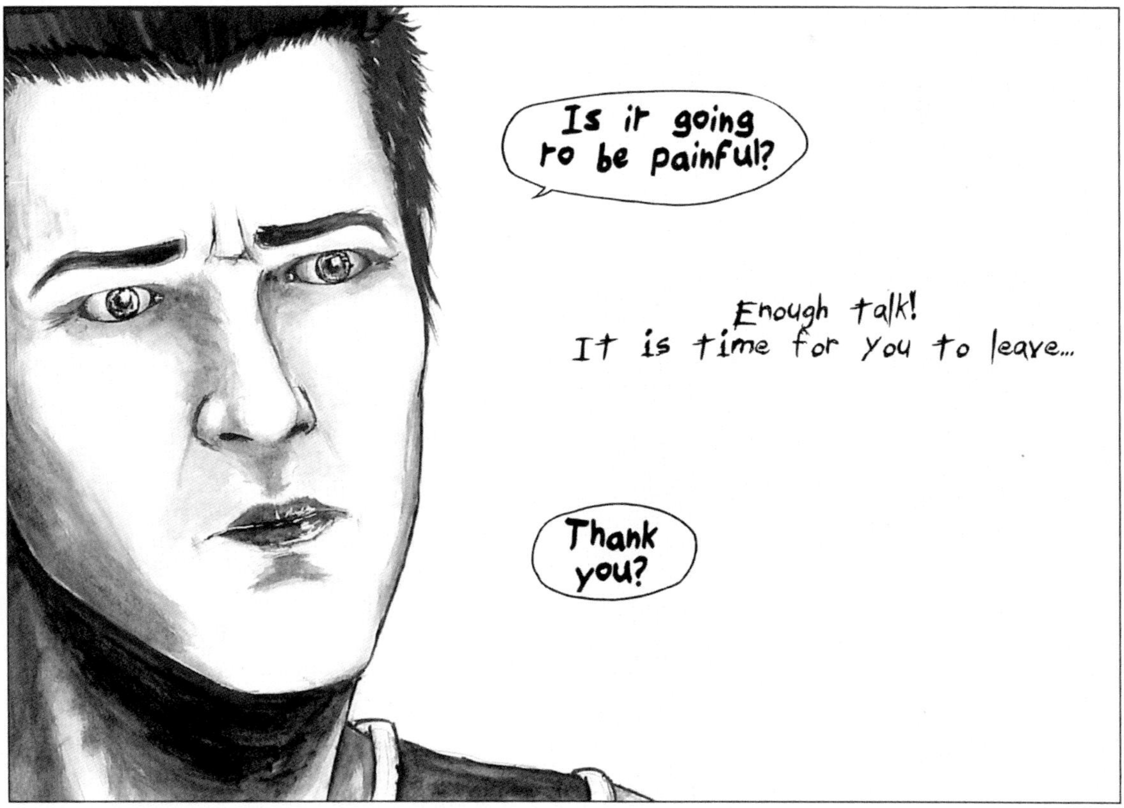
Is it going to be painful?
Enough talk!
It is time for you to leave...
Thank you?

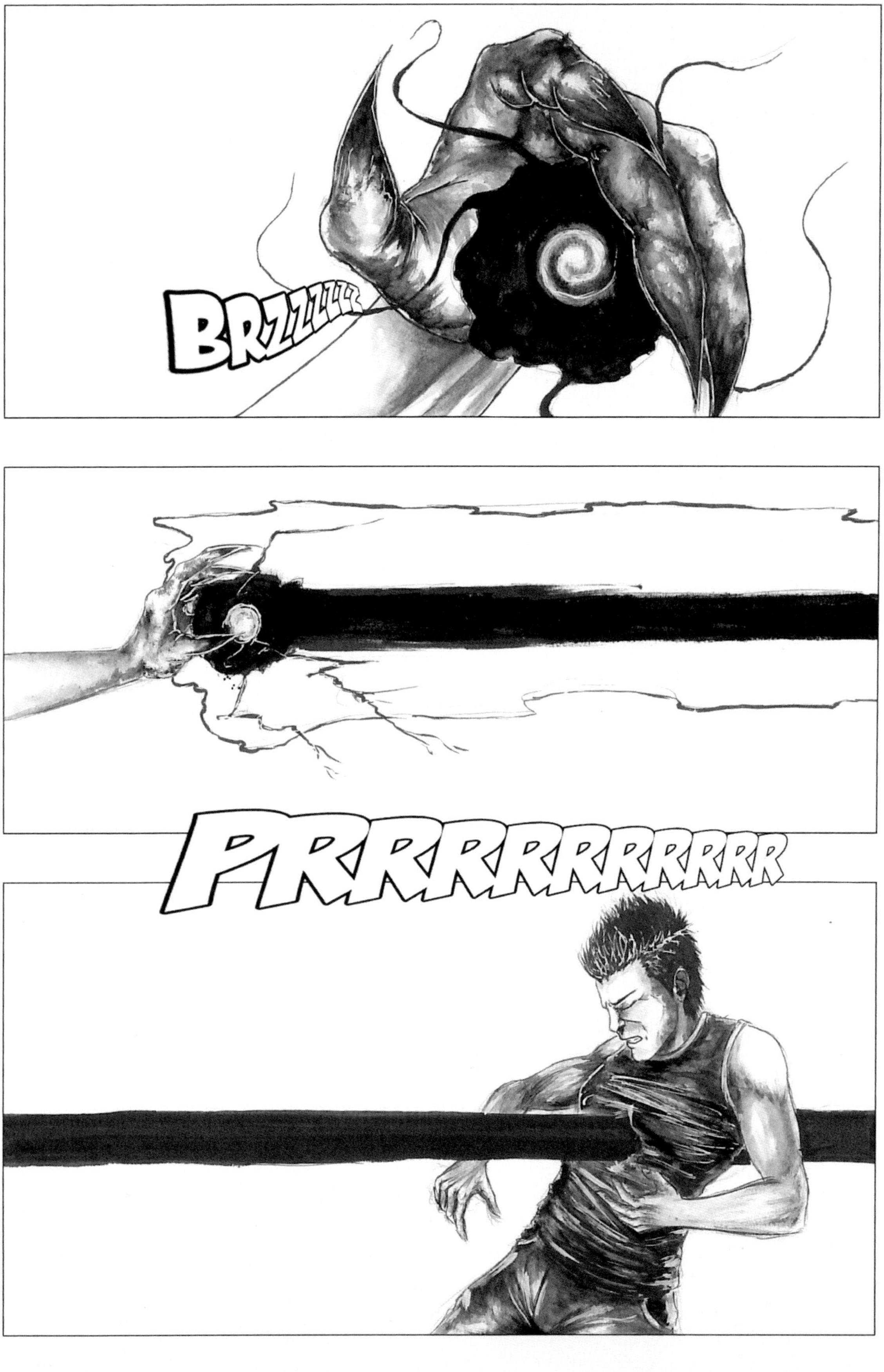
BRZZZZZZZ
PRRRRRRRRRR

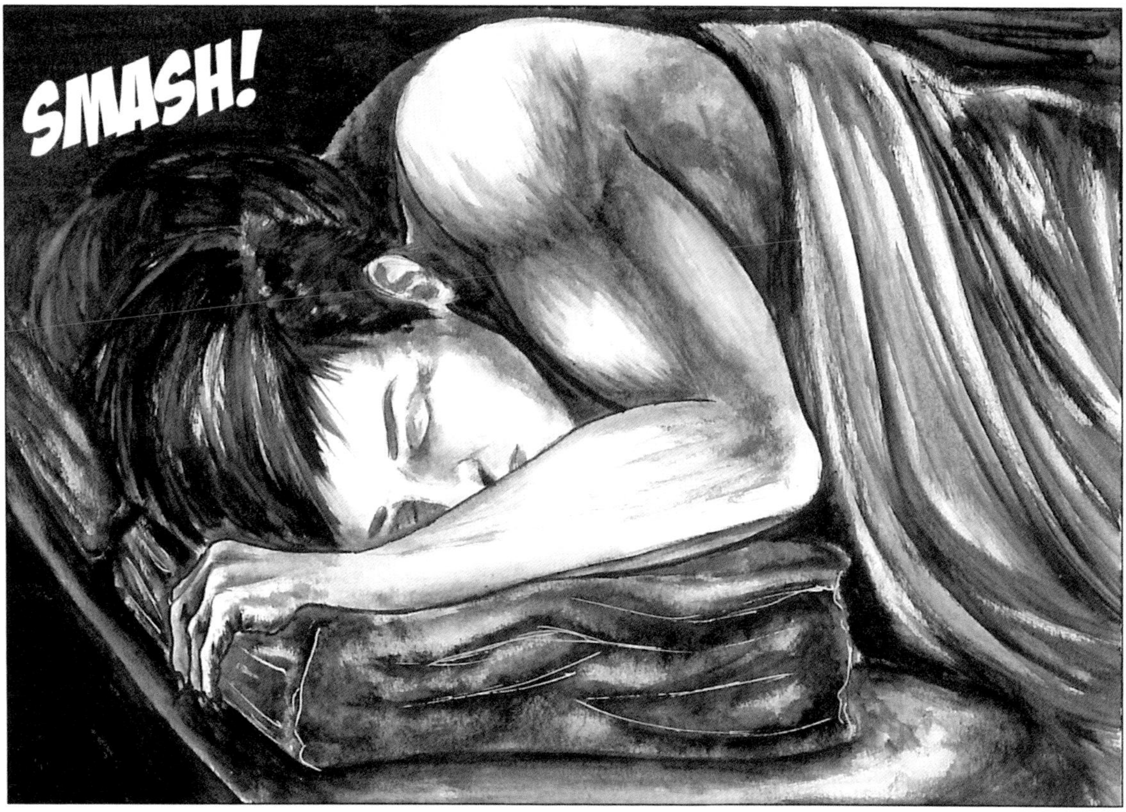
SMASH!

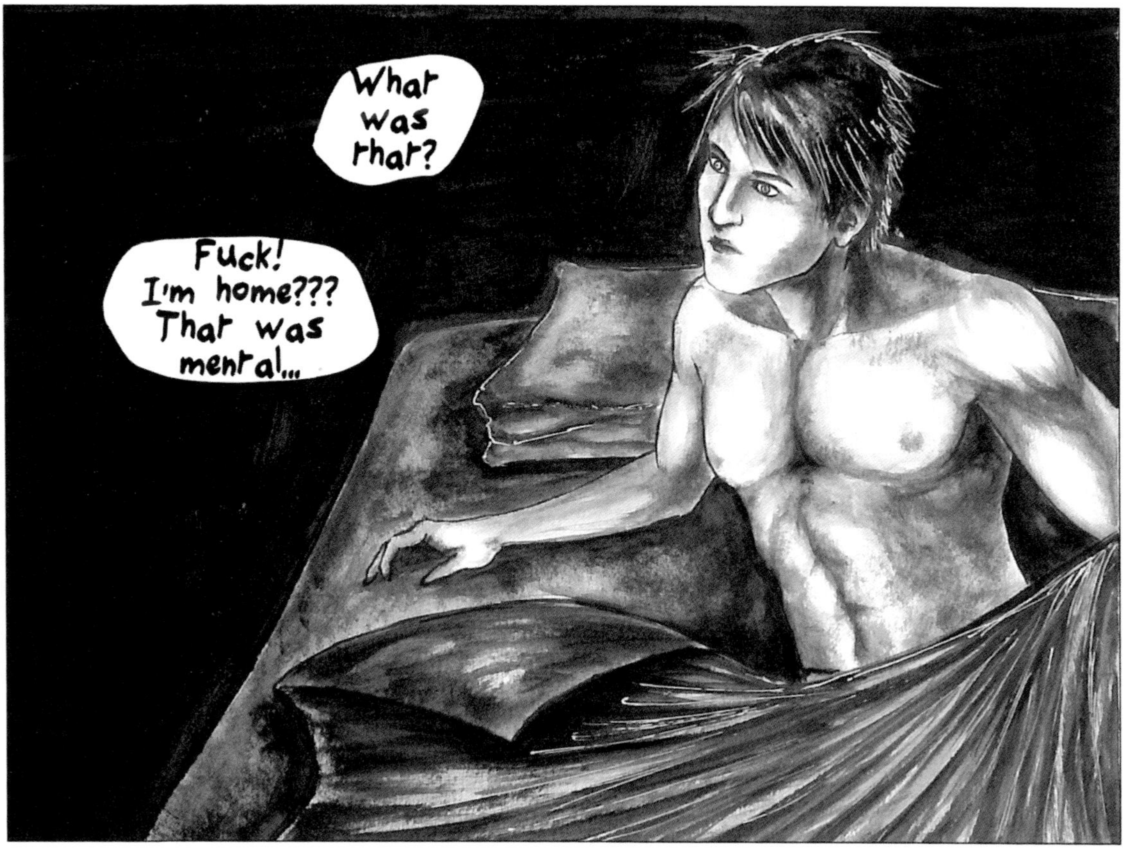
What was that?
Fuck! I'm home??? That was mental...

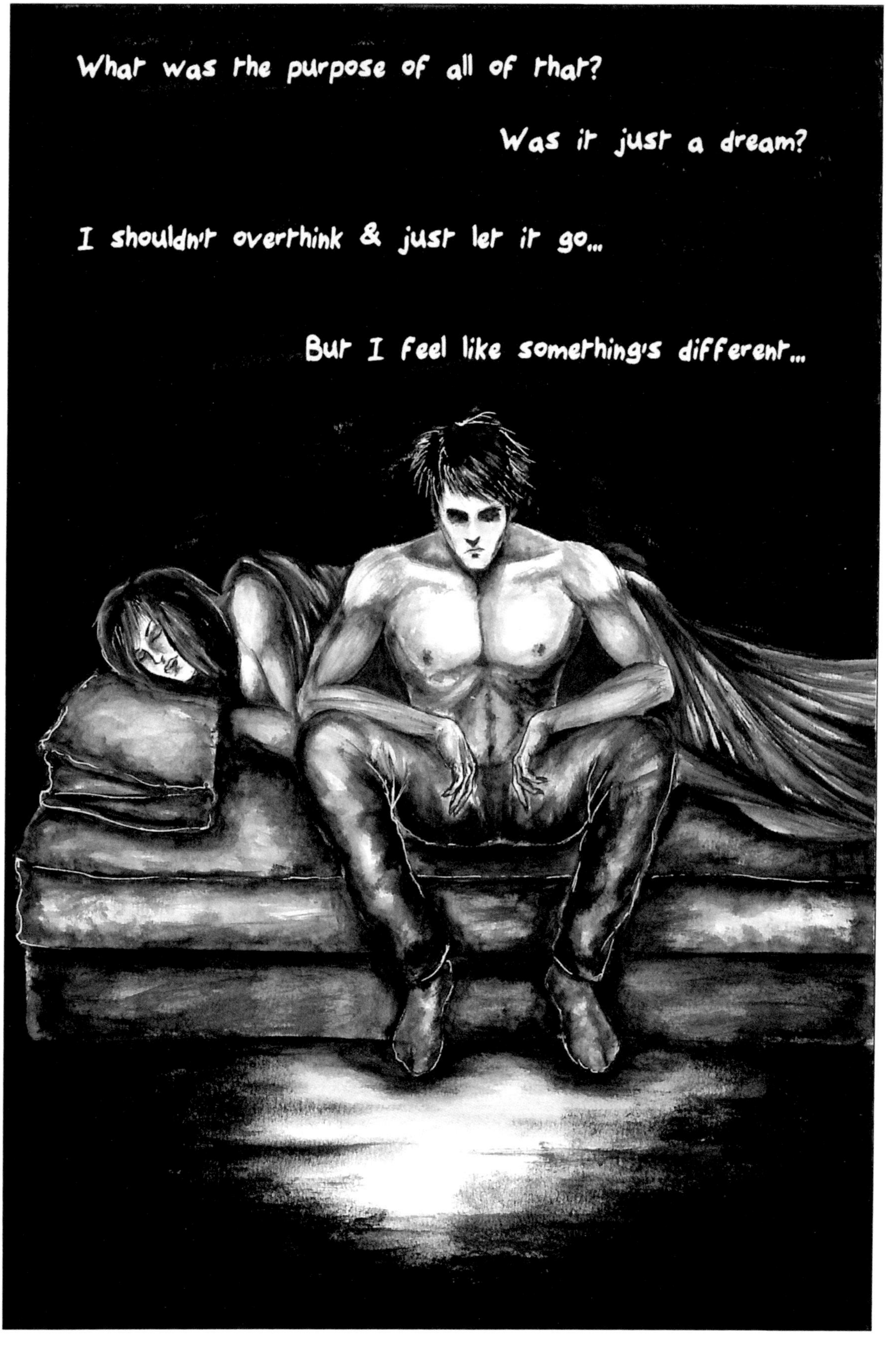
What was the purpose of all of that?
Was it just a dream?
I shouldn't overthink & just let it go...
But I feel like something's different...

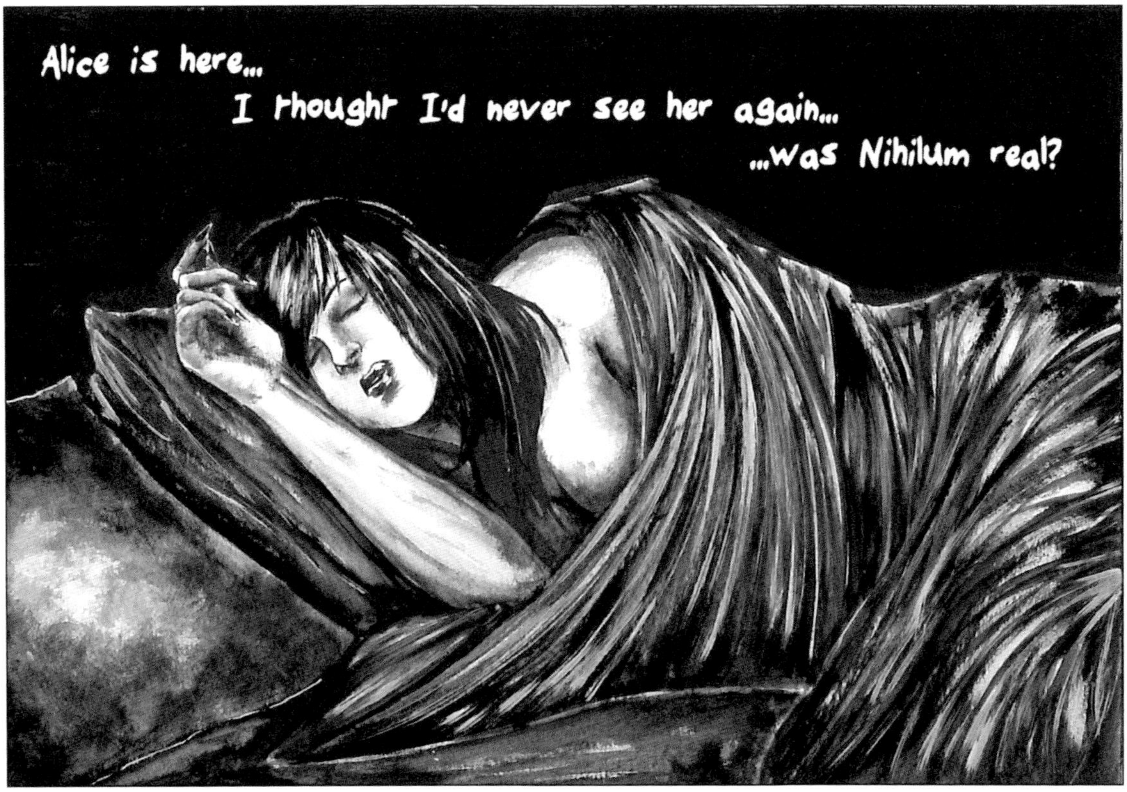
Alice is here...
I thought I'd never see her again...
...was Nihilum real?

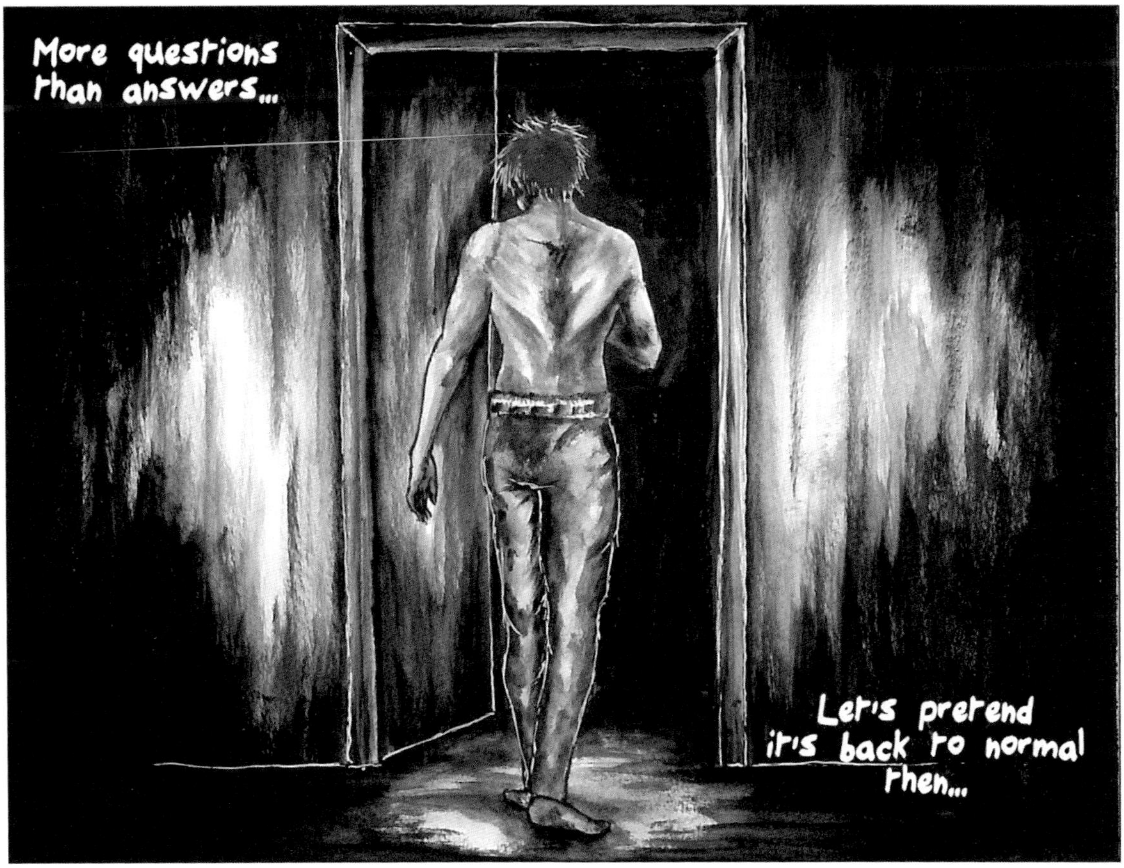
More questions than answers...
Let's pretend it's back to normal then...

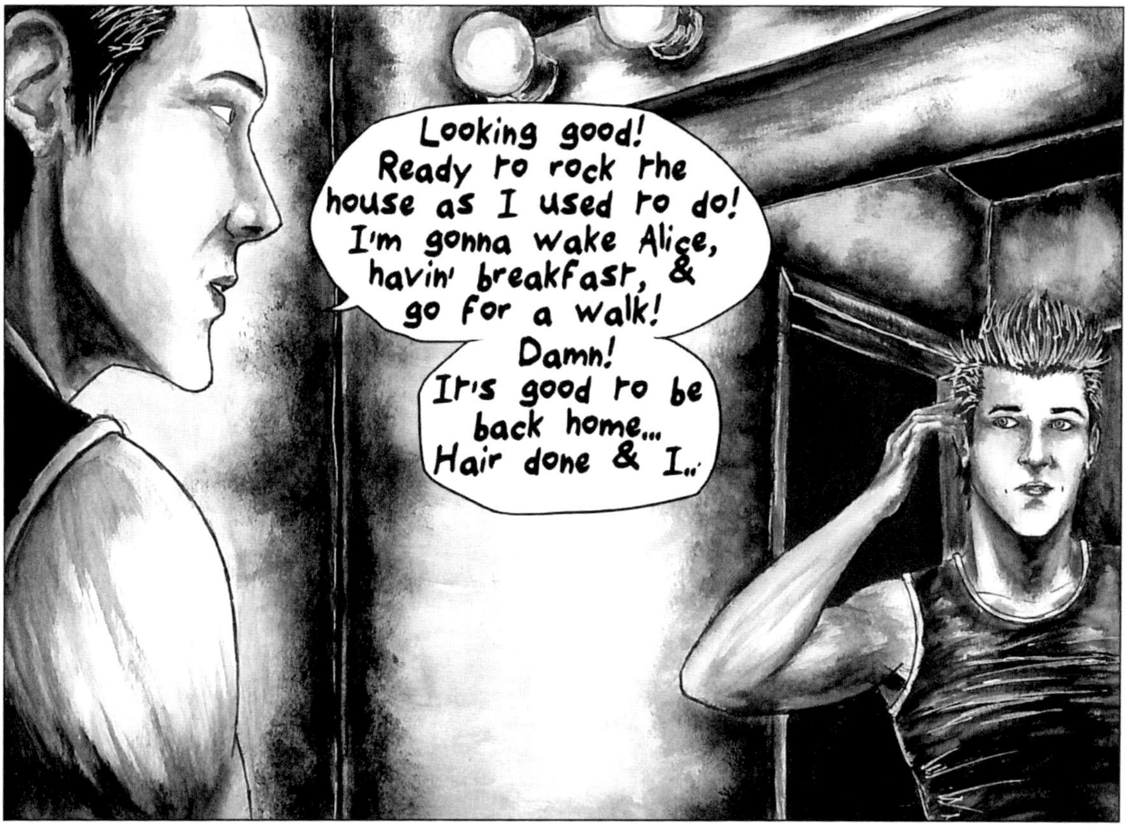
Looking good! Ready to rock the house as I used to do! I'm gonna wake Alice, havin' breakfast, & go for a walk!
Damn! It's good to be back home... Hair done & I...

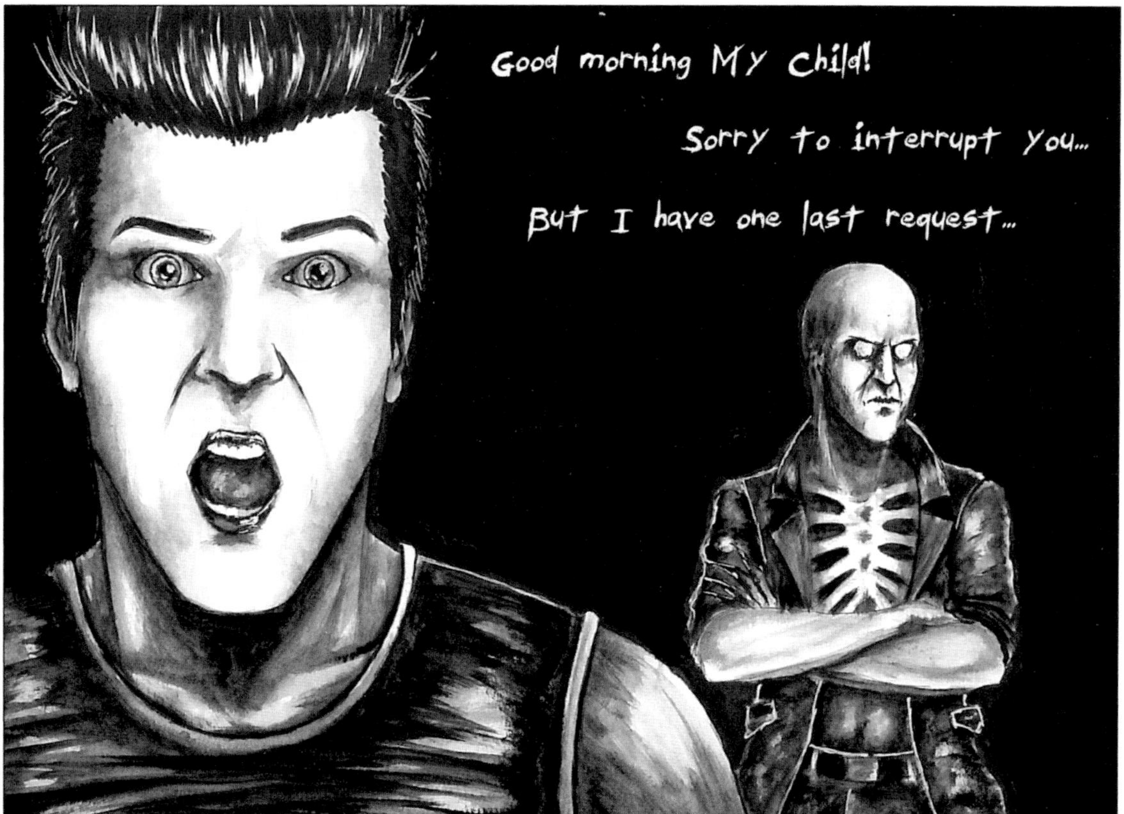
Good morning My Child!
Sorry to interrupt you...
But I have one last request...

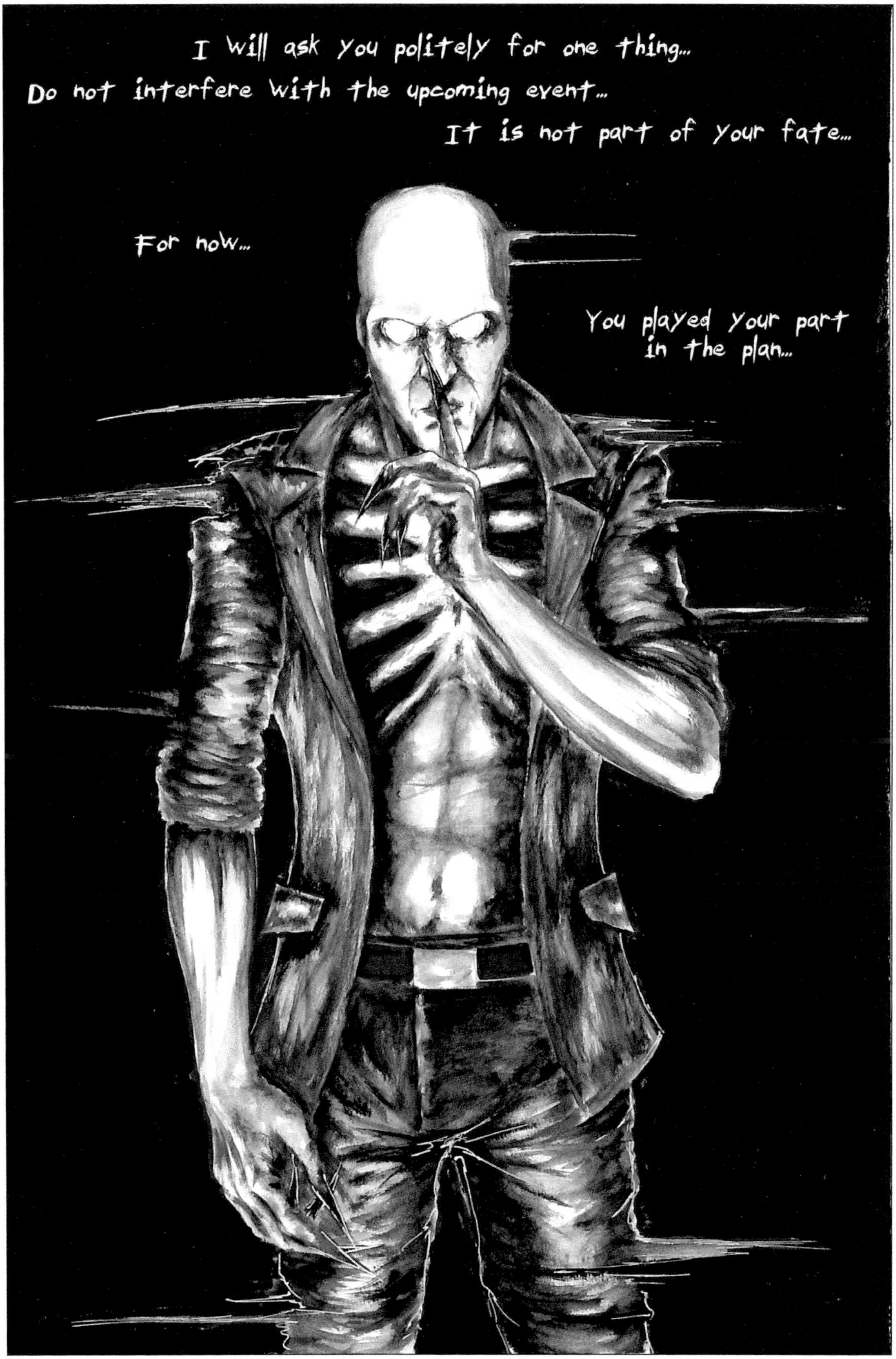
I will ask you politely for one thing...
Do not interfere with the upcoming event...
It is not part of your fate...
For now...
You played your part in the plan...

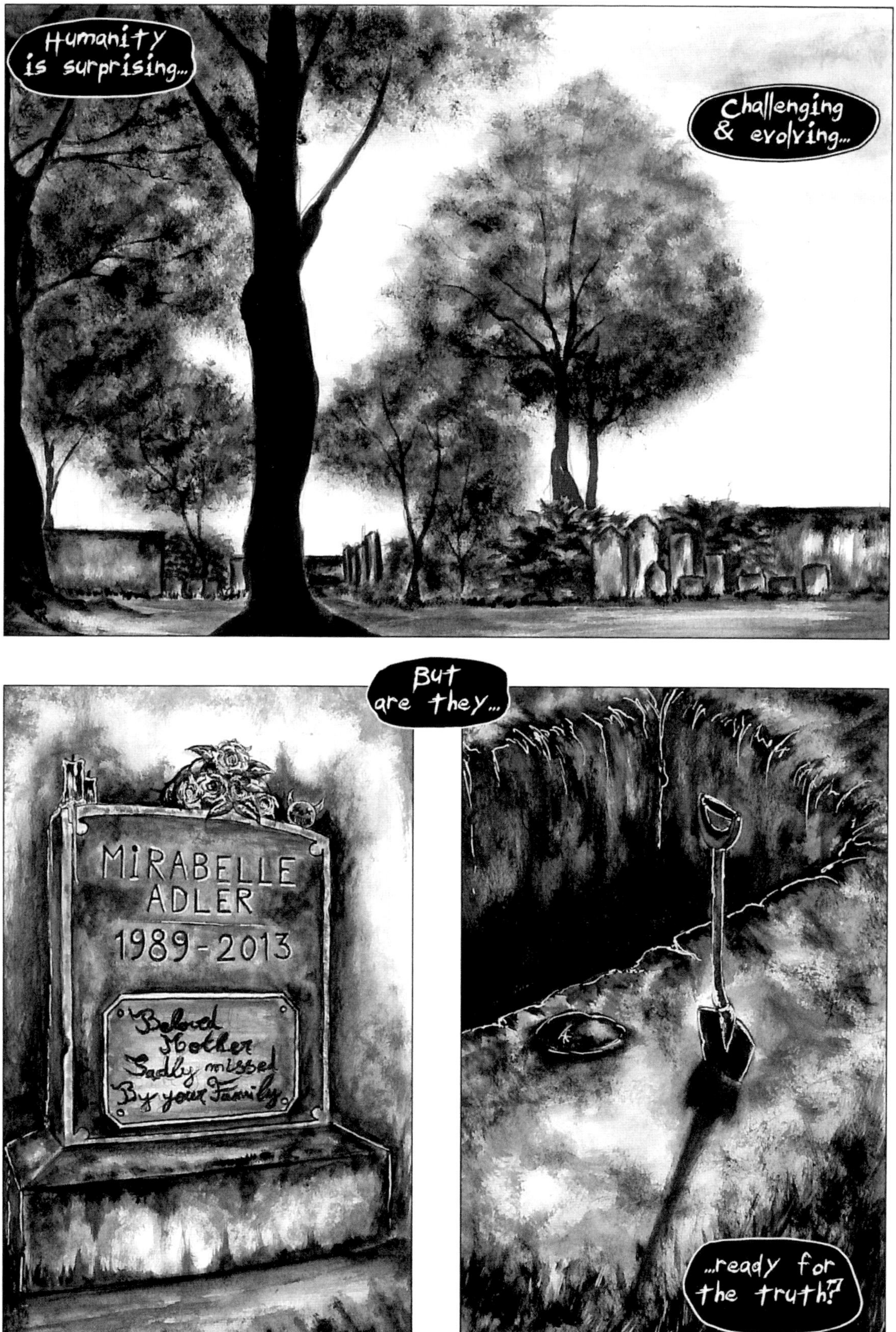
Humanity is surprising...
Challenging & evolving...
But are they...
MIRABELLE ADLER
1989-2013
Beloved Mother Sadly missed By your Family
...ready for the truth?

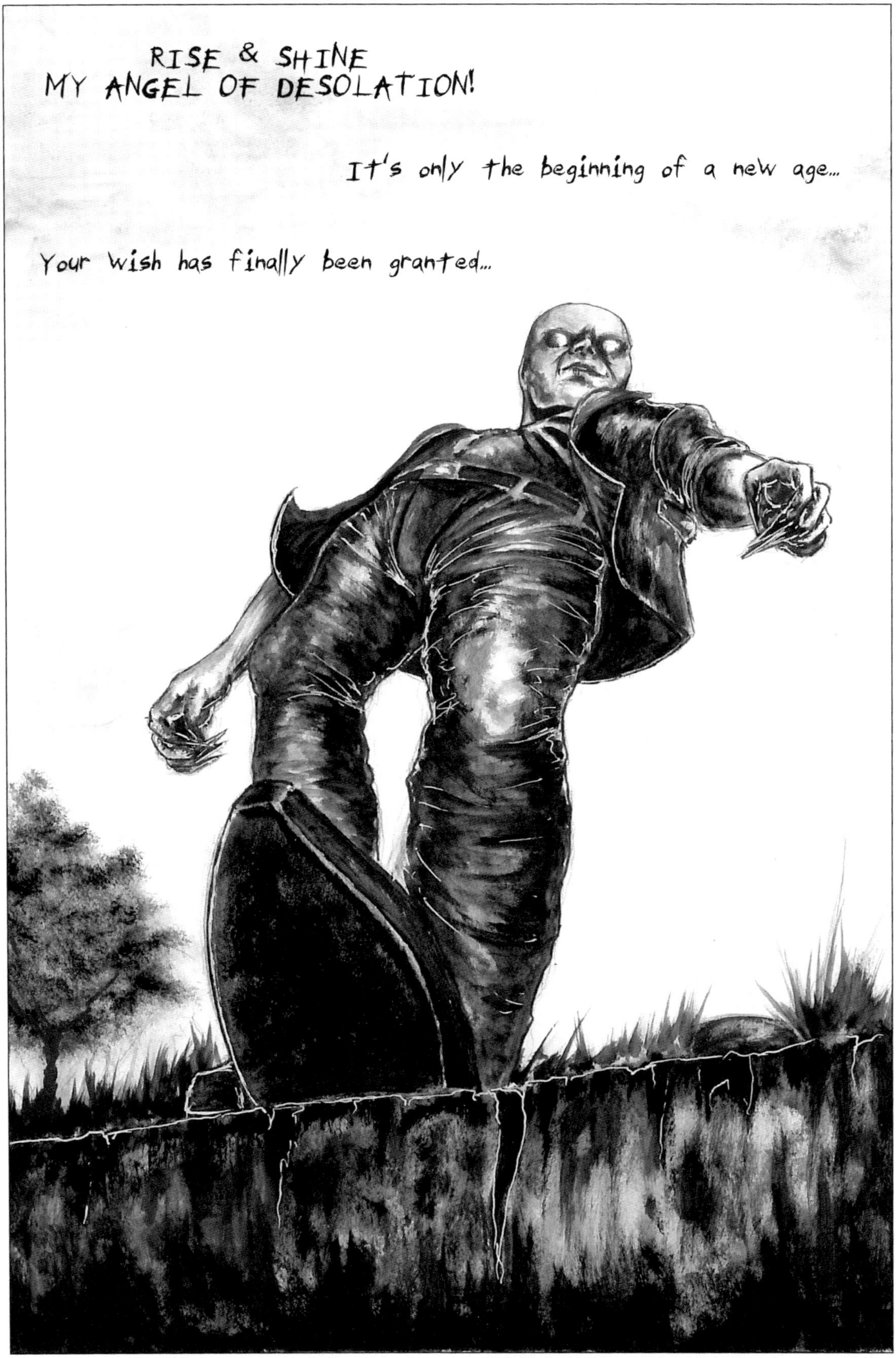
RISE & SHINE
MY ANGEL OF DESOLATION!
It's only the beginning of a new age...
Your wish has finally been granted...

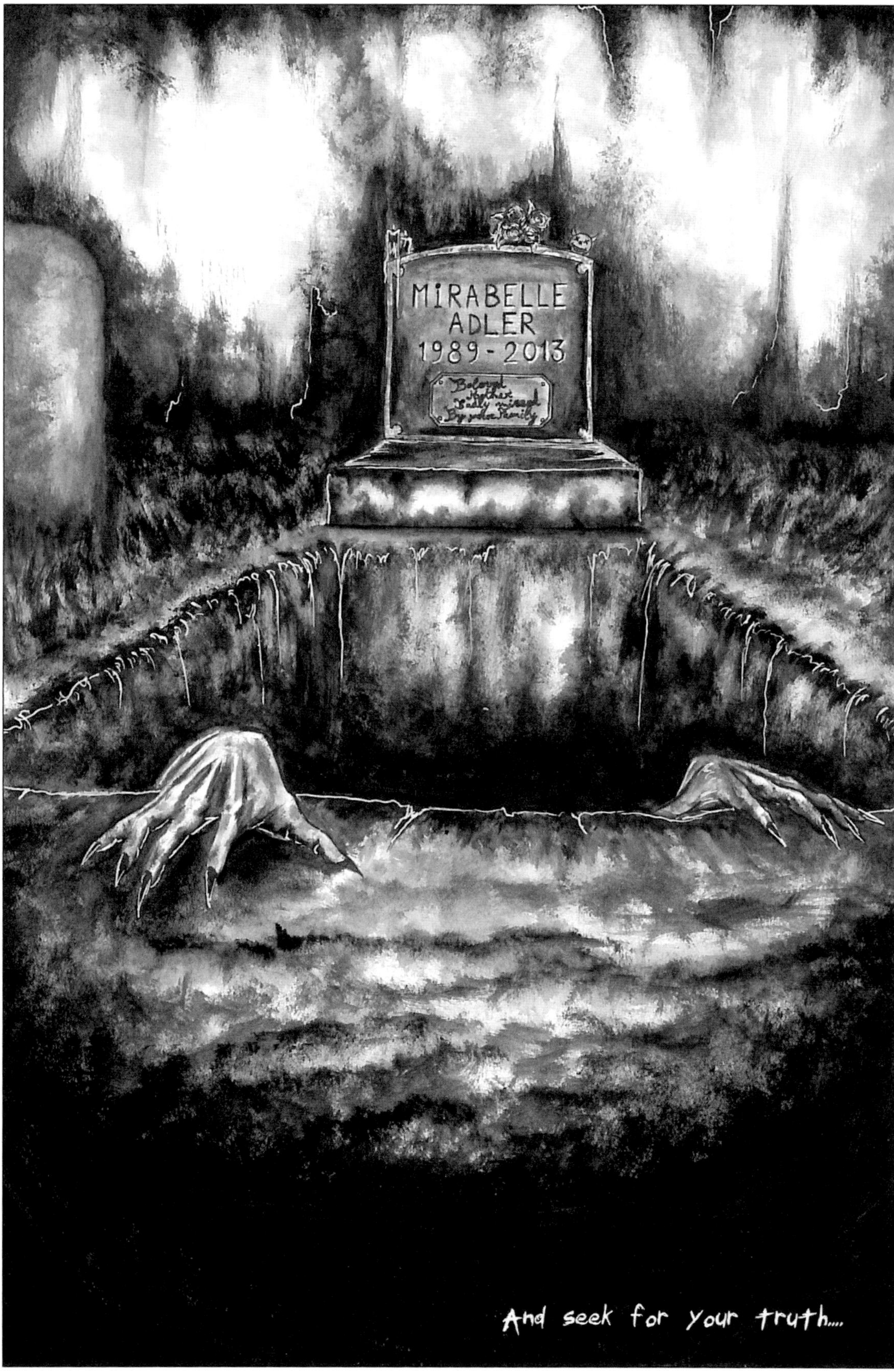
MIRABELLE
ADLER
1989 - 2013
And seek for your truth....

NIHILUM OMNIPOTENS, OMNIUM CREATURUM DIVE PATER, PIETAS TUA VENIAT SUPER ME QUI A PRO NIHILUM BEATUS SUM DEPRECOR TE, UT ME DEFENDAS DE ADVERSARIIS TUOE PROTEGES ME SECUNDUM PIETATEM TIBI COMMENDO ANIMAM MEAM ET CORPUS MEUM QUI NULLAM SPEM NE QUE HABERE VOLO NISI IN TE, NIHILUM, ADJUVA ME ET PER TUAM IMMENSAM CLEMENTIAM ET MISERICORDIAM TUAM NE DISCESSERIS A ME INTENDE IN ADJUTORIUM NIHILUM SALUTIS MEOE INDUE.NIHILUM, VISCERA MISERICORDIOE TUOE UT AD VOLUNTATEM BENEGNITATEM PRUDENIAM, JUSTITIAM, FORTITUDINEM, TEMPERATIAM, MODESTIAM, PATIENTIAM, CONCORDIAM, PACEM ET PRO OMNIBUS PERSEVERANTIAM ET CANTITATEM TRIBUERE DIGNERI QUI VIVIS ET REGNIS IN AETERNUM

NIHILUM OMNIPOTENS, OMNIUM CREATURUM DIVE PATER, PIETAS TUA VENIAT SUPER ME QUI A PRO NIHILUM BEATUS SUM DEPRECOR TE, UT ME DEFENDAS DE ADVERSARIIS TUOE PROTEGES ME SECUNDUM PIETATEM TIBI COMMENDO ANIMAM MEAM ET CORPUS MEUM QUI NULLAM SPEM NE QUE HABERE VOLO NISI IN TE, NIHILUM, ADJUVA ME ET PER TUAM IMMENSAM CLEMENTIAM ET MISERICORDIAM TUAM NE DISCESSERIS A ME INTENDE IN ADJUTORIUM NIHILUM SALUTIS MEOE INDUE.NIHILUM, VISCERA MISERICORDIOE TUOE UT AD VOLUNTATEM BENEGNITATEM PRUDENIAM, JUSTITIAM, FORTITUDINEM, TEMPERATIAM, MODESTIAM, PATIENTIAM, CONCORDIAM, PACEM ET PRO OMNIBUS PERSEVERANTIAM ET CANTITATEM TRIBUERE DIGNERI QUI VIVIS ET REGNIS IN AETERNUM

NIHILUM OMNIPOTENS, OMNIUM CREATURUM DIVE PATER, PIETAS TUA VENIAT SUPER ME QUI A PRO NIHILUM BEATUS SUM DEPRECOR TE, UT ME DEFENDAS DE ADVERSARIIS TUOE PROTEGES ME SECUNDUM PIETATEM TIBI COMMENDO ANIMAM MEAM ET CORPUS MEUM QUI NULLAM SPEM NE QUE HABERE VOLO NISI IN TE, NIHILUM, ADJUVA ME ET PER TUAM IMMENSAM CLEMENTIAM ET MISERICORDIAM TUAM NE DISCESSERIS A ME INTENDE IN ADJUTORIUM NIHILUM SALUTIS MEOE INDUE.NIHILUM, VISCERA MISERICORDIOE TUOE UT AD VOLUNTATEM BENEGNITATEM PRUDENIAM, JUSTITIAM, FORTITUDINEM, TEMPERATIAM, MODESTIAM, PATIENTIAM, CONCORDIAM, PACEM ET PRO OMNIBUS PERSEVERANTIAM ET CANTITATEM TRIBUERE DIGNERI QUI VIVIS ET REGNIS IN AETERNUM

PEACE IN THE VOID

After a decade, it felt like an endless race to complete this piece.
I almost lost faith in what I grew from, & let my dreams slip away.
Few souls gave me warmth, hope, strength & motivation to finish what I believe in. Reminded me the purpose of all of it, building a monument in memory of the forgotten... It started with Amnesia, went into the loss of a brother. To here... NIHILUM.

I'm grateful for the support & want to give a very special thank to :

My parent for their support, & believing in me.
Ludovick Carrier, who's a living Hero to my eyes.
Cindy Carrier, who's strong and unpredictable.
Ophelie Dehud, with whom I saw the edge of the world.
Molly G. Brown, for her patience and correcting my grammar.
Richard A. Morgan, for his precious advices & support.
All the souls who been always here cheering me up.

Also, to all the amazing Kickstarter backer who made my dream becoming true.

But most importantly, this graphic novel is dedicated:

In memory of my beloved brother Sebastien Carrier,
who left us unknown of the world and way too early.
To his talent & dreams.
To his eternal rest in void &
may he forgive who ran off with his legacy.

REQUIESCAT IN PACEM

NIHILUM OMNIPOTENS, OMNIUM CREATURUM DIVE PATER, PIETAS TUA VENIAT SUPER ME QUI A PRO NIHILUM BEATUS SUM DEPRECOR TE, UT ME DEFENDAS DE ADVERSARIIS TUOE PROTEGES ME SECUNDUM PIETATEM TIBI COMMENDO ANIMAM MEAM ET CORPUS MEUM QUI NULLAM SPEM NE QUE HABERE VOLO NISI IN TE, NIHILUM, ADJUVA ME ET PER TUAM IMMENSAM CLEMENTIAM ET MISERICORDIAM TUAM NE DISCESSERIS A ME INTENDE IN ADJUTORIUM NIHILUM SALUTIS MEOE INDUE.NIHILUM, VISCERA MISERICORDIOE TUOE UT AD VOLUNTATEM BENEGNITATEM PRUDENIAM, JUSTITIAM, FORTITUDINEM, TEMPERATIAM, MODESTIAM, PATIENTIAM, CONCORDIAM, PACEM ET PRO OMNIBUS PERSEVERANTIAM ET CANTITATEM TRIBUERE DIGNERI QUI VIVIS ET REGNIS IN AETERNUM

NIHILUM OMNIPOTENS, OMNIUM CREATURUM DIVE PATER, PIETAS TUA VENIAT SUPER ME QUI A PRO NIHILUM BEATUS SUM DEPRECOR TE, UT ME DEFENDAS DE ADVERSARIIS TUOE PROTEGES ME SECUNDUM PIETATEM TIBI COMMENDO ANIMAM MEAM ET CORPUS MEUM QUI NULLAM SPEM NE QUE HABERE VOLO NISI IN TE, NIHILUM, ADJUVA ME ET PER TUAM IMMENSAM CLEMENTIAM ET MISERICORDIAM TUAM NE DISCESSERIS A ME INTENDE IN ADJUTORIUM NIHILUM SALUTIS MEOE INDUE.NIHILUM, VISCERA MISERICORDIOE TUOE UT AD VOLUNTATEM BENEGNITATEM PRUDENIAM, JUSTITIAM, FORTITUDINEM, TEMPERATIAM, MODESTIAM, PATIENTIAM, CONCORDIAM, PACEM ET PRO OMNIBUS PERSEVERANTIAM ET CANTITATEM TRIBUERE DIGNERI QUI VIVIS ET REGNIS IN AETERNUM

NIHILUM OMNIPOTENS, OMNIUM CREATURUM DIVE PATER, PIETAS TUA VENIAT SUPER ME QUI A PRO NIHILUM BEATUS SUM DEPRECOR TE, UT ME DEFENDAS DE ADVERSARIIS TUOE PROTEGES ME SECUNDUM PIETATEM TIBI COMMENDO ANIMAM MEAM ET CORPUS MEUM QUI NULLAM SPEM NE QUE HABERE VOLO NISI IN TE, NIHILUM, ADJUVA ME ET PER TUAM IMMENSAM CLEMENTIAM ET MISERICORDIAM TUAM NE DISCESSERIS A ME INTENDE IN ADJUTORIUM NIHILUM SALUTIS MEOE INDUE.NIHILUM, VISCERA MISERICORDIOE TUOE UT AD VOLUNTATEM BENEGNITATEM PRUDENIAM, JUSTITIAM, FORTITUDINEM, TEMPERATIAM, MODESTIAM, PATIENTIAM, CONCORDIAM, PACEM ET PRO OMNIBUS PERSEVERANTIAM ET CANTITATEM TRIBUERE DIGNERI QUI VIVIS ET REGNIS IN AETERNUM